The Chosen Few

By

Col. Cline Williamson

Other works by the author available on Amazon.com at booksbyclinewilliamson or Legionbooks.net

SOG Series
Tempting the Devil
Don't Mean Nothing
Private Enterprise
Driving On
Last OP, Armageddon
Code Word Prairie Fire
Shadowman

RVN Series
A Hard Way to Die
Men of Iron
Code of Honor
The Chosen Few
Hired Help
Bad Moon Rising
The Frenchman

Adventure Series
A Crying Shame
Hitler's Revenge
Bishop

Stecker's Run
Sadler's Gold
Finder's Keepers

RVN Series
III

"One shot, one kill."
"We deal in lead."

These are the unofficial mottos of US Marine Corps snipers, who are collectively the most skilled marksmen in the world. During the Vietnam War, they eliminated the NVA and Viet Cong in large numbers for a mere thirteen cents a round: the cost of one 7.62 mm bullet. That made them the most efficient killers in modern history. Their reach was country-wide, their reputation was legendary, and they never missed. This is the story of one of them.

Background

The Korean War is probably the most forgotten and least memorable in America's modern history, and several possible explanations exist. First, it was not viewed as, much less called, a war by the United States Government when it first began. Instead, it was labeled as a "police action" by both President Harry Truman and the press in an attempt to downplay its seriousness to the American public.

At the time, the US government had the mistaken impression that North Korea was simply a third-world country with a fourth-rate army. They held it in such disdain they declined to even listen to its rhetoric. Consequently, when North Korea began explicitly stating its intentions to invade South Korea and unify the divided country, our national leadership dismissed its claims as pompous threats. If they attempted to conduct it, the US felt it would take little more than a show of force by the United States military to deter their threats. If they invaded, the American troops could easily force the North Koreans to give up their designs on South Korea and return to their own country without difficulty.

Those assumptions proved to be completely unrealistic and massive errors in judgment. Just as labeling the war, which followed, a police action proved to be a completely erroneous and unrealistic nomenclature. As usual, the politicians were wrong. Now someone had to rectify their mistake.

The "police action" was quickly renamed a conflict when Americans discovered that defeating the North Korean Army would not be as easy as the US government and its military had initially envisioned. Especially after the North Korean invasion began sweeping through South Korea like a runway freight train, the US military couldn't stop.

Finally, when the American and Republic of Korea, or ROK, forces were forced to retreat into a small pocket around the port of Pusan and were in grave danger of being thrown completely off the entire Korean peninsula, the conflict began being referred to as a war.

Secondly, when the Korean War started, WWII had ended barely six years earlier. Consequently, war, death, and casualties were subjects that were still fresh in most Americans' minds. Most had lost friends or relatives in that conflict and weren't very amenable or enthusiastic to repeat that experience. Especially since WWII had been a long and bitter struggle for America and its Allies. One in which millions were killed, maimed, or wounded worldwide during its seven-plus years of suffering.

Entire families had been wiped out, lineages ended, cities erased, races subjected to genocide, and entire nations rendered nonexistent during and after its conduct. In the process, much of Europe and Asia were left in utter shambles.

As a result, America and the rest of the western world were more than tired of conflict by the end of that climactic event. They certainly weren't either receptive or eager to hear about, much less engage in another conflict, having barely recuperated from the previous one. So, war, in any form, name, nation, or region, was a subject that was not a popular one.

Americans were so disgusted with conflict they didn't want to hear, read, or even think about it anymore. They certainly did not want to listen to their national leadership try and explain why we needed to engage in another war in Asia. Particularly one between two Asian countries they neither cared about nor were interested in. Hell, most Americans couldn't even find Korea on a world map.

Given that, when the war began, they had great difficulty identifying with it or even understanding why the United States was involved. Particularly since it was a war fought between two small Asian nations, some four thousand plus miles away and didn't affect America's security. Moreover, the United States seemed to have no significant reason for interfering or supporting either side other than the newly recognized threat of communism. Lastly, regardless of which side ultimately prevailed, nothing would change viz a viz the United States. At least, that was the public perception at the time.

As such, Americans were leery of getting involved in the conflict. Especially since it would again require the commitment of major US military forces and equipment to solve another foreign nation's problems. We had already gotten ourselves involved in two World Wars for similar reasons. When they ended, we had extraordinarily little to show for it. So, there was little public support for our involvement in another foreign conflict that didn't directly concern us.

Even the advent of communism threatening to engulf the entire world didn't seem to matter since most Americans were uninterested in political ideology as a basis for going to war. Therefore, they had little concern regarding two small Asian nations supposedly fighting over that concept. Unfortunately, this wasn't just a sign of the times. Americans had a long history of loathing war in a foreign country based on political ideology. WWI and WWII were prime examples. Korea was just the latest iteration.

During World War I, there had been great anguish within our citizenry when the idea of sending United States soldiers to fight in a European conflict between England, France, and Germany was first proposed. In most Americans' eyes, the war itself was a European problem that they had brought on themselves. They viewed it as an internal conflict confined to the three European nations involved that had nothing to do with the United States.

It was being waged in Europe, had started there because of European problems, and was being fought there by European rulers who disagreed about European politics. Worse, even the two rulers of England and Germany, who were its primary protagonists, were related by blood, yet still at each other's throats. Given all that, most Americans saw no reason America should involve itself.

That same feeling existed in the early years of WWII. Initially, most Americans viewed that as almost a repeat of WWI. We were again being asked to fight in Europe for the same reasons we had fought in WWI. Those reasons didn't sit well with the American public in either conflict. Especially since we had massive economic problems of our own at the time and no apparent way to fix them. Unemployment was a national crisis and business stagnation, a fact, so another foreign war didn't interest us.

Despite all that, there were other significant reasons we didn't want to get involved. Britain, Germany, and France had already been at war for over two years before the Japanese attack on Pearl Harbor. Worse, the Axis powers were winning. Besides, since we had the Atlantic Ocean protecting us, there was little danger of a

European conflict spilling over onto our shores. Lastly, the war was viewed strictly as a European problem, similar to WWI, because, Americans were still, by and large, isolationists. They didn't consider Germany, or the war in Europe, to be a conflict that threatened the security of the United States and as such, they didn't want to get involved in it.

Instead, they viewed the war as another dispute between Europeans that they could resolve without outside assistance or interference. Certainly, without the United States having to send troops to assist them. And especially since we had already done that once before and hadn't even received a polite thank you for all our efforts.

Had not Pearl Harbor occurred, a declaration of war on Germany alone might never have happened because Germany was not considered a direct threat to the United States since the Atlantic Ocean separated us and prevented Nazi Germany from importing their war onto American soil. Given that, it took the Japanese sneak attack on American forces at Pearl Harbor to arouse the furor of the American public and get Congress to declare war on Japan. And even then, America declared war on

Germany only because she was Japan's axis partner by a mutual defense Pact.

Consequently, until Japan's sneak attack on Pearl Harbor, most Americans hesitated to get the United States involved. They were still quasi-isolationist and more concerned with America's stagnant economy than Europe's or Asia's ongoing wars. More importantly, they felt safe because they had two oceans separating them from the rest of the world and their conflicts. The Atlantic kept all of Europe's problems from overflowing onto our shores, and the Pacific kept us separated from all the problems existing in Asia.

In addition, we had already assisted the Europeans in fighting the Germans and winning WWI a decade earlier. Afterward, we had extraordinarily little to show for that effort except for boatloads of dead and wounded citizens, a whopping bill for all the material and supplies we expended, and not even any thanks from either the French or the English for saving their nations from the German threat. Consequently, we weren't very enthusiastic about doing it again, twenty-odd years later.

Only President Franklin D Roosevelt and a few like-minded Democratic, progressive political cronies saw any urgent need to get America involved in another war with Germany. Especially one that Germany was winning at the time. Most Americans vividly remembered WWI, when US troops had been sent to the European continent to fight an earlier war with Germany. A war that, at the time, many Americans had regarded as none of America's business. They also remembered its conclusion, after which America had virtually nothing to show for our sacrifice and efforts.

Exacerbating the problem, President Roosevelt was a known and ardent Anglophile and a vocal and public supporter of the British. So his political views regarding Germans in general and the English, in particular, were not only biased but widely known. More importantly, they were largely unsupported by the American public. As such, the US population was unwilling to involve themselves in what they considered another internal European problem that didn't concern us. Especially since they viewed the primary reason for US pending involvement as Roosevelt's admiration and sympathy for the English.

Roosevelt's administration's primary propaganda theory and reason for our involvement was based on a lie. The US was being forced into the war because German U Boats were sinking our merchantmen. However, after examining the facts, that reasoning didn't hold much water with the public. Germany began unrestricted submarine warfare against the US only *after* Roosevelt transferred an armada of US destroyers to the British and afterward began supplying them with war materials *using American merchant shipping*. That act made the US an overt supporter of the British war effort. Consequently, our merchant ships became legitimate U- Boat targets. Legally, to the dismay of Roosevelt, even the world court in The Hague agreed with that premise.

That meant German U Boats sinking US merchant ships loaded with war supplies bound for England was an appropriate response for Germany. However, there was an easy and reliable fix to remedy that problem, although it was never considered, much less adopted.

All America needed to do was stop shipping war materials on US ships and use British ships instead. Again, that option was neither considered nor publicly advocated by Roosevelt or his administration since it was in direct opposition to their plans to get America involved in the war. Consequently, they continued, and even increased, their propaganda efforts towards that end, aided by a sympathetic media and an apathetic public.

Only the Japanese sneak attack on Pearl Harbor aroused America's national fury and caused them to go to war with Germany and Japan. And even then, our primary motive was revenge against the Japanese, not hostility towards the Germans.

However, the real hidden reason Roosevelt wanted a war with Germany was economics. The US economy was in shambles, we were in a major recession, unemployment was rampant, and the best and quickest way to recover from all that was a war. It would rapidly would invigorate and expand our GDP and solve our problems. That has been a Democrat solution to domestic economic problems since the party was first formed, and it was used once again.

Yet once war was declared, once again, Roosevelt again erred dramatically. He allowed his Anglophile bias to enable the US to be manipulated by English Prime Minister Winston Churchill to pursue a Germany First policy. Despite the fact that Japan had been the nation that attacked us and not Germany! Primarily because Britain was losing its oil fields in the Middle East while being defeated in France and the low countries and feared an invasion.

And although America's own military leaders openly challenged that strategy, Roosevelt pursued it regardless throughout the remainder of the war. As a result, even though that mistake had massive repercussions, it soon became just another forgotten footnote of history that few Americans remember today. .

Regardless, ten years after WWII ended, America entered the Korean War with many of those same misguided political missteps and flawed reasoning, thanks primarily to our own thoroughly inept State Department. They again produced the usual uninformed and mistaken national predictions and projections to the US national leadership, and our stupid politicians based our strategy on them.

However, unlike WWI and WWII, the Korean war was vastly different in the way the North Koreans conducted it. It was America's first attempt at a "limited war" and was something we had never experienced before. That type of conflict would soon prove to be considerably different in several ways, all of which were detrimental to the US.

For example, when we entered the Korean War, politically, we never considered the enemy's total defeat as our goal, followed by unconditional surrender. Instead, we only wanted a return to the status quo, as it had existed before the North Korean invasion of South Korea. In short, we wanted a limited war with limited goals. What's more, we told the North Koreans that when we entered the war, so it became a win-win situation for them. Win or lose, their government and national boundaries would remain the same. That massive error proved to be a costly and irrevocable disaster we not only refused to learn from but were destined to repeat in the future in Vietnam, Afghanistan, and Iraq. Evidently, governmental and bureaucratic stupidity has no boundaries or time constraints, and our politicians are so inept they can't or won't learn from their past mistakes.

So, the question remains. Why did America elect to fight a limited war in Korea? The answer is politics, incompetence, and greed. Especially since we were utterly unprepared militarily, both in men and materials, when it began to even attempt such an effort.

Massive post-WWII defense cuts by progressive Democrat politicians had slashed our military to the bone, leaving it only a hollow shell of its previous self. To regain at least a semblance of our pre-WWII capability and deploy the necessary troop strength would have required reinstituting the draft, which was a political nonstarter. The public would have never stood for any such action.

However, reviving the military-industrial complex was another matter. There was support for that, especially in government and among the politicians. There was massive amounts of money to be made from that, and the politicians wanted their share.

Secondly, according to the State Department, a full-fledged war with the North Koreans might have brought Communist China into the fight and triggered a nuclear conflict. That was something the US was utterly unprepared to accept, much less deal with. Especially over a reunification issue regarding two third world countries. However, history proves that assessment was totally false. It was yet another example of the State Department's incompetence and stupidity. Yet, ironically, again, thanks to State Department and CIA intelligence failures, that happened anyway when China sent three hundred thousand "Chinese volunteers" to the Chosin Reservoir to block a UN invasion across the North Korean border. That is just another glaring example of the stupidity and incompetence of the State Department's personnel and the subsequent inaccuracy of their intelligence estimates.

Unfortunately, US military support to America's friends in Asia was not apparent to many Asian nations at the time, most notably North Korea. In fact, quite the reverse. The US Secretary of State, in a speech to the world had already openly admitted that US military support for South Korea was nonexistent. Even Worse, the US State Department's own gross negligence was a primary factor in the US having to enter the Korean conflict in the first place.

Months before the war, Secretary of State Dean Atcheson made a major foreign policy speech to the worldwide media that admitted that fact. In that speech, he deliberately listed the Asian nations that fell within what he called the *"United States Asian Defense Perimeter"*; in other words, those Asian nations the United States would support and defend militarily in the event they were attacked.

However, because of a wholesale and completely inexcusable blunder by his own incompetents in the State Department, *the nation of South Korea was not included on that list when it was officially published!* Therefore, it appeared to the other countries in Asia, particularly North Korea and China, that the United States felt no responsibility for defending South Korea against any threat to their national sovereignty.

That alone gave the North Koreans all the motives and excuses they needed to invade South Korea and attempt to reunify the two countries. In effect, our own State Department had told them it was acceptable! Consequently, what happened next was perfectly understandable and reasonable from their point of view.

Considering all our strategic blunders in strategy, unreliable intelligence, unrealistic goals, and erroneous national intentions, the war in Korea became inevitable. Worse, it was our own fault. With all the mistakes we made before, during, and after that conflict, our "limited war" in Korea turned into a worldwide disaster. Therefore, it was no surprise that America had to end it by signing an armistice. One that was not only unpalatable to the American people but also repugnant to our national senses because, in the end, it solved nothing and humiliated and disgraced us.

When the war ended, the combatant Koreas still had the exact same boundaries, the same political ideologies, and the same leaders. The only real difference was that North Korea remained virtually intact while South Korea lay in shambles. That's the usual result of a limited war, as vividly demonstrated in Vietnam, Afghanistan, and Iraq. That made the war a complete failure and total waste of time and effort.

So, politically, when the Korean War ended, the United States was right back where we had started, five years earlier. We had two separate Koreas, a whopping bill for all our wartime expenditures, multitudes of dead and wounded, and egg on our face for all our efforts. A perfect ending to an idiotic strategy.

Asians laughed their ass off at us, along with Europeans and Russians. Consequently, the United States was viewed as a weak, eunuched giant incapable of even defeating a third-world country's military. Thus we became a standing joke in the eyes of the other Asian nations and a sizable portion of the rest of the world, and rightly so.

Once again, large numbers of American citizens had been either killed or wounded, we had expended vast amounts of material and money, and we had nothing to show for it except our national disgrace and a continuing global problem that still exists today.

Furthermore, we experienced a monumental loss of status and standing in the eyes of the world diplomatically, militarily, and politically. Worse, after the signing of the armistice, the North Korean government and China despised us, and in the future, would go out of their way to cause problems for us on the world stage. That is yet another situation that still exists today.

In summary, the Korean War was a complete disaster in every possible arena. We helped create the war from the very beginning, when we allowed the Russians to claim half the Korean peninsula in repayment for their finally declaring war on Japan *only ten days before WWII ended, then demanding a full share of the war's spoils in Asia as repayment.* Unbelievably, we let them get away with that.

In fact, that is how the nation of North Korea came into being. The Russians demanded the separation of the two portions of the nation-state to advance their communist model. We again caved in and gave it to them! Yet the Russians never sent one single soldier to fight in the entire Pacific theater during the war. Despite that, we let them claim the lion's share of its spoils in Asia when it was over. That was an unbelievably insane decision and monumental strategic error our Democrat politicians were again responsible for.

Capping that self-inflicted disaster, we later told the world that we would not support South Korea if it was attacked. All because our politicians were so goddamned stupid, incompetent, and spineless and our State Department so incompetent it should have been disbanded.

Adding to that collection of monumental missteps, the post-WWII United States still had the gall to call itself the ultimate defender of the entire noncommunist world after the war ended. That was another grossly false claim since we no longer had the military power to back it up. Although we erroneously viewed ourselves as the bastion of democracy, the freer of the oppressed, and the defender of the weak, that was utter propaganda and a huge lie. We didn't have either the military power or the national resolve necessary to protect ourselves, much less the free world. All that evaporated after WWII when we cut our military to the bone and mistakenly told ourselves that we were safe since we had the atomic bomb. However, that was the thinking prevalent in most Washington bureaucrats, even though it was short-sighted and erroneous. Even worse, we continued to project that image through our policy statements, foreign speeches by our diplomats, and our civic, political, and military actions. Unfortunately, we didn't have the military capability or the national will to back it up.

Three primary post-WWII cases illustrate that erroneous point of view. First, there was the Berlin airlift we were forced to conduct when the Soviets shut off Berlin to the rest of the world, and we did nothing to stop them. Secondly, there was the unsuccessful attempted communist takeover of Greece, which we again did nothing about. Finally, there was the aborted Chinese invasion of Taiwan to eliminate Chaing Kai Chek and the remnants of his Kuomintang government. That was prevented only because our Navy still had some teeth left despite efforts to emasculate it.

In all these cases, however, the US proved to be little more than a paper tiger even though we were supposedly the world's first superpower with the atomic bomb. Given that, we mistakenly saw ourselves as both impregnable and unassailable. We viewed ourselves as a gentle giant and mistakenly thought no nation, especially a third-world country like North Korea, would dare challenge us. As history shows, we were completely wrong.

To the Russians, Chinese, and North Koreans, we were simply a tired, worn-out old pussy cat, declawed and defanged by our massive post-war defense cuts and rapid demobilization. Our spineless actions after WWII had proved it. Although we once growled loudly, we no longer had the means to scare anyone nor the will necessary to accomplish that using our military forces. Primarily because most of them no longer existed. Even the remaining ones were sorely undermanned, poorly trained, and unprepared. The Korean War proved that.

Consequently, after the Berlin airlift, Russia wanted to test just how firm our resolve was and saw South Korea as the perfect venue. In addition, the Chinese, still stinging from their aborted invasion of Taiwan, also despised us and wanted revenge. They wanted another chance to save face before the other Asian nations because they had lost so much of it and viewed the war in Korea as a convenient way to regain it with little impact on them.

Consequently, both these nations openly supported Kim Il Sung, the North Korean leader, when he went to China and publicly enlisted their political, military, and logistical support. Both he and the Chinese government even officially announced their intentions before the actual invasion began!

However, thanks to typical US State Department inefficiency and incompetence, President Truman dismissed all their warnings, even with their explicitly stated intentions in the world media. Thanks to our idiotic and incompetent State Department and CIA, he saw all that as simply communist blustering, unworthy of even a stern warning, much less a military show of strength to prevent any military action. Not that it would have made any difference, given how weak our military was at the time.

Adding to the problem, while the bureaucrats in the State Department had been busily proselytizing for democracy, the liberals in

Congress had been hard at work dismantling the American military and stripping its capabilities. So, while we talked big publicly, we had nothing left militarily to back it up.

We found that out in spades when Kim il Sung fulfilled his promise to reunite the two separate Koreas and made good on his intention to invade. Within weeks, he ran over the US and South Korean forces like a freight train and almost threw them off the entire Korean peninsula because we had too little troop strength to stop him. Worse, the few divisions we had to oppose him were so poorly trained and exercised; they weren't even a match for the third-rate North Korean Army.

The North Korean advance was so successful all resistance in South Korea collapsed, and the remaining units were forced to retreat into a small pocket surrounding the port of Pusan, a stinging example of their reputed capability. Once there, we soon found ourselves in grave danger of being thrown off the Korean peninsula! Only air support kept that from happening. Even then, we were hanging on by our fingernails until additional ground forces from the US finally arrived.

On the ground, we had gotten our ass kicked initially. Only our Air Force had saved us. Later, an involuntary recall of some of our WWII vets, a political euphemism for another draft, eventually saved us from being completely defeated before an armistice was finally declared. And considering who we were fighting, that was a military humiliation and a political disgrace of monumental proportions.

Sadly, those two significant embarrassments resulted from our first "limited war." However, they would not be our last nor our worst. A place called Vietnam would ensure that. In that "limited war," we would again exhibit even greater levels of stupidity, incompetence, and flawed strategy. Once again, we would prove that limited and war, in the same context, was an oxymoron. It would also demonstrate just how corrupt, stupid, and totally incompetent our politicians were and still are. So, we have no one to blame but ourselves since we elected them.

Prelude
The Corps gets the call.

Prior to the Korean War, US Army forces in Japan, our primary ground forces in Asia, were a hollow shell. Although formidable looking on the surface, they were a mere skeleton of their previous wartime strength and capability. Unexercised, lacking training and having poorly maintained and somewhat obsolete equipment, they were totally unprepared to fight a war on the Korean peninsula. Yet, by necessity, they were the first to be called.

They were primarily post-WWII occupation troops in Japan and had become parade ground soldiers who were there mainly for show. They looked good but had forgotten how to fight. Their combat edge, earned during WWII, had been severely dulled by over five years of inactivity. This was especially true of our ground forces. As a deterrent in Asia, they were pitifully inadequate.

Adding to the problem, the US's only military forces in Korea were infinitesimal by comparison. They consisted of members of a very small MAAG (Military Army and Air Force Advisory Group), numbering less than five hundred personnel. Their mission was to reequip and train South Korea's fledgling Army and Air Force and upgrade their capabilities. They were trainers, not warriors.

Consequently, when the war began in Korea, it became immediately apparent America would have to have some major external military support to help fight it since its existing forces were too small and unprepared. It was either that or reinstitute a nationwide draft to furnish enough military personnel to fight it unilaterally. That was primarily due to the vast post-WWII cuts in our military, which left us with very few assets to fight anyone. However, there wasn't time. The war had already started and would be over before a draft could be instituted and produce any significant results

Given that, in theory, the newly created United Nations, the successor to the ill-fated and useless League of Nations, was the obvious answer. After all, it had been created for just that purpose. But, like its predecessor, the UN was a lot of talk with little action, not the world's policeman it had been touted to be. Although charged with maintaining peace in the world through its members' collective force, it had no real power of its own nor the will to use it. It was as useless as the League of Nations had been before it and still is.

As a result, only a few of America's stauncher allies provided any real troop strength and combat power to aid the United States in its brand-new war in Asia. However, to at least portray the UN as a workable entity to the world, America and its allies elected to fight the Korean War under the United Nations' collective banner.

Soon after the North Korean invasion, when MacArthur began sending various US Army units stationed in the Far East to Korea to stem the North Korean onslaught, the need for more significant numbers of allied ground forces on the peninsula became readily apparent. Over the dismal months that followed, that need moved from the "necessary" into the "urgent" category as the North Korean advance swept through South Korea like an avalanche.

When the newly created ROK Army, aided by the US division hastily sent from Japan, failed to stop the North Korean onslaught, as had been so highly touted by the west in earlier military estimates, even the public at large soon realized it would require a great deal more troop strength than had been initially envisioned to turn the tide.

When that happened, the United States Marine Corps got the call. They were ordered to reinforce General Macarthur with a Marine Division. However, unknown to most outside the Corps, the Marine Corps, like the Army, had already been stripped of most of its WWII troop strength and assets and was only a shadow of its former self.

Instead of boasting multiple Marine Divisions and dozens of Air Wings, the Corps, like the US Army, was now an understrength and poorly equipped organization, struggling to barely survive. The overall military situation in the United States was so bad there had even been an earlier unsuccessful attempt to persuade Congress to do away with the Marine Corps entirely and fold its assets into the steadily decreasing ones of the Army. That would have given the US at least one force capable enough to go to war if the need arose. Fortunately, Congress had prevented that from happening.

Consequently, when the Corps was tasked to supply a Division for service in Korea, there was a mad scramble for assets within its ranks.

Marine reservists were hastily called up, and Marine units headquartered all over the US were stripped clean of their personnel. The 1st Marine Division was then hastily reformed at Camp Pendleton, California, from all these diverse entities. Even then, they were barely enough to flesh out its ranks.

Regardless, after it had been hastily established, the Division, with no time for refresher training, promptly loaded onto troopships bound for the port of Pusan. By that time, South Korea had already been entirely overrun by North Korean forces. The remaining allied troops had been forced to retreat into a small perimeter around the southern port of Pusan, where they were hanging on by their fingernails. This was the strategic situation facing the 1st Marine Division when it departed San Francisco.

When the convoy sailed, the Division boasted a troop strength of approximately 22,000 Marines, including a supporting Air Wing and other combat and support assets. Part of that contingent was a young buck Sgt named John Casey, a squad leader in 1st Battalion, 5th Marines. Casey had joined the Corps as soon as he had turned eighteen, wanting to fight in WWII and avenge his brother's death on the island of Tarawa.

Unfortunately, by the time he got through boot camp and was ready to be assigned to a Marine Division in the Pacific theater for combat duty, the war was suddenly over, thanks to the atomic bomb. Consequently, he never got the chance to fight. Instead, like a good Marine, he served the remainder of his hitch, going where he was told, in the peacetime Marines. Unexpectedly, however, after that first enlistment, Casey discovered he liked the organization and regimentation in the Corps and decided to reenlist with the intention of making it a career.

After his re-enlistment, because he was a fantastic shot, he received additional training as a sniper and practiced his craft until the Korean conflict rolled around. He realized he would finally get the chance for action that he had narrowly missed in WWII.

But when Casey was hastily transferred to the 1st Marine Division, he discovered that he would not be going to war as a sniper. Instead, he would be assigned as a noncom, in charge of an ordinary Marine rifle squad, as part of a Marine rifle platoon. There he would operate as a squad leader and lead his rifle squad in conventional combat operations against the enemy. Unfortunately, that wasn't his only surprise.

The Korean War would not be what Casey had envisioned it. It would not be a glorious, flag-waving, patriotic war involving entire continents and a multitude of nations fighting for liberty and world freedom on a grand scale. Nor would it be a fight for America's survival, as WWII had been. Most American citizens wouldn't even herald it as a worthwhile endeavor worthy of committing her soldiers to active combat. Even the President had labeled it as a "police action. As such, it would not be a publicly endorsed conflict by most of the war-weary American public.

Asians fighting other Asians, in a place most US citizens had barely heard of, for control of territory they could care less about, was not a subject high on most Americans' priority list. Thus the war there was a conflict they thought unworthy and unnecessary.

Lastly, it would certainly not represent a conflict over anything vital to the United States' national interests. That was particularly true after we had already been told, by our own Secretary of State, that South Korea was not even worthy enough of our concern to be included in our area of national interest! That fact alone had been a clear and overt signal to the North Koreans that the US wouldn't oppose them if they wanted to attack South Korea and reunite the country.

In the end, however, the United States opposed them when that happened. A portion of that opposition was supplied by the 1st Marine Division, with young Marine Buck Sergeant John Casey as a part of that effort.

So, Casey finally got his war, one he had so desperately yearned for, but one which, in the end, he wished he had never heard of. Because, as he soon discovered, the war in Korea, in the middle of the worst winter seen in over fifty years, was not going to be either glamorous or self-satisfying. Instead, it would be savage and brutal, almost exceeding the imagination, in its conditions and level of bloodletting.

The suffering he was about to witness would be so widespread and catastrophic; that it would defy the boundaries of acceptable human behavior. In the end, having lived through and endured all that, Casey and the rest of the western world would be utterly dissatisfied with the results of its dismal conclusion.

The war's end would leave a horrible taste in America and the rest of the world's collective mouth. One that was so distasteful and foul would cause them to regurgitate it from time to time in the future. However, that was Casey's concern. He had been sent just to fight it. In the process, Casey would learn valuable lessons that he would remember the next time he went to war in Vietnam.

Chapter One
Learning the trade

The unchecked wind roared in off the North Korean icy plateau in conjunction with the subzero temperatures prevalent in the area, sliced right through a man. The below zero cold, alone, was bad enough, butll, when combined with the howling wind, it attacked a man's skin like acid, burning into it with a ferocity almost as intense as a red-hot piece of steel. That chilled him to the bone in less than a minute. There was no defense against these terrible conditions and no relief. Korea was experiencing the wrost winter in fifty years, so men just had to endure somehow, until even that was no longer possible. It was bad enough having to fight the Chinese and North Korean hordes trying to kill you daily. Having the weather trying to do the same thing at the same time made the situation insufferable.

Casey gasped as he awakened from another night of semi-sleep. Because of the cold, he had dozed intermittently but never fell asleep because he was shaking too badly. That left him groggy when he arose, but that feeling vanished as his body recoiled from the wind chill factor.

"Another miserable day in the Division's retreat from the Chosin Reservoir and the same forecast," he thought angrily." Freezing and miserable with a chance of death."

"Christ, Marines having to retreat anywhere is terrible enough, but having to do it in the worst goddamn winter Korea has experienced in over fifty years makes it unbearable."

"Especially with two hundred thousand Chinese all over your ass."

As his eyes teared, the drops instantly turned to ice crystals as they tried to run down his white, bloodless cheeks. So his frozen tears just clung to his face as it turned numb. Moments later, his lungs began burning as they tried unsuccessfully to ingest the icy air. But the cold was so overwhelming, his body shook and quivered as it tried unsuccessfully to adjust to the glacial temperature. To breathe, he had to put a woolen scarf over his mouth to prevent his lungs from freezing.

The frigid climate and severe conditions were not only too much for Casey to bear, but for the rest of the Marines in the 1st Marine Division as well. They could barely accept and cope with the sudden shock their bodies were being forced to endure continuingly. As a result, most Marines in the Division, who were still mobile, were barely aware of their legs anymore. Their feet were barely controlable blocks of ice attached to their numbed legs. That was assuming they weren't already suffering from frostbite or their limbs, and lower appendages hadn't already frozen solid, which wasn't uncommon.

It was the same with their arms and hands. All their appendages had little to no perceptive feeling, thanks to the bitter, unrelenting weather. Even their stiff, aching fingers stung unmercifully when they tried to hold something. Like they had just grabbed a live electric wire. But there was no decrease in relief. The weather and conditions continued daily and even worsened.

The constant cold they were being forced to endure was relentless, creeping into their torsos, freezing their feet and fingers, and causing their entire bodies to shiver uncontrollably. They were on the very edge of freezing to death, and they knew it, yet couldn't stop it. There would be no abatement from the frigid landscape and no escape from the Siberian temperature because the forecast was for more of the same. Something to really look forward to. The constant, mind-numbing, glacial environment enveloped everything, so you were forced to either endure it or die.

Casey had never known cold like this before. It was all-consuming, ruthless, and continuous. It attacked everything: men, equipment, morale, even the will to live. It eventually ground everything into submission with a constant, relentless, mind-numbing force that seeped through the tiniest hole, crept into the slightest crevice, and slithered its way into the heaviest clothing. Once there, it bit into the skin, gnawed at bones, and shriveled innards, all in a matter of seconds. What it didn't freeze outright; it numbed within moments, with a sudden chilling seizure that took a man's breath away.

There wasn't even a remembrance of ever having been warm with no relief in sight. That was a longed-for but forgotten luxury, that had been erased from most Marine's memories. And the arctic rawness now encompassing them not only affected their bodies but also affected their minds. Now even their brains were becoming sluggish and lazy because of the cold. Their bodies were slowly shutting down, and their minds turning to the equivalent of frozen oatmeal. So, to stay alive, Casey and the rest of his Marines were forced to concentrate on only one thought, movement.

Movement was required for continued survival. Marines had to keep their blood flowing if they wanted to stay alive. Because movement produced body heat, and heat kept you from freezing. So those that wanted to live forced themselves onward, regardless of what their brain was telling them. If they stopped for rest or sleep, as their mind wanted them to do, they'd freeze to death. It happened every day, all around Casey and his men.

But even with that hideous knowledge, every step they took was exquisite agony. Frozen socks glued to the insides of ice-encrusted boots made their cold feet almost uncontrollable. The relentless numbing that made even their joints ache was never-ending, and their desire for rest remained constant yet unfulfilled. They stumbled along on the icy ground and in the freeing wind, reeling like drunkards and forcing themselves forward in a frozen stagger. Somehow, they kept going; they had to; they had no choice. There was no more room on any of the vehicles for the weak or those who couldn't keep up. They were already overloaded with the frozen dead.

Consequently, hardened Marines cried as they plodded onward, heads down, bodies aching, and jaws clenched. Their teeth had long since stopped chattering, and their appendages had already stopped shaking. They were already in the first stages of hypothermia. Their tired, brutalized bodies were now losing heat faster than they could generate it. They continued to endure only by sheer will.

As the snow continued to fall and the wind continued to howl, the temperature continued to drop. The conditions continued to worsen. It was a daily, never-ending nightmare, repeating itself with deadly monotony. North Korea was amid the worst winter in half a century. Marines had to fight their way out of it through a horde of over fifty thousand Chinese that Mao Tse Tung himself had explicitly dispatched to kill them. Supposedly, they were the Chinese Army's elite troops and outnumbered the Marines over six to one!

That made the Marines' days long, sunless, and bitter as they tried to endure the agony of their withdrawal. And when the bleak sun went down, Marines knew from painful experience that the cold and their desperate situation would get even worse.

The Chinese would attack again when darkness fell, as they did every night. They outnumbered the Regiment over six to one and had it surrounded. Undercover of darkness, when Marine air support was useless, they would come in endless human waves, as they did every night. With bugles blaring and whistles blowing, the mountainsides would erupt with hordes of screaming fanatics, charging down the icy slopes and firing blindly. The sudden surge of human bodies on the white snow would look like a deadly toxic stain spreading on white linen or a nest of ants surging towards a jar of spilled honey, crawling all over themselves in a frantic rush to consume it. That's when the killing would begin in earnest.

There would suddenly be so many targets; there wouldn't be time for Marines to aim, just fire and reload, fire and reload, fire and reload. The Chinese formations were so dense, and the bodies packed so closely together, it was nearly impossible to miss. So, it was kill, and keep killing; stop the human surge with a wall of lead before they could get to you. Annihilate the screaming maniacs until they either retreated or there was no one left to kill. Keep firing as long as you have the strength or until you run out of ammo. It was a race whether the Marines would run out of bullets first or the Chinese would run out of soldiers.

Afterward, when the action was over, the bleak snow- and ice-covered hills and mountainsides would run red with blood, and the snow would turn crimson. Chinese bodies would cover the slopes like black dots on them. They would freeze where they had fallen, in grotesque positions with limbs pointed everywhere and looking like modern, abstract sculptures in a surreal winter landscape. Eventually, the howling wind would blow away the blue gun smoke and the stench of death. The falling snow would cover their pitiful remains within hours, freezing them in place for eternity. The area would then become just one more frozen unnamed Asian graveyard in the pitiless landscape of North Korea. When that happened, the Marines would stop shaking and be able to take a deep breath again, realizing that against all odds, they had survived another vicious attempt to kill them and were still alive. It was the same every night.

"Is staying alive even possible anymore?" *Casey asked himself after surviving another night*

onslaught. *"Or am I just fooling myself and delaying the inevitable?"*

He remembered the last attack as he sucked on a cigarette. Its burning ember was the only thing warm within five miles. Before the previous attack, the temperature had dropped so low that many Marine's weapons had malfunctioned, the oil on their bolts turning to gel and freezing them shut, effectively turning M-1 Garands into nothing more than nine-pound clubs. But clubs were no match for Chinese Burp guns that spewed death at twenty rounds a second. So, many Marines died, swinging wildly, unable to fire a single shot.

"Maybe they were the lucky ones," Casey thought bitterly. *"Their suffering was over in a split second."*

"We survivors are the poor bastards that must remain and endure, and our suffering has only just begun."

But endurance was becoming harder and harder for the young Buck Sgt and his fellow Marines. The brutal, arctic weather was making even a Marine's primary weapon malfunction, and without a functioning weapon, he was as good as dead. Since Casey didn't want to die, he urgently wanted to check his piece and ensure it was still operational. Still, he was hesitant even to do that.

"If I take my hands out of my pockets," he cautioned himself. "my fingers will probably stick to the metal extractor rod if I try to open the breech,"

"And if that happens, I'll lose skin at the very least, and frostbite will probably soon follow."

"Then I won't even be able to hold the weapon, much less fire it," He reasoned.

"If that happens," he told himself. "I'm screwed."

So, he weighed his options, tried to find a suitable compromise, and finally decided on a solution.

"Better to press my piece close against my body."

"Try to keep it out of the wind and warm enough to still function."

"Hopefully, that'll be enough."

"I'll tell my men to do the same"

Fortunately, Casey's plan worked, but it left him unsatisfied. He had other deadly problems facing him and his men that he couldn't solve. Questions he couldn't answer. Worries that wouldn't go away and couldn't be resolved.

"What are we even doing here?" he asked himself bitterly.

"Why are Marines even in this godforsaken place?"

"What have we done to incur such a terrible wrath?"

"Why has God singled us out for such horrible suffering?"

But there was no answer. Evidently, God wasn't listening, didn't care, or had other matters to consider that had a higher priority. Consequently, there was just the continual, howling wind taking the wind chill factor down even lower into the area where even survival was questionable. When it reached its nadir, death would ultimately follow.

The 5th Marine Regiment's situation was desperate and growing worse by the hour because the conditions were indescribable and the cold unrelenting. Men froze to death daily with never a whimper. Buddies beside them didn't even know they were dead until they tried to wake them. Then they saw their cold, lifeless eyes, frozen open and staring accusingly at those still living. That was unnerving; dead men spying on the living to see how much longer they could last before joining their ranks. It was macabre, and it was grotesque. It was unthinkable and gruesome, yet it happened daily and regularly.

"This isn't war any longer," Casey told himself angrily. "Not in these conditions."

"Instead, it's a bizarre, time-delayed suicide, but on a mass scale."

"It's a king-sized version of "You Bet Your Life," and we're losing."

But Casey was wrong. This was no game. Groucho Marx wasn't in North Korea, and this was no TV quiz show, broadcasting his humor and giving out prizes to the winners. The stakes here in the Chosin Reservoir were much higher.

"Here, if the Chinese don't kill you, the weather will," Casey thought bitterly.

"There's no third option."

"It's simply a race to see which one will finish the job first."

That was reality, and unfortunately, Casey could do nothing to change it.

Casey didn't mind fighting and possibly dying. He was prepared for that because it was his job. That's why he had enlisted, and that's what he had been trained to do. Marines pay for freedom with their blood and their lives. They know that when they put the uniform on and accept it. But no one had ever said anything about fighting like this. This wasn't a modern battle anymore. This was sheer butchery, blind savagery almost on a medieval scale, and under conditions so brutal they were barely describable.

When the Chinese human wave attacks came at night, there was so much constant killing; it resembled genocide. It happened on a nightly basis, and Casey was physically exhausted by the sheer magnitude of it when it was over. But there was no alternative. It was either endure all that butchery and continue to function or die. And Marine's primary mission was not to die for his country but to make the other poor bastard die for his.

"But here, in this godforsaken place called the Chosin, literally everything is against us," Casey reminded himself. *"the enemy, the temperature, the terrain, the wind, the precipitation, the conditions, even the ground."*

"It's frozen so solid, you can't even dig a foxhole in it."

"That makes things so horrific that sometimes you have to use the frozen dead for cover instead."

"That makes the situation so horrible and macabre it is almost surreal."

"Sometimes, it makes you wonder if there is any point in even trying anymore."

"How can men continue to fight in this arctic wasteland, where weapons won't fire because they're frozen, water-cooled machine guns malfunctioned because there was no antifreeze for their water jackets, and vehicles had to be cranked and run every thirty minutes just to keep their crankcases from freezing?" Casey wondered fearfully.

"Who could survive when hardened Marines who could endure no more just finally gave up, laid down, and died, letting themselves fall into the blissful oblivion of an endless cold sleep?"

"Hell, even some of those who fought on, often bled to death, their bodies so numbed by the cold, they never even knew they'd been hit until it was too late."

"The poor bastards' bodies were so numbed by the cold, they never felt the pain; an almost unbelievable fact, yet true."

"Survival in this environment is already marginal." Casey realized. "but with no relief in sight, and conditions worsening by the hour, it will soon become impossible."

"It's only a matter of time," he told himself miserably.

"Christ, fighting the Japanese on Guadalcanal in WWII must have been a luxury compared to this," Casey thought.

"At least there, Marines had been warm when they died, unlike here."

"Here, men had forgotten what warm ever felt like."

"During daylight, we battle our way down an icy, single lane, windswept, dirt road. The rocky soil is frozen so solid it is akin to torn up, concrete, uneven, jagged, and slick."

"Worse, these narrow winding passages are often deathtraps perfectly suited to channeling retreating Marine units into deadly ambushes."

"Regrettably, none of that matters," he thought disgustedly.

"It's the only way out and the only route home."

So, Marines trudged on, fighting their way forward when they had to, as they wound their way down steep mountains and treacherous snow-covered ridges and ravines in temperatures that were below zero. They struggled or fought their way onward in a chilled stupor every pain-filled day. When night fell and they were forced to stop, the savagery continued as they fought off Chinese human wave assaults on the road's shoulders or in small burned-out villages, whose names they couldn't even pronounce, even if they could find them on their maps. Here, Marines sometimes outnumbered twenty to one, blindly killing until sheer numbers overcame them.

Here even heroes eventually succumbed to the Chinese hordes or the brutal, arctic weather. Here courage was not measured by heroic deeds but by continued endurance in brutal conditions. Here Marines' failing bodies, finally overruled their sluggish minds and just quit functioning. Here, even their vaunted espirit de corps was flagging because they were always retreating, and that was a bitter pill for any Marine to have to swallow.

Marines didn't retreat; they attacked. They didn't give up ground; they took it and held it. That tenet had been drilled into them since they were boots, and it was part of the age-old Marine Corps ethos. That was something they were renowned for. But that was not the case in this barren, mountainous, God-forsaken place, where ice covered everything, and the raw, unforgiving conditions were just short of being unbearable.

This was the Chosin Reservoir. In conjunction with the 9th Chinese People's

Volunteer Army, the weather had suddenly changed all the rules. Here the temperature never even rose to freezing. That would have been a good day, and there weren't any of those. It was thirty-five degrees below zero, and the wind was a continuous, howling beast. That put the wind chill down to fifty degrees below zero.

On top of that, Marines were surrounded by over seventy thousand Chinese regulars bent on their destruction. They were the elite of the Chinese Army and had been especially dispatched to North Korea by Mao Tse Tung himself, to wipe out the 5th Marine Regiment. Between them, the unrelenting weather, and the Marines' suffering, death often seemed like a tragic but welcome luxury.

When Casey looked over the pitiful collection of Marines he now commanded, he almost wept. His Platoon leader, a Second John named Issacs, had been killed four days ago. His frozen body was now strapped onto the fender of deuce and a half, like some macabre, misplaced hood ornament. The truck was somewhere in the column up ahead, along with all the other vehicles hauling the dead. There were already so many there was no more room left for the wounded, so many were forced to walk, another reminder that only death offered any relief.

Casey was the only noncom left in the platoon, all the others had been killed in the first few days of the withdrawal. The unit, with an original complement of over forty men, now numbered less than twenty Marines. Even they were all half-frozen and hollow-eyed, continuing to function primarily by rote, training, and Casey's constant hounding.

The rest were gone, killed, wounded, or frozen to death. And of those remaining, Casey knew that he would probably lose one or two more the following day. That was the usual standard, and the way casualties had been running in the 5th Marine Regient as it retreated it's way back through the mountains by day and then fought off Chinese human wave attacks by night.

Those Marines still alive at dawn, would patch up their wounded, collect their dead, and put their stiff, frozen bodies on vehicles like stacked cordwood. Afterwards, the retreat would begin all over again. It was a brutal and never-ending cycle.

Marines never left their dead. It was an unwritten code. So, the dead retreated along with the living. And the living now consisted of those Marines that were *certain* to die soon, and those that would *probably* die shortly after that. Being a potential survivor was no longer considered possible. Instead, most Marines felt like they were already dead men walking, simply living on borrowed time while they waited their turn.

After this ordeal, very few, if any, would live to talk about the Chosin Reservoir. It was a disastrous, magnificent, bloodletting of the first order, one destined to be recorded in the annals of Marine Corps history. It would go down as a brutal but gallant effort and be remembered as an epic saga of courage, suffering, and endurance, the stuff of military legends. They might even have to add a new verse to the Marine Hymn if anybody left to tell the tale and sing it.

But to those living through the horror, it was none of that. It was simply a never-ending, living nightmare that would make Christians out of atheists and believers out of sinners, all in the blink of an eye. It would cause hardened Marines to cry at the mass suffering evident all around them if they had any tears left. God himself would cringe at the carnage and the heartbreak he witnessed nightly, and he would wonder at the savagery of his creation.

Casey wasn't much Christian, but he believed in God. Everyone else around him did too. If they didn't, here in the hell of Chosin, they were fools. With everything else against them, God was the only thing left that seemed to still be on their side. But Casey had begun to wonder about even God lately. It appeared that even He had given up on the Marines and gone somewhere else, probably just to get warm again. If He had, Casey couldn't blame him. The frozen Chosin was no fit place for anyone, mortal or otherwise. Here, there were only the dead and those waiting to die. Sometimes, it wasn't easy to differentiate between the two.

Both Heaven and Hell would have long waiting lines when this brutal struggle was over, the entrances to both clogged with weary Marines. If admittance to the pearly gates were measured in good deeds or heroics, then the extenuating circumstances of Chosin would provide entire new battalions of Marines to guard Heaven's portals. Afterwards, God could listen to war stories that were so terrible; had they been told anywhere but Heaven, no one would have believed them.

And as for Hell, the Marines headed there would laugh at the Devil when they arrived and probably give him rude one-fingered gestures and catcalls. He certainly wouldn't scare them. He would be doing them a favor by letting them in. At least they would be warm again.

Chapter Two
A Brand new War

The crosshairs in the scope were centered on the target, and the Winchester Model 70 was as steady as a rock. The man shouldering it was an experienced shooter, so as soon as he pulled the trigger, the target was a dead man. He was that good. Hell, he was better than good. He was phenomenal because he never missed. Buster always aimed for the head and was so accurate he could shoot the balls of a male mosquito at a hundred yards.

That meant accuracy wasn't the problem. Neither was the killing. All that was a done deal. Getting away after the shot was the problem. Especially here, since this place was a deathtrap, to begin with.

Operating as a sniper in your own territory was hairy enough. But at least you had fire support and friendlies there to call on if you needed it. At least you had safe havens to run to if you needed one. That wasn't the case in Laos. Here you had nothing. You were all alone out in the heart of Indian country, and your ass was flying solo and swinging in the breeze. You could only depend on yourself or your spotter because there was no one else. If you got into a jam, you'd have to get yourself out of it. That was reality, and that was the problem.

All that made operating in Laos extremely different. There was nothing there for you except maybe death. No artillery, no reinforcements, no firebases, nothing. Maybe air support, if you were lucky enough to contact it if it could get to you in time if it could find you in the lousy jungle when it did, and if it was accurate. That was a lot of ifs to bet your life on. Probably too many. But that scenario was the norm out here in the Twilight Zone. More importantly, that was probably exactly what was about to happen, and Buster knew it

"Can we still get out of here after I kill this asshole?" he asked nervously.

"He's got a lot of friends down there and our extraction LZ is four klicks from here through virgin jungle."

"That's a long haul all by itself."

"It's even worse with a wagon load of pissed-off NVA chasing you."

"And what if the little shits have troops watching the LZ before we get there, just as a precaution?"

"What then?"

"Can Dunaway and I still make it out of this shithole without getting shot to pieces or killed?"

"And if so, how?"

Those were serious questions worrying Buster that he had no answers. Gut wrenchers causing him to sweat and start doubting himself and his future. He and Dunaway, Mutt to Buster, were in Laos covertly, which meant they were expendable. They would be written off and disavowed if the mission went south or they were compromised. Unfortunately, currently, that's the way things seemed to be headed.

Buster glanced over at his spotter, who was eyeing the target carefully through his spotting scope. His friend was sweating too, the strain evident on his face. However, outwardly he still appeared calm and collected, because he was all Marine and careful to project that image. Buster wondered if Mutt had asked himself those same questions.

"Probably," he thought.

"After all, he's smart and a professional."

"By this time, he would have assessed our situation accurately and figured all the possibilities."

"He had probably done that before we were ever inserted."

Buster hadn't. He was just a shooter and didn'usually think that far ahead. He was still a teenager, thought he was immortal, and usually lived for the moment. His favorite pass time off duty was drinking booze and getting laid. Up to now, he had considered his job as something exciting and new yet he had concentrated on his liberty time. Now, the full impact of his primary job was sinking in.

"Two against maybe up to fifty NVA is shitty odds," Buster thought nervously. *"And that's if the intel was right."*

"And good intel about this shithole of a country is generally lousy."

"So there's probably a lot more of the little shits down there we don't even know about."

"That wouldn't surprise me."

Dunaway had considered that possibility too. Just as he had considered exactly what his shooter was looking at. It was big trouble with "watch your ass" written all over it. He and Buster were outnumbered, outgunned, and in an extremely dangerous and risky position. The goddamned NVA owned the entire fucking area, so they had nowhere to run if things went sideways. Given the odds, that was a definite possibility. He had already considered all that carefully and didn't like the conclusions he had arrived at since they were all negative.

Still, he was a hard ass and mission-oriented, as most Marine corporals usually were. With them, the mission came first, regardless. But that was the rule in South Vietnam and not necessarily not Laos. The situation here was vastly different and much more dangerous. That changed everything. Still, as the team leader, he was in charge and would make the final decision because that was his job. However, he was running out of time, and he knew it. Consequently, he judged the odds one last time but still didn't like the answers. If he gave consent to fire, they'd have to run over four klicks just to survive. If he aborted, it was a failed mission, and Dunaway didn't like failure.

"Will Mutt still give me consent to fire, considering the numbers and our location?" Buster wondered. *"Especially with the extraction LZ four goddamn klicks away through the damned jungle?"*

"More importantly, with the two of us thirty fucking miles inside Laos all by ourselves?"

Mutt looked at him grimly a moment later, his face an emotionless mask. He had weighed the odds and decided.

"Send it," he ordered.

Buster was surprised but remained stone-faced, having expected nothing less. Still, he felt like he had been sucker punched. He sucked in his breath and turned back to the scope.

"Here we go," he thought grimly. *"Full speed ahead and fuck the consequences."*

"It's root hog or die time, with no holds barred."

"Typical Marine Corps thinking."

"We're about to get our asses handed to us," he told himself disgustedly. *"and I'm only nineteen."*

"We are gonna get buried in this fucking place because of this cluster fuck of a mission and Dunaway's hard-ass attitude."

"Shit," he moaned. *"I may have just had my last shot of Jim Beam and my last piece of ass."*

"And I'm damn sure gonna miss all that."

A second later, he reacquired the target in the scope, steadied himself, and squeezed the trigger. A nanosecond later, the target's head exploded in a technicolor rainbow of red blood, white bone, gray brain matter, and black hair. The NVA Major standing next to him died a second later, the same way. A nearby Captain followed him. All three were dead before the first shot echoed through the valley.

Dunaway just stared in astonishment and awe. Buster could throw a bolt faster than anyone he had ever seen and remain on target. And as a past member of the USMC Rifle Team, he had seen thousands of world-class shooters. None of them even came close to matching Buster's skill. He was in a class all by himself and didn't even work at it. It just came naturally.

As the shots echoed across the valley, all three target's heads exploded. Immediately afterwards, a thousand hostile eyes began searching for the shooter. AK fire erupted from the valley floor immediately, drowning out everything and chewing up the landscape. Fortunately, it was all blind, a gut reaction based on the desire for revenge. The NVA had no real target. They only knew the general direction the shots had come from, if that. They had no idea of Buster's shooting position. Still, they were pissed, there was a shitload of them, and now they all wanted revenge.

Unexpectedly, after the three shots, an army of previously unseen NVA troops popped up from the foliage everywhere, seemingly hundreds of them. A hell of a lot more than the mere platoon Buster had been briefed on. Their Officers and NCOs began shouting frantic orders as the troops hurried to obey. They started coming out of the foliage and moving towards the ridge Buster and Mutt were on like a small tidal wave.

"Oh shit," Buster exclaimed nervously as he eyed the unexpected surge in his scope. "We've just stirred up a hornet's nest, Mutt."

"There must be over three hundred little fuckers down there."

"They're popping up everywhere."

"Not the one lousy platoon we were briefed on," he said heatedly.

"The goddamn intel was wrong," he said angrily. "and we're about to get fucked because of it."

"I can see them," Mutt confirmed disgustedly. "But it's too late to worry about that now."

"They know we're here somewhere, and they're coming to find and kill us."

"We've got to move immediately, or we'll never make it to the LZ."

"Not with all those bastards chasing us."

"Grab your shit and ruck up," he ordered angrily.

"We may never make it anyway," Buster thought fearfully as he donned his rucksack.

"Four klicks is a long goddamn way to run through the jungle with over three hundred pissed off NVA trying to run us down."

"Maybe you should have considered that before you ordered me to fire."

As the pair took off, Dunaway was already calling for their extraction chopper on the radio. Thirty seconds later, both men were tearing through the foliage headed for the LZ, balls out and running for their lives. It was a race now, pure and simple. If they got there first, they lived. If not, they died.

"Goddamn Marine Corps," Buster thought angrily. "they've been fucking me since the day I joined."

"They don't call it "The Crotch" for nothing."

"Maybe I should have taken the chain gang instead."

Chapter Three
Welcome to the Corps.

Buster Macklin was miserable. It was July, it was firecracker hot, and the broiling South Carolina sun had turned the converted school bus he was riding into a portable, rolling oven. The temperature was spiking, and the macadam road he was on only exacerbated the situation. It was another prime reason for the extreme heat. Its black asphalt absorbed the sun's heat like a thirsty sponge. Eventually, it became so hot; it was gummy to the touch. That was the case now. The tar in it was already running out and pooling on the road's shoulders which only raised the ambient temperature.

Of course, that wasn't unusual. The road was in a state where summer temperatures routinely hit the hundred-degree mark in the height of summer, and this summer was especially hot. Even with all the windows cranked down, when the hot outside air poured into the heated bus, it didn't cool anything off. Instead, all it did was move the sweat around on your face and arms and made your skin tingle.

As a result, the back of Macklin's thin print shirt was already so wet, it was plastered to the fake leather seat he was sitting in. That, in turn, made the miniature rivers of sweat inching down his back and stomach, pool at the waistband of his faded blue jeans, and form a dark wet splotch that made it look like he had pissed himself.

However, although miserable, Macklin wasn't very aware of the heat. Instead, he was more concerned about his current circumstances. He was still angry and resentful over the series of events that had gotten him here. In a word, they had been bizarre.

Oh, he realized he had fucked up and brought it all on himself, primarily by his adolescent and stupid behavior. Still, in his mind, his punishment was a harsh and unrealistic penalty to have to pay for something he considered so trivial.

As a result, he now found himself in an equally impossible situation. He felt like an alien on his way to some outer world penal colony to serve his three-year sentence. He had sinned and was now being forced to atone. As a part of his repentance, he suddenly found himself in a situation and an environment where everything around him was completely new and totally upsetting. The bus was a prime example.

It was painted olive drab, not yellow, as was the norm. In addition, it had strange little signs plastered all over the inside of it. They told its passengers, who were obviously morons and couldn't think for themselves, what they could and couldn't do while riding in it. They ordered:

"No hands or arms outside the windows."

"No swearing or spitting."

"Stay seated when moving."

It even had a large one over the aisle that read.

"This vehicle's maximum speed is 45 MPH."

"What the hell is a vehicle?" Macklin *wondered angrily.*

"This is a fucking school bus, for Christ's Sake!"

But obviously, the bus didn't hear him. Accordingly, it maintained a steady 45 mph that never varied as it rolled down the hot, black South Carolina macadam. It was then that Macklin finally realized he had involuntarily entered an alien world that he had no control over. One that was about to affect his life and his future significantly. Because both were now in the hands of total strangers. The bus was just the first taste of his new situation, and he didn't like what it portended.

Accordingly, he cursed the events that had brought him here because he certainly wasn't here by choice. That option had never presented itself. Instead, his presence here had been forced on him. Primarily because he had let his teenage hormones and out-of-control mouth get him into a pissing contest, he couldn't possibly win. Now, he would have to pay the piper for his stupidity. Unfortunately, he didn't know if he had enough ass to cover the bill.

It had all started a mere six days previous. A period that, in reflection, now seemed like a lifetime. At the time, Macklin had been in some no-name, honky-tonk, red-neck dive, just across the state line, in the north Georgia mountains. The slop chute was in the heart of shit-kicker country and in a town so backward that the schoolteachers had to be imported.

Worse, the locals were xenophobic and resistant to change. They were typical rednecks, had names like Bubba or J.T., were barely literate, and didn't cotton to strangers. Especially ones from out of state. Worse, they protected their own, regardless of right, wrong, or circumstance. They enforced their laws with biased discretion, excessive force, and mostly on nonresidents.

Mostly, they liked things just the way they were. Consequently, anyone trying to change them was aching to get his head busted, his ass beat, or enjoy life on a Georgia chain gang for a few months. Of course, Buster, full of piss and vinegar and with all those teenage hormones just begging to be turned loose, fell right into that category.

At the time, he had been drinking illegal moonshine whiskey and talking shit to a ten-dollar whore named Connie. She was telling him in delicious detail what she would do to him if he had the money. They were sitting in a dive so essential; it could only boast a sawdust floor. That should have been a red flag for Buster, but he was so drunk and lusty, he ignored it

Macklin, floating in rotgut and with a raging hard-on, was fascinated by her vivid, detailed descriptions and more than ready. Especially since she had already told him that she'd screw him till his little brown eyes crossed, in just about every position imaginable. Now she was telling him what she'd do for dessert. It all sounded so delightful Buster could hardly wait. So, after he had inspected her perky little breasts and squeezed her tight little ass, Macklin was already reaching for his wallet with a youthful lust that was ready to explode.

About that time, some fat little, pig-eyed asshole named Earl had shown up with a pissed-off look plastered all over his huffing, red face. He wore a dirty white shirt with pinstriped pants and was built like a beachball. Worse, he sported a bald head, projected a lousy attitude, and had a foul mouth.

He angrily walked right up to Macklin's face and told him that Connie was his woman. That the out- of-town youngster had better keep his evil little thoughts and his roaming hands to himself. If he didn't, he'd get a giant-sized ass whipping. Since Macklin had already consumed about half a quart of bust head by then, the whiskey, in conjunction with all his teenage hormones, made him stand up and say something stupid.

"Why don't you go take a flying fuck at a rolling donut, fat man," He snorted.

"You don't look like you got enough gas left in your tank to scare a girl scout."

"Much less whip somebody's ass."

"Now git, before I swat you like a fly."

"You little sonofabitch," Earl screamed.

A second later, he threw a wild punch at the youngster that would have taken his head off had it connected. But, with the agility of youth, Macklin easily dodged the blow. Afterward, with a lazy smile, and the outrageous, hundred-proof courage brought on by the moonshine, he proceeded to beat the living shit out of the loudmouth, with Connie screaming the entire time.

Of course, the fight didn't last long. The bartender had immediately called the cops before the first punch was thrown. It was that kind of place. Naturally, thanks to the bar's reputation, they arrived in record time, then got right down to business. The next thing Macklin knew, he was cuffed in the back seat of a police cruiser and had a knot the size of a hen's egg on his young, hard head as the police car headed for the county jail, siren wailing.

However, even in his half-drunk condition, when the cruiser passed a county road gang dressed in prison stripes and pouring asphalt a few minutes later, Macklin quickly realized he was in deep shit. Obviously, the law in this town was serious when it came to troublemakers, especially if they were outsiders. When the cell door clanged shut behind him ten minutes later, and he looked out from behind the iron bars, he was dead sure.

Southern jails don't have deluxe accommodations, and they certainly aren't known for their luxurious amenities. They boast only the bare necessities. So, with an aching head and an oncoming hangover, Macklin sat down on the steel cot in his cell and started to contemplate his sins while he worried about his future and rubbed the knot on his skull.

A long hour later, a pot-bellied deputy, wearing cowboy boots and a tan, sweat-stained Stetson, came walking down the cellblock, his heels clicking on the cheap linoleum. When he arrived at Macklin's cell, he unlocked Macklin's cell door without a word, then put a set of cuffs on him. A moment later, he frog-marched him across the street to the county courthouse.

Macklin had been in Georgia for a total of exactly three hours. In his opinion, their version of southern hospitality sucked. Unfortunately, things were about to get worse.

The judge turned out to be a leathery-faced old-timer with a shock of white hair, yellowed teeth, and a dry sense of humor. He smiled when Macklin walked in as the deputy perp-marched

Macklin up in front of his rostrum. Buster winced as he realized it was time to pay the piper.

"What's your name, boy?" the black-robed old-timer asked.

"Roan Macklin," Macklin answered with a drunken grin of his own. "But my friends call me "Buster."

"Is that so?" the judge asked, squinting.

"Well, I ain't yore friend, Macklin," the judge snapped nastily, obviously totally unimpressed with Macklin's full name.

"I'm the law here, and you're in a shit pot fulla trouble, boy."

Buster's smile disappeared even faster than the judges.

"Where you from, Macklin?" the old coot asked.

"Burl," Macklin answered. "Burl, Tennessee, just across the state line, about forty-five miles north of here."

"It's a small tow....."

"Thought so," the judge said huffily, cutting him off. "I don't recall ever seeing you around here before."

"Woulda remembered iffen I did."

"Cause you look like the kind that gets his ass into trouble regularly."

Macklin remained silent, groaning inwardly at the remark. The old fart sitting in front of him was about to hand him his young ass, and he knew it. He suddenly remembered the chain gang he had seen earlier and realized he had made a monumental goddamned mistake when he decided to drive down to north Georgia for a bit of hell-raising. Now he was going to pay dearly for his error. The old white-haired coot in front of him would ensure that.

As Macklin groaned, the judge adjusted his readers and looked down at Macklin's charge sheet. He carefully studied each line, his lips moving silently as he read every single word. When he finished, he looked back up at Macklin with a face that would have soured fresh milk.

"Had yourself quite a little time, didn't you, boy?" He said, squinting nastily.

Buster remained quiet. One attempt at cordiality had been enough. There was obviously no fuck around in this old boy. He looked like he'd been weaned on a pickle.

"The deputies got you charged with underage consumption of alcohol, drunk and disorderly, assault and battery, and resisting arrest." The old judge grunted.

"You're practically a one-man crime wave, ain'tcha, boy?"

"Oh shit," Buster thought, but he didn't answer.

It wouldn't have made any difference. He was shit out of luck, and he knew it! The old fart seated above him was about to hand him his ass.

"What you got to say about all that?" the judge asked, his face revealing he had already heard every excuse known to man about every unlawful act committed in the last decade.

"Well, judge, I was drinking with a lady friend," Macklin explained, hoping against hope that the judge would at least hear him out.

"When this fella, calling himself Earl, came up to the table and told me Connie was his woman."

"He called me a dirty name and told me to clear off, or he'd beat my ass."

"I was going to judge…. honest."

"But when I stood up to leave, he took a swing at me," Macklin said, describing the scene just as it had happened. Well almost.

"So, to protect myself, I hit him back," Buster stammered.

"The whole thing was self-defense."

"Self-defense, Huh?" The judge said, doubt written all over his face. "Got any witnesses to that?"

"The whore I was with, er, the woman I was with, name of Connie," Macklin said hopefully, as he remembered her name. "She was there."

"She saw the whole thing," Macklin said happily.

"She can tell you exactly what happened."

"Oh," the judge said disgustedly. "that Connie."

"Earl's wife, you mean."

Buster's heart skipped a beat when he heard that. He hadn't known Connie had even been married. She was obviously a whore, so he hadn't bothered to even ask. Now, with the truth coming out, even as young as he was, Buster could feel his entire future headed south at the speed of light. He was up to his eyeballs in shit, and he knew it. So, he braced himself for what he felt sure was coming. He wasn't disappointed and didn't have long to wait.

"Well," the judge continued. "there wasn't nobody around when the deputies got there, boy."

"Female or otherwise."

"Everybody else had cleared out except the bartender, who claims he didn't see shit."

"There was just you and Earl, and you'd done beat the shit out of him by that time," He added.

"He's still down at the hospital getting patched up."

"And it will probably be a week before he can even work again."

"Wonderful," Macklin thought. *"more good news."*

"I'm fucked, sure as shit."

"I'm about to become a Georgia jailbird," he told himself as he weighed his chances.

"How old are you, Macklin?" the judge asked unexpectedly.

"Eighteen," Macklin replied, a ray of hope suddenly presenting itself. Maybe.

"Got something you can show to prove it?" The judge asked.

Macklin nodded eagerly.

"My Tennessee driver's license," he replied quickly, reaching for his wallet.

"Maybe there's a chance after all." He thought excitedly, eagerly reaching for his wallet.

"Maybe the judge will take my youth into account."

"Maybe he'll even let me go because I'm barely eighteen," Macklin prayed.

"After all, boys will be boys."

"Surely the judge will understand that."

Fat chance! The judge smiled thinly as he gazed at Buster's laminated license, then he dropped the hammer.

"Well, Buster," he said, his smile widening delightedly at some hidden joke. "you've already admitted you were guilty of drinking."

"Hell, you're still half-drunk."

"I can smell the liquor on your breath from way up here," He confirmed.

"Since your driver's license proves you're underage, you ain't even supposed to be drinking, to begin with," He cackled nastily, holding up Macklin's license as the evidence.

"So that just about takes care of the first two charges."

"Oh shit." Buster suddenly realized in disgust. *"This old fart doesn't give a tinker's damn about how young I am."*

"He's gonna throw the book at me, and he's gonna use my own driver's license to help him do it."

"And you damned sure beat the shit outta Earl," The judge continued.

"He'll probably be laid up for at least a week, maybe more, which means he won't be able to work."

"My deputies can attest to that."

"I'll also bet cash money that Earl will testify that you were lying about who started the fight too."

"Him being a good tax payin' citizen of this here county and all, and Connie bein' his lawful wife."

"Since my deputies had to pull you off him when they arrived, and you took a swing at one of them in the process, that takes care of the other two charges too."

"So, all things considered, that means your side of the story is weaker than cat piss, Boy."

"And all that adds up to you being shit outta luck," The old judge said with a smile so thin it was slit in his face.

"Pears to me, you're guilty as sin of everything listed here on the charge sheet," He barked.

Buster groaned when he heard that. He had obviously fucked up one too many times, just as his Pap had warned him. Now he was about to pay for all his previous bad behavior. The old judge sitting in front of him would see to that.

Consequently, Buster suddenly saw his entire future going down the drain like old dishwater. His life along with it. Unfortunately, there wasn't a damn thing he could do about it.

A second later, the old judge confirmed all his fears.

"With nobody else around to corroborate your side of the story, boy," old White hair told him. "that means you're guilty as charged."

"Hell, we don't need a trial to determine that."

"So, unless you plead "Not Guilty" and demand one, I can sentence you right now and get this mess over with."

"Otherwise, you'll go back to jail and await a trial date."

"And that could take another month or two because my calendar is full for at least that long."

"So what will it be, boy?

"A trial a month from now or a sentence after you plead guilty."

"Do you want a trial, boy?"

Buster shook his head. "No." That would prolong the inevitable and mean more jail time while he waited.

"Road gang, here I come," Macklin thought, wincing.

"All your charges mean you're looking at about two years on the county road gang, near as I can tell, boy," the old coot snorted at Macklin, confirming his prediction. "and that's if I go lenient on you."

Although he had already been expecting it, that got Buster's immediate and undivided attention. One year wearing leg irons and pouring asphalt on a Georgia chain gang was goddamn near medieval. He didn't even want to think about having to do a two-year stretch on one. Christ, he had heard tales of men dying while trying to serve just one!

"Around here, boy," the judge explained testily. "we don't take kindly to underage juvenile delinquents coming down here from Tennessee, getting drunk, raisin' hell, then beatin' up on our citizens."

"We don't tolerate that kinda shit in these parts."

"So, when that happens," old white hair explained patiently. "we usually just throw their asses in jail for a year or two and teach 'em some manners."

"Pouring asphalt for the county in hundred-degree heat in the summer and digging out frozen drainpipes in the winter seven days a week generally gets their minds right and straightens their young asses right out."

"Gives them an entirely new attitude and outlook on life."

"Cause if the guards on the chain gang can't teach you right from wrong by working you half to death, then they'll beat it into you."

"And believe me, son, that's an education you don't want any part of."

"It's a real ball-buster and life-changer," he cackled.

Macklin could feel his sphincter tightening as he thought about it and winced.

"There it is," he thought glumly.

"My Pappy tried to warn me I'd get my ass into deep shit if I didn't straighten up and change my attitude and ways."

"Told me to quit drinking and hell-raising more than once."

"I was just too smart-assed to listen."

"Now I'm about to find out what he said was true, and I'm going to do it the hard way."

"Course, it doesn't have to come down to that," the judge said unexpectedly a moment later, with a sly smile.

Macklin's head popped up so fast he hurt his neck. Unbelievably, the judge was offering him another choice.

"I could let you enlist instead," The judge told him.

"If you did, I'd drop all the charges."

"Enlist," Buster thought in alarm. *"In what?"*

"What the fuck is this old coot talking about?"

"The organization I'm referring to will make a man outta you, boy," the judge said, smiling as if reading Macklin's mind.

"Get rid of all that excess energy and all them teenage hormones that are getting you into so much trouble."

"Teach you how to act in public, and learn you some manners in the process."

"Grow you some too and make a man out of you."

"Give you a whole new outlook on life and get you back on the good road."

"It's the proudest band of cutthroats in this country," He said, smiling widely.

"Used to belong to it myself," he said proudly, showing Macklin a faded tattoo on his arm. "And right now, it's got a big need for fresh meat."

"So, make up your mind, boy," The judge said expectantly.

"Which one will it be?"

"The county road gang for two years, or the United States Marine Corps?"

Buster's heart sank.

"Shit," he thought angrily. "Some choice."

"I'm screwed either way."

Ten minutes later, the deputy escorted Macklin across the street to the local recruiter's office. There he showed his ID, proving he was eighteen, then signed the appropriate paperwork. Afterwards, the deputy took off his cuffs and laughed as he walked out. Apparently, this wasn't the first offender he had escorted into the waiting graces of the US Marines.

After he left, the Marine recruiter told Macklin to find a bunk in the back of the building and sack out. He told him he'd depart for the recruit training depot the following day. He also told him not to even think about leaving before then. The Marine MPs were not as gentle as the county deputies were, and they would prove that when they found him again. When they did, he would find himself in worse trouble than before he enlisted. The look on the recruiter's face convinced Buster he wasn't lying.

Chapter Four
The New Breed

After signing his enlistment papers, the young hell raiser Tennessee with a penchant for booze and babes, changed dramatically. Before the ink was dry, he became Macklin, Roan, A. Serial number: 4456178. Rank: Marine recruit trainee. Destination: Marine Corps Recruit Training Depot, Parris Island, South Carolina. Status: Fucked!

That had been two days ago. Now the living nightmare Buster had enlisted for was in the process of unfolding. In the process, his entire way of thinking, acting, talking, and way of doing everything else, along with his overall attitude, was about to take a radical right-hand turn. He would soon discover everything he had learned or done previously had been wrong. But there was hope.

His Marine DIs would teach him the correct way of acting, doing, thinking, speaking, and obeying. When his transformation was complete, Roan Macklin, the young hell riser from

Tennessee, would be no more. He would become Macklin, Roan A, Pvt, United States Marine Corps, a certified life-taker and heartbreaker.

First, however, he had to survive Boot Camp. Fortunately for Buster, he had no idea what that entailed. Had he, he might have gone AWOL immediately and fled the recruiting station. All that had been two days ago. Now, his future was about as firm as a diaper full of baby shit.

Forty-five minutes later, the bus went through Parris Island's main gate. It was manned by two smartly dressed man-mountains, who looked capable of running the bus down and stopping it with their bare hands if they had to. After they waved the bus through the checkpoint, it traveled another mile or so, then pulled up to a puke yellow, WWII vintage wooden building with peeling paint. There, it stopped with a squeal of brakes. Afterwards, the inquisition began.

When the bus door opened, a gorilla dressed in a snappy uniform came aboard and screamed to everybody that they had exactly three fucking seconds to unload the *"Vehicle"* and fall out onto two yellow lines painted on the parking lot outside.

"Last man off this bus will rue the day he was fucking born and give me fifty pushups for being so goddamned slow," he threatened menacingly.

A second later, it was assholes and elbows as everybody ran for the door. Obviously, this man was not a person to be fucked with. Failure to obey his commands would undoubtedly result in him handing you your ass. Painfully.

Naturally, as raw recruits, Macklin and his contemporaries soon proved incapable of even lining up correctly once outside. Even with yellow lines showing them exactly where to stand. Of course, they were immediately corrected by their helpful DI. He not only showed them how to dress right and cover down, but he also showed them the correct, Marine way to execute pushups and squat thrusts for their ignorance. Exercises they continued for at least ten minutes until they were all bathed in sweat, and he was satisfied he had their undivided attention. Afterwards, they were herded into a building for the next step necessary to enter the Marine Corps.

After emptying their pockets of any suspected "contraband," ten minutes later, they found themselves standing inside a room with their right hands raised, being sworn into the Corps by a Marine officer. When the small ceremony concluded, they discovered they had all just become certified pieces of United States Marine Corps property. Like it or not, their asses now belonged to the US Marines. After that, things went downhill at about the speed of light, and their lives changed immediately and dramatically.

In the space of the next six hours, Marine Recruit Trainee Macklin, Roan A., along with thirty-eight other ignorant, miscreant assholes, who had the misfortune to be with him, went through a whirlwind of initial orientations, equipment issue, medical inspections, and barracks assignment. They were accompanied by a level of verbal and physical abuse issued by their friendly Drill Instructors that was almost biblical in its proportions.

They ran everywhere, did pushups for every imagined infraction possible, and were told loudly and regularly that they were worthless pieces of useless, prehistoric, amphibian shit. Fucked up abortions that had somehow managed to crawl out of the cesspool they were born in and were now, by some unknown miracle, United States Marine Corps trainees!

Since they had just become certified applicants to the Corps, from now on, they would do what they were told, how they were told, when they were told. Exactly! If they didn't, the entire world would fall in on their worthless asses. As recruit trainees, there would be no relief, escape, or going back. They were at Parris Island to prove they had what it takes to become Marines or die trying in the attempt.

To stay there, they would have to prove they were ready to walk through fire and piss napalm, eat steel rails and spit thumbtacks, whip Superman's ass daily, and do every other fucking thing they were told to do by their omniscient Drill Instructors. It was almost a religious experience.

For the remainder of that miserable day, Macklin and the thirty-eight idiots with him were treated to a never-ending, minute-by-minute barrage of physical and verbal abuse, the likes of which they had never dreamed possible. Macklin felt like he had just entered the Twilight Zone and had been abducted by aliens. Hard men who had every intention of eventually killing him but wanted to completely grind his ass into dust before doing so.

In the next few hours, he had his stature, looks, personality, lineage, education, and his constant and ever-increasing list of errors, all colorfully described to him in language that was so vulgar and profane that he never knew some of it even existed. All this confirmed that he was now living in another universe. One in which he would be lucky to survive during the next twenty-four hours.

After a visit to the post barber shop, where it took a shearer precisely twelve seconds to remove every single hair on his head, Macklin soon found himself and his platoon entering a mess hall to eat what the Corps colorfully called. "Chow."

Chow was the Marine Corp's creative term for breakfast, lunch, or dinner. It was an absolute culinary delight that closely resembled vomitus. It was served in huge portions that overlapped the steel trays it was slopped onto.

Fortunately, Macklin was ravenous. So, despite the food's dubious looks and taste, he consumed everything on his tray. However, half of his platoon didn't, a cardinal offense in the Corps. Their lack of hunger proved that the Marine recruits didn't really care about the Mess Sgts that had gone to so much trouble to feed them. Thus they were thus sorely disappointed that all their time and trouble had not been appreciated.

As a result, the offenders had the privilege of licking their trays clean with their hands behind their backs and the trays on the mess hall floor. They lapped it up like dogs, all under the watchful eyes of their DIs who screamed at them to eat even faster. In this manner, they were forced to remove every single scrap on the stainless-steel tray before they turned it back into the KPs. It was an educational experience none would ever forget, and few would repeat.

After that painful lesson on the consequences of failure to consume all the delicious food the Corps had graciously provided them, the platoon then enjoyed an exhilarating two-mile run back to their barracks. During it, over half of them threw up what they had just eaten. Another gross error they would soon regret!

Consequently, on arrival, everyone was treated to a highly motivating verbal counseling session. It concerned all the sins they had committed during their previous six hours in the Marine Corps, and there were many. Afterwards, they atoned for them in the leaning rest position while they did endless pushups. All while they were offered constant, helpful, corrective advice by their concerned DI's to motivate them.

While they listened to this thirty-minute fairy tale of abject sloth and unbelievably moronic behavior on their part, they knocked out endless repetitions of the exercise until their muscles failed. All the while being screamed at by the senior Drill Instructor's two chief assistants. An exciting pair of psychotic, muscle-bound Neanderthals who continually threatened to rip all the trainee's balls off if their so far dismal performance didn't improve immediately and dramatically.

Overall, the platoon's collective first-day experience as new prospective Marines was, in a word, catastrophic. Shortly after lights out, when they were finally allowed the luxury of sleep, whimpering and soft sobs could be heard in the otherwise dark barracks. It came from some of the recruits who had never endured anything remotely like this before.

But not Macklin. He wasn't scared or disoriented or even apprehensive about what else was in store for him. Instead, he was furious. At himself for the juvenile antics that had gotten him there and at the old man who had been responsible for his election to join the Corps.

"*If I could get my hands around that white-haired old judge's neck,*" he told himself angrily. "*I'd strangle the sonofabitch!*"

The following day, after another round of delicious "chow," the Platoon got its first lesson on learning how to march. It was the first of many such sessions because the Marine Corps is big on marching. The Drill Instructors absolutely live for it. As such, they treat their undertrained recruit charges to mindless repetitions of it at every available opportunity.

Unfortunately, a mere three minutes into the training, Macklin suddenly discovered he was out of step with the rest of the platoon. He knew this was an absolute fact because his drill instructor suddenly appeared an inch in front of his face and began screaming at him!

"Macklin," the DI roared, his face so contorted with rage, the veins in his neck visibly inflated as it turned crimson with rage.

"Are you actually trying to tell me you are so fuckin' dumb you don't even know your left from your right?"

"No, Drill Sergeant," Macklin bellowed.

Macklin felt a hard slap against the left side of his head and his cheeks stung as his ears rang.

"Which side is that asshole?" the DI screamed.

"My left side, Drill Sergeant," Macklin roared.

There was an immediate hard slap to the right side of his head, which also stung unmercifully.

"And which side is that?" the DI yelled.

"My right side, Drill Sergeant," Macklin thundered.

"So, you _were_ lying to me, weren't you, you miserable little prick," the DI roared.

"You do know your right from your left."

"Yes, Drill Sergeant," Macklin responded automatically, suddenly realizing that any answer he gave would be wrong.

"You miserable little insect," the DI thundered.

"You're deliberately trying to fuck with my head, aren't you?"

"No Drill Sergeant," Macklin screamed in abject fear.

"Then you better have your screwed-up brain housing group tell your fucked up, irresponsible feet they had better get their goddamned act together, Macklin," the DI roared.

"Otherwise, I'll teach you your left from your right in a manner that's so goddamn painful you won't ever forget it."

"Is that perfectly clear, you little backwoods cockroach?" the DI screamed.

"Yes, Drill Sgt," Macklin roared

"You fuck my formation up again with your half-assed, civilian idea of marching; I will personally gouge your eyes out and piss in the empty sockets," The DI warned.

"You got that, you little jerk off?"

"Yes, Drill Sergeant," Macklin responded as he cringed, uncertain if he would even survive the remainder of the day.

"Get your sorry ass back in formation, you little maggot," the DI screamed.

The DI then stormed back to the head of the formation, screaming at the rest of the fuck ups in Macklin's platoon and promising them that he would march their sorry asses around the parade ground until they either wore ruts in the asphalt or their miserable attempt at marching in formation improved to a point it didn't resemble some dyslexic, Chinese fire drill.

"Welcome to the United States Fucking Marine Corps, you stupid asshole," Macklin *thought to himself in complete disgust.*

"Christ, even the chain gang would have been better than this!"

And so, it went. The situation never improving and continually deteriorating. From then on, Macklin and his fellow recruits wondered if they would ever do anything right again. Of course, that question was re-emphasized daily over the next few weeks. During that time, Macklin and every other recruit in his platoon continued to screw up by the numbers despite themselves.

Accordingly, their Drill Instructors continued to correct their totally screwed up and irresponsible attempts to do as they were told with endless rounds of pushups, squat thrusts, and other delightful, sweat-producing exercises. They were always accompanied by volumes of screaming lectures designed to correct them. But, no matter how hard they tried, the new trainees couldn't do anything right. Worse, they were constantly reminded of that fact by their helpful DIs in simple, direct, and highly profane language.

Since none of the recruits seemed able to follow simple instructions and do what they were told on their own, the DI's deliberately set about teaching them the correct way of doing things, the Marine Corps way.

Over time, they were taught how to act, how to speak, how to walk, how to dress, how to eat, how to think, how to accomplish even the most basic of tasks, and how to organize and maintain their newly issued Marine Corps equipment until it was absolutely spotless, among other things.

During those agonizing lessons, Macklin and the rest of his platoon were all firmly convinced they were complete and worthless fuck ups. Ugly, little useless pimples stuck on the ass of the world who were incapable of correctly accomplishing even the most basic of tasks. Simple-minded morons whose only purpose in the world was to provide sadistic amusement for their rabid drill instructors, who were desperately trying to teach them, but obviously failing.

Finally, in their sixth week of training, they were marched to the rifle range, where their marksmanship training began. There, suddenly, Macklin's world abruptly changed.

As the platoon marched onto the range complex, Buster smiled for the first time in almost seven weeks.

"I have finally found something that I can do right," he thought excitedly. *"even to Drill Sergeant Kimmel's exacting standards."*

"Even he won't be able to fault me on my performance," Macklin thought to himself in excited anticipation.

"Wait until he sees me shoot."

But that was a pipedream. Drill Sergeant Kimmel was an absolute expert at finding faults with everything. He could find ten separate moral turpitude violations in five seconds with Jesus Christ himself if he put his mind to it. The man was almost supernatural in his abilities.

After an initial lecture on basic marksmanship, followed by an hour of dry firing, everyone in the platoon zeroed their weapon. They were then paired off, one firer and one coach, and assigned a numbered firing lane. Macklin's was number fourteen.

Three hundred yards downrange was his target. A six-foot white circle with decreasing intermediate rings, ending in a six-inch black bull's eye at its center. Theoretically, following their initial marksmanship instruction, the trainees were supposed to place five shots out of their initial seven, somewhere on their target, with the aid of their "coach."

Unfortunately, their coach was a fellow trainee just like them. Another idiot who was undoubtedly even more ignorant than they were regarding marksmanship. So, the trainee's ability to hit much of anything was in serious doubt. But their weeklong training here would rectify that.

"Firers," the loudspeaker in the tower blared, "lock and load your seven-round magazine."

An audible, collective click on the firing line signaled the twenty-five firers had seated their magazines into their weapon's magazine well, then pulled back their extractor rods and charged their pieces.

"Ready on the right. Ready on the left. Ready on the firing line," The loudspeaker blared.

Heads nodded their preparedness, and red flags were raised as shooters shouldered their weapons. Buster settled in, snuggling the steel butt plate of the M-14's dark stock into his shoulder like an old girlfriend. Then he got a tight spot weld on the rifle's stock, acquired a good steady sight picture, and shallowed out his breathing. Finally, he snicked off the safety and took up the slack in the trigger.

"Commence firing," the loudspeaker ordered.

Buster commenced firing all seven rounds in rapid but controlled succession. It took him less than ten seconds. He then safed the weapon, checked the chamber, and removed the magazine. When he did, his coach timidly raised his hand, signaling Buster had finished firing. Meanwhile, every other firer on the range was just getting their second round off.

When Buster looked up, Kimmel was standing over him, glaring. His face was so angry looking he looked like he was Mount Vesuvius getting ready to erupt.

"Just what in the *fuck* do you think you're doing, you little Dickweed?" He roared at Macklin.

Macklin was stunned. So astonished, his smile of expected congratulations disappeared abruptly.

"You are supposed to be trying to place accurate, controlled fire on your target, you goddamned moron," Kimmel screamed.

"That means slow and deliberate aiming and firing, with good sight alignment and a soft trigger squeeze."

"But No," he screamed sarcastically. "Not you, you simple-minded little turd."

"Instead, you're trying to play Machine Gun Kelly."

"Oh Shit," Buster thought in terror. "what have I done?"

"Didn't any of the marksmanship lecture you just received sink into that pea-sized brain of yours, you incompetent little maggot?" Kimmel thundered.

Now Buster was crestfallen.

"Obviously not," Kimmel roared, now really getting into it because he was so angry.

"Because instead of trying to learn to be a Marine marksman," he screamed. "You're acting like you're Wild Bill fucking Hickok at some goddamn half-assed wild west gunfight."

"Some cowboy trying to impress everybody with how fast you can empty your piece."

"That," Kimmel screamed, pointing at Macklin's M-14, "is a semi-automatic rifle, numb nuts."

"Not a goddamn machine gun."

"That means that you don't try and shoot the sonofabitch as fast as you can pull the trigger."

By this time, Buster was unsuccessfully trying to melt silently into the ground.

"Is any of this getting through to you, shit-for-brains?" Kimmel screamed hopefully.

Macklin just stared straight ahead at rigid attention, wholly bewildered and afraid to answer. He had intended to impress Kimmel with his shooting. Not anger him off so badly he would go postal. Obviously, that wasn't happening. Now what?

"Get off the firing line; you little jerk off," Kimmel screamed.

Then he really lit into him.

Moments later, as he stopped to get his second wind, Kimmel glanced downrange at Macklin's target, intending to use it as a teaching point in Buster's monumental ass chewing. Amazingly, the scorer in the pits was signaling seven bull's eyes. Kimmel's eyes bulged in total astonishment, and he could hardly believe it. But before he could say anything, the tower loudspeaker blared again.

"Firer on lane fourteen, report to the tower immediately."

"Oh, shit," Macklin cringed. "that's me."

"I'm about to get an even worse ass-chewing than Kimmel's."

"If that's even possible."

"Permission to report to the tower, Drill Sergeant," Macklin screamed.

"Get your fucking ass up there, you insignificant little worm," Kimmel thundered.

"And when they've finished with you, report back to me," He added.

Ten seconds later, Macklin stood at attention in front of the range NCOIC. He was a grizzled, leather-tanned Gunnery Sgt. who looked like he had been sent by God as his personal enforcer for any ignorant asshole attempting to fuck up his marksmanship training. One look at him told you there was no fuck around in this old boy. He was all Marine and all business.

The Gunny was inspecting a target when Macklin marched up. Glancing down quickly, Macklin suddenly realized it was his target because it had the number 14 written across its top.

"Oh shit," he thought. "Here it comes."

"I'll probably be glad to see Sgt Kimmel again when the Gunny gets through with me."

"So much for my idea of trying to impress him."

"Recruit trainee Macklin, Roan A, reporting as ordered," Macklin bellowed loudly as his sphincter tightened in preparation for the colossal ass-chewing he knew he was about to receive. Imagine his relief when, amazingly, that didn't happen.

"At ease, Macklin," the Gunny ordered calmly, "and answer me in a normal voice from now on."

"Jesus Christ," Macklin thought in complete disbelief.

"He's treating me like a normal human being."

"He's not even screaming at me."

"Is he drunk, or am I dreaming?"

But it turned out to be neither.

"Where are you from, Macklin?" the Gunny asked calmly.

"Burl, Tennessee, Sergeant," Macklin replied, still stunned.

"Who taught you to shoot like this?" the Gunny asked as he showed Macklin his target.

It had seven small holes in the center of the black bull's eye you could have covered with the bottom of a Campbell's soup can.

"My Daddy, Sergeant," Macklin replied.

"What did you usually shoot at back in Burl?" the Gunny asked.

"Rabbits, squirrels, turkey, possum," Macklin replied, "sometimes a deer, Sergeant."

"Anything to put food on the table."

"We hunted pretty near every day if we wanted to eat."

The Gunny nodded and said, "Ummm, I thought it might be something like that."

"Ever shoot at paper targets before? the Gunny asked a moment later. "Like this one?"

"No sir, Gunny," Macklin replied. "Today was my first time."

"We didn't have money for things like that; no ammo, neither."

"And nobody but your father has ever taught you anything about shooting?" The Gunny continued.

"You're sure about that?"

"No sir, Gunnery Sgt," Macklin replied. "Just my Pap."

The Gunnery Sgt took a long look at Macklin, then another look at his target and the seven closely spaced holes in it. He then shook his head in wonder.

"All right, Macklin," the Gunny ordered. "report back your DI and tell him to come see me."

"Aye, Aye, Gunny," Macklin responded.

Afterwards, he did a smart about-face, came to port arms, and ran back to the platoon area to find Sgt. Kimmel and relay the message.

Fifteen minutes later, as Macklin cleaned his weapon, Kimmel walked up and motioned him over to where he stood.

"Macklin," he said conversationally. "get your ass over here."

Macklin put his weapon down and ran over to where Kimmel was standing, a good twenty yards from the rest of the platoon.

"My God," Macklin thought in amazement. "Kimmel has just spoken to me in a normal voice for the first time."

"Am I hearing correctly?"

He then wondered what the hell was going on and how much trouble he was now in.

"Listen up, shitbird," Kimmel said in a low voice, his eyes boring into Macklin.

"You keep your mouth shut and your nose clean for two more weeks, and you're gonna graduate and become a real Marine."

"You impressed the Gunny with your shooting just now, and believe me, that doesn't happen very often around here," He told Macklin unexpectedly.

"So, after you graduate, you're going to get some specialized training from some people who are going to teach you how to *really* shoot."

"If you learn enough, you might make something out of yourself in the Corps."

"Understand?"

Macklin nodded, not quite believing this was happening.

"Now, get your piece cleaned up and keep your mouth shut about all this," Kimmel ordered in a low whisper.

"You run off at the mouth about any of this to your moron friends," he threatened. "I will hear about it."

"When I do, I will take you out behind the nearest tree, rip your fucking head off, then shit down your neck!"

"Got me?"

"Yes, Drill Sergeant," Macklin answered with a slight smile.

That started it.

Chapter Five
A Brand New War

When Gunnery Sergeant Casey awoke, he was shivering. That was odd because the temperature outside the hut was almost ninety degrees in the nearby jungle. The nights in Vietnam were like that, hot, sultry, and uncomfortable, with humidity so high, you sometimes felt like you were drowning instead of sleeping. But Casey hadn't been swimming. His slumber had been deep but restless, troubled by his past. During it, his numbed body had been far away in another place and another era. It was that same, ageless, recurring dream he had never been able to rid himself of. It lay burned into his brain permanently, a constant reminder of misery and death.

The specter of stiff frozen bodies, strapped onto trucks, with their icy, lifeless eyes staring upwards, and their exposed, waxy-looking skin, stretched white and taut, was a picture impossible for him to erase. Fortunately, the dreams always ended. The memories, however, didn't. The Chosin Reservoir was an experience that would never be forgotten or erased, no matter how many years had passed.

But the youthful buck sergeant in charge of twenty-odd, half-frozen Marines had somehow lived through that nightmare and fought his way out of the Chosin Reservoir along with the rest of the 1st Marine Division. They had chopped and hacked their way through what seemed like half the Chinese Army, and done that under the bitterest and most severe weather conditions imaginable. In doing so, they had forever made a name for themselves in American military history. They had fought every step of the way as a unit against impossible odds. They had endured until what was left of the Division had finally reached the LSTs in the port of Hung Nam and been evacuated.

That had been the young Casey's first taste of combat, and he had seen it at its worst, experiencing the extremes of war, both in climate and savagery. He had killed. He had overcome the brutal conditions in which he had to fight, and he had somehow survived. He had not only fought his way back to safety, but he had also led the rest of his platoon in doing it.

Take care of your men, the first basic rule of command.

Consequently, that leadership exercise was forever imprinted in his brain housing group.

After that ordeal, Casey knew he would never fear death again. He had already looked it straight in the eye, laughed at it, and finally welcomed it. Death had stalked him for too long on that frozen march out of hell, but in the end, he had beaten it. So, it didn't scare him anymore.

The Chosin had forged him, tempered him, and forever shaped him. It had been his first taste of fear, his first command, and his first war. Now, Vietnam was his second.

He was older, wiser, and more experienced now. A certified life taker who was an expert at dispensing death. He had learned his skills in the most demanding of war's classrooms and then honed them to a fine edge over the ensuing years through relentless practice. Now he and the men he commanded were cold-eyed, efficient killers who took lives with practiced ease, not only in ones and twos occasionally but usually in greater numbers and regularly.

They were merciless and deadly. He had made them that way. He had trained them, mentored them, and practiced them until they were experienced single-shot killers of the first order. He had taught them that war was the same in almost every respect, no matter where it was being fought. In the final analysis, if you were at the tip of the spear, you either killed or got killed. It was the same at Chosin, or here in the Asian jungle, with only one fundamental difference. Now, instead of freezing to death as you fought, you sweated.

Casey was convinced there would never be a war in a temperate country that boasted a moderate climate. God wouldn't allow that because Marines were meant to suffer. It was part of their contract with him.

Gunnery Sergeant John Casey thought briefly about his career as he shook off the last dregs of sleep and climbed out of his rack. He was a career Marine, a "lifer." A young man who had enlisted in the Corps when he had turned eighteen, mainly because he didn't know the difference between exotic and erotic.

He had mistakenly believed that Marines sent overseas would be besieged by bevies of beautiful erotic women throwing themselves at them. Instead, he quickly discovered that women in Asia, although exotic, were not erotic. Instead, they were slight slant-eyed females who distrusted westerners intensely, usually didn't wear makeup, and rarely bathed.

The nations they lived in were vastly different, too, at least to the average National Geographic-reading westerner. The glossy photographs typically featured in those types of publications were primarily myths. Deliberate advertising propaganda displayed in staged photos, all designed to sell magazines and lure tourists.

Unfortunately, the real Asia was something altogether different, and it wasn't pretty. It was a sea of unwashed humanity, where life was cheap, thinking was fatalistic, illiteracy was rampant, wars were commonplace, and crops were fertilized with human shit. So, the words erotic or exotic hardly applied to either it or its women.

Casey had spent most of his adult life in the business of killing. Asians mostly. They were small, slant-eyed, yellowish-skinned men who never appeared to tire and always seemed prepared to die. They were never-ending, seemingly able to breed faster than you could kill them. Worse, they were always fighting for a piece of land that no one else seemed to want or even care about. But the price paid by the US for real estate like that was far too high. Especially since we usually gave it away after we had tried so hard to win it.

Vietnam was a prime example. No one cared about the place except the Vietnamese, and even most of them didn't give a damn who ran the country. The vast majority just wanted to be left alone. Free to grow their rice and raise their kids. Communism or democracy was all the same to them. They were both simply hollow words and inane concepts; they could neither fathom nor explain. Certainly nothing worth dying over.

Governments had never given them anything anyway, regardless of what political system they espoused. Politicians were just vain men dressed in suits who lived in big cities and yearned for power. To achieve it, they always had to take it by force from other politicians, and when they did, men fought and died in the process.

So, conflict, and all the ills that came with it, were, by now, a way of life for the Vietnamese. They had experienced it for generations, ever since their tiny country had been born. They had been an occupied people forever. First by the Chinese, then the French, then the Japanese, then the French again, and now the Americans;

the latest foreigners come to rule and tell them how their country should be run.

Now there were decades piled upon decades of continuous foreigners, who always brought the war with them when they arrived. Great grandfathers, their sons, grandsons, and great-grandsons had all perished in the eternal struggle. Death was never-ending, and as a result, the country had never known peace. Even worse, more would die before this latest conflict ended. War had exterminated generations in its past and was now headed towards eliminating record numbers in the future, as Western technology made killing more efficient.

Unfortunately, their leaders during all that time had been the same: sly, cunning, evil men with giant egos. They desired wealth and power and routinely used simple peasants to obtain it for them. Once they had achieved it, they usually disenfranchised the people who gave it to them. It was a vicious and never-ending cycle, with the only real losers being the innocents. They remained the ultimate victims, regardless of what political system governed them.

However, as inhumane and regrettable as it might have sounded, all that was a political or a social issue, and Casey didn't deal with those types of problems. He was a professional Marine, and his job was not to mandate, contemplate, advocate, or even negotiate. He was sent to simply exterminate. He couldn't afford the luxury of even wondering why. Therefore, all his energy and concentration were focused on that task, as well as on keeping himself and the men under him alive. At the same time, they eradicated their targets as efficiently and quickly as possible. What the poor Asian bastards were dying for was their problem. His job was simply to hurry them along in the process. As the senior NCO of the most elite band of killers, the world had ever known that task was an easy one.

Casey and his men were all members of the 1st Marine Division's Scout Sniper Platoon. Their unofficial motto was *We deal in lead,* and they lived up to their reputation. They were cold-eyed, world-class killers of the first order. They saw their victim's agonized faces in their scopes, as a one hundred and fifty-grain slug plowed into him at over three thousand feet per second, and he died before their eyes. As snipers, they espoused *One Shot, One Kill,* and they were experts at their trade.

Pound for pound and man for man, they were the most efficient killers in Southeast Asia, maybe the world. For thirteen cents a round, the average price of a single .308 bullet, they killed as cheaply and as efficiently as possible. A trail of dead North Vietnamese Army Dog Soldiers stretching from the DMZ in I Corps, all the way down to the mountains of II Corps, was a testament to their prowess and their efficiency.

Enemy privates, corporals, sergeants, officers, even an NVA General had all been their victims at one time or another. They had all died the same way, from a single round through their head or chest. With eyes bulging from the shock of a .308 round impacting their skulls or upper torsos, they had all exploded in a panoramic burst of red as the copper jacketed round plowed into them and flung them backward. When that happened, their comrades around them were at first shocked but later terrified by the suddenness of it all.

No one was immune, and no one was safe, not even in their secret sanctuaries hidden across the border in Laos. That made the members of the Scout Sniper Platoon equal opportunity eliminators who had an international reach. It also made the entire North Vietnamese Army and their surrogates, the Viet Cong, simply potential targets.

So effective were Casey's killers that the North Vietnamese government had put bounties on their heads to try and stem the slaughter. Their soldiers were regularly butchered from ranges up to a thousand yards, and they had no other remedy. The poor unsuspecting bastards died in explosions of blood before their comrades even heard the shot. Those kinds of death were taking a deadly toll on both morale and combat effectiveness.

With each new killing, the NVA Dog soldiers lost more and more self-confidence, ensuring morale was at an all-time low and sinking fast. It was almost impossible to remain courageous when you never saw your friend's killers, and their heads exploded around you in a rainbow of red blood, gray brain matter, black hair, and white bone. After that terrifying spectacle, it was difficult to force your body to stand up and resume the fight. Especially when you didn't know where the shooter was, and you realized you could be next!

But even bounties for their scalps hadn't deterred the 1st Marine Division Scout Sniper Platoon's snipers. Instead, it had only boosted their morale and spurred them on towards achieving even higher body counts. Now there was an unofficial competition within the unit to see who could record the greatest number of confirmed kills in a single twelve-month combat tour.

Consequently, numbers were already nearing the high eighties, and there seemed to be no end in sight. After all, it was what snipers termed a *target-rich environment.* Because, in their tight, close-knit community, the world was divided into two categories: targets and all others, and business was booming!

Regular Marines fought in units and used teamwork and tactics to close with, attack, and kill their opponents in conjunction with massive firepower. In contrast, Marine snipers worked alone or in pairs, a sniper and a spotter. They killed from long distances with no warning and a single shot. One that was almost always unexpected and usually one hundred percent fatal. Because of that, there was usually no way for the NVA to retaliate because the sniper was too far away or too carefully camouflaged. Besides, he was always concealed. So, trying to even locate where the shot had come from was generally impossible.

As a result, it was maddening having to watch your comrades around you suddenly die from a lone shot and not being able to exact any revenge or even see their attacker. It was terrifying when a round blew the back of a man's head off, and you didn't know where it had come from or who would be next.

Model 70 Winchesters chambered in .308 caliber and fitted with 7x 50 Redfield scopes, or 30-06 Remington Model 700 BDLs with advanced Urtel optics were the weapons of choice. The ammunition was Lake City Match Grade, the specially made rounds typically used in National competitions. Each one had been specifically loaded and neck turned, then its brass and projectile checked for imperfections before being selected. Finally, the rounds were boxer primed to ensure accuracy. Sometimes, even the weapons themselves had been specially constructed, with their actions pearled, their triggers and sears reworked for smoothness, their receivers bedded in fiberglass, and their chambers fitted with heavy barrels to give them increased accuracy and a minute of angle grouping. That made them capable of killing at extreme distances.

With sophisticated implements such as these, a scout sniper platoon member could shoot the balls off a male mosquito at three hundred yards! That made killing a normal human being at that range mere child's play. The actual shot was, in fact, the easy part. The stalk and getting yourself into a secure position where you could make it was the problematic end of the equation, along with getting your ass back to safety afterward. But Casey's men had been trained in the fine art of stalking, too, so they were generally able to locate, maneuver to, and then engage any target they were sent after. And when they found it, they killed it!

The North Vietnamese soldiers despised Casey's killers, but at the same time, they were terrified of them. After all, the NVA Dog soldiers were supposed to be the ones who typically fought from hiding and were rarely seen by their American counterparts. They were the ones who usually killed at a time and place of their choosing, then faded back into the concealment of the jungle. That's what they were known for.

But Casey's killers were now using their own tactics against them. Now the NVA were the ones being butchered regularly using those same methods. Moreover, those killings weren't from chance meetings or random encounters and firefights with Marine units in the field. They were being deliberately hunted and surgically eliminated by cold-eyed, merciless killers who were rarely seen and never missed.

They weren't safe anywhere. Casey's men even stalked them across the border into neighboring Laos, where the NVA had hidden sanctuaries that were supposedly sacrosanct. Americans were supposedly forbidden to enter the country because it was neutral in the war, but obviously that was just a myth. The American snipers followed them there too, and when they found them, the North Vietnamese died as quickly and as easily there as they did back in South Vietnam. No tactic the North Vietnamese government had yet devised was effective in eliminating the American killers. So, in the end, the NVA were all simply targets, in Laos or elsewhere.

Chapter Six
A brand new Concept

The scout sniper ideology in the Marine Corps was a relatively new concept in military thinking back in 1965. Marines had always had sharpshooters and snipers, going back to their creation. The Corps was even renowned for its fabled reputation of making a Marine a rifleman first and then training him in his essential military skill afterward. But until Vietnam, becoming a sniper had been just a learned skill that selected individuals who were good shots had been hastily trained for, then sent to Marine units to employ. When and if they were available.

Being a sniper was not a formalized Marine occupational specialty that required specialized training. At that time, snipers were usually just non-standard add-ons to Marine units. They had no permanent home and no formal training. Thus, they were generally considered the red-headed stepchildren of the Corps, not even having a formal military classification.

Although their skills were admired, their popularity and association were often shunned.

Somehow, in the convoluted thinking of regular Marines, snipers were more akin to assassins than soldiers. Apparently, to them, it was acceptable to kill as a member of a Marine unit engaged in a firefight, with hundreds of rounds going downrange towards indiscriminate targets. But to deliberately stalk and then kill a solitary enemy soldier with a single shot from a concealed position was unacceptable.

So, for various reasons, some reasonable and others completely unsustainable, accreditation of the sniper as a trained and coded military occupational specialty had never been formalized as a standard military occupational specialty in the Marine Corps. That would have required attendance and training at a specialized school created to produce such individuals and then award them a special personnel skills identifier when they graduated. However, neither the school nor the military occupational specialty existed. Then Vietnam came along, and attitudes suddenly changed about all that. Not only for the Marines but the Army as well.

Because the US Army had snipers, too, as well as scouts. They used both these specialties in much the same manner as the Marine Corps, normally informally. Because the Army didn't have military occupational specialty codes for snipers either. They were good marksmen added to regular units too.

But the Army divided those two tasks into two separate categories, with different personnel trained and assigned to conduct each of them. They even gave each position a different name and assigned an individual to accomplish it.

The Marine Corps didn't. Instead, it combined the two tasks and charged a single Marine to accomplish them both. Therefore, a Marine scout sniper was a specially trained and highly efficient sharpshooter charged with the mission of placing long-range precision fire on a selected target. He was also an accomplished scout, capable of performing reconnaissance missions and sending valuable combat-related information back to his headquarters. At least he would be if the concept of Scout Sniper was ever validated and adopted within the Corps.

A mustang Captain by the name of Ed Land had proposed the original idea and was now its foremost proponent in the Marine community. As a Marine NCO, Land had been an accomplished shooter in his own right and had been on the Marine Corps Rifle Team. He won numerous trophies at the Camp Perry matches and other shooting venues. As a result, he had the background and credentials to promote the idea and try and get the required backing within the Marine Corps leadership to set up a working test bed to find out if it would work.

Because of all that, it came as no surprise that later in his career, when he was assigned to the 1st Marine Division in Vietnam as an officer, Land realized the potential for snipers in that war and convinced his superiors that Vietnam was a perfect venue to create a Scout Sniper Platoon to prove his new concept in combat.

Since the Marines prided themselves on marksmanship as an essential pillar of their fundamental capabilities, the idea itself was readily accepted and was, therefore, soon adopted. The Scout Sniper Platoon was then formed as a result and designated as the unofficial combat testing ground for Land's theory. If the concept proved workable in the hell of Vietnam, it would undoubtedly work in other environments, or so Marine Corps thinking went. As a result, Land began putting together a unit to illustrate and prove his theory.

Once he got the go-ahead, Land began recruiting world-class shooters from the ranks of the Corps and the 1st Marine Division to flesh out his newly created test bed.

Gunnery Sergeant Carlos Hathcock, and Sgt Chuck Mawhinney, both already known as world-class shots, were among the first personnel assigned to the Platoon. They were soon followed by other less well-known Marine shooting notables as part of the list of potential personnel Land wanted.

"But I want the creation of a scout sniper capability in the Marine Corps to be a permanent change." Land had told Casey as they discussed the formation of the new unit.

"My ultimate goal is the creation of a formal military specialty adopted in the Corps that will endure long after Vietnam ends."

"I also want the means to ensure this creation becomes institutionalized and its traditions and skills are carried forward."

"We'll have to recruit some younger Marines to accomplish all that," Casey told him.

"And, of course, they'll have to be excellent shots, but with no reputation."

"They'll need to be assigned to the unit, along with the old hands like Hathcock and Mawhinney," Casey explained.

"So, they can be mentored by the old hands."

"That'll ensure their shooting skills get honed to perfection."

"Later, as the new generation, the legacy they form here in Vietnam will continue."

"Once they're trained and grow to be world-class shots and long-range killers in their own right," he finished. "their skills and knowledge can, in turn, be passed on to other younger generations of Marines, we'll recruit and train later on."

"Eventually, if we do it right," the Gunny had concluded. "after Vietnam, your concept will have been proven, and as a result, scout sniper training will occur in a permanent, formalized school founded to produce world-class shooters."

"Therefore, your legacy will endure, and the Marine Corps will have a permanent scout-sniper capability added to its ranks."

"That's exactly what I want, Casey," Land had said. "And we'll never have a better opportunity."

"Make it so, Gunny," He had ordered.

Consequently, to ensure that legacy was begun and carried on, Casey began recruiting carefully selected young bloods into the platoon.

They had been carefully scrutinized and later recommended by grizzled range NCOs back at Boot camp in the states, like the one Buster had met. Even then, they weren't accepted until they were checked out by Casey and his old hands first.

Once assigned, they were mentored by Hathcock, Mawhinney, and other experienced shooters. Eventually, they would grow, in their own right, to the point that they could replace them.

Lance Corporal Martin Dunaway and PFC Roan Macklin both fell into that category. Both youngsters were excellent shots, and once word of the new unit filtered down the Corps' ranks, they had been recommended for the assignment. They soon proved to be eager to not only further their shooting skills but also to learn from the experienced pros. Based on their records and their ability, both men were soon accepted. Afterward, their shooting education began in earnest, and they improved their skills accordingly.

Dunaway was a tall, thin, blue-eyed drink of water who had joined the Corps after he had graduated with honors from a private high school in Boston, Mass. His parents were both career educators and had raised their only son in a relatively sedate and cloistered intellectual environment in hopes of him also becoming a teacher. In the process, they had tried to instill in him the belief that life was sacred and that peace was the only acceptable path for humanity. They had also tried to impress on him that teaching your fellow humans to accept and promote a doctrine like that was a noble and gratifying profession.

Unfortunately, Martin had wanted a more exciting life. After graduating high school, he unexpectedly joined the Marines to find one. That act alone had shocked his parents, who had expected him to enroll in an Ivy League college to finish his education. That didn't happen, either. Later, when Dunaway became a trained sniper, they were appalled at his choice of profession.

Dunaway had never handled a firearm in his life before he joined the Corps. However, under his marksmanship instructors' watchful eyes during boot camp, he was quickly recognized as a shooter with extraordinary potential. That skill was honed during his next assignment, and he soon became recognized as an excellent shot with a fine eye for deflection. Later, he made a minor name for himself by winning the Division

Shooting Championship and placing seventh at the National Matches at Camp Perry in the heavy-caliber Division. That had started his shooting career.

Macklin, however, was almost his exact opposite. Short, muscular, and with a hair-trigger temper, he had barely managed to graduate from a rural county high school in southern Tennessee, which was not exactly a focal point for intellectual achievement to start with. As a result, his upbringing and formal education were sorely lacking, with his experience and knowledge base acquired mainly in the school of hard knocks. Although he had good common sense, he was still young and naïve enough to fail to employ it on most occasions where it was sorely required. As a result, his young life had been full of disappointment, hardship, and helping his family eke out a bare bone, backwoods existence, where social graces were almost non-existent. Because of that, he was not known for his intellect, compassion for his fellow man, or worldliness. Instead, young Macklin was a raw-boned, ill-educated hell-raiser with a penchant for trouble.

"You better get a hold on yourself, boy, and quit all that wild-assed traipsing around and drinkin'," His Daddy had often told him.

"You don't; you're gonna fumble fuck around until you screw up bad enough to earn yourself a trip to the state pen."

"And believe me, boy, that's that last place you want to wind up."

"Them boys up there don't play."

"You give them any lip; they'll take the hide right off you."

"And once you're there, if they don't wind up killin' you, the only thing you'll do is make little rocks outta big ones."

"And believe me, son, that makes for long, hard days and miserable nights."

"You best mind what I say, boy," He warned.

"I already done three years up there, and I know what I'm talkin' about," he said bitterly.

But Buster had laughed and ignored all his father's warnings. He told himself he'd never do anything stupid enough to warrant a trip to the state pen. He was more intelligent than his illiterate father, and a lot smarter. Or so he thought.

"You best mind what I say, Buster," His Pappy had warned one last time.

"You ain't near as smart or as tough as you think you are, boy."

"Pretty soon, if you ain't careful, you're gonna get yourself in a pack of trouble, and somebody's gonna pull you up short and yank a knot in yore smart little ass."

"And when they do, it won't be pretty, and it damned sure won't be funny."

"You won't be a laughin' then," he told Buster.

"Instead, you'll wish to God you'd listened."

However, contrary to all his father's advice and warnings, Buster hadn't listened. He had done just the opposite and laughed at his father's warnings and ignored his advice instead. He was eighteen, full of raging hormones, and out to prove himself. So naturally, thinking he was wiser than his elders, he had done nearly everything wrong. Consequently, almost all his father's prophetic warnings had come true, and a lot sooner than Buster had expected.

Although he had not wound up in the state pen, he had almost ended serving two years on a Georgia chain gang for his youthful delinquent antics. Only a lenient judge had saved him by offering him the chance to join the Corps instead. Because of that, Macklin had entered the Corps under much different circumstances than Dunaway. With him, voluntary enlistment had not been an option, at least not in the usual manner.

Macklin had been involved in a bar fight with another man over a woman in a no-name dive that served up moonshine liquor and two-dollar whores. The incident had occurred in a small mountain town on the Georgia-Tennessee line, and Macklin had wound up getting arrested as a result. He had severely beaten the other man, who he claimed had attacked him first.

Unfortunately, the whore they had fought over and who could verify his story had long since disappeared by the time the cops had gotten to the scene. As a result, the judge hadn't agreed with Macklin's unsupported claim of self-defense and had offered him a choice: the Marine Corps or a speedy trial and a subsequent two years on a chain gang.

It was 1964, the Corps needed bodies for Vietnam, the rural county Macklin was locked up in still boasted a county road gang, and the judge, a former Marine, was happy to oblige. Forcing

Macklin into the Marines was an easy and inexpensive way to get rid of the county's troublemakers and let the military teach them how to grow up.

"Besides," the judge had told Macklin. "you're from just across the line in Tennessee and shouldn't have come down here and caused trouble in Georgia, to begin with."

"Since you young, smart asses never seem to learn, a three-year hitch in the Marines is just what you need to get your mind right."

He had reminded Macklin of his father, who had already told him almost the same thing. He hadn't listened then either, and look where that mistake had gotten him.

"But the Marines will lern you better, boy," The judge had promised with a smirk. "Take some of the bark off you too."

"You may think you're tough, boy," the old judge had told him laughingly.

"But you don't even know what tough is!"

"But you'll learn; I can guarantee that."

"The Corps is practically legendary for curing problem children like you."

Macklin, better known as "Buster" to his friends, was ignorant but not stupid. So, when he had been offered the choice between a chain gang or the Marine Corps by the obliging judge, he had promptly elected to enlist. He was no doubt thrilled at the chance to serve his country and have the opportunity to be sent to Vietnam as part of that obligation.

Therefore, as his handcuffs came off, his uniform soon went on. He quickly found himself wearing olive drab Marine Corps utilities and being treated by the hardened drill instructors at Parris Island as the worthless and useless piece of pre-historic, amphibian shit they told him he was.

Boot camp was an eye-opening and humbling experience for the young tough guy, Macklin thought himself to be. It took about twenty-four hours for him to realize he had better do exactly as he was told, or the world as he knew it would cease to exist.

"Just like the old judge had promised," Buster remembered.

As Buster quickly learned, the Marine Drill Instructors had no sense of humor and did not play. You did what they told you, or they busted your ass, and at that, they were consummate professionals. Under their less than gentle tutelage, Macklin learned an entirely new series of skill sets, but he was quickly recognized out for his marksmanship.

Unlike Dunaway, Macklin had been around firearms all his life and grown up shooting them almost daily. He and his father had helped feed the family that way from their rural mountain home in the Tennessee-Georgia backwoods. As such, the marksmanship training he received during boot camp had only polished an already natural and defined talent. Like Dunaway, Macklin's instructors had been impressed by his shooting skill, and he had been singled out for further training.

He was a superb shot when he entered the Corps. Still, after a few months serving under the careful instruction of some of the Marine Corps' better shooters, his ability improved to a point where it approached being world-class.

He had honed those skills over those next few months. But when the Marine Corps Rifle Team had approached him to join them officially and participate in the National Matches at Camp Perry, he had turned them down. He had surprised everyone by saying that he had no interest in competitive shooting. Punching holes in paper silhouettes did not appeal to him. He preferred live targets instead.

Of course, that attitude had infuriated the Marines on the rifle team. So, after a phone call to the Marine Corps Personnel Section, the Corps had granted the brash mouthed Buster his wish and promptly sent him to Vietnam. There, he would have ample opportunity to fulfill his desires to shoot at live targets. If they didn't kill him first!

When both these men had arrived at Division Headquarters, their records were checked, and they were singled out for further possible assignment to the newly formed Scout Sniper Platoon. During their processing, they had been paired up as a potential shooting team by some Division admin joker who had laughingly dubbed them Mutt and Jeff as a joke because of their different sizes. However, the name stuck, and they were soon training in the Platoon as a team until they were comfortable working with each other and finally accepted.

Deemed ready several weeks later, the shooting team of Dunaway and Macklin were dispatched to support various units in the 1st Marine Division on operations in I Corps. Once in the field, over the next few months to sharpen their skills, they quickly began to make a name for themselves in that role. Especially Macklin.

On one operation, Buster had calmly dispatched sixteen NVA, one after another, in a little less than five minutes, as they attempted to transit the DMZ in northern I Corps. The remainder of the unit had fled back across the border in terror before he could kill them. The battalion commander of the unit he and Dunaway were attached to at the time had witnessed the entire incident, observing the action through binoculars. Then noted that feat in his later report to Division Headquarters.

"You're a helluva shot, Macklin," the Lt Col had said as he eyed the sixteen dead NVA strung out in front of him.

"Sixteen in a row, and you never missed once."

"I've never seen anything like that before." He admitted admiringly.

"You're a world-class killer, boy," He told Macklin.

"So, we're wasting your talents in the boonies working with a battalion."

"Division's got more important things you should be doing."

As a result, Macklin and Dunaway were soon pulled from regular sniper support missions for units in the Division and selected to begin taking out specific high-value targets given to them by Division Intelligence. Of course, they did that as assigned members of the newly created Scout Sniper Platoon.

That was the beginning. From then on, they would operate as a two-man team on their own. Their mission would be to find their assigned target, kill it and then return to base camp for another mission. To Macklin, it was a time of giants. Hunting game as a teenager in Tennessee had been fun, sometimes even exciting. Hunting men, however, was the ultimate experience, and he reveled in it.

Chapter Seven
A license to kill.

After two months of working together in the bush as a team with Marine units, Dunaway and Macklin had each settled into their roles as scout snipers. Dunaway, as a corporal, was the team leader and acted as the spotter. His job was to locate and identify targets, give consent to fire, confirm any kills, and control the overall mission. Macklin was the shooter. It soon became apparent to Dunaway and everyone else in the Platoon that Macklin was exceptionally well suited to that role.

Back at the Division's base camp, while they practiced their craft on the range, even Hathcock and the other old-timers had marveled at Macklin's skills. The youngster had an almost unnatural gift with a weapon. If you could see it, Macklin could hit it. He never missed.

Unfortunately, he was still young, and sometimes his youth and inexperience with life caused him problems. Especially when he was on liberty. Macklin was barely nineteen years old, in the middle of a war, and still had an enormous amount of teenage hormones controlling his emotions.

Consequently, when he was in downtown Da Nang on liberty, with both liquor and cheap pussy available in record numbers, he acted like most other teenagers in that environment in every slop chute in town. He went hog-wild and couldn't get enough of either. Since his inexperience and youthful exuberance were uncurbed in those situations, invariably, he wound up in trouble.

That was usually true of the first ten days of every month. On those days Buster partied hard, trying to screw every hooker he met, and drink every bar dry he went into. However, when he ran out of money, he had to spend the remaining twenty days of the month storing up his energy until his next payday. Once the eagle shit greenbacks again, Macklin would head downtown and resume his hell-raising. It was a monthly routine that never varied when he wasn't in the field and operational.

Contrastingly, in the field, Macklin was a completely different animal. A consummate professional: adult, composed, efficient, and deadly. He killed every single target he was sent out to eliminate with apparent ease. But off duty and in the rear, he was a train wreck, just waiting to happen.

In his first few forays into downtown Da Nang, Macklin accompanied his partner Dunaway, who was only two years his senior. But Macklin's wild behavior and unquenchable thirst had soon proved to be too much for Dunaway. So, after two separate outings with him, Dunaway let Macklin do his drinking and wild carousing independently.

Buster and his idea of a good time were too wild for his partner Dunaway.

"I can't stand the pace," Dunaway *admitted to himself.*

"But I'm not going to interfere either."

"Because no matter how drunk or hung-over Macklin is off duty, when mission time rolls around, he's always back at base camp, sober, alert, and ready to go."

Once in the field, the red-eyed, drunken, wild man disappeared, and the cool, efficient stalker and killer emerged. On every single mission, Macklin continually amazed Dunaway with his ability. The youngster seemed to blend with the jungle and become one with it. He moved like smoke through the thick foliage with never a sound. His senses were on the alert for the slightest movement, missing nothing. For those reasons, Dunaway always let Macklin handle movement to the target area and the actual creep to their shooting position. Macklin never let him down. He was as good at stalking, as he was at shooting. Probably a result of years of stalking game in the backwoods to help feed his family.

After Dunaway and Macklin had been pulled from the Division support detail, their first assigned mission had involved locating an NVA unit that had supposedly transited the DMZ and was en route to an unknown location farther south. According to Division intelligence, the unit was Company sized, but that report was unverified. Dunaway and Macklin got inserted by chopper below the unit's assumed direction of march after kitting up. Their mission was to locate it, then take out its officers.

Their insertion went off without a hitch, and the two men soon found themselves alone in the jungle, searching for their target. Within an hour, Macklin had located a well-used trail at a choke point, and Dunaway decided to set up in a position where they could observe it. Since it was the only route through the terrain they were in, it was a logical choice.

"We'll wait here," He told Macklin.

"See if the NVA Company uses this route."

"If they do, we'll engage."

"If not, and they aren't in this area, we'll extract and move further south tomorrow evening and try again."

Macklin nodded his agreement. Then they had set up a camouflaged shooting position that afforded a good view of the trail, with Macklin satisfied he could see anyone coming down it. Nothing happened for almost five hours. But just before dusk, Macklin sat up suddenly and sniffed the air.

"You smell anything, Marty?" He asked, his nostrils flaring.

Dunaway sniffed several times.

"No," he finally said. "I don't."

"Do you?"

"I smell wood smoke," Macklin said.

"Coming from that direction," he said, pointing.

"Are you sure?" Dunaway asked doubtfully.

"Positive," Macklin said, standing up.

"Let's go take a look."

Minutes later, both men were crawling up the slope of a long, high ridge in the direction of the smoke. When they reached its crest, they could see several small fires, winking in the dusk, in the broad valley below.

"I think we just found out target," Macklin told Dunaway.

"But that's an awful lot of cook fires for just a Company."

"That looks more like a battalion of men to me."

"We'll wait here until morning," Dunaway replied in a whisper.

"Then we'll get a visual ID and a count on whoever's down there."

"But meantime, we'll crawl down the slope a bit and get into a better position where we aren't so exposed."

"That little outcropping about sixty yards below us looks like a good spot," Buster said, pointing.

Twenty minutes later, both men were in position. They stayed there the next ten hours until dawn, alternating on who slept and who kept watch, continually camouflaging their position in the meantime.

When dawn broke, and the sun came up, it was to their backs, and they were virtually undetectable. That was good, because there would be no reflection off their scopes as they searched the valley below. Good thing, too, because as both men soon discovered, the valley held an entire battalion of NVA. Over four hundred and fifty North Vietnamese Dog Soldiers, and not the hundred-man Company they had been sent to find.

Dunaway set up the radio and passed the information back to Division through an airborne radio relay with that discovery. An NVA battalion usually consisted of over four hundred men, way too many for a two-man sniper team to tackle. If they were to try, chances were, they would get shot to doll rags in the process.

But unexpectedly, the word came back from headquarters for him and Macklin to take out as many officers in the battalion as possible without exposing themselves. An airstrike would supposedly take care of the rest.

"Without exposing ourselves?" Macklin snorted in disbelief.

"What the hell does that mean?"

"Those jokers back at Division don't know shit from shoe polish when it comes to operating in the field."

"That's a bullshit order, Marty, and you know it."

"As soon as we start shooting," he told Dunaway. "we're gonna be exposed."

"And when that happens, we're gonna have over four hundred pissed off NVA we're gonna have to deal with!"

"Or does Division think the NVA are going to think the Good Fairy is the one shooting at them?"

Dunaway shrugged, not knowing how to answer. He knew Buster was right but hesitated to criticize the order. But he also realized that as soon as they started shooting, they would become the hunted ones. He wondered what he should do because, in his eyes, it was a lose-lose situation. Then, unexpectedly Macklin made his decision for him.

"We better get damned creative on this one, Marty," Macklin said quietly after some more thought.

"There's over four hundred, well-trained assholes down there that will kill us if we don't."

"Once we start lighting them up, if we're not careful, we'll be knee-deep in the little fuckers before you can say Jack Shit!"

"How do you want to handle this?" Dunaway asked, ignoring Buster's comments but basically feeling the same way. He was waiting to hear his plan since he didn't have one of his own.

In the past, Dunaway had always asked Macklin for his suggestions because Macklin seemed to instinctively be able to come up with a workable plan. One that would allow them to accomplish their mission and still get back to base to talk about it. It was like Buster had some special ingrained gift. Now he hoped that Buster would have a workable idea concerning how they would have to deal with their current predicament.

Buster thought for another moment.

"First, let's try and locate the battalion commander," Buster said a moment later.

"If we can find him, I'll take him out first."

"Then I'll concentrate on everybody around him."

"Hopefully, that will include his staff, who will probably be officers too."

"I'll keep shooting as long as I have targets," He explained.

"If I can kill enough of them, the battalion will be leaderless."

"At least until someone else steps up and takes over."

"Meanwhile, I'll kill some more until they get a fix on us."

"When they finally locate us," he explained. "if we start taking accurate fire, we'll move."

"But when we do, we'll move down the slope."

"Towards them, but to another position."

"Not up it like they'll figure us to."

"They won't expect that."

"See that old dead tree to our left, about fifty yards down the ridge?" Buster said, pointing.

"That's where we'll head."

"When we get there," Buster continued. "we'll just hunker down and let them shoot until they think they've run us off."

"Later, when the battalion reforms and starts to move," Buster explained.

"We'll hit them again."

"I should be able to take out at least another six or seven more without them spotting our new position."

"Then we'll cease-fire and wait again."

"We won't move a second time because they'll be looking for that."

"Afterwards, we'll wait for them to reform again." Buster continued.

"And while we're waiting, you can call for air support."

"When it gets here," Buster explained. "we'll call an airstrike in on their asses."

"And while it's going in, we'll use it for cover and crawl back to the top of the ridge."

"The NVA will be too busy running and hiding from the airstrike to see us move," He predicted.

"After the airstrike is finished," Buster concluded. "we'll wait and see if anybody is still around."

"If they are, I'll shoot some more while you call in our extraction bird."

"When it gets here, we'll let the gunships rake this side of the ridge and the valley while we extract from the other side."

"They can mop up while we exfil."

"How does that sound?" Macklin asked, smiling.

Dunaway looked at his young partner in utter astonishment. Buster's previous ideas had all sounded workable. This one said like he had gone insane.

"It sounds like you're fucking nuts," Dunaway replied in amazement.

"We'll never get away with a stunt like that."

"When we hit the NVA a second time, they'll be all over us."

"After that, we'll never get out of here."

"Not if I'm careful," Macklin replied, explaining.

"Remember, the sun is behind us, so it'll be in their eyes while I'm firing."

"And it'll also be in their eyes when they start looking for us up here," He reminded Dunaway.

"My guess is they won't be able to see shit because they'll be looking directly into it," He said with a grin.

"And if I can shoot five or six quickly, then quit, they'll never spot us."

"They might figure out we're somewhere on this ridge," Buster admitted.

"But this is a big hill, so they won't know exactly where."

"Besides," he added. "they'll never think we'd be dumb enough to stick around and hit them a second time, or even worse, a third."

"They'll never think we'd be that stupid."

Dunaway just stared at him.

"Macklin, you got balls on you the size of cantaloupes," Dunaway finally said.

"Either that, or you're just plain crazy."

"We'll never get away with a stunt like that."

"Trust me, Marty," Macklin said calmly. "we can do this."

"If I didn't think so, I would have never suggested it."

"Believe me; I know what I'm talking about."

Dunaway looked at Macklin closely.

"Is he that good," he thought.

"Or is all that just teenaged bullshit talking?"

Moments later, the sun blossomed fully, and daylight flooded the valley. Suddenly, it was too late to move again when that happened, and Dunaway knew it. Consequently, it was either go with Macklin's plan or devise another on his own. Since Dunaway quickly realized that anything else would involve moving to another shooting position, and it was light now, there was a danger of them being spotted if they tried. Besides, he couldn't think of any other better-sounding option.

"Shit," he thought. "like it or not, we'll have to go with Buster's crazy-assed scheme."

"It's either that or do nothing because it's too late to try anything else."

"You better be right about this, Macklin," Dunaway finally said reluctantly.

"Otherwise, we're dead, you crazy little redneck."

Buster smiled as he shouldered the Winchester and put his eye to the scope. Moments later, both men were carefully scouring the valley for the NVA battalion commander's CP location. It took them a few minutes, but finally, Dunaway located it.

"I've got three NVA wearing red collar tabs at two o'clock at six hundred yards," Dunaway said three minutes later.

"They're standing by an old dead tree."

Macklin shifted his rifle to the spot, his eyes never leaving the scope.

"Got them," he said a moment later. "What do you think?"

"Well. I don't know what an NVA battalion commander's rank insignia looks like," Dunaway replied. "But I haven't seen anybody else wearing red tabs on their collars." "

"So, to me, that means they're officers."

"And since they look older than a normal soldier, that fits too," He added.

"Besides, the way they're acting and gesturing, it looks like they're giving orders and getting ready to move."

"To me, that means they're leaders of some kind."

"I agree," Buster replied.

"Give me the word, and I'll take them out."

"Stand by," Dunaway said, giving the area around the intended targets one final sweep.

"Range seven hundred yards. Targets stationary. Wind negligible." He said in a flat no-nonsense voice a moment later.

"Drop is approximately twenty-five inches."

Buster dialed the information in on his scope., then got a good sight picture of his first target.

"Ready," he said a moment later.

"Fire," Dunaway softly ordered a few moments later.

Suddenly, there were three loud Cracks in rapid succession as Macklin fired. Dunaway was amazed at the speed Buster could throw a bolt, reacquire another target and squeeze off another round while remaining on target. His skill was phenomenal.

Below in the valley, one officer's head exploded, showering everyone around him with a spectacular burst of blood and gore. However, before anyone could even react, a second officer standing beside him went down too, his head suddenly erupting in a bloody mist and gray brain matter, white bone and black hair splattering everywhere.

As the third officer suddenly realized what was happening and turned to run, he too went down as his head evaporated. Afterward, two more quick Cracks from Macklin's Winchester, and seconds later, two more nearby soldiers died. Both their faces were a picture of bewilderment at the sudden onset of killing.

When there were no more nearby targets, Buster stopped firing. The remaining NVA in the vicinity had finally figured out what was happening and gone to the ground, their faces registering sheer terror. Dunaway watched the entire thing in his spotting scope in awe.

"Jesus Christ, he's fast," Dunaway thought.

"But he hit everything he aimed at."

"I knew he could shoot before, but all that was just on the range or in the slow fire mode."

"This is the first time I 've seen him in action against multiple live targets in a combat situation and at any distance."

"Christ, the little shit is a natural-born killing machine."

After Buster finished firing, there was silence for a moment while he reloaded. Seconds later, however, the entire valley erupted in a wild barrage of weapons fire, seemingly in all directions. Rounds began flying everywhere, clipping foliage and smacking loudly into trees all along the ridge he and Dunaway were on, along with all the other ridges surrounding the entire valley.

The NVA were shooting everywhere, but they were shooting blind. They had no idea of Buster's position. Still, 7.62 parabellum Chicom tracer rounds punched green rainbows in the air as they zipped through the sky like miniature rockets. The shocked NVA fired at everything in every direction, but all their firing was wasted effort. They had no target. Their firing was just a knee-jerk reaction to them being shot at, and several killed. As a result, not a single round came anywhere near Dunaway and Macklin's position.

Worse, initially, when the firing began, there was uncontrolled, frenzied bedlam within the NVA ranks. People were running, while others dived for cover. Still, others were standing and firing. Some were even throwing themselves to the ground instinctively, even where there was no cover or concealment. All of it was an utterly futile gesture. But after a few minutes, the firing finally fizzled out, then stopped altogether, as the remaining officers and NCOs in the battalion finally regained control.

When they did, Buster waited a few minutes, then popped back up from cover, put his scope back on the valley, and surveyed the scene carefully.

"Un-fucking-believable," Macklin said as he stared at the valley below through his scope.

"There's no need for us to move, Marty."

"Nobody down there saw shit."

"They have no goddamn clue where we are."

"They were all just shooting at shadows," He chuckled.

"Let's wait and see what they do next."

As it turned out, what the NVA did next was absolutely nothing. For almost another five minutes. They were leaderless now, so no one was issuing any orders. Instead, the entire valley floor consisted of four hundred men all bent on hiding and afraid to move, lest they suddenly become the next victim. Buster could see an occasional foot, or a hand partially revealed in the dense foliage, but little else. Those still alive were glued to the ground and hiding behind some cover to save their own lives. They were terrified.

Finally, the seemingly frozen scene ended as orders in Vietnamese filtered up the valley on the wind. Hearing them, the NVA lying on the valley floor began crawling around, seeking better cover. They had been too afraid to move before, for fear of getting shot, but now that it was once again quiet, some of their courage was returning. Buster watched them through his scope smiling, their terror evident in their stubborn and hesitant movements.

A few minutes later, when someone finally retook command, a few brave souls stood up and started looking at the ridges around the valley. Shielding their eyes with their palms and vainly trying to spot their unseen attackers as they gazed into the bright sun. But since Macklin and Dunaway were well concealed, with the morning sun to their backs, and over six hundred yards away, it was a futile effort.

A few minutes later, another series of faint commands in Vietnamese drifted up from the valley, and troops began getting up out of the foliage on its floor. They were tentative at first, looking around fearfully and expecting to get shot any second.

But when there were no more shots forthcoming, they began moving around usually. Shortly after that, a series of whistles were blown, more faint commands, and the troops began forming up into unit formations. Evidently, the remaining officers had finally gotten their act together, taken charge, and were getting ready to move. That was what Dunaway and Macklin had been waiting for.

"Ready?" Buster asked Dunaway as he chambered another round.

Dunaway nodded, turning back to his spotting scope.

"I got another two officers," He said a few moments later.

"One at o'clock at five hundred and fifty yards, standing beside a big coconut palm."

"The other one is standing next to him."

"Got them," Macklin said after another second of searching.

"Stand by," Dunaway said.

"Fire," he commanded a moment later.

Macklin rapidly cranked off another series of six shots. Dunaway watched as the two officers and four other soldiers around them went down. Their heads exploded, and their lifeless bodies were thrown backward violently as the one hundred and fifty-grain slugs plowed into them. Once again, the valley floor erupted in a wild barrage of weapons fire, this time even more frantic and savage than before.

"That pissed them off," Macklin said, smiling as he ducked.

Dunaway was already on the radio, calling for air support.

Shots were still being fired randomly ten minutes later when a FAC with four Marine F-4s showed up over the valley. The FAC, directed by Dunaway, then marked the center of the valley with WP rockets. The F-4 Phantoms rolled in and started unloading on it with five-hundred-pound Snake eyes. When they did, Buster spoke again.

"Time to move, Marty."

"Follow me and keep low."

Dunaway grabbed his weapon and spotting scope. Without comment, he followed Macklin back up the hill in a low crouch as the air-delivered ordnance impacted the valley below.

Soon, both men were back at the crest of the ridge and hidden in the shadows of a stand of bamboo. They crouched there and again watched the valley below as the airstrike continued.

After the first four fast movers expended the last of their ordnance, they were soon joined by a second flight of F-4s. Minutes later. They, too, had unloaded all their ordnance into the valley. It was quickly blanketed by a thick layer of dense black smoke that hung over it like a dark cloud, obscuring everything.

"Shit," Macklin growled angrily as he gazed down at the thick black cloud.

"You might as well call for the extraction bird, Marty."

"We can't see shit now, so I guess we're finished here," he said reluctantly.

"Time to haul ass."

Chapter Eight
After Action Report

"Where the hell did you come up with that half-assed plan we used back in the valley?" Dunaway asked Macklin as he soaped himself up again.

"It just came to me," Macklin replied as he scrubbed his close-cropped head.

"I figured the NVA would never think we'd be dumb enough to stick around and hit them twice."

"And I was right," he said, beaming.

Both men were back at the Platoon area in the Division's base camp after their extraction two hours previous. After they had landed and had been debriefed, it was then time to try and rid themselves of the sweat, dirt, and grime they had accumulated on their three-day mission. So, they were showering back at the Platoon area.

Not real showers, of course, but field-expedient ones. They were made by placing used 55-gallon drums on wooden stands about eight feet off the ground. A pipe with a shower head on the end of it was then welded around a hole in the barrel's bottom, and the drum filled with water. The sun heated the water, and gravity did the rest. After you turned the small valve on the pipe, you stood on old wooden pallets and let the warm water cascade over you as you bathed. It was Holiday Inn, Marine Corps style.

"I'm amazed we're still alive," Dunaway told Macklin, shaking his head in disgust as he thought about what had just happened.

"We lucked out," he reasoned.

"That's the only logical explanation."

"I should have never let you talk me into a screwball stunt like that, you crazy little shit," he said angrily.

"Christ, I knew better."

"You could have gotten us both killed, you dumb redneck."

"We were never in any real danger," Macklin corrected him.

"The sun was behind us, so the Dicks couldn't see shit."

"They were staring right into it every time they looked at the ridge."

"That's the reason I knew they'd never spot us, even if we stuck around for a second hit."

"Shit, if it hadn't been for that damned smoke caused by the airstrike, we could have hit them a third time and nailed a few more before we extracted."

"Nailed a few more," Dunaway said in disbelief. "You killed eleven, for Christ's sake!"

"How many more did you want?"

"As many as I could get," Macklin snapped.

"That's what we're here for, Marty."

"Remember?"

"Our job is to kill Dicks, whenever and wherever we can."

Dunaway just stared.

"Is that just teenage bravado talking, brought on by a young, reckless mouth?" he wondered. *"Or is it something else?"*

"Is Macklin starting to enjoy the killing?"

"You getting a rush from taking out targets now?" Dunaway asked Macklin as he reached for a towel.

"Starting to enjoy it?"

"No," Macklin answered. "I'm not."

"I'm just doing my job." he huffed.

"What *"the Crotch"* trained me for and ordered me to do."

"I just want to kill a few more of them, that's all," He said in a pout.

"Why?" Dunaway asked, puzzled.

Buster remained silent, but his silence didn't satisfy Dunaway. He wanted an answer.

"I asked you a question, Buster," Dunaway persisted.

"I'm trying to beat Hathcock and Mawhinney's records," Buster finally reluctantly admitted a moment later.

"They've each already got over sixty confirmed kills."

"So, I got a lot of catching up to do."

"Jesus Christ," Dunaway thought to himself in disbelief.

"The dumb little bastard thinks it's some sort of game."

"See who can kill the most Dicks in twelve months, and the winner gets the bragging rights."

"I was right about him after all."

"He is just an irresponsible, out of control, little wild man; the crazy little fucker."

But as he glanced at Buster, he realized his partner had already forgotten the incident.

"I'm headed for town," Macklin said, toweling off, all thoughts of his job and confirmed kills now vanished.

"I'm thirsty, and I wanna get laid."

"You coming, Marty?"

"I think I'll pass," Dunaway said, not wanting to tell Buster he wanted nothing more to do with his wild-assed behavior, especially on liberty.

"I'm not in the mood."

But he was still worried about Buster's earlier statement, and his worry showed on his face.

"Suit yourself," Macklin said, pulling on a clean set of utilities.

"But you don't know what you're missing."

"I know a whore who could suck the chrome right off a trailer hitch," He boasted.

"She ain't a bad screw either."

"She'll stay all night for twenty bucks, and she humps like a bronco."

Dunaway sighed as he looked at his young partner, now putting on his boots.

"Possibly getting killed doesn't bother him at all," Dunaway thought to himself.

"He's so young; he thinks he's immortal."

"Hell, he's still acting like a horny teenager."

"How many times have you had the clap in the last three months, Buster?" he asked disgustedly, trying to make a point.

"Two, maybe three times," Macklin answered. "I'm not sure."

"What's that got to do with anything?"

"Has it ever occurred to you where you're getting it from, you dumb little fucker?" Dunaway asked in an exasperated voice.

Macklin looked up in surprise.

"Well, of course, I know where I'm gettin' it from," Buster replied indignantly.

"I ain't that dumb, you know."

"Well, if you know," Dunaway said logically. "then why don't you stop."

Buster looked at him like he was crazy.

"Because a man's gotta get his ashes hauled regularly," Buster replied in all seriousness, missing the point entirely.

"Otherwise, he'll swell up till his balls explode."

"And I sure as hell don't want that to happen to me."

"Who the hell told you that?" Dunaway asked, not quite believing what he had just heard.

"It's common knowledge, back in the hills," Buster said.

"I'm surprised you didn't already know about it, Marty."

"You being so smart and all."

"Everybody where I come from does."

"That is complete and total bullshit, you dumb little backwoods peckerhead," Dunaway said in complete exasperation.

"That's the stupidest thing I've ever heard."

"If you don't get laid regularly, your balls won't explode, you dumb little shit." He told Macklin.

"It's a physical impossibility."

"There's no danger of that ever happening."

"That's just some old wives' tale from some ignorant hillbilly."

Macklin looked at him doubtfully.

"Maybe so," he finally said. "but I ain't takin' no chances."

"Besides, I like fucking." He said with a smile.

"Drinking too."

"And here in Vietnam, I don't have to be twenty-one to do either one."

"I don't have to worry about getting thrown in jail for it, neither," he added mysteriously.

"So, I'm heading out to get my fill of both while I have the chance."

"See you later, Marty," He said, putting on his cover and departing.

Dunaway sat on the cot and watched his youthful partner depart. He'd be back in the

173

morning, red-eyed and broke. But he'd be smiling. Buster rarely got serious about anything when he wasn't in the field. He was a typical teenager, living for today with no thought for tomorrow. He thought he was invincible and would never die. He was about as carefree, reckless, and unconcerned as you could get.

The fact that he was in the middle of a war didn't seem to faze him. It was like he was out on a lark, back in the backwoods and hunting squirrels. Except here, liquor was plentiful, and there was more pussy than you could even dream about. On top of all that, he got to shoot people for a living instead of squirrels. It was a macho male teenager's idea of heaven.

"So, what the hell suddenly happens to Buster when we get a mission and go to the field?" Dunaway wondered.

"Where does all that adolescent immaturity and unconcern go all of a sudden?"

For when Macklin was on a stalk or in a shooting position, he was all business. He didn't even *think* about fucking around. He took his job of eliminating the NVA seriously. Take that last mission. Although Dunaway was supposedly in charge, it was Macklin who had made all the decisions. When he had smelled the wood smoke, it had been Macklin who had said, *"let's go find out where it's coming from."*

And when they had found the battalion, Macklin had been the one that had decided they were going to attack it. He had even devised the means. Even when Dunaway had tried to talk him out of it, Macklin had overridden him, finally convincing him it could be done. The little shit had even come up with that near-suicidal plan that Dunaway had wound up agreeing to. And unbelievably, it had worked!

"Where was my brain?" Dunaway asked himself as he thought about it.

"What in hell was I thinking?"

"Or was I even thinking at all?"

"Apparently not."

"I was just along for the ride," He finally decided.

Dunaway suddenly realized that because of his rank, he was supposed to be the one in charge. The one who made all the decisions and gave all the orders. However, it was the other way around. Macklin was the one who ran things when they were in the field on a mission. That wasn't the way it was supposed to work, but that was the way it was. Worse, Dunaway had deliberately let things happen that way.

That should have never happened. He was a Corporal, while Macklin was still a Private. So, he was the one that supposedly made the decisions, formulated the plans, and gave the orders. That's the way things worked in the Marine Corps.

"Trouble is," Dunaway rationalized.

"Macklin is so damned good in the weeds."

"He moves like a ghost."

"He always picks the right route to the target."

"He avoids enemy contact like he had some sixth sense."

"And he always nails who we were sent to get."

"In truth, he keeps us alive the entire time we're out there."

"So, do I want to fuck all that up?" Dunaway asked himself pointedly.

"As long as we complete the mission and get back alive," he rationalized. "who cares who runs the mission and makes the decisions out in the middle of nowhere?"

"Nobody but me and Buster knows anyway."

"I want to come out of this war alive," Dunaway told himself.

"That's my priority."

"So, if I have to bend the sacred and hoary Marine Corps tradition of always letting the ranking Marine be in charge, then I'm gonna do that."

"And as far as what Macklin does on liberty," he told himself.

"I'm not going to worry about that either."

"He's a big boy."

"If he wants to screw his brains out, get the clap so often his pecker falls off, or drink himself into a stupor every time he goes downtown, then let him."

"He's not hurting anybody but himself."

"As for me," Dunaway thought. "I'm smarter than that."

"I'll do my drinking in the NCO club here on base."

"It's cheaper, the booze is better, and it's a hell of a lot safer."

"When I want to get my ashes hauled occasionally," he thought.

"I'll be a lot more cautious and prudent about that too."

"Not fuck some cheap whore who I know has the clap just because she gives world-class blow jobs."

"I like the Marine Corps," Dunaway admitted to himself.

"So, if I decide to re-enlist after my hitch here is up, I don't want anything on my record that will prevent me from doing that."

"I'm not an ignorant, hillbilly dumb ass like Buster," He thought.

"He doesn't give much of a shit about anything, or at least that's the way he acts when he's in the rear."

"If the Skipper is okay with his wild-ass behavior and outrageous conduct downtown, then who am I to argue."

"Let the little fucker screw himself till he goes blind," Dunaway thought with a chuckle.

"If he doesn't know any better, that's his problem."

"And the same goes for his drinking; it's his liver."

"As to his conduct when he's downtown," Dunaway thought. "as long as he accomplishes his duties in the field, I don't give a shit what he does in his off-duty time."

"If he fucks up often enough or bad enough, the Corps will eventually pull him up short and teach him his manners."

"Besides," Dunaway thought to himself. "you can't talk to the little shit anyway."

"He won't listen."

"You can't reason with him either," he thought disgustedly. "He's too goddamn ignorant."

"That comment about your balls swelling up and exploding if you didn't get laid regularly is a prime example."

"How could anybody with half a brain believe shit like that?"

"Buster only has two redeeming traits," Dunaway told himself.

"Despite all his other faults and his teenaged outlook on life, he's a nice kid."

"I've never heard him gripe or bitch about anything."

"And in this fucking country, in the middle of this shitass war, that's saying something."

"Secondly, he's the best goddam shot I ever seen or even heard of."

"And amazingly, all that comes naturally to him."

Chapter Nine
Back to the Grind

Macklin itched in the Ghillie Suit. The Asian sun was a fiery golden orb trying to sear everything beneath it, making the humid jungle environment hot and uncomfortable. Macklin even more so because the Ghillie was an extra layer of clothing.

Since there was no shade to offer any relief, with the Ghillie on, the sun was broiling everything, making it nearly unbearable. Macklin, lying on the exposed ridge's slope and surrounded by low scrub, felt like a fillet in a frying pan. He was bathed in sweat, and there was not even a hint of a breeze. That made the hot air stifling and the Asian sun relentless. Worse, the Ghillie suit he was wearing seemed to suck up every single degree of heat the sun emitted and keep it trapped against his already sweltering body.

When he was first issued the Ghillie and later schooled its purpose, the young Marine had hated it immediately. That feeling had only intensified with age. It had been designed to provide a shooter with a partial cloak of invisibility in the field by disguising his shape and making him blend in easily with the surrounding foliage. It had not been initially intended for use in a jungle environment. But being flexible, like all Marines, the scout sniper advocates had adapted it to fit anyway and trained their snipers to employ it on missions.

Despite all that, Buster disliked it intensely, preferring to stalk in just his jungle fatigues instead. They were infinitely cooler, blended with the jungle foliage easily, and were much lighter. He had hunted wearing similarly camouflaged clothing all his life. He had never needed any special equipment or apparel then to either conceal himself in the forest or to stalk his intended prey.

"And I don't need it now," he reasoned.

However, when he had arrived at the Platoon, the instructors there had trained both him and Dunaway on the Ghillie's use and then required them to wear the suits when in the field and on a mission. It appeared, like it or not; he was stuck with the damned thing.

Macklin had been in the same position for almost two hours without moving, Dunaway lying right beside him. Both men were concealed on the slope of another ridge, also covered in scrub vegetation. It was almost a twin to the one they had been on during their last mission. Their position overlooked a broad valley below them, just as it had a month before in another location.

But this valley was different. It was mostly open, the only dense foliage grew along the small stream's sides that ran down its center. The only cover available was a few crumbling, rice paddy dikes crisscrossing the valley floor and the banks of the stream itself. At one time, years earlier, it had probably been a rice field.

The valley also boasted a well-used dirt trail that paralleled the stream and came from its northern end and disappeared back into the jungle on its southern end. In addition, the far end of the valley contained some old deserted, run-down straw huts. The remains of a little, now-deserted village that some peasant farmers had once called home before the war came.

Apparently, the entire village had long since been abandoned, just another casualty of the war. The entire scene seemed so idyllic and serene; it was a typical picture of the Southeast Asian countryside and worthy of a fine watercolor in normal circumstances.

Unfortunately, it was now in the middle Indian country, over twelve klicks across the South Vietnamese border in a neighboring country called Laos, an NVA stronghold.

Laos was a country the US government had told the world was neutral in the war. They respected both its sovereignty and neutrality. Accordingly, the United States military had no troops operating in the country. They were forbidden to operate there by US edict. Supposedly, the country favored neither the North Vietnamese nor the Americans and their South Vietnamese allies. Furthermore, Laos demanded all the warring parties respect its sovereignty.

But that was just propaganda put out by all the parties involved. US troops were operating in Laos. Both the Army and the Marines did it regularly, but not openly. Macklin and Dunaway were proof positives.

So did the North Vietnamese, but on a much larger scale. Ho Chi Minh had established a network of logistic complexes, training areas, and staging bases for his guerrilla cadres in the country as early as 1942, and had expanded and enhanced them a hundred-fold since then.

He had used them first against the French, and now, he was using them against the Americans. They were, in fact, vital to his current war effort against the South Vietnamese. Because they were the primary logistic artery for moving war materials from North Vietnam. Although the North Vietnamese called the trail network the *"Troung Son Road,"* the Americans had labeled it the *Ho Chi Minh Trail.*

Furthermore, the Laotian government was aware that both the Americans and Vietnamese were violating their eastern border at will. Still, they elected to turn a blind eye to all this activity and ignore it. That was because they either couldn't do anything to stop it or because they chose not to even try for fear of becoming involved in the War itself. That meant both the US and the North Vietnamese continued their illegal activity with impunity. Both Macklin and Dunaway were current proof of that.

They were in Laos and carefully watching a small trail that ran through the valley below them. It was a part of the significant NVA logistics artery called the Ho Chi Minh Trail that had branches running off it all through eastern Laos. This trail was the main supply route that ran between a hidden NVA logistics site hidden deeper inside the country and the northern portion of South Vietnam. Although it served as an NVA resupply route between the two countries, its secondary purpose was an infiltration passage into South Vietnam for NVA troops transiting the area.

Division intelligence, working in concert with the CIA, had already identified the trail as a favorite infiltration route for NVA entering the I Corps' neighboring section. They had also told Macklin and Dunaway that there was reliable intelligence that a party of high-ranking NVA officers would be using the trail to transit the area sometime in the next few days.

The officers were supposedly the advance party of a major NVA unit, preparing to move into South Vietnam in the next few weeks. That made the advance party high-value targets, and that's why Macklin and his partner had been sent here. Their job was to ensure the officers in the advance party never made it to South Vietnam.

Once inserted, it had taken both men almost half a day to inch their way down the slope of the ridge they were on to the location they now occupied. Then another hour to get themselves into a concealed position to engage and take out their targets. The time involved in making that move had been excruciatingly long because their movement had been snail-like to avoid detection.

The entire border region was almost alive with NVA patrols and security elements to ensure its safety, so any excessive movement was always a risk. This valley and trail were no exception. Consequently, Macklin's and Dunaway's efforts had been tiring because they had been forced to low crawl the entire way at a sloth-like pace. Worse, they were wearing their Ghillie suits when they did it.

That was imperative because the entire area was alive with NVA patrols that crisscrossed the area regularly, observing and securing it. Now, withthe creep concluded, both men were exhausted and sweating while resting in their newly created and camouflaged shooting position.

All that effort, as difficult and extreme as it had been, had not included the day and a half they had spent earlier, silently stalking their way from their insertion point just inside the Laotian border. Afterward, they had sneaked their way through the Laotian jungle to the ridge they now occupied. That journey had proved to be an ordeal that had presented its own challenges.

Although the vegetation, foliage, and terrain in the Vietnamese jungle and the Laotian jungle were the same, that's where the similarity between the two areas ended,

The NVA heavily patrolled the entire border area of Laos/South Vietnam. Still, the Laotian side of the border was even worse. It was infested with them. They had been so numerous that after the team had beeninserted, they had been forced to go to ground and hide four separate times to avoid being detected. All on the same day!

That had all been yesterday. Then early this morning, on the last part of their movement to the target area, they had silently watched two separate NVA patrols pass their hidden positions so closely they could have reached out and touched them. Afterwards, they had finally been able to get to the ridge they now occupied. Now, after all that effort, they were in position, and the tense waiting game that always precedes a kill shot had begun.

Macklin had not minded the move to the target area, but now that he was in position, he despised this part of the hunt. He was not a patient person by nature, plus he was young, and still a teenager. So, waiting in one place without moving for hours on end required almost monumental concentration and effort on his part. By contrast, Dunaway, only slightly older, seemed unfazed by the requirement.

Both men were almost a case study in opposites, but they each used their partner's strengths to offset their weaknesses. That was one reason why they so effective. Macklin's ability with a rifle and his skill in the weeds was another.

Dunaway, as the spotter, let Macklin doze as he watched the target area. He knew Buster hated waiting, so he let him rest until he had sighted the target. That was his part of the contract. Buster's skill in the weeds was much better than his, so Dunaway always let Buster take charge of getting them to the target area. The man had an almost uncanny ability to blend in with the environment, avoid the enemy, and silently navigate his way through the maze of the jungle to the objective. That was Buster's part of the deal.

But once there, both men seemed to homogenize into a single weapons system. Dunaway located, identified, and assessed the range to the target while noting any deflection or wind. Macklin then made all the required calculations, dialed in all that information into his scope, and then did the shooting. The results were invariably the same. The targets died.

Today would be another repetition of that success-based formula, but with one difference. With multiple targets and considering the proximity of the NVA patrols in the area, Dunaway might have to be prepared to shoot too. There was also the possibility of too many targets for Macklin to handle alone in the short amount of time the targets would be visible.

In addition, once the firing began, the area would probably come alive with NVA reinforcements rushing to the sounds of the shooting. If that happened, keeping them at bay while Buster downed all the primaries would be Dunaway's job. If that occurred, then just getting back out was going to be a major problem for both men.

Of course, they had a plan for that. One that they had carefully developed back at base camp before the mission started. It considered the area's terrain, the natural camouflage and cover available, the probable location of any NVA reinforcement units near the kill zone, their reaction time, and a possible escape route. It also had some built-in contingency plans should the need arise. But plans often went tits up once the shooting started.

The NVA would have their own plans and they rarely coincided with the ones developed by either Macklin or Dunaway. That was usually the way of things. But Dunaway had confidence in his partner. He was the best he had ever seen in the weeds. If a firefight developed after the primary targets had been taken out, and push came to shove, Buster would get them out of Dodge safely. Even if he had to kill everyone in their path to do it. Dunaway had supreme confidence in that.

Dunaway glanced over at Buster, who was half dozing. The young Tennessee redneck was often crass and uncouth, but he had quickly become his friend. Buster's drawl was as thick as honey dripping off a biscuit, it was so southern, but he was a likable sort. Generous and usually smiling, even being a rowdy when he was on liberty, didn't matter. The bond between the two was intense. Even with that, it was difficult to visualize the boy-faced Macklin as a cold-eyed deliberate killer. But that's what he was.

Put a rifle into Buster's hands, and he almost became a living extension of it. That was what probably accounted for his unique ability.

When Buster zeroed in on his target, all his friendliness disappeared, and Macklin, the killer, emerged. The friendly southern boy from Tennessee vanished, and Buster turned into a cold-eyed, deadly efficient, man-killer. One that never missed.

He was unique in other ways too. Unlike the old pros like Hathcock and Mawhinney, Macklin always went for the headshot instead of the center of mass in the chest. In addition, he could throw a bolt faster than anyone had even seen. Always remaining on target while did. That's how good he was.

Dunaway had watched through his spotting scope as NVA's heads had exploded like ripe melons when Buster pulled the trigger on previous missions. Gray matter and blood flew everywhere in a sudden crimson mist of Technicolor as brains got blown out in rapid succession. Buster never missed, and he was fast. No one, not even the old pros, could throw a bolt any faster or smoother and remain on target.

Macklin had an uncanny ability at that. Sometimes he had three rounds on the way before his targets had even heard the first shot. When there was no wind to offset, Buster was a killing machine. He was like someone shooting clay ducks at a kiosk at a county fair. The huckster running the stand couldn't wait for him to go away. The NVA probably couldn't wait for Macklin to go away either. He had already killed enough of them to move himself from the "nuisance" pigeonhole into the "major fucking problem" category.

When Macklin went to work, targets were knocked down like bowling pins, each dead before hitting the ground. Dunaway had personally witnessed Buster take out five targets in less than seven seconds, all of them headshots.

Then, after reloading, Buster would kill some more. Finally, when there was no one left to kill, the affable smiling young boy from southern Tennessee would reappear as if by magic, and Buster was his usual, joking, generous self once again. Dunaway often wondered if Macklin had a hidden on-off switch somewhere that controlled his Jekyll and Hyde-like personality.

Dunaway considered himself to be an extremely gifted shooter. After all he had placed in the National Matches at Camp Perry just a year earlier. That feat alone ranked him as one of the best in the world. But, when he compared himself to Macklin, it was no contest. Macklin was not only a better shot; he could throw a bolt so fast he was able to kill five people in the same amount of time it took Dunaway to kill one! That's how good he was.

More importantly, Macklin hadn't gotten his reputation punching holes in paper targets on some long-distance range in Ohio. He earned his killing of men, a talent he seemed born for! There was a hell of a difference.

Suddenly, out of the corner of his eye, Dunaway caught a hint of movement at the far end of the valley. He put his spotting scope on it, adjusted the range to maximum, and waited. A full minute later, a party of five NVA officers with a ten-man security element loomed up in his scope.

They were moving quickly but with no hint of fear. After all, Laos was their backyard, so they undoubtedly felt safe there, especially considering all the parols in the area. They also knew their government had publicly forbidden Americans to cross the border, so only added to their sense of safety. But Macklin would soon change that perception.

Dunaway watched the party move towards him for another full minute before finally nudging Buster.

"Time to go to work, Dickweed," he whispered.

"Targets in sight."

"Twelve hundred meters at your two o'clock."

Macklin didn't reply. He just opened his eyes, rolled over, shouldered his rifle, shifted it to the right, and then watched.

"Got them," he said moments later.

As he slowly panned the rifle and scope around the valley and the trail to his front, he finally settled on a spot.

"We'll take them at about five hundred yards," he told Dunaway, taking charge, once again.

"When they reach that old dead tree at our one o'clock."

"The stream is about two hundred yards from the trail at that point," he noted. "and there's no other cover or concealment that's any closer."

"So, they'll be in the open the entire time."

"It's an easy shot, so I should be able to get every one of them before they can get to any cover."

Dunaway looked at the area through his spotting scope and nodded. As usual, Buster was right, and the spot was perfect.

"I'll take the last officer in the formation first," Buster explained. "then work my way forward."

"When they start to run, it'll be towards the stream, so watch where they go in case I miss one."

"I think I can get at least four out of the five before they get to the foliage."

Maybe all five if they're slow to react."

"I'll call for the guns and the extraction bird now," Dunaway responded, knowing that after the shooting started, the area would come alive with NVA patrols, and there would be no time.

"They're on strip alert, but even so, it'll probably take them at least twenty minutes to get here."

"Hopefully, we'll finished by that time."

Buster nodded in agreement.

"After I start taking out the primaries," Buster ordered a moment later. "watch the wood line at our nine o'clock, Marty."

"That's where the NVA security patrols will probably comie from when they hear the shots."

"If I'm still busy," he warned. "you may have to knock down the first two or three to slow them down some."

"Otherwise, we'll be up to our ass in the little fuckers and have no way to move."

"As soon as I'm done with my five, I'll help you if you need it."

Dunaway nodded and unzipped his rifle case, unlimbering the Remington 700 BDL. He preferred it to the Winchester Macklin carried. Then he laid two extra stripper clips with 30-06 rounds beside it Afterwards, he returned to his spotting scope.

"They're at six hundred yards now," he said a few minutes later, checking the range to the steadily advancing NVA group of officers.

"The wind is negligible."

"Drop will be eleven inches."

Buster acknowledged by dialing the info into his scope, then flicking off the safety on his Model 70. He then snuggled the weapon into his shoulder, put his cheek against the smooth walnut stock, and got a good spot weld. Satisfied, he shallowed out his breathing and gota good sight picture. An NVA officer's head was suddenly dancing in the reticule of his scope moments later as he steadily tracked his forward movement.

A few moments later, Dunaway whispered.

"Five hundred and fifty yards now, Buster."

"Stand by."

Buster was silent, his crosshairs glued to his target. He didn't acknowledge, but Dunaway knew he had heard him.

Moments later, Dunaway whispered, "Fire."

The word wasn't even out of his mouth completely before there was a loud Crack beside him, then the sound of a bolt being thrown. A split second later, another Crack and Buster's second round was on the way. Then a third. Dunaway watched as the last NVA officer in the formation was suddenly thrown violently backward as his head exploded. The small column stopped in shock when that occurred, not quite believing what had just happened.

But before they could react, a second NVA officer went down too, flying off the trail as if he had a hidden wire attached to his ass and someone had just jerked it. The remaining NVA knew what was happening then and were terrified as they turned to run.

As the remainder of the small column quickly wheeled to their right in a frantic effort to find cover near the stream, they had barely taken their first steps when there was another Crack. The third dead NVA officer hit the ground, splattering brains and blood all over his comrades. Afterwards, the remainder took off running like jackrabbits. Buster calmly shot the remaining two in the back of their heads just before they reached the concealment of the stream, a scant three seconds later.

By that time, the ten-man security element accompanying the now dead officers was in total pandemonium. They were firing blindly in all directions and trying to run, duck, and shoot all at the same time. It was a complete cluster fuck for them.

As one suddenly loomed up in Buster's scope, he took him out too. That only added to the confusion. Then he watched the remainder of the terrified soldiers scatter everywhere, still trying to figure where the shots had come from. A few seconds later, the valley was quiet again as the last of the security element slithered along the ground headed for the streamline and concealment, still trying to locate their unseen attacker and scared witless.

"Company," Dunaway whispered a few moments later. "at our nine o'clock."

"Ten men in the open and running."

"It's an NVA patrol," He confirmed.

"They obviously heard the shots, and they're coming hard."

"I'll spot for you," Buster said unexpectedly.

"You take them."

"You need the practice."

Dunaway snorted as he shouldered his weapon. But he was delighted that he'd get the chance to shoot.

"Range seven hundred yards at nine o'clock," Buster said, staring through the spotting scope. "Targets are moving at about six miles an hour towards us."

"Remember, Slick," he told Dunaway. "you're shooting downhill, and they're moving towards you, so don't forget to aim low."

"You just keep an eye on the bastards," Dunaway said, his eyes never leaving the scope.

"I already know how to kill them; thank you very much."

"Fire when ready," Macklin ordered, a smile creeping across his freckled face. He knew Dunaway was good. He was just needling him.

A moment later, the 700 BDL barked loudly, and the first NVA Dog soldier in the line was flung backward as the 30-06 slug plowed into him.

"Hit," Buster said, "Center of mass."

"Good shot."

Three seconds later, there was another flat Crack, and another soldier went down.

"Hit," Macklin reported. "Center of mass."

"The rest are scattering."

Dunaway shifted slightly to get a better angle on a new target, then fired again.

"Hit," Buster said, "Center of mass."

"That was a heart shot," buster told him excitedly. "I saw his back get blown out."

Dunaway prepared to fire again, but Buster put his hand on his partner's shoulder.

"That's enough fun for one day, Marty," He said.

"Anymore shooting, and the Dicks will figure out where we are."

"If that happens, we'll have a hell of a time getting back up this hill."

"Let's pack it up, then beat feet." He ordered.

"The guns will be here in a minute anyway, and they can take care of the rest of them."

Dunaway nodded and put the Remington back on Safe.

A moment later, Dunaway whispered on the radio to their extraction bird and the lead gunship pilot. Meanwhile, Macklin was putting his partner's Remington back into its cloth case.

"You're sacked up," he said when he finished.

"How much longer?"

"Two or three more minutes," Dunaway answered.

"When the gunships get here, I'll signal them with my mirror."

"When they have our location, I'll have them rake the streamline and the far end of the trail."

"While the Dicks have their heads down," he explained. "we'll break for the top of the ridge."

"The Slick will pick us up when we get there."

"Get ready to move."

"I'll move as soon as I take off this goddamn rag mop," Buster snarled as he began shedding his Ghillie.

"I can hardly breathe in the damned thing, much less run in it."

"I'd forgotten about that," Dunaway admitted as he began getting out of his.

"I'm telling you, Marty," Buster bitched angrily. "this is the last goddamn time I'm wearing one of these damn things."

"They drive me crazy."

"They're just too goddamn hot."

"Christ, I'm sweating like a pig and itching all over."

"I feel like I got the heebie-jeebies."

Dunaway smiled.

"That's my Buster," he thought.

"We're eight miles inside Laos, a country that legally we aren't even supposed to be in."

"He's just killed six men.

"Every Dick within five miles of us is on his way here to waste our asses, and he's more worried about getting heat rash from some silly Ghillie suit than he is about getting out of here."

"There's no doubt about it; the little fucker is crazier than a shithouse rat."

Ten minutes later, Dunaway and Macklin were aboard the Slick, and the two escorting gunships were tearing up the real estate below. The extraction had been effortless. The few Dog Soldiers left alive were hiding or running for their lives as the Slick departed the area moments later.

After a few more minutes of flight time, the copilot yelled back and told them they were back across the border in South Vietnam. When Macklin looked out of the chopper at the jungle below, he shrugged. He couldn't tell the difference between Laos and South Vietnam since the terrain and jungle were the same. The border separating the two countries was just an imaginary line drawn on a notoriously inaccurate map anyway, and that didn't mean shit to him. He killed them where he found them.

Besides, he wasn't concerned with the mission anymore. That was over and ancient history now. He was now thinking about the pussy he would get once he got back to base camp, got cleaned up, and went downtown. A good shot of cold Jim Beam and a young Vietnamese hooker with a tight little ass was much more important.

There would always be another mission, but there might not always be another chance to drink and get laid quite so easily.

"You had to take it where you found it when you got the opportunity," he thought.

"A man had to get his priorities straight."

Chapter Ten
Failures

Dunaway was in the NCO club nursing a beer at a table by himself when Gunnery Sgt Casey walked in unexpectedly. It was the next day after the mission, and he was relaxing. At first, the Gunny squinted, his eyes unaccustomed to the darkness inside the club after the bright sun outside. But in another second, as his vision readjusted to the inside of the building, he scanned the nearly vacant bar's interior. Finally, he spotted his target and began moving towards it. Dunaway looked up as Casey made a bee line towards his table with a disapproving look plastered all over his leathery face.

"Oh Shit," Dunaway said to himself as the Gunny walked purposely towards him. "here comes trouble."

"Casey looks pissed."

He was right. The hard-looking Gunny started talking to him even before he reached Dunaway's table.

"I just read the after-action on your last mission, Dunaway." the senior NCO said conversationally when he arrived at the table and stopped abruptly.

"Nice job."

"The old man said to tell you, "Well Done," too."

"That's two in a row."

Dunaway nodded his thanks, but he was still leery. Gunnery Sgts don't have time to find subordinates when they are off duty. Much less when it is only to tell them Well Done for a previous mission. Instead, they have their subordinates report to their office.

"Where's your running buddy, Macklin?" Casey asked conversationally.

"I'm not sure," Dunaway replied with a shrug.

"Downtown getting drunk or getting laid," he offered. " probably both."

"That's where he usually is when we're off duty, and he's got the money."

"The little fucker loves the juice and the broads."

"And you're not with him because?" Casey asked curiously.

"I wasn't in the mood," Dunaway said off-handedly, not catching the hint of steel in Casey's voice.

"He's a little too wild for me when he gets drunk and starts carousing."

"Is that so?" Casey asked, with a slit on his face that resembled a smile.

"Funny," he said tersely. "that's the very thing that I came over here to talk to you about, Corporal."

"Here it comes," Dunaway thought incorrectly.

"Buster's fucked up again, and since I'm his partner, Casey wants me to go downtown and get his ass."

But he was wrong. Casey had not come just to see Dunaway about his rowdy partner. The Gunny also wanted a piece of Dunaway's ass too, a fact that soon became readily apparent.

"I put you two together for a reason, Corporal Dunaway," Casey began in a low voice filled with menace. "And that reason was for you to keep young Macklin out of trouble."

"Considering how young he is, along with the close availability of liquor and pussy, getting into trouble is normal for someone his age," he explained.

"Unfortunately, as you already know, Macklin tends to go overboard every chance he gets."

"The little shit needs a keeper when he's not in the field because he's a fucking accident waiting to happen back here in the rear."

"But since he's your partner, and you're his NCO, I expected you to be the one that would fill that role and teach him how to act like an adult at the same time."

"He's a big boy," Dunaway said jokingly, still not getting it.

"Am I supposed to be his keeper or something?"

Casey stared at him for a long moment before he replied. A moment later, his face clouded up, and the veins on his neck stood out.

"Well, you're right about him still being a boy, Dunaway," Casey said, half in exasperation and half in anger, barely able to control his rising temper. "and as a Marine NCO, I expected you to understand that, and try and teach him how to grow up and start acting like an adult, instead of some oversexed juvenile delinquent."

"Unfortunately," Casey snapped angrily, "that hasn't happened."

"Oh shit," Dunaway thought, *now starting to get it.*

But he was too late. He had fucked up. He had gotten caught. Now he was in deep shit as a result.

"You're the educated and thinking part of a unique team, Corporal," Casey started to explain as he tried valiantly to contain his anger. "Supposedly, that means you have the brains and the experience to set the example."

"Private Macklin is just the young and immature gifted tool that's the other half."

"What that means, Corporal," Casey continued as he felt himself losing it. "is that you're supposed to be the one in fucking charge."

"Macklin's inexperience and youth almost got him thrown in jail before he joined the Corps," Casey explained hotly, now starting to really get into it.

"He came about that close to spending a couple of years in the penitentiary because he couldn't control himself when he was drinking."

"But a lenient judge offered him the Corps instead."

"That's the reason he's now a Marine."

"It was either us or jail."

"But since he enlisted," Casey continued in a cold voice. "Macklin hasn't had much of a chance to work on any social amenities or develop much maturity."

"For two reasons," Casey said hotly.

"First, because shortly after boot camp, he found himself over here in the middle of a war."

"And second because no one has taken an interest in helping him grow up."

"So basically, he's still a kid."

"That's what most young Marines are when they enlist," Casey revealed.

"But, unlike Macklin, once they make it through boot camp, their noncoms make an effort to try and turn them into adults and give them a sense of pride and accomplishment."

"They try to get them to at least start thinking about making something of themselves and show them where to start."

"They do that, Corporal," Casey said hotly. "because it's part of their fucking jobs as Marine NCOs."

"In case nobody told you," he said angrily. "that's part of the responsibility that goes with the rank."

"But you haven't done that with Macklin, Corporal," Casey continued heatedly.

"Instead, you've doped off and evaded your responsibilities as an NCO."

"Rather than trying to help educate Private Macklin, you've tried to act like his buddy instead."

"Consequently, you've let him do pretty much as he pleases, especially when he isn't in the field."

"As a result, he's like a kid in a candy shop every time he goes downtown on liberty."

"Basically, you've just coasted along and done absolutely nothing to help him become an adult," Casey said fixing Dunaway with a merciless stare.

"In other words, Corporal Dunaway," Casey said, now really getting into it. "you have failed totally in your responsibilities as a Marine Non-Commissioned Officer."

Now Dunaway was listening intently. The light bulb had suddenly clicked on and was burning brightly. He was in deep trouble, and he knew it. Casey was so angry with him; he looked ready to destroy his ass.

"The Corps has invested a great deal of time and money training Macklin to do a specific job," Casey continued.

"That makes him a valuable piece of Marine Corps property."

"But without the benefit of any mature guidance, he's pretty much of a loose cannon when he's off duty."

"And that makes him a problem child."

"I've had three separate reports of his juvenile antics downtown already, and he's only been here four months," The Gunnery Sgt revealed.

"And there's probably more on the way that I don't even know about yet."

"That is totally and completely unacceptable," Casey thundered.

"I didn't do anything about those reports when I received them, Dunaway," Casey explained tersely.

"As his direct supervisor, I kept hoping and expecting *you* to straighten him out and help him grow up."

"After all, that's your fucking job," the Gunny roared.

Dunaway cringed. He was getting it loud and clear now. Casey's simple way of explaining things to him had illuminated everything perfectly. Not to mention Casey's volcanic anger at having to hunt him down and explain something to him that he should have already been acutely aware of.

"As an NCO and his partner," Casey said, his voice getting angrier as he spoke. "I expected you to not only lead Macklin but to also set the example, and mentor him."

"Teach him how to not only become an adult, but also learn how to conduct himself when he's off duty."

"That's what those two stripes on your sleeve are there for, Corporal," The Gunnery Sgt pointed out hotly.

"They are not some goddamn decoration designed to dress up your fucking uniform and make you look pretty!"

Dunaway was sitting up and listening very intently now, almost at attention.

"Gunnery Sgts did not give lectures like this because they are in love with the sound of their own voices," he thought nervously.

"Nor did they like to waste their valuable time explaining things to numb nuts like me who should already be aware of them."

That pisses them off immensely."

"So, when they had to hold a come-to-Jesus meeting like this, it behooves the listener to pay very close attention."

"I am in serious trouble," he moaned.

"But it is now readily apparent," Casey continued hotly. "that I made the wrong assumption when I expected you to act like a Marine NCO and take care of your subordinate, Corporal Dunaway."

Dunaway gulped. It had gotten incredibly quiet in the club now, with other patrons edging towards the door. They didn't want to be in the blast radius when the Gunnery Sgt really exploded.

"You obviously never had any intention of correcting your subordinate." Casey continued.

"That's because you've never had anyone explain exactly what your duties and responsibilities are as a Marine NCO before, Corporal."

"But I intend to rectify that situation, starting right fucking now," Casey snarled.

Dunaway was barely breathing now and sitting stock-still.

"Please God," he thought. *"let this pass, and I will atone; I swear it."*

"Don't let Gunny Casey rip me a new asshole so large I'll have to have it surgically repaired just to be able to shit normally again."

But by this time, it was past the point of worrying about ripped assholes. The Gunny was now well into his sermon, and they would be no prisoners taken and no quarter given. Sinners would be named, and repentance would begin. It was now root hog or die time. No holds barred. Dunaway's future was about as firm as a sneaker full of baby shit, and he knew it. He had fucked up royally, and he knew that too. Unfortunately for him, so did Gunnery Sgt. Casey.

"Macklin hasn't had the advantages of a real education or a comfortable lifestyle like you had before you joined the Corps, Corporal," Casey began initiating his re-education campaign.

"Nor has his family ever given him much guidance."

"They were just backward hillbillies and probably too busy just trying to provide for the bare necessities."

"That's because his people are as poor as Church mice, Dunaway." the Gunnery Sergeant revealed.

"Not comfortable like yours."

"They live in a back woods cabin up in the mountains, kill or grow their own food, and normally don't have two nickels to rub together at the end of every month."

"That's where Macklin was born and raised, and that's the f conditions he faced growing up."

"As a result, he's had to scratch and claw for everything his entire life."

"And in reality, he's probably never gotten very far out of that place and experienced very much about life in the process."

"Because of all that," Casey explained in a menacing voice. "he's still very rough around the edges."

"He's undereducated, doesn't know how to conduct himself in public, and in reality, he's not even an adult."

"He's just an oversexed, under-aged, hillbilly teenager who is trying to find his own way around in the world because he doesn't have anybody to tell him what to do or show him how to act."

"On top of all that," Casey roared." he's in the middle of a war."

"So, he has that "*live today because I might die tomorrow*" attitude."

"All that makes him act like a fucking dyslectic crossing guard at a Chinese fire drill when he's on his own in a social environment."

"If he acted as he acts right now back in the States," the Gunny snorted. "he'd be in jail."

"Because, unsupervised, he is a complete, unmitigated fucking disaster!"

"Macklin only has one saving grace," Casey said. "his skill with a rifle."

"If it weren't for that, given his current lifestyle, he wouldn't be worth a shit, and you and I wouldn't be having this conversation."

"Hathcock has seen him shoot and has told me that Macklin is the best natural shooter he has ever seen."

"He's that rare, one in ten million, that was born with the hand-eye coordination and body control it takes to be world-class."

"And Hathcock said he had never seen *anybody* throw a bolt any faster and still be able to stay on target as accurately."

"And believe me, Dunaway, coming from a shooter that has won the Wimbledon Cup and is the best in the world, that means something."

"It means that dumb little juvenile hillbilly has an extremely rare and unique talent."

"One that five, maybe six people in the entire world can match."

"But even with all that extraordinary skill," Casey continued. "Macklin's immaturity and penchant for acting like a juvenile delinquent when he is off duty will probably prevent him from ever being able to take advantage of all that talent and make a decent life for himself in the Corps."

"And believe me, the Corps is his only chance."

"That can only happen if he grows up and keeps his nose clean," Casey explained.

"And he can't do that by himself because he doesn't know how."

"So, the Corps is the only place someone like Macklin has to make a decent life for himself."

"He wouldn't last a month back in civilian life."

"So, he either makes it with us, or he doesn't make it at all."

"And right now, he's headed in the wrong direction."

"You are his closest friend, and he respects you, Dunaway," Casey pointed out.

"You are also his direct supervisor."

"You could teach him a lot if you put your mind to it or if you cared."

"Or," Casey said in disgust. "you could simply continue to do what you've been doing, which is fucking nothing."

"You could just continue to be his spotter until your tour here is up and continue to let him do what he pleases when he's downtown until he fucks up in some spectacular way and ruins any chance he has for a career."

"Then the Corps will pull him up short with a court-martial, he'll spend a few years in Portsmouth Naval prison."

"Afterwards, when he goes to the brig, and your tour is up, you could go back to the states and forget all about him."

"And if you do that, then Macklin will ruin his life, and the Marines will lose a very gifted shooter."

Dunaway sat stock still, barely breathing. Praying he would survive this monumental ass chewing and ashamed that he had failed so miserably in his duty.

"Is any of this getting through to you, Corporal," Casey asked in a low dangerous voice. "or am I just talking for my health?"

"Because if it isn't," Casey snarled. "I will explain it to you in much simpler and more direct language to ensure you understand back in my office."

"I'm reading you loud and clear, Gunnery Sgt," Dunaway replied.

"Excellent," Casey replied. "then get up off your ass and get on with it."

"Start acting like an NCO," Casey ordered.

"Do your fucking job for a change and make something out of your partner that both you and he can be proud of."

"Teach him how to be a real Marine."

"Impress me with your leadership skills from now on, Corporal," Casey thundered.

"Save Macklin from himself."

"And while you're at it, try and discover what the duties and responsibilities of a Marine NCO are and get your own act together."

"Otherwise, I will explain them to you in graphic and minute detail," Casey promised.

"And if I have to do that, I can assure you, that lesson will be a very long and penal one."

"One in which you will find Jesus and beg to be forgiven."

"Do you understand me, Corporal Dunaway?"

"I understand, and I will correct my deficiencies immediately, Gunnery Sgt," Dunaway promised, almost sitting at rigid attention now.

"From now on, I can promise you that taking care of my partner, Private Macklin, will become my primary responsibility."

"I will get him to grow up, and train him to be an exemplary Marine."

"That will become my primary duty."

"I will also start conducting myself accordingly as a Marine NCO."

"That's what I wanted to hear, Corporal Dunaway," Casey said with a thin smile.

"You can start by going downtown, finding the irresponsible little sonofabitch, and then getting him sobered up, cleaned up, and presentable."

"The old man wants to see both of you, and I want that to be sometime before the sun sets today, although I'm not very hopeful."

"Do I make myself clear?"

"Crystal, Gunnery Sergeant," Dunaway replied., reaching for his cover.

A long and tedious hour and a half later, Dunaway finally found Buster in a cheap dive off Quoi Lon street in the bar district of Da Nang. He had already combed out most of the other bars and whorehouses in the area in a vain effort to locate his partner with no luck. So, by this time, he was hot, sweaty, angry, and still stinging from Casey's ass chewing. Consequently, when he spotted Buster with his arm around a young Vietnamese hooker and a silly grin plastered on his face, he was not in a very forgiving mood. The little redneck was obviously shit-faced!

"Whattaya say there, Marty?" Buster asked drunkenly when Dunaway walked up to the table.

"Changed your mind, Huh?"

"Decided to have a little fun anyway, despite yourself!"

"Well, it's about time," Buster said happily before Dunaway could reply.

"You need to learn how to relax a little, Dunaway."

"You act like an old maid with a corncob jammed up her ass half the time; you're so fuckin' stuffy," he joked.

Dunaway answered with a strained smile.

"Relax, boy," Buster invited. "Sit down and have a snort."

"I'm buying, and I can tell you, the hooch here is pretty damned good."

"And if you wanna get your oil changed," he said, nodding at the hooker wrapped around him. "this little cutie is just the ticket."

"She could suck a golf ball through a garden hose, and she just loves to make the beast with two backs."

"Ten minutes with her, and you'll wanna get married," He promised.

Dunaway rolled his eyes in exasperation.

"*The little shit is slobbering drunk,*" Dunaway thought as he looked down at Buster, completely unamused. "*and he's probably already got a world-class case of the clap.*"

"*How the hell am I going to pry him outta here and back to base without him starting a riot?*"

"*He sure as hell won't leave voluntarily,*" Dunaway realized as he continued to smile at Macklin.

"*He's too drunk, and he's having too good of a time.*"

"*And I damned sure don't wanna have to try and force him outta this shithole.*"

"*I try that I'll not only have to fight him but everybody else in the place.*"

"*So, I'll have to think of something that will lure him out.*"

"*Make him want to leave.*"

Meanwhile, Buster continued to smile drunkenly and paw at the whore's tits.

"I've been looking all over for you, Buster," Dunaway began a moment later, turning on the bullshit.

"I just got us dates with two Red Cross Donut Dollies I met at the PX."

"Both of them are built like brick shithouses."

"Have tits that are like mountains."

"We got less than thirty minutes before we pick them up," He said, glancing at his watch.

"So, we got to move, boy, or we'll be late and miss them."

"Donut Dollies," Macklin parroted, grinning lopsidedly as his eyes lit up.

"You mean real American round-eyed females?" he slurred eagerly.

"As ever was," Dunaway swore, holding up his right hand.

"And believe me, they are hot to trot, son."

"They're waiting for us right now; both of them all fired up and ready to party."

"Hot damn," Buster said eagerly, struggling to get up. "where's my cover?"

"I ain't had no American pussy in six months."

"You stay here, GI," the Vietnamese hooker screamed angrily, grabbing his arm.

"I love you too much, if you do, Mackleeen."

"You no need, American girl," She pouted.

"I make beaucoup love with you myself."

"I give you number one fuck suck."

"Keep it warm, sweetheart," Dunaway said, helping Macklin up.

"We'll be back later," he promised.

"You lie," The hooker screamed angrily at Dunaway. "You no come back later."

"You steal my number one boyfriend, Mackleeen, and go to meet American whores."

"You number ten, Marine asshole."

But Dunaway was already steering Buster out of the door with the whore still screaming. He hailed the Vietnamese version of a taxi moments later.

"Where are the round eyes?" Buster slurred drunkenly when they were in a pedicab headed back to base minutes later.

"We're already on the way to join them," Dunaway lied.

"We'll be there in just a minute."

"Relax and save your strength, Buster."

"You're gonna need it," He promised.

Buster fell asleep two minutes later as the pedicab chugged through the heavy traffic, rocking gently on its old worn-out suspension.

Ten minutes later, they pulled up at the base's main gate with a squeal of brakes. When the cyclo stopped, Buster woke up and quickly figured out where he was. Puzzled, he looked at Dunaway.

"I thought you said we were on our way to get round eye pussy, and I was gonna get fucked, Marty," He said suspiciously.

"Oh, but you are, Buster," Dunaway said, throwing a right cross that hit Macklin right on the button and cold-cocked him.

"But not by any Donut Dollies, you drunken little shit."

"Help me get this asshole across my shoulder so I can carry him back to our unit," he told the gate guard a moment later.

"The CO wants to see him, and I've got to sober him up first."

The MP shook his head as he walked over.

"Jesus," he said, shaking his head disbelief as he took in Buster's condition. "Good Luck."

"He looks like a ragbag and smells like a fuckin' still."

"What fucking dive did you have to dig him out of?"

"Just help me pick him up, Private," Dunaway ordered disgustingly.

Chapter Eleven
Necessary Corrections

Two and a half hours later, Macklin and Dunaway were standing at attention in front of Gunnery Sgt Casey's desk. That task alone had taken a monumental effort on Dunaway's part because he's the one that had been forced to sober Buster up. Given the degree of Macklin's drunkenness, that had been no mean feat.

As a result, a tired and red-eyed Private Roan Macklin looked like he had been washed, pressed, and then dry-cleaned uniform-wise. But his face told the real story. It looked like he was just recovering from a month-long bout with distemper.

"Private Macklin," Casey bawled, eyeing a wobbly-legged, red-eyed Buster trying valiantly to stand at rigid attention in front of him, but failing.

"You look like you just crawled out of a fuckin' sewer someplace."

Buster moaned inwardly. He was in no condition to receive an ass chewing. But he realized he was going to receive a monumental-sized one anyway.

"You reek of alcohol, Private," Casey said angrily.

"Did Corporal Dunaway have to drag you out of some goddamn bar?"

"Yes, Sir, Gunnery Sgt," Macklin replied in embarrassment. "About an hour ago."

"I thought so," Casey said disapprovingly. "Christ, you still don't appear sober."

"He's sober enough, Gunny," Dunaway barked as he interrupted.

"He's had three cold showers and about a gallon of black coffee poured into him."

"And he's already puked all the rot gut out of his system."

"Most of it on me!"

Casey said "Ummm" and nodded, doubt evident in his eyes.

"Private Macklin," Casey began. "I have already had a little *"come to Jesus"* meeting with Corporal Dunaway earlier, and part of it concerned you."

"Now, we are going to discuss your shortcomings."

"Not all of them, you little maggot," Casey said, seething. "Because there are so many that we don't have the time."

"So, we will confine ourselves to talking about your most recent glaring deficiencies."

Buster gulped as he saw the look on Casey's face.

"Oh Jesus," he thought.

"Let me start by saying that you are an absolute, total fucking disgrace, Private," Casey roared. "to the Marine Corps, to this unit, and yourself."

"Your conduct during your off-duty time since you have been assigned to this unit has been nothing less than a spectacular fucking abortion."

"That is completely unacceptable and will no longer be tolerated; you shriveled up little turd."

Buster started to cringe.

"Are Gunny Casey and Drill Sergeant Kimmel related?" he wondered.

"I have had no less than three separate delinquency reports on you cross my desk in as many months," Casey thundered. "all of them concerning you and your half-assed activities downtown on liberty."

"But because of your past performance in the field, and because I had hoped that your half-assed partner, Dunaway, would help you clean up your act and teach you to start acting like an adult," Casey said angrily. "I let those reports slide."

"That, however, has turned out to be a colossal error in judgment on my part," Casey hissed.

"Because I can now see that neither you nor Corporal Dunaway is capable of conducting yourselves responsibly."

"You're both world-class fuck ups."

"So, it's a case of the blind leading the blind."

"Neither one of you could find your own ass with both hands and a fuckin' flashlight in the area of personal responsibility."

"You, because you don't know how, Macklin," Casey explained tersely. "and Dunaway, because he doesn't know what the duties of a Marine NCO are."

"But, that all ends, Private Macklin," Casey said in a low deadly voice. "right fucking now."

"From this moment on, you will start acting like a man and not some drunken little juvenile delinquent who thinks he can chase pussy, get drunk, wreck bars or do anything else he pleases."

"From this moment on, Private," Casey snarled. "you are going to start acting like a Marine, a real Marine."

"And you are going to start conducting yourself in a like manner, both in the field and when you are off duty."

"Is all this sinking in, Macklin?" Casey said eyeing Buster, with a face so cold it could have frozen water.

"Am I getting through to that pea-sized brain of yours?"

"Yes, Sir, Gunnery Sgt," Buster said, now standing at rigid attention and starting to sweat alcohol-tinged bullets.

Buster was in real trouble now, and he knew it. Once again, his drinking and carousing had gotten him into an exceedingly difficult situation. When would he ever learn?

"Whether you know it or not, Macklin," Casey continued in disgust. "you were specially selected for this unit."

"And after that happened and you joined us, it was hoped by both the Skipper and I that you would behave like an adult and act like a professional."

"That hasn't happened," Casey roared.

"You haven't even come close, you little fucking worm."

"Therefore, you have embarrassed both your commander and me personally."

"And that is something I won't tolerate, you little shit."

"Because it reflects on my personal judgment in selecting you, and on my professional reputation."

"And it goes even farther than that."

"For your information, Private," Casey snarled. "the entire Marine Corps is watching this Platoon to see whether or not they ought to adopt the scout sniper concept as a full time Marine military occupational specialty and make it a permanent part of the Marine Corps."

"So, you and the childlike behavior you have been exhibiting since you arrived, are preventing us from presenting ourselves in a very favorable light, Private."

"Instead of looking and acting like seasoned Marines and dedicated professionals," Casey explained. "you two are making us look like a bunch of Neanderthal cowboy fuckups at some goddamn wild west, goat rodeo."

"Complete total malfunctions who are not only incapable of conducting themselves as professionals, but who aren't even smart enough to pour piss out of a boot if it had directions printed on the heel!"

"That makes people think of this entire unit as some fucked up comedy act that has no business even being considered a future part of the Corps."

"But I can assure you that you are not going to fuck things up for us and embarrass the Skipper any longer," Casey snapped.

"Because I am personally going to ensure that doesn't happen."

"Instead, from this moment on, you will become the epitome of a well-turned out and adult-acting Marine, Private."

"Starting right fucking now!" He screamed.

Macklin's heart sank.

"Jesus." he thought. "I was wrong."

Kimmer and Casey aren't related."

"Casey was probably Kimmer's DI when he was a boot.

"That's where he learned his trade so well."

"Casey taught him."

"And when you learn how to behave like a well turned out Marine, Macklin," Casey continued. "you are going to make us all proud, and in turn, make this unit an exemplary one." the Gunny roared.

"Is that absolutely fucking clear, you miserable little ignorant shit?"

"Yes, Sir, Gunnery Sgt," Macklin barked loudly, fervently hoping that he was going to survive the next few minutes.

"That means that if I ever even hear of you being drunk again, or causing trouble because want into Mary Jane Rottencrotch's panties," Casey thundered. "then I will personally supervise at your crucifixion and laugh as I rip your miniature dick and balls off and feed them to you."

"Is that also clear, you little maggot?"

"Yes, Sir, Gunnery Sgt," Macklin roared.

"Excellent," Casey said, his voice returning to normal.

"Now, you and the half-assed Lance Corporal who has the dubious honor of supervising you, will now return to your quarters."

"When you get there, you will both clean every single piece of your equipment until it is absolutely spotless, and it shines."

"I mean, it better be pristine, mister."

"Afterwards, you will notify me you have finished," Casey ordered.

"After I have personally inspected all that gear, and it is up to my personal standards, you will hold yourself in readiness for a meeting with the Skipper."

"That will probably be sometime tomorrow," Casey said, looking at his watch in disgust. "since you have already fucked the majority of today up."

"This is the first, last, and only time I ever expect to have to counsel you on your sins like this, Private," Casey continued, coldly eyeing Macklin like some shark eyeballing its prey.

"If I ever have to take up my valuable time doing it again, I can promise you that you will be extremely and profoundly sorry."

"Because if that ever happens again, you will spend the rest of your tour in Vietnam cleaning every shithouse in the entire 1st Marine Division."

Buster almost barfed at the thought of that.

"You will scrub out three-hole shitters until your fingernails turn brown," Casey threatened. "because that will be your only duty, Macklin."

"And you will shovel shit until your arms ache."

"And you will smell it too, every single hour of every day."

"For so long, its odor will form brown crusts in your nose."

"And even when you've finished cleaning every day, you will have to sleep outdoors because no one will be able to stand being anywhere near you because of the stink."

"Eventually, you will become a pariah: unwanted, unapproachable, and unable to be tolerated by your fellow Marines."

Buster moaned.

"Do you understand what I'm telling you, Private?" Casey roared.

"Yes, Sgt," Buster snapped loudly. "completely."

"You better "shit- for- brains," Casey told him. "because from now on, your entire future is in your own hands."

"So, you better do everything humanly possible not to fuck it up!"

"You are now officially on my shit list, Macklin," Casey snarled.

"So, you would be well-advised not to piss me off any further in the future."

"Do you understand me, you little toad?"

"Yes, Sir, Gunnery Sgt." Macklin thundered. "Loud and clear."

"Good," Casey said, his eyes fixing Macklin like some insect pinned to a specimen board.

"Now get your sorry little ass out of my sight and get busy."

Chapter Twelve
A chance at redemption

"I've fucked up really bad this time, haven't I, Marty?" Buster asked later as they sat on their bunks, reviewing how badly he had screwed up.

"Yeah, Dickweed," Dunaway replied. "you sure as hell have."

"World fucking class this time."

"I haven't heard an ass chewing like that since I was a boot."

"And I don't have to tell you," he warned. "Casey was as serious as a heart attack about what he said."

"You pissed him off, Buster," Dunaway told his young charge.

"So, you better shape the fuck up, and you better do it immediately."

"You fuck around with Gunny Casey," he said. "and life as you know it will cease to exist."

"That man means exactly what he says."

Both men were back in their hooch, furiously cleaning their equipment. Buster had been quiet for almost half an hour after they got back. Dunaway had soon realized his partner was probably too embarrassed to speak, so he had remained silent too. Besides, he had been thinking about his own failures and sins.

Unfortunately, Casey had been right about him too, and he realized it. He was as much a failure as a Marine NCO as Buster was of a being drunken skirt chaser. He was utterly embarrassed and humiliated about that, especially since he had been publicly reminded about it by Casey himself. So, he wasn't in the mood for casual conversation.

Macklin's behavior had not only gotten him in trouble, but it had also brought Dunaway's failures as an NCO to light for everyone to see. And although he didn't want to admit it to himself, Casey had made him feel like a failure too. And he was. The trouble was, unlike Buster, he should have known better.

"We both fucked up," Dunaway finally admitted a minute later.

"You, because you don't know how to behave yourself in public, and me, because I don't know how to behave as an NCO. "

"So, neither of us has any excuse."

"We're both screw-ups."

Buster looked up from his scrubbing. He knew Dunaway was right, and he was ashamed. Of himself for his behavior and because his actions had also landed Dunaway on Casey's shit list.

"I don't know about you, Buster, but I'm ashamed of myself," Dunaway said in disgust.

"Unlike you, I knew better."

"I got you into trouble, too," Buster asked. "didn't I, Marty?"

"No," Dunaway said. "I got my own self into trouble."

"I should have known better, so it's my own goddamn fault."

"Maybe," Buster said.

"But it was all *because* of me." He insisted.

Dunaway didn't reply.

"I'm sorry about that, Marty," Buster said a moment later.

"Gunny Casey was right."

"I just don't know how to act when I get to drinkin'."

"I almost got throwed in jail because of it before I come in the Corps," Buster admitted, not knowing Dunaway already knew about his checkered past.

"Fact is, that's really why I'm in the Corps."

"In fact," he revealed. "seems like I been a fuck up ever since I started drinking."

"I'm just sorry I got you into trouble because I'm such an asshole."

"But I promise you, Marty," Buster said in an apologetic and embarrassed voice a moment later.

"I'll make it up to you."

"From now on, I ain't gonna do nothing that will cause you or the Gunny any more embarrassment."

"I swear it."

"I ain't drinking no more; I ain't gonna chase no more pussy, and I'm gonna do my best to make you and the Gunny proud of me from here on," He vowed.

Dunaway eyed him doubtfully.

"I never listened to anyone about my faults before," Buster admitted. "not even my old man."

"He tried to tell me to straighten up when I first took to drinking and started acting wild-assed."

"But I didn't pay him no mind."

"Thought he was just an ignorant hillbilly."

"Later on, after I nearly got throwed in jail in my hometown, he tried talking to me again."

"But I was still too much of a smartass to listen to him," Buster explained.

"Thought I already knew every damned thing and had all the answers."

"Didn't need no advice from anybody."

"Told him I was all growed up."

"But I was wrong," Buster revealed.

"I wasn't."

"Finally, when I got throwed in jail down in Georgia later, I found out he was right."

"That's the reason I'm in the Corps."

"It was either the Marines or a chain gang for two years."

"I didn't know shit then," he admitted. "and I ain't learned very much since."

"At least about how to act in public."

"So now I've gone and done the same goddamn thing again."

"Cept this time I got somebody else in trouble too, and that ain't right."

"But no more, Marty," Buster vowed. "I promise you that."

"This is the last goddamn time."

"All that kid-actin', wild-assed shit stops right now."

"I ain't gonna do no more of that kinda shit, ever."

"I like the Marines, and I wanna stay in," Buster told Dunaway.

"Because there sure as hell ain't nothing for me back in Tennessee."

"And I damned sure don't wanna have to clean no shithouses here in Vietnam," Buster said emphatically.

"I don't even want to think about having to do that kinda job."

"I ain't much, but I know I'm better than that."

"So now I'm just gonna have to start busting my ass to convince Gunny Casey, the Skipper, and the Corps to let me have another chance."

"And I sure could use some help trying to do that."

"I ain't smart like you, Marty," Macklin said, embarrassed.

"Barely got through school back in Burl, and it wasn't much of a school to start with."

"Fucked off, farted around, and didn't even try to learn nothing even as bad as it was."

"Never grew up either," He admitted.

"Never thought I'd have to."

"So, I sure as shit don't know how to act when I get into public and start drinking."

"I was just a smart mouth little red neck who didn't give much of a shit about nobody or nothing back then, and I ain't learned very much about how to act since."

"Never thought I'd have to."

"Thought I'd be just like my Pappy and never get outta Burl."

"Wind up going to the state pen like he did."

"But I did get out," he said. "courtesy of some old white-haired judge."

"He offered me two years on a chain gang or the Corps."

"So here I am."

"But I still ain't much smarter than I was back in Burl," Buster revealed grudgingly.

"So, I need somebody to teach me how to act."

"And I'd be pleased if you'd oblige me because I ain't got nobody else."

Afterwards, he stopped talking and went back to scrubbing his web gear.

"If you mean that," Dunaway said a moment later. "then I'll help you, Buster."

"But if you're just bullshitting me, or trying to con me, then Lord help your sorry little ass."

"Because I'm gonna be all over you every time you even think about screwing up in the future," He said, eyeing Buster angrily.

"I mean it."

"I don't ever want to get on Casey's bad side again," Dunaway told Buster. "especially because of you fucking up."

"So, I'm going to clean up my act and start acting like an NCO.

"And that means you're gonna clean up yours and start acting like an adult."

"If you don't," Dunaway promised. "I'll have you cleaning shithouses myself!"

"Now," Dunaway said. "enough talk."

"Let's get this gear cleaned up."

Buster smiled as he started scrubbing again.

Two hours later, Casey was at their hooch inspecting both men's efforts. He examined every piece of equipment they had, eyeing it critically, but he paid particular attention to their weapons. When he had finished, he handed the Model 70 back to Macklin.

"If you want to keep using this, Private," he warned. "you better make damned sure I don't ever have to counsel you again."

"I meant exactly what I said earlier."

"Understand?"

"Yes sir, Gunnery Sgt," Macklin roared.

"Excellent," Casey said.

"The old man will see both of you at 0900 hrs. tomorrow morning," Casey told both men a moment later.

"He's going to assign you two a new mission that will involve you working with some specialized Army people."

"They'll be in charge," Casey explained. "but they want a sniper team to assist them in their mission."

"A really good one."

"The old man asked Hathcock who he thought was the best shooter in the Platoon, and he said you, Macklin," Casey continued.

"Fortunately, your off-duty conduct didn't enter into the equation."

"So, based on that, the old man is sending you two."

"So, you both better absolutely shine on this new mission," Casey warned dangerously.

"Because if you don't, or if you even think about fucking this up, then I'll have both your asses when it's over, and you two get back here."

"And if that happens, I promise you both you will regret the day you were born," Casey said in a low and menacing voice.

"Do you read me?"

Macklin and Dunaway nodded their understanding.

"This mission is highly classified, so it must be pretty damned important," Casey explained.

"So, you keep your traps shut after the old man briefs you."

Macklin and Dunaway nodded again.

"The old man told me that scuttlebutt says approval for it had to come from Washington," Casey revealed.

"So, see to it that you conduct your part of it in a completely professional manner."

"And remember that you're Marines."

"That means you are held to a higher standard and expected to do more than just what is required."

"Instead, you will do your absolute best."

"See that you remember that too," He added.

"Don't this fuck up, girls," Casey warned. "This is too important."

"To your future as well as the future of the Platoon."

"It could go a long way towards validating the Skipper's concept as far as the Marine Corps is concerned."

"So, I expect both of you to excel in your performance."

"Anything less is not acceptable."

"Do you read me?"

"Yes, sir, Gunnery Sgt.," both men replied loudly.

Of course, Gunnery Sgt Casey was correct in everything he told Macklin and Dunaway about the mission. The Skipper repeated what the Gunny had said to them when he briefed both men the following day.

Unfortunately, the Skipper did not tell them anything new about the mission. That was because, as he admitted, he did not know anything more himself. He had just been told the mission was classified, it had an extremely high priority, and that he would provide a top-notch shooting team for it.

The mission, any of the details concerning it, and the target would be given to them when they linked up with the other half of the Team and got briefed by the mission controllers. That would probably occur sometime in the next day or two since Macklin and Dunaway were scheduled to fly to Saigon on an afternoon flight that same day to link up with the remainder of the team.

Three hours later, after noon, chow, Macklin, and Dunaway, along with all their gear, were driven to the airfield by Gunnery Sgt Casey. As they waited for the flight to be called, Casey had a few parting words for them. He surprised both men by not only what he said but the way he said it.

"If you two stay in the Corps," Casey told them. "there will likely be other similar missions assigned to you."

"That's because you are both specialists."

"You are Marine Snipers, and that means you are some of the best shots in the world."

"You kill deliberately and with surgical precision, and that places you in a category that is outside the mainstream of anything in the rest of the military."

"That's the reason I have tried to impress on both of you just how serious your job is."

"Consequently, you, in turn, have to be serious about *it.*"

"All the time."

"Normal Marines and soldiers are taught to kill as a part of their jobs," Casey explained. "so, when they see the enemy or meet him in the field, they engage him and try and kill him as part of a unit."

"But what you do, as compared to what they do, is completely different," He explained.

"When you take out a target, you do it very deliberately, and you do it all by yourself."

"You don't do it by accident or because of some chance meeting, and you aren't surrounded by your friends who can protect you."

"You deliberately stalk your target," Casey said. "

"You locate him; then you see the color of his eyes and the shock on his face as you deliberately kill him."

"Gentlemen," Casey told both men. "that's about as serious as it gets."

"To be able to do what you do regularly and then live with it," Casey explained. "takes a very serious person."

"One that is in complete control of his faculties as well as his emotions at all times."

"And that means when he on duty or off duty."

"That's why I demand the best from all my people, all the time," The Gunny explained.

"When you fully understand what I'm telling you right now, you'll realize that what I demand of you is critical to your job."

"Whether or not you both realize it," Casey continued. "you each have a rare gift."

"Only maybe two or three hundred people in the entire world can shoot as well as you do."

"And even the majority of them can't do what you do daily."

"Because we're not talking about shooting at some paper target in some competition on a long-distance range somewhere," Casey said.

"We're talking about deliberately hunting and then killing somebody at a range of up to a thousand yards or more."

"Then watching his chest or head explode when we take him out."

"We can see the agony and shock on his face when the bullet we just fired hits and kills him."

"That's what you two have been trained for," Casey said. "and that's why you are assigned to the Platoon."

"You are handpicked, certified man killers of the highest order."

"That means that you are the best in the world at what you do," Casey said.

"Now, go and do this job and make us proud of you in the process."

"When it's over, bring your asses back in the same condition as when you left."

"Consider that is an order, gentlemen," Casey said as he smiled.

"Good Luck."

Chapter Thirteen
New Friends

Before either of them could speak, the Gunny drove off in a cloud of dust. Afterwards, Macklin and Dunaway shouldered their gear and walked into the terminal. Once inside, Dunaway inquired about their flight, and after getting the information, both he and Macklin sat down to wait. While they did, Buster thought about what Gunny Casey had told them. For the second time in his young life, Buster realized he had screwed up badly but was being given a second chance. This time he was determined not to waste it.

Twenty minutes later, both men were on a C-130, bound for Tan San Nuht Air Force Base just outside Saigon. After they took off, Dunaway also thought about Casey's farewell remarks. He also remembered his ass chewing and the reason he had gotten it. He knew he had deserved it, and he also knew he had to change if he wanted to make the Corps his career. He had to take charge and show some leadership for a change.

"Private Macklin," he said, a moment later, looking directly at Buster in all seriousness. "starting right now, we are both going to begin acting and behaving like real Marines, both on and off duty."

"We will think, talk and act like professionals from now on."

"Is that clear?" He asked Buster.

Buster was so surprised all he could muster was a nod. Dunaway was shit serious, and he knew it.

"Since I am the Non-Commissioned Officer in this detail, from now on, I will do all talking, most of the thinking, and I will make *all* the decisions," Dunaway told him.

"I will do all those things because that's my job." He thundered.

"That doesn't mean I won't ask for your advice or take any of your suggestions from time to time."

"Especially when we are in the field," He added.

"It just means I will be responsible for making the ultimate decision."

"We are a team," Dunaway continued. "and a damned good one, so we will continue to operate as a team."

"I am also your friend and will continue to be your friend, Buster."

"But I am also your supervisor," Dunaway reminded Macklin, his voice ringing with authority.

"That means it is my responsibility to look out for your welfare and to instruct you in those areas you need help with."

"And in your case, that means I am going to ensure that you grow up, start acting like an adult and clean up your act."

"Especially when you are off duty."

"Do you understand what I'm telling you, Private?" Dunaway asked in a curt voice.

Macklin looked at Dunaway with newfound respect.

"Yes, sir, Corporal," he said.

"Excellent," Dunaway responded.

"Then, from now on, we understand each other."

"Accordingly, I will expect nothing less than absolute professional behavior from you on or off duty."

"That means you will start acting like a well-turned-out Marine and not some juvenile delinquent in uniform."

"Anything less, wherever you are, will not be tolerated."

"Is that clear?"

"Yes, Corporal Dunaway," Buster bellowed loudly.

Those were the new rules, and Buster realized he would have to abide by them. Dunaway would ensure that. It was an entirely different ballgame now. Buster had already had his two strikes and he wouldn't get a third one.

A little over an hour later, the aircraft landed, taxied to its parking spot at Tan San Nuht, AFB, and shut down. Once the rear ramp was lowered, the pair were met by a hard-looking Army NCO wearing a green beret.

"You two Dunaway and Macklin?" he asked as they stepped off the aircraft.

Dunaway nodded.

"I'm Breslan," He said. "I'm here to pick you up."

"Grab your gear, put it in the carry-all, and get in," He ordered.

"Afterwards, I'll take you to the compound."

Thirty minutes later, Breslan pulled the carry-all through a guarded gate into a walled and fortified compound secured by a company of

Nung mercenaries who looked like they knew their business.

As they passed the Nung gate guards, Macklin nudged Dunaway and pointed. He had never seen a Nung before and was curious. But since Dunaway hadn't either, he just shrugged too.

"We're here," Breslan said, as he stopped a moment later.

"Grab your gear, follow me, and I'll show you where you'll be bunking."

Minutes later, Breslan led them into an air-conditioned barracks building containing three other people. As they put their gear down on two empty bunks, a tanned man about thirty, wearing camouflaged pants and an OD T-shirt, walked up and stuck out his hand.

"I'm Captain Jim Taylor, your Team leader," he said with a smile. "Welcome to Saigon."

Both Dunaway and Macklin snapped to attention, and then Dunaway barked.

"Corporal Dunaway, reporting with a detail of two, Sir."

Taylor smiled and then said.

"At ease, men."

"We're not that formal around here."

"What are your full names?"

"I am Corporal Martin Dunaway, and this is Private Roan Macklin, Sir," Dunaway replied.

"Glad to meet both of you," Taylor said.

"I'll let everybody else on the team introduce themselves to you in a moment."

"But first, let me tell you that Sgt Breslan and I are Army Special Forces and our two Nung counterparts, Chuy and Lop, are SCUs."

"We are all members of SOG."

Both Dunaway and Macklin just looked puzzled since the acronyms meant nothing to them.

"I'm afraid we don't know what SOG is, Sir," Dunaway finally replied. "SCUs either."

Taylor laughed again.

"That's right," he said. "you're Marines, so you wouldn't know."

"I forgot that for a moment."

"SCU is short for Special Commando Unit," He explained. "That's where our two Nungs, Chuy and Lop, come from."

"That means they are highly trained, mercenaries hired by Special Forces to work in various classified assignments."

"Specifically, they work for SOG as members of a cross-border recon team."

"Mine to be exact," He explained.

"SOG is short for the Military Assistance Command Special Operations Group," He explained further.

"We do all the covert and dirty jobs here in the theater."

"What we call unconventional warfare." He continued.

"We work mainly in Laos, Cambodia, and North Vietnam conducting classified and covert special operations."

"In our case, he explained. "that means cross-border reconnaissance missions into northeastern Laos."

"Is that where we'll be going on this mission, Sir?" Dunaway asked.

"To be truthful," Taylor replied unexpectedly. "I'm not sure where we're going, Dunaway."

"And I don't know what our mission is either," he admitted.

"They haven't told us yet."

"They?" Dunaway said in a surprised voice.

"I was told the Army was in charge of this mission, Sir."

"No," Taylor replied. "My men and I are simply requested Department of Defense assets for this party, just like you and Macklin."

"The Agency is in charge and will be running things."

"We'll all be working for them."

"You mean the Central Intelligence Agency, Sir?" Dunaway asked, his eyes widening.

Taylor nodded.

"Didn't your people tell you that before they sent you down here?" he asked.

Dunaway looked at Macklin. Buster looked back at him and just shrugged since he did not know what to say. No one had said a word about the CIA being a part of this mission. Dunaway wondered if either the Skipper or Casey knew. If they did, they didn't tell him.

"No sir," Dunaway finally replied. "they didn't tell us anything."

"Not even our Skipper knew."

"All he was told was to provide a shooting team to some specialized Army assets for a high priority mission."

"We don't even know what we'll be doing on the mission."

"Jesus," Taylor said. "You mean you didn't even know what you were volunteering for?"

"We didn't volunteer, sir," Dunaway replied unexpectedly.

"We were just given the tasking and told to report."

"We're Marines, so that's what we did."

Taylor just shook his head.

"Apparently, the Marine Corps handles missions like this one much differently than us Army pukes," he said, grinning.

"At least we're given a choice on something like this."

"Anyway, Welcome aboard," Taylor said with a smile.

"We're glad to have you."

Afterwards, the Nungs walked over and introduced themselves.

"What's a Nung?" Buster asked them right off.

"I never heard of that before."

Chuy and Lop laughed, then they explained. Buster was fascinated.

Chapter Fourteen
Joint Covert Ops

After breakfast the following day, the entire team assembled in a secured briefing room in another building on the compound. When everyone was seated, a tall thin civilian, who appeared to be in his mid-thirties, and wearing rimless glasses, walked into the room, stationed himself behind a small podium in its front, and began to brief them.

"Good Morning, gentlemen," he began. "Welcome to Saigon."

"My name is Chambers, and I work for the Central Intelligence Agency."

"The Special Activities Division, to be exact."

"And as of this morning, so do all of you," He explained.

"We requested several assets from the Department of Defense to perform a special mission here in theater, and MACV sent us you people."

"We were told you are all experts in your career fields, and after reviewing your records, I feel satisfied you will be able to complete this mission with little to no trouble."

"You men have now been detailed to the Agency to perform that mission and will do so under our command and control."

"I am your control officer, so all your dealings with the Agency will be conducted through me."

"Any questions or problems with that?"

There was silence in the room.

"Good." Chambers said.

"Before we get into specifics about the mission, let me also tell you that everything you see here, hear here, or do hear, especially about the mission itself, is classified Top Secret and will not be discussed or referenced with anyone outside your team."

"Now or at any time in the future."

"That includes anyone in your chain of command when you return to your unit."

"Before leaving this room, all of you will be required to sign non-disclosure statements to that effect."

"Any violation of those agreements, and you will go to prison."

"Does everyone understand that?"

Everyone on the Team nodded.

"Excellent," Chambers said. "now to the reason why you're here."

"You men have all been selected to perform a special mission here in Southeast Asia that is critical to the war effort in the theater," Chambers revealed.

"The mission itself will be conducted in the country of Laos, and for that reason, it will be covert."

"That means that it will be conducted in a manner that is plausibly deniable."

"That's trade talk meaning nothing about the mission or its participants can ever be traced back to the United States."

"To ensure that happens, you will conduct it using all sterile equipment."

"It also means that if something goes wrong, you get captured, or the mission gets blown, you are on your own."

"Neither the Agency nor the United States government will ever admit knowing you."

"In other words, in simple terms, if you fuck up, you're screwed.

"We never heard of you."

"Wonderful," Dunaway thought.

"What have Buster and I gotten ourselves into?"

"After this briefing," Chambers continued. "Under the guidance of Captain Taylor, you will study all the intelligence we have concerning the mission and the target and develop a suitable operations concept."

"After you have developed a concept of operations for the mission, and it has been approved, you will all be taken to our equipment warehouse in Cholon and issued whatever equipment you deem necessary to conduct that mission."

"Now, let me tell you exactly what that mission is," He said.

"Finally," Buster thought.

"This asshole sure likes to hear himself talk."

"This man," Chambers said, pointing to a picture of an Asian man in uniform that had appeared on a screen behind him. "is General Thu Trang Pao."

"He is the commander of all Pathet Lao forces in northern Laos."

"And, as we all know, the Pathet Lao are the North Vietnamese surrogates in the country."

"That makes General Pao the primary military leader of all the communist forces in Laos."

"He takes his orders directly from General Giap, the leader of all the North Vietnamese forces, and that makes Pao a critical man and a high value target."

"The Pathet Lao are the North Vietnamese allies in the country," Chambers explained. "and Laos has a full-fledged ongoing insurgency of its own because of them."

"To conduct that insurgency, they are supplied by the North Vietnamese with arms, equipment, and other military wherewithal to conduct their operations."

"They use all that material to conduct guerrilla warfare against the legitimate Laotian government, and they take their orders from General Giap and the North Vietnamese government, who want to take over Laos as well as South Vietnam eventually."

"However," Chambers revealed. "the insurgency in Laos is slightly different from the one here in South Vietnam."

"In addition to their military activities, the Pathet Lao also control a large portion of the drug trade in the country, opium growing, harvesting and conversion into heroin to be specific."

"Once it has been converted, it is sold on the world market, and the profits from those sales are staggering."

"The Pathet Lao use the money they make from that effort to enhance their capabilities."

"Those funds, gentlemen," Chambers explained. "are quite substantial; literally, multi-millions of dollars annually."

"That makes Pao not only a military threat but also an international criminal since the drugs he produces ultimately end up on the world market."

"And every year, that market continues to get bigger and bigger," Chambers emphasized. "which means Pao's capabilities also get larger."

"Therefore, the decision has been made at the highest levels of our government to eliminate him."

"That will be your job," He said in a flat, unemotional voice.

"Through our own, as well as DEA assets," Chambers continued. "we have learned that soon, Pao, along with several of his top advisors, will be attending a meeting that will be held in a village located very near the Thai-Laotian border area."

"To get there, he will have to travel overland from his headquarters in northern Laos,"

"Since the distance between this village and his headquarters is substantial, most of his journey will, by necessity, be conducted by vehicle."

"But since there are very few roads in that portion of the country," Chambers explained. "Pao will be limited as to his choice of routes."

"Fortunately for us, all these roads intersect near the Burmese border near the actual meeting site."

"According to our intelligence analysts and some of our Paramilitary assets, that will probably be the most logical place for you to take him and his people out."

"But the final determination on an exact shooting location will be left to you." He added.

"We just want him dead."

"Where you kill him will be your call."

"However," Chambers said. "the area surrounding that point, along with the village where the meeting will take place, is entirely controlled by hostiles."

"That makes getting a shooting team into any position where they can eliminate their targets extremely difficult."

"That's why we requested a Team from MACVSOG." Chambers told everyone, nodding at Taylor.

"It will be their job to get our two Marine snipers to that position, protect them while they eliminate the targets, and then get them back out again."

Dunaway nodded unconsciously as he gazed at Pao's picture on the screen.

"Now I understand Taylor's role in all this," he thought

"The meeting General Pao will attend," Chambers continued. "is scheduled to be conducted in a little over five weeks."

"According to our sources, Pao will meet with a prominent drug lord in the region, probably to either enlist his support or to negotiate the sale of Pao's opium for the year."

"Either way, it makes no difference as far as you're concerned."

"We want him dead regardless."

"That gives you a little over a month to plan, rehearse and then get yourselves into position to accomplish that," Chambers continued.

"You will stage for the mission here in South Vietnam, but you will launch from one of our Agency bases in either Laos or Thailand," Chambers explained.

"Once the mission has been completed, you will recover to a base in Thailand," He added.

"The helicopter assets for your exfiltration have already been coordinated."

"Whatever else you need to complete the mission," Chambers concluded. "you may request through me."

"Planning will be done here in the compound, but rehearsals and any training necessary will be conducted at other suitable nearby locations," He explained.

"Now that you know the mission and the area of operations," he continued. "I recommend you take the next few days to develop a concept of operations."

"Once you have that, I'll arrange for you to be taken to the equipment warehouse in Cholon where you can requisition the necessary equipment."

"Now, what are your questions?" the case officer asked.

The room was silent for a few moments as everyone thought about Chamber's briefing. Finally, Dunaway spoke up.

"Just how many targets are we talking about, Sir?" Dunaway asked.

"We don't know for sure at this point," Chambers replied. "but we anticipate no more than five, including Pao."

"However, they will undoubtedly have a large security detail protecting them."

"Regardless, first and foremost, your primary target is Pao."

"You take him first," he ordered. "everybody else is gravy,"

"What do we know about this village where the meeting will take place?" Taylor asked.

"We have satellite photos of it," Chambers replied. "but that's all."

"To our knowledge, it's nothing special, just another medium-sized Laotian village."

"As far as we know, it was selected because of its location, since it's still in Laos, but midway between the headquarters of the Thai drug lord Pao is meeting with, and Pao's headquarters in the northeastern part of the country."

"Have you got a source you can access for more detailed information about Pao and his plans if we need it?" Taylor asked.

Chambers hesitated before he answered.

"Possibly," he finally admitted.

When there were no more questions, Chambers passed out the non-disclosure forms, and when they were all signed and collected, the meeting adjourned.

Ten minutes later, the entire team was assembled around a large table back in their billeting area. On the table, now located in the middle of the room, was a stack of maps, photos, intelligence folders, and satellite imagery that had been put there while they were being briefed. Evidently, they would use it to develop a suitable plan.

"Okay," Taylor said. "now we know where we're going and what they want us to do."

"The rest we'll have to figure out for ourselves."

"But before we get into all that," he said. "I think it would be a good idea if we acquainted ourselves with each other's capabilities."

"That will affect how we plan and execute this mission."

"I'll begin," He said.

"My team and I have been running reconnaissance missions into northern Laos for over six months now," Taylor began.

"We have eleven missions across the fence under our belt, so we are all well acquainted with what it takes to move and operate in denied territory without getting detected."

"Presently, we are short three men for the team." He added. "our radio operator was killed on our last mission, and two of our Nungs were wounded and are still in the hospital."

"However, that hasn't degraded our capabilities to the point we can't perform this mission."

"The two remaining Nungs on our team are both experts in the jungle and can read NVA and VC trail sign, so they will keep us out of trouble.

"And for this mission, Sgt Breslan will handle the radio."

"Mostly," Taylor explained. "for the past seven months, we have been locating NVA logistic sites, then calling in air strikes to destroy them."

"However, let me say that just surviving and moving in that kind of environment without getting detected, much less locating, and marking a target in it, is extremely difficult."

"About on a par with trying to paint a moving train and not get spots on your clothes while you do it."

"That's a close comparison."

Breslan chuckled, and both Dunaway and Macklin were suitably impressed.

"Our FOB, or forward operating base," Taylor continued. "is called Command and Control North, or CCN for short."

"CCN has lost over five complete teams in the past six months on similar missions."

"Other CCN teams have had multiple KIAs and WIAs trying to accomplish those same types of missions."

"That should tell you how dangerous our job is and what kind of people it takes to perform it."

"Running recon is not a task for the faint-hearted, nor is it anything like trying to operate here in South Vietnam."

"It is dangerous, tedious work that has to be conducted right under the NVA's noses in their backyard, which they protect fiercely."

"That should give you some idea of the kind of environment we'll be going into and the risks involved on this mission," Taylor explained.

"Laos is dangerous, and the terrain is a nightmare."

"Most of it consists of steep ridges, one after the other, all covered in vegetation that ranges from short scrub in open areas to triple canopy jungle in low ones."

"Some of it is so dense, it is impassable."

"Worse, there isn't a hell of a lot of open areas, at least not where we've been operating."

"So, finding a suitable LZ to either infill or exfil from is damned difficult."

"To make matters worse, the area fifty or so miles inside the Laotian-Vietnamese border is entirely controlled by the NVA," He continued. "And when I say entirely controlled, I mean just that."

"Most of their sanctuaries have at least a battalion of NVA guarding them and securing the area around them."

"Some sites have even more."

"I've also been told that the Pathet Lao equally secure the area west of these sanctuary locations, all the way to the Thai and Burmese borders."

"At least in the northern section of the country."

"That means that wherever we are on the ground on this mission, it will be extremely difficult to move, navigate, and remain undetected."

"Also, bear in mind that this mission will be covert," Taylor added.

"That means that if we get hung up somehow or get into it with the Pathet Lao, we are on our own."

"There will be no help or support coming," He emphasized.

"We either get ourselves out of whatever jam we're in, or we're dead."

"If that happens, there won't even be a body sent home to your parents afterward."

"You'll just simply cease to exist as far as anyone is concerned."

"Those are the rules we'll be operating under the minute we set foot in Laos," Taylor concluded.

"In summary, since we have been operating in northeastern Laos for the past seven months as a team," Taylor summed up. "we know how to move, how to communicate, and how to survive in denied territory, and we also know what the rules are."

"I guess that means that if there are any experts at operating in northern Laos, we're about as close as you're likely to get to them," Taylor concluded.

"That's why we got the job of taking you two in, and bringing you back out safely."

"Now, how about you two? Taylor asked.

"What's your experience base?"

"We are a scout sniper team assigned to the 1st Marine Division's Scout Sniper Platoon," Dunaway began.

"The Platoon's mission is to support the battalions in the Division with long-range precision fire and also eliminate high-value targets assigned by Division intelligence."

"In addition, we collect valuable combat-related intelligence about the area we operate in and pass it back to our headquarters elements."

"The Platoon itself is composed of Marines who are expert snipers and shooters; some of them world-class."

"We work primarily in teams of two men each, a shooter and a spotter, and our area of operations is in I Corps and along the DMZ."

"However, we also get tasked to perform missions in Laos from time to time, so we are also somewhat familiar with operating in denied territory too."

"Private Macklin and I have performed two such missions in the past," Dunaway explained.

"On one, we eliminated several targets near the Laotian border, and on our last one, we eliminated a five-man advance party of NVA officers eight miles inside Laos, along with several of their security detail."

"*Well, I'll be damned,*" Taylor thought. "*I never knew Marines operated across the border too.*"

"*I thought only SOG did that.*"

"*These guys aren't cherries at this like I thought they were,*" He thought, smiling.

"What kind of ranges are we talking about here?" the Sgt named Breslan asked.

"We normally like to shoot from at least four hundred yards because that gives us time to get away afterward," Dunaway replied.

"But we have eliminated targets at up to eight hundred yards, and we are capable of taking out targets at up to fourteen hundred yards with our current weapons."

"Are you the spotter or the shooter?" Breslan asked.

"I'm the spotter," Dunaway replied. "Private Macklin is the primary shooter."

"You don't talk much, Macklin, do you?" Breslan asked, turning to Macklin.

"No, Sgt," Macklin replied. "Corporal Macklin is in charge of our detail, so he answers most of the questions."

"Well, since you're the shooter, just how good are you?" Breslan asked.

"He's the best in the Platoon," Dunaway answered for Macklin. "and that's saying something."

"Because we have at least five Marines assigned there that have placed in the International Matches at Camp Perry."

"One has even won the Wimbledon Cup."

"That means they are all world-class shots."

"And since they have been in Vietnam, their number of individual confirmed kills is nearing the seventies."

Breslan nodded appreciatively.

"Corporal Dunaway is also one of those shooters, Sgt Breslan," Buster interjected. "He placed seventh in those same matches a year ago."

"In the Marine Corps," Macklin explained. "shooting teams are composed of two shooters; one just acts as a spotter."

"Corporal Dunaway eliminated three moving targets on our last mission from a distance of over seven hundred yards."

"That should give you an idea of how good he is."

"And Private Macklin is a much better shot than I am," Dunaway added.

Breslan whistled appreciatively.

"Well," Capt. Taylor said, smiling. "I guess that answers all our questions about whether or not you two can do the job."

"It sure as hell does," Breslan said.

"I'm a qualified Army sniper, but I'm not even in these guys' league."

"I can't wait to see them shoot."

Chapter Fifteen
Mission prep

Three days later, Breslan got his chance. By that time, the team had developed a working concept of operations for the mission, gotten it approved by Chambers, and had gone to the Agency's equipment warehouse in Cholon to draw the equipment they would need to execute it.

Since the Pathet Lao had no actual uniforms common to them all, Taylor elected to dress the Team in East German camouflage fatigues. They blended well with the jungle and the terrain in the area, and they were lightweight yet durable enough. Most importantly, since the mission was covert, they were made in Europe and not the United States.

He aslo decided everyone on the team would wear modified Chinese web gear and personal equipment and carry Chinese rucksacks. The team would also carry an East German radio for communications and would be armed with AK-47s, the weapon common to most Pathet Lao.

However, that did not include Macklin and Dunaway. They would carry Sako rifles chambered in .308 caliber with Leupold 7x 50 wide-field scopes and illuminated reticules. The optics, weapons and ammunition had been specially constructed by Agency armorers back in the States and sent to South Vietnam specifically for the mission.

Buster was almost agog when he was issued his. That was the first time he had ever seen one of the legendary Finnish rifles before, much less held one. But he knew its reputation for both precision and accuracy, and he could not wait to shoot it.

The Sako Buster was issued had a heavy barrel chambered in .308. It was fitted to a pearled chamber attached to a polished action and trigger group that was as smooth as glass. The trigger had a three-pound trigger pull with no slack. The entire assembly was glass bedded into the walnut stock on titanium pillars, which made the barrel free floating from chamber to the forestock. The scope was fixed mounted onto the weapon and had oversized, marked churls for both elevation and deflection, along with an illuminated reticule.

The rifle also had an adjustable leather sling with brass stays, suitable for stabilizing the shooter's left arm when he was shooting from an unsupported position. It was evident that whoever had constructed the weapon was an expert gunsmith, skilled in the fine art of accuracy. Buster thought it was the most beautiful thing he had ever seen.

There was even an attached paper target in the weapon's package, with three holes in it and marked at four hundred yards to verify the weapon's accuracy. The grouping was minute of angle, proof that the weapon was capable of extreme accuracy at long distances. Dunaway's weapon was an exact duplicate. In addition, there was a Leupold spotting scope in his package, along with two pairs of long-range Zeiss binoculars.

When Dunaway examined his and Buster's Sako's and then looked at their construction and optics mounted on them, he was impressed. When he saw the targets enclosed with the weapons, he was satisfied the weapons could hit targets out to and beyond a thousand yards. So, like Buster, he could hardly wait to shoot them and see how they performed. Fortunately, he didn't have to wait long.

Shortly after the Team was outfitted, they were trucked to a closed range at Taylor's request to test fire their weapons. Although the range wasn't designed for long-distance shooting, Dunaway and Macklin set up behind its rearmost point, the placied their targets at the range's furthest point downrange. When they paced off the yardage, it was just a shade over nine hundred yards.

First, the rest of the team test-fired their AKs by running two thirty-round magazines through them, one on semi-automatic and the other on fully automatic. They all performed flawlessly, as expected. Taylor would have been amazed if they hadn't because the AKs had a well-deserved reputation for both reliability and accuracy out to three hundred and fifty yards.

Meanwhile, Macklin and Dunaway readied their weapons. After the Nungs had test-fired their AKs, they set up a series of E silhouette targets for Macklin and Dunaway. Two were at five hundred yards, and the others were at nine hundred.

Looking at the tiny targets in the barely visible distance, Taylor had his doubts, while Breslan openly scoffed.

"Hell, Macklin will be lucky to even hit anything at that range," he predicted.

"Those far targets are over nine hundred yards from here."

"That's over half a mile, and he's got a brand-new rifle he hasn't even broken in yet."

"Even money says he won't hit half of them."

Taylor remained silent.

Both Macklin's and Dunaway's first series of shots were to zero the weapons and dial in the scopes. That was done at a hundred yards at a fixed circular target pasted onto each E silhouette and took about ten minutes. Even so, when the Nungs brought the target back for inspection, the groupings were impressive. After they were zeroed, Macklin settled down to engage the targets at nine hundred yards by himself, with Dunaway spotting.

After Dunaway gave him all the firing data, Macklin first fired a series of three slow fire shots at the first target. They were all hits to the head of the first E silhouette. Then he got down to business.

Timed by Breslan, he fired five shots at five different E silhouette targets as fast as he could. The five shots took a total of seven and a half seconds. Afterwards, Breslan had the Nungs collect all the targets and brought them in for inspection. The walk down and back took nearly twenty minutes. Later, when the Nungs handed Breslan the targets, there was much excited Chinese chatter between them. When Taylor and Breslan examined them, they saw why.

Macklin's first target, at four hundred yards, had three holes in the head portion that you could have covered with a quarter, but the remaining nine hundred yard targets were the big surprise. Macklin's five targets in the timed fire mode each had a hole dead center of its forehead.

"Jesus H Christ," Breslan said in amazement as he examined them.

"I apologize, kid."

"I was dead wrong and I apologize."

"You really can shoot."

"Better than anyone I have ever met."

"Goddamn," he exclaimed in awe to Taylor as he showed him the targets. "I've never seen anyone any better in my entire career."

"And I've never seen anybody throw a bolt any quicker, anytime."

"Man, you're fast, Macklin."

"I thought at first that you were just showing off with that, but you weren't, were you?" Breslan asked.

"You can shoot that fast and still be that accurate."

"Yes, Sgt, I can," Macklin replied. "and don't call me kid."

"I'm a Marine, and I try very hard to conduct myself as a professional."

"So, I would appreciate you treating me like one."

Dunaway suppressed a smile when he heard that. Gunnery Sgt Casey had impressed Macklin after all. The kid was trying like hell.

"Sorry, Macklin," Breslan said with a slight smile. "No offense intended."

"It won't happen again."

"Anybody who can shoot like you deserves to be called whatever he wants."

"Macklin will do," Macklin said. "but my nickname is Buster."

"That's what my friends call me," He said, smiling.

"Well then," Breslan said, holding out his hand. "If it's Okay with you, that's what I'll call you."

"You're a helluva shot, Buster."

"The best I've ever seen."

Buster smiled and shook the Sgt's hand.

"Thanks," he said.

Later, when they were back on the compound and discussing the planning, Taylor asked Macklin.

"Can you shoot like that in the field, Buster?"

"Consistently, I mean, and hit people when you do?"

"Yes, Sir," Buster replied truthfully. "I can."

Taylor looked doubtful.

"He can, Captain," Dunaway confirmed. "I've seen him do it more than once."

"He took out his last five targets in seven seconds, at six hundred yards, and two of them were running."

"And they were all head shots."

"God a mighty," Breslan said in awe.

Taylor nodded.

"Well, that puts an entirely different complexion on how we can conduct this mission," he said.

"Before today," he explained. "I thought we'd probably have to engage the targets at three, maybe four hundred meters, tops, to guarantee first-round kills."

"Now that I've seen you shoot, Buster, it seems like we have a whole new set of options available to us."

"But I'm a novice at working with snipers," Taylor revealed. "This is my first time."

"And in my experience, it's always proven best to listen to the experts before you decide what to do."

"So, I think we should listen to you and Dunaway's take on what you think about taking out the targets before we come up with any real operations plan."

"With that in mind," Taylor said. "how about educating Breslan and me about how, where, and at what range you want to engage your targets."

"And while you're at it, you can fill us in on all the other factors that we're going to have to consider when we pick a shooting position."

Buster smiled but didn't reply. Instead, after thinking a moment, Dunaway did.

"There are several factors I think we need to consider before we pick a position, Sir," Dunaway began.

"First," he explained. "if our targets are in a vehicle like Chambers told us, then we'll need to stop it and force them to get out of it before we engage them."

"And when we do that, ideally, we won't want them to suspect they've deliberately been stopped."

"Explain," Taylor said.

"If they suspect their vehicle has been deliberately stopped," Dunaway explained. "They will immediately become suspicious."

"When that happens, everybody in the entire party will be on the alert, both the targets and their security detail."

"So, the targets will be cautious when and where they exit the vehicle, because they will suspect something's wrong."

"And even then, their exit will be shielded by their security detail as well as the vehicle itself.

"That means the target will get out of the vehicle on the side that we can't see."

"Or, depending on the terrain, he may not even exit it at all."

"If there are hills masking portions of the vehicle they may just get on the floorboard where we can't engage them."

"In addition," Dunaway continued. "their security detail, if they're any good, will probably surround them even if they do get out."

"That will make it very difficult, if not impossible, for us to get a decent sight picture, much less a clear shot."

"If they do that, they'll probably also make the targets use the vehicle itself for cover after they have helped them exit."

"In addition, when they exit, it will be from only one side, and that side will have the nearest and best cover," He added.

"In either case, just acquiring a target in a situation like that will be extremely difficult, if not impossible," He concluded.

"Okay," Taylor said. "I get it."

"What else?"

"Even if we can stop the vehicle in a way that Pao or his security detail won't think there's anything wrong," Dunaway continued. "we still have to have a position to fire from."

"That position will have to be located where we can engage all five targets before they can get to any cover."

"That means we'll have to have an unobstructed view from where we are, all the way to the targets."

"Ideally, they won't be near any covered position they can hide behind."

Taylor again nodded his understanding.

"Since you've already told us the majority of the terrain in northern Laos is a jungle, just like South Vietnam," Dunaway explained. "that will mean that the area the targets are in will have to be open, and by necessity, we will have to be located above them."

"From that location, the foliage and trees won't interfere with the flight of the round."

"And ideally, the place we will be shooting from will also be a concealed position."

"Since most of northern Laos is jungle, and there are very few roads going through it, finding a spot like that on any road is going to be extremely difficult, if not impossible, in my opinion."

"And frankly, if we can't find a spot like that," Dunaway remarked. "then you won't need a sniper team."

"You'll be forced to start shooting at the targets from the jungle, probably at a distance of less than a hundred yards, if you want to get confirmed kills."

"When you do that," Dunaway predicted. "the security detail protecting the targets will probably shoot you to doll rags before you can engage all the targets, much less get away."

Taylor nodded.

"That's exactly what will happen if we try something like that," he thought to himself.

"This kid is pretty damned smart."

"Next," Dunaway continued. "we'll have to make the shot during daylight, for obvious reasons."

"We don't have night scopes, and even if we did, they don't work very well at distances over two hundred yards."

"Lastly, we need to make the shots in good weather."

"If it's raining or foggy, that could screw up everything because it could adversely affect the flight of the round, in addition to making visibility, and therefore, target identification more difficult."

"Those are the primary considerations that I can think of right off the top of my head," Dunaway said. "but there are others."

"However," he told Taylor with confidence. "if we can solve the primary problems, I think Buster and I will be able to handle the rest of them."

"That was a very informative little lecture, Dunaway," Taylor said, obviously impressed.

"Those parameters narrow down our potential shooting positions considerably."

"And the fact that Pao will be in a vehicle is a problem that we'll also have to solve."

"To be honest, I hadn't even considered that," Taylor admitted.

"So, first, I think we should look at this road Pao will be traveling on more closely and see if there are any spots that appear to be suitable."

"If we can't find any," Taylor said. "we'll have to think of another option."

"But, on the off chance that we can find some suitable spots on the road," Taylor said. "I'll order some more overhead imagery of them so that we can take a close look at what they have to offer."

"Meanwhile, we'll also try and figure out a way to stop the vehicle in an unsuspicious way while we're waiting for the photos to arrive," He added.

"I'll have to admit," Taylor said, scratching his head. "when I first got this tasking, I figured it was going to be a simple escort and protection job."

"Now, I realize it will require much more thought and creativity."

"I'm just glad I have somebody like you two that can not only illuminate all the potential problems but help me come up with solutions for them."

"You've got quite a head on your shoulders, Corporal."

"Thank you, Sir," Dunaway said.

Later, after evening chow, Buster asked Dunaway.

"Did I do good today, Marty?"

"Am I starting to act more like an adult?"

"Yeah, Buster," Dunaway said, surprised at the question. "You are."

"You acted like a complete professional today."

"I was impressed, and so were Taylor and Breslan."

"Keep it up."

"Gunnery Sgt Casey's words must have sunk in," he thought. *"Maybe you're starting to finally grow up.'*

"You did good, too, Marty," Buster said, beaming.

"The Captain was impressed with what you told him about shooting positions and all."

"I could tell he knows you're smart."

"Yeah," Dunaway thought. "he was."

"Maybe I did a little growing up myself."

"What do you think of our two young Marines now, Bob?" Taylor asked Breslan on the other side of the room.

Breslan thought about the question for a moment.

"Dunaway has a first-class head on his shoulders," Breslan finally replied.

"He's going to be a real asset when it comes down to actually selecting a spot that Macklin can shoot from."

"And I think he can help in planning the mission too," He added.

"Hell, he'd already thought about the targets being in a vehicle and figured what we'd have to do, even before you asked him."

"And something tells me he's already figured out some alternatives if we can't find a way to take Pao out on the road," Breslan said.

"He's pretty goddamn smart for a Corporal."

"As for Macklin," Breslan continued. "what's there to say."

"He's young, still a kid, really."

"But he's trying very hard to act like a professional, so I can't fault him there."

"And as for ability," Breslan continued. "I've never seen anybody shoot like that before, ever."

"He's world-class, no doubt about it."

"Did you see that shot group?" he asked, shaking his head in admiration.

Taylor nodded.

"The amazing thing about him is that it's all natural to him," Breslan said in awe. "he doesn't even think about it."

"Lastly, he can throw a bolt and get back on target faster than anyone I've ever seen before."

"I've watched the Army's Marksmanship Unit shoot at Ft Benning," Breslan told Taylor. "Even shot with them a couple of times."

"And believe me, those guys are no slouches."

"But Macklin is head and shoulders above any one of them by a long shot."

"But what impressed me the most," Breslan said. "is that Dunaway told me that's the first Sako Macklin had ever seen."

"He'd never even shot one before today."

"And remember, the one he shot today hadn't even been broken in yet," He said in awe.

"It's a brand-new weapon."

"There's no doubt in my mind that if we get those two in a good shooting position, Jim," Breslan concluded. "Pao and his entire staff are dead men."

"I'd bet my pension on that."

"That kid could drive nails at three hundred yards with that Sako, so killing Pao won't even be a challenge!"

Chapter Sixteen
Mission planning

"Dunaway," Taylor said. "Breslan and I went over the maps last night in detail, looking for a shooting position on or near that road that meets the criteria you laid out yesterday."

"We couldn't find a single one."

"Of course, the satellite photos I requested may reveal something the maps missed, but I doubt it."

"So, I'm not very hopeful," Taylor concluded.

"That being the case," he continued. "and given your expertise, what other spots should we be looking for as potential shooting sites?"

"I mean ones that will guarantee that Macklin can take out Pao."

"I did some thinking last night too, Sir," Dunaway admitted. "about the very same thing."

"Mainly, because I also doubted, we could find a suitable spot on the road to stop that convoy either."

"Much less find a way to make the targets get out of the vehicle and then engage them successfully."

"Just like I thought," Taylor thought to himself. *"Dunaway is as smart as a whip."*

"He anticipated us not finding a suitable shooting position on the road, so he's already worked out some other options."

"All in all," Dunaway told Taylor. "I don't consider the CIA's plan very feasible."

"Even if it did come from their experts."

"Why?" Taylor asked, anxious to hear Dunaway's reasoning.

"There are just too many things that could go wrong with it," Dunaway replied flatly.

"In addition, the site they recommended to us as a shooting location has too many negatives associated with it."

"Explain, please," Taylor urged.

"For starters," Dunaway began. "it's a road junction of all the roads in the immediate area."

"The one nexus for all the vehicular capable routes out of northern Laos that lead down into the Thai border area."

"To me, that means it is also a hub for trade as well as traffic in the region."

"Given that, I'd be very surprised if there weren't several other villages somewhere near it, and that means a ton of people and a lot of traffic both in the target village and on the road itself."

"That's something we don't need," he explained.

"Because either of those things could easily interfere with the shot or endanger the entire mission."

"However, that's not its worst fault," Dunaway continued.

"Its location is."

"When I measured it on a map, that road junction is over a hundred kilometers from the Thai border."

"We get wrapped around the axle that far from the border; we'll never get out," he explained.

"It's just too far for us to move through all those Pathet Lao," Dunaway explained. "Especially after we have just eliminated their top leader."

"We'd never make it."

"In addition, like you," Dunaway added. "I have serious doubts we could find a suitable shooting location anywhere near the road junction even to attempt it."

"So, given all that," Dunaway said. "I came up with a few alternatives."

"I'm all ears, Corporal," Taylor said smiling.

"First," Dunaway said. "I think we should take a close look at any bridges or any natural obstacles that Pao is going to have to negotiate along his route."

"I'm talking about things like passes, gorges, streams, and especially rivers," Dunaway explained.

"Places where he will either have to either slow up or even better, exit the vehicle to negotiate."

"Ideally, these locations should be close to the Thai border."

"The closer, the better, in my opinion."

"Chokepoints or gorges offer the advantage of height," Dunaway explained.

"If we can find a suitable one near a cleared area of the road or even somewhere on his route to the village after he has to leave the vehicle and travel overland, they might offer a good possibility."

"However, after looking at the map, in my opinion, that possibility is remote."

"What I'd really like to find is a river he has to cross," Dunaway said. "Preferably one located before he gets to the village."

"We catch him trying to cross a river," Dunaway explained. "even if he's still in his vehicle, we can make him stop it and then force him out."

"If nothing else, Buster and I can shoot the tires flat."

"And once Pao realizes he's not going any further in the car, he'll have to get out to escape, and there's not very much cover on a bridge or a river."

"If there isn't any bridge over the river," Dunaway said. "That's even better."

"He's wide open because he'll have to cross it by boat."

"Either way," Dunaway said assuredly. "he's an easy target, and that means he's dead."

"A river, even one with a bridge over it," Dunaway explained. "has everything we need: concealment for us along its banks, an unobstructed view of the target, and no cover for either Pao or his security detail."

"They won't even have any place they can run to once we start shooting."

"Buster will kill every one of them before they can spit."

Taylor smiled when he heard that.

"This Corporal definitely knows his shit when it comes down to planning a hit."

"He's smart, and he's adaptable, and I like both those qualities."

"If we can't find a suitable spot in any of those areas," Dunaway continued. "then, by necessity, we'll need to take a close look at this village Pao is headed for."

"But," Dunaway stressed. "I would consider that only as a last resort, Sir."

"Why?" Taylor asked, already knowing the answer but wanting to know just how intelligent Dunaway was.

"We'd probably have to take General Pao either going in or coming out of the village itself," Dunaway explained.

"While he's in the village unless it's in a wide-open area, we probably won't even be able to see him, much less get a shot at him."

"Of course, when we take him in or near the village," Dunaway concluded. "we'll not only have his security detail to deal with, but the drug lord's as well."

"I don't like those kinds of odds at all, Sir," Dunaway said in conclusion.

"That could mean up to a company of men, maybe more."

"And that's way too many for us to either have to deal with or run from."

"Especially since we'll be in their own backyard."

"Then I guess maybe we better go over his entire route again and see what we can find," Taylor suggested, having already arrived at the very same conclusion himself earlier.

Dunaway nodded in agreement and smiled.

"Thank God Taylor is easy to work with and takes suggestions from his subordinates." he thought.

It took three more days before Taylor's request for additional satellite photos of the river crossing to come in. After a thorough search, he and Dunaway found it on the map and later verified that it was part of the route Pao would have to take to get to his meeting site. Later, when they reviewed the crossing site's satellite photos, they also determined the spot he and Dunaway had finally selected was ideal for a shooting position.

The river itself was almost half a mile wide at that point and was nearly the same distance from the nearest large village. Best of all, it had no bridge. It also had no large ferry, so it could only be crossed by small boat. Pao's vehicle would have to be left behind once he reached it.

The usual method of crossing was hiring a sampan and then being ferried across. From there, it was a short walk to a large village where vehicle transportation could again be arranged for, thus allowing Pao and his party to continue to the meeting site by road, which was still some twenty fifty-five kilometers away. And since there were no other roads capable of vehicular movement in the area, Pao would be forced to take that route.

Now that the primary shooting position had been selected, the team spent the next few days discussing the best way to infiltrate themselves into the area undetected. That proved to be another problem. Since the entire area was under Pathet Lao control, whatever method they eventually decided on would, by necessity, have to be clandestine.

One option was to go in by helo to a suitable LZ located somewhere near the river and then walk overland to the crossing site and the shooting position. However, the only open areas near the river were cultivated rice fields with their owners living in houses near by. That meant the helo would undoubtedly be heard when it overflew the area and especially when it landed. That alone ensured that the team's presence would undoubtedly be compromised immediately. Once detected, someone, probably the local farmers initially, but certainly the local Pathet Lao later on, would eventually come looking to investigate the noise. When they did, that could screw up everything. It could even force Pao to change his route to avoid the Team.

In addition, if the helo itself was seen and identified, the entire covert nature of the mission might be compromised. So, Chambers would probably never approve that insertion method anyway. That ranked the option exceptionally low on the team's probable insertion methods.

Another alternative was to walk in from Thailand, whose nearest border was the Mekong River which was approximately seventy miles away. But once again, the danger of detection during the required trek to the shooting position would be extraordinarily high because the Pathet Lao patrolled the entire area. In addition, the team would have to deal with numerous villages scattered throughout the area, whose inhabitants either willingly or unwillingly supported the Pathet Lao. So, if the team was detected en route to the shooting position, and given the circumstances, that was highly likely, they would again be forced to abort.

Parachute drop into the area was also ruled out since neither Dunaway nor Macklin was airborne qualified. Besides, Taylor didn't consider it a very safe option anyway. So, in any form, it was also a nonstarter.

Lastly, air landing by a STOL capable aircraft was also a negative because there were no suitable locations available to use as a field expedient airstrip anywhere remotely near the river. And using one farther inland would again involve a long overland trek that would create the same problems already associated with walking to the shooting site. So that left no other choice but to go in by boat.

Fortunately, rivers and navigable waterways were quite common in the region. The Mekong River itself was the actual border between Laos and Thailand to the south and Burma and Laos further to the north. Additionally, it had numerous unnamed tributaries flowing off it almost everywhere in the region. All these intersecting waterways served as replacement road networks. They were filled daily with various watercraft hauling trade goods to market or ferrying people, foodstuffs, and anything else of value to the stores and shops in all the villages in the region.

Therefore, a native watercraft carrying supplies as cover and also carrying a well-hidden team shouldn't arouse any undue suspicion, especially if a native crew manned it. That was the method of infiltration Taylor decided on.

After the hit was completed, the team would vacate the area immediately, go to a hide site, and remain there the rest of the day. After sunset, they would move overland for approximately a klick and a half to a nighttime exfiltration site where they would be extracted by helicopter. Following the exfiltration, they would recover to a Thai airbase and return to South Vietnam the following day. At least, that was the plan.

The team spent the next few days sanding off its rough edges, fleshing it out, and polishing it. Taylor then briefed it to Chambers, who took it to the Station Chief in Saigon for approval. Two days later, Chambers informed everyone that it had been accepted and approved. After that, the entire operation shifted into high gear.

The Agency arranged for a boat and a reliable crew already on the CIA's payroll for the Team's insertion. They would depart Thailand by boat and navigate up the Mekong, crossing into Laos on a smaller river that emptied into the Mekong. They would follow that river to a point downstream of the crossing site and their shooting position. On arrival, the craft would drop the team off, then continue upriver on a trading expedition. The night of the hit, it would return to pick up the team if something happened to screw up the helo extraction.

Meanwhile, Chambers had more photos taken of the proposed shooting site and its area, but in much greater detail. The team pieced them all together into a giant collage and then taped them to the barracks wall. When you looked at it all together, you could see the entire shooting site and the area around it for half a mile, in detail. The team members studied it for days, familiarizing themselves with the entire area and its features.

At the same time, Macklin and Dunaway spent at least two hours a day on the range firing to loosen up the Sakos and get themselves familiar with the various types of ammunition tthe Agency had provided. They went through several different ammunition brands, test-firing various loads and types of projectiles, trying to determine which combination fitted the rifle best for the shots Macklin would have to make.

They finally settled on a 168-grain boat tail hollow point Winchester, manufactured by Partizan Arms in Europe, a firm known for its precision and accuracy. The rounds were all Match Grade and were brass-cased, neck turned, and boxer primed. With them, Macklin was capable of easily shooting minute-of-angle three-round groups at five hundred yards. And, they had one other advantage.

When the hollow points hit anything, especially a hard target, they mushroomed evenly. They created a maximum exit wound as they plowed through it at over 2500 feet per second, delivering almost 2600-foot pounds of energy when they impacted. That was equivalent of a concrete block going through a plate glass window at a hundred and seventy-five miles an hour. Therefore, a hit anywhere in a human head guaranteed it would be one hundred percent fatal.

At night, both Buster and Dunaway spent hours studying General Pao's various photos, and memorizing his face. According to the date stamps on the pictures, many were older shots, taken as much as two years previous according to the date stamps. Still, some were less than a month old, confirming Dunaway's suspicion that the Agency had a well-placed asset in Pao's headquarters feeding the Agency information about the Pathet Lao General regularly.

Taylor had already reached the same conclusion and had already requested a detailed itinerary for the General, giving the team the General's exact route to his meeting site and a timetable for each day's travel. In addition, he had asked for the precise number of people in the General's entourage and details of his accompanying security detail. If he could get all that information before the team had to launch, that would certainly make their job easier, and they could narrow down the time the targets would be in the kill zone.

However, Dunaway realized they couldn't count on that. More probably, they would have to plan on launching several days in advance of the General's projected crossing time and then spend hours in the shooting position waiting for their target to arrive. That was not a prospect he looked forward to, but there was no other option. It was a normal part of a hit.

He and Buster were used to waiting in a hide site for a target. They had been trained in it. But Taylor and his men were an unknown quantity. They might not be able to spend days in a shooting position without revealing themselves. He warned Taylor about that.

However, there was one good scrap of intelligence. The Laotian peasants, who controlled the crossing site and ferried people across the river for pay, only worked in the daytime. According to the Agency source, they weren't even around the site after sunset because they returned to their village, three miles upriver. That meant Pao and his party would have to cross the river in daylight. When they did, they would be clearly defined targets.

The last few days before launch, Macklin and Dunaway spent hours on the range with Macklin shooting at moving silhouettes attached to ropes and pulled across the far berm by the Nungs to simulate targets in a sampan being paddled across a river.

The Nungs and Buster rapidly became friends because of their daily association and their closeness in age. They were a happy twosome named Chuy and Lop and were senior to Buster by only three years. But there, the similarity ended. Both Nungs worked for Special Forces for over five years and had combat experience up the ying-yang. Chuy had already been wounded twice, once in that year alone. So, both men were combat-hardened veterans even though chronologically they weren't even twenty-one yet.

Both marveled at Buster's ability with a rifle and would bring him the spent targets after each shooting session, happily poking their fingers in the bullet holes that Buster had drilled through the targets. Buster, in turn, gave them packages of their favorite menthol-flavored Salem cigarettes for their efforts, which they loved and called "Saleeems."

And each evening, when offered some Jim Beam as an appetizer before supper by Breslen, Buster turned the offer down, saying that he didn't drink when he was prepping for a mission. It was something that took steely determination on his part, but he did it. Dunaway was extremely proud of Buster's refusals and his newfound resolve.

Chapter Seventeen
Staging and Launch

Finally, seven days before the Team's anticipated movement to the Thai launch site, Chambers brought the Team a rough itinerary for General Pao's trip, sent by the Agency's asset. Barring complications, it placed the General and his entourage at the river crossing in the late morning, six days hence. Accordingly, Taylor told Chambers they would depart for Thailand on a scheduled Agency flight in two days. Chambers agreed and arranged to have them met, then ferried to their link-up point with the Thai trader who would, in turn, carry them to their shooting site in his boat. The night before their departure, Chambers arranged a steak dinner for the chow hall team as a farewell gesture.

After eating, Buster told Dunaway jokingly that they should have been working for the Agency all along. They had air-conditioned billets, real beds with mattresses, hot showers, top-of-the-line equipment, and steak dinners. On the other hand, the Platoon offered tents to live in, folding cots to sleep on, occasional hot meals that were rarely steak, and cold water to wash in. Even its best weapons were still used, rather than new, and they certainly weren't Sakos. Dunaway was unimpressed with the joke but laughed dutifully.

The following day, the team, dressed in non-descript army fatigues with no rank or nametags and carrying all their equipment in prepackaged boxes, boarded an Agency C-47 with no send-off or fanfare at Tan San Nuht Air Force Base, just outside Saigon. During the flight, Dunaway learned by accident; they weren't even listed on the aircraft's manifest when he saw a copy of it by chance. At the time, he thought it was just another operational security procedure implemented by the Agency to ensure the overall security of the mission. A little over two and a half hours later, the Team landed at Nakom Phanom Royal Thai Air Force Base in northern Thailand.

After the aircraft had landed and taxied to the far end of the runway, well away from the main terminal and hanger facilities, they were met by a nondescript Agency spook who didn't mention his name. He had a one, and a half-ton, stake bed truck with a canvas-covered cargo compartment that took them and their gear directly from the aircraft to a back road at the end of the airfield, then to a point out of site of the runways and terminal.

Once out of sight of the airfield itself, the spook stopped the truck to allow Breslan to set the radio up and get a commo check with the Agency base station back in Vietnam. After that had been successfully accomplished, the spook drove them off the base. They neither saw nor met anyone else while on the Thai Air Force base, something that Dunaway also wondered about afterward. But again, he put it down to operational security.

Three hours later, they arrived at a moderately sized Thai village located on the northern Mekong River banks that smelled heavily of fish. There, the spook turned them over to a smiling Thai boatman who spoke rudimentary English and told them that his name was "Charlie." Afterward, the spook left without another word, not even wishing the team Good Luck.

"I'll be your guide for your trip to Laos," Charlie told them.

"We'll be leaving as soon as it gets dark."

Accordingly, the Team dressed in their East German fatigues and then ate a spicy dinner of beef, hot peppers, and rice, courtesy of their host. Since they were all ravenous after their long trip, they wolfed it down appreciatively. Shortly after sundown, they did a final equipment check, then boarded Charlie's boat and departed.

The craft was about forty feet long, about eight feet in its beam at the widest point, had high side walls, a small, enclosed cabin, and was loaded with an assortment of trade goods, ranging from foods to farming implements. They were either hung on, strapped to, or stacked against just about anything on the boat, making finding a comfortable place to sit difficult. Still, the team managed.

The craft was powered by a forty-five horsepower two-stroke gasoline engine attached to its stern on a fixed swivel. It had a length of pipe attached to its crankshaft on one end with an attached propeller on the other. The other side had a steering arm with a throttle control strapped to it. With it, the boat was capable of about nine knots.

"You can relax now," Charlie told the team. "I never get stopped on a trip like this."

"Much less searched."

"I have done this many times, and the Pathet Lao know me and like me."

"Because I usually give them gifts when I make a trip."

Everyone on the team almost believed him.

The night aboard the boat was typical of the region, balmy and warm, with a slight evening breeze that blew off the water and made things reasonably pleasant. After a while, the team relaxed.

An hour after departure, the Team crossed the watery non-descript border into Laos without incident, motoring up the smaller unnamed river that led to the crossing site some sixty-odd miles distant. However, that was straightline distance measured on a map. In reality, the distance was significantly further.

Just like Charly said, they were unchallenged at the border itself, which was the far bank of the Mekong. They didn't even see anyone or anything their first three hours of the journey because the moon had set, and the night had become a sea of darkness. It was so black that Dunaway idly wondered how Charlie could navigate and keep the boat in the center of the river.

Charlie kept them moving most of the night past five, small, dimly lit river villages. Finally, an hour before dawn, he pulled the boat into the riverbank, shut off the engine, and told the Team that they were at their drop off point. Although Taylor tried to get him to show them their exact position on his map of the area, that proved impossible. Charlie claimed he couldn't read a map. He told Taylor he didn't need one because he was thoroughly familiar with not only the area but all the various waterways that ran through it.

That seemed odd to Dunaway, but since Charlie apparently knew where to drop them off, Dunaway kept his concerns to himself. Still, there certainly weren't any visible landmarks in the area that he could find on his own map.

The blackness of the night was so complete; the brightest thing on the boat was his watch that had a tritium dial. However, Dunaway didn't comment because Taylor was running the operation, and it probably wouldn't have made any difference anyway. They were at their presumed drop-off point, and that was that.

After reaching it, Taylor reluctantly offloaded the team on the lonely spot on the dark riverbank and then listened to Charlie, and his boat chug off into the darkness minutes later.

He was obviously unhappy about the situation because he had no real idea where the Team was. Worse, until the sun rose, and he could locate some nearby landmarks and then find them on his map, he had no way of finding out. Accordingly, everyone hid themselves in the reeds growing along the riverbank to await the sunrise and find out exactly where they were.

The Team was supposed to send an Initial Entry Report to Chambers by radio, letting him know that they had been safely inserted once they reached their drop-off point. Taylor nixed that idea since he couldn't verify his exact position. They would do it later when they knew their location.

An hour later, when the sun came up, the team found out they were in the wrong place. Despite his supposed knowledge of the river, good old Charlie had dropped them off at the wrong spot. And not by just a little bit, but by a considerable distance! When Taylor finally fixed the team's actual location, a long hour later, he discovered they were at least seven miles downstream from their preplanned drop-off point and another two to three miles from their actual shooting position. Good old Charlie had dropped them off at entirely the wrong place by almost ten fucking miles!

"So much for his vaunted complete familiarity with the area," Dunaway thought.

However, a moment later, another thought struck him; an odd one. Before the team departed from Thailand, Dunaway remembered that Taylor had shown Charlie the team's desired drop-off point on a map. Charlie had told him that he knew where the place was. Yet a few hours ago, that same old Charlie had told Taylor that he couldn't read a map! So, what the hell was going on? Was Charlie just trying to save face because he didn't want to appear ignorant, or was it something else? Dunaway wondered.

At any rate, Taylor was furious at discovering he and the team were miles from where they were supposed to be. Still, there was nothing left to do except hide in the reeds the remainder of the day until nightfall so they could move to their correct position under cover of darkness and avoid possible detection. They couldn't risk movement in the daylight for fear of being spotted by the locals and subsequently compromised.

Consequently, the team members spent the rest of the day hiding near the water's edge, which was a miserable experience. Initially, half the team tried to sleep while the other half kept watch because no one had gotten any sleep the previous night. That tactic proved to be a complete waste of effort for everyone. Eventually, it degenerated into a nightmare because of the insects.

Later, when the sun rose fully, it got so hot it was impossible to sleep or to do much of anything else except broil in the rays of the hot sun reflecting off the nearby water. So, everyone stayed awake all day and sweated instead.

To make matters worse, everyone soon discovered they had a raging case of the shits, thanks to the meal Charlie had fed them the night before. That made the day almost perfect. As a final straw, to top everything else off, the mosquitoes and gnats came out in droves when the sun came up to feast on the new meat now hiding in the reeds and stinking of feces. As such, the entire team spent a thoroughly miserable day at the water's edge, fighting off hordes of ravenous insects while they shit themselves blind regularly. Dunaway wondered absently what else could go wrong as the first pangs of worry eventually turned to suspicion. Worse, the more he thought about all the bizarre things, the more questions popped up in his mind. And he already enough to worry about since the mission had started.

The torture finally ended at sundown when they were able to move. Maintaining a careful pace count to ensure their exact location, Taylor moved them out in an Indian file. They slowly and stealthily made their way upriver, staying close to its bank, hidden by the reeds, and stopping at regular intervals to listen.

They avoided a large village close to the river they found an hour into the move. They eventually relocated themselves to their correct shooting site, nearly six long hours later. When they finally arrived, everyone was exhausted. Half the spent team fell into an exhausted slumber while the other half kept watch as soon as they set up. Five hours later, they rotated.

Dawn brought with it blessed relief from the diarrhea. Evidently the hot peppers had gone through everyone's system like an express train, so they were able to keep the freeze-dried rations that made up breakfast, and later lunch, in their digestive tracts without any trouble. And since they were literally on the river, water to keep hydrated wasn't a problem. Accordingly, they spent that day and the following night recuperating from the lack of sleep, dehydration, and the effects of the diarrhea.

The following dawn, gazing through a pair of binoculars and looking at his map, Taylor confirmed that they were at their correct shooting position. An hour later, people showed up with sampans at the crossing site and began ferrying other people across the river farther upstream, proving that the team was finally in the correct location. Taylor then ordered Breslan to send their long-overdue Initial Entry report back to the Agency base station, reporting their safe arrival. That's when the Team discovered their second major problem.

Unexpectedly, even though he had tested it at the airfield two days earlier, the East German radio the team had been issued no longer worked! Breslan, who had been carefully tutored on its operation during the staging phase, tried everything he knew to make it function correctly, even changing the brand-new battery, shifting transmit locations, and setting the radio on an emergency transmit band.

Still, the radio stubbornly refused to operate correctly. It would only receive on an occasional basis, usually just random bits of static, but would not transmit at all. Breslan was furious, taking the malfunctioning radio as a personal affront to his ability to operate it.

"Goddam it, Sir," he told Taylor angrily. "this sonofabitch worked fine before we left Saigon."

"I got a comms check with the Agency's base station and read them five by five before we even left for Tan San Nuht."

"Later, after the spook picked us up and took us out to the end of the airstrip at NKP, I did another one, and it was still working perfectly."

"I read Saigon five by five from there too, and they reported the same for me."

"So, I don't understand what the hell's wrong with it now."

"Maybe it's atmospherics, Taylor suggested hopefully.

"Shit," Breslan replied. "Look at the sky, Sir."

"It's clear as a bell, so I know damn well it isn't that."

"It's the goddamn radio itself."

"Something's wrong with it."

"Did you drop it after we left NKP?" Taylor asked, grasping at straws.

"No," Breslan said adamantly. "I took pains to take care of it."

"I even gave it to the spook driving the truck to carry up front in the cab in the passenger seat because I didn't want it bouncing around with us in the cargo compartment."

"I didn't want to chance it getting banged up."

Taylor thought for a moment.

"Screw it," he finally said. "We're already in position and have got the target area under surveillance."

"So, we'll know when Pao gets here tomorrow, even if he's late."

"We don't have to contact the base station to give us any last-minute changes concerning his arrival time because we don't need them."

"So, after the mission has been completed," Taylor explained. "instead of calling for the helo like we originally planned, we'll let Charlie pick us up tomorrow night at the drop-off point and extract that way."

"We'll just do the mission without the damned radio," He said hotly.

"We don't need it anyway."

"The Agency will just have to wait until we get back to Thailand to find out how things went."

Dunaway listened to the entire exchange without comment, but his worry meter went up several more notches.

"First the manifest, then Charlie claiming he couldn't read a map, then the wrong drop-off point," he thought. *"now the fucked-up radio."*

"Are we jinxed, or is it something else?" he worried.

"This mission is going downhill at the speed of light."

"What the fuck else is going to go wrong?" he wondered.

However, since there was nothing he could do about anything, and Taylor was in charge, Dunaway concentrated on his and Macklin's part of the mission. He knew for sure that it would go right.

He and Buster had already decided he would act as Buster's backup shooter on the operation in training. With a platoon of Pathet Lao as a security detail, after Buster took out the General, all hell would probably break loose. So, Dunaway had to be prepared to start taking on the security detail before they could get themselves organized, identify the shooting site, then start moving elements to a range where they could bring accurate fire on it, especially if

Buster was still occupied with taking out the five primaries.

After the General went down, if the remaining targets bailed out of the sampans into the water once they realized they were being shot at, that might be another problem. Lastly, if the General had a more extensive security detail than Dunaway had planned for, that could complicate matters.

Dunaway and Taylor had both estimated the general's security detail to be at least a platoon of Pathet Lao, commanded by an officer. That was at least thirty men. If the detail was more significant, say two platoons or even a company, that could create even bigger and more serious problems. When Dunaway had discussed that possibility with Taylor during the planning phase, he had told the green beret Captain that his real worry wasn't the size of the security detail but how well trained they were. Taylor agreed.

Because Buster would be firing at around five hundred yards, that put the team outside of the range of the security details AK-47's, presuming, of course, that was what they were armed with. So even with sixty or more men, initially, there wouldn't be a problem. He could probably keep them out of rifle range until Buster finished off the primaries using his own Sako. But that was assuming they were just ordinary soldiers, drafted as security for the General's trip.

On the other hand, if they were a trained security detail, that put an entirely different complexion on the situation. A sixty-man detail could conceivably have an advance element sent ahead to the crossing site to check it out before the General arrived. If that turned out to be the case, there was a strong possibility that they would check the area of the crossing site thoroughly, looking for an ambush. Possibly even finding the team itself or forcing it to move rather than being discovered.

In addition, that large of a security detail raised the possibility of them having one or two counter-sniper teams of their own, armed, of course, with scoped sniper rifles. If that were the case, then the entire mission could be in jeopardy because once Buster took out the General, the team itself would come under fire from the counter snipers.

In any event, Dunaway had to be prepared to keep the NVA security elements out of range long enough for Buster to complete his mission. That was essential. If he could accomplish that, the team could most likely escape with relative ease, especially since Lop had already stolen a sampan the night before and had it concealed in the reeds nearby to use as a getaway vehicle to take the team back to their original drop off point.

Three or four minutes after Buster took out, the General would be all they would need. And given the confusion that would ensue once Buster killed the General, that should be something that should happen automatically. But you never knew. There was always the unexpected. Considering the way this mission was going, Dunaway wasn't hopeful everything would go as planned.

Later, Buster surveyed the crossing point using the spotting scope and gave estimated ranges to it and various other points in the area to Dunaway, who wrote them down in a small notebook. Afterwards, he and Dunaway switched roles, and Dunaway estimated the same ranges to the same locations while Macklin wrote. Both men then checked the numbers and averaged them. Then Dunaway drew a small diagram of the entire shooting site, including all the areas of interest and checkpoints. He wrote the average distance to each location from the shooting site underneath each point when he finished.

The diagram would serve as his quick reference guide to the entire killing zone once the action started. Dunaway would have no time to estimate ranges to new targets with the spotting scope once Buster fired his first shot. Using the diagram, he wouldn't have to.

Using the calibrated spotting scope, both he and Buster had estimated the distance to the center of the river where the crossing point was located to be four hundred and ninety yards. Accordingly, Buster set his scope on five hundred yards. That's where he planned to take them. After he shot the General, even if the other four targets jumped in the water to get away, they would still have to surface to breathe. When they did, their heads would pop up, and when that happened, Buster would blow them off. At five hundred yards, given the position he was in and the weapon he had, Macklin was confident he could kill all five targets quickly. He was ready. Now his targets just had to show up.

The following day dawned bright and clear. This was the day the Agency's asset had said Pao and his entourage would arrive at the river crossing. Taylor had everyone in position ten minutes after sunrise to ensure they were ready. Everyone except Lop, who was tending the sampan and providing rear security, and Dunaway and Macklin, who would be doing the shooting, had a set of binoculars. They were using them to watch the road in shifts for the General and his party. Even so, they had to be extremely careful to keep the sun from reflecting off their lenses and exposing their position. As it turned out, their wait time was shorter than expected because the General and his entourage showed up early, a little after ten.

Chuy, one of the Nungs, spotted the vehicle convoy first as it came up the road that led to the crossing site. Moments later, everyone was watching it. The small convoy consisted of two Russian-made two and a half-ton trucks, each with fifteen Pathet Lao soldiers in the rear. The two trucks had four-wheel drive carry-all sandwiched between them. Dunaway guessed correctly that the carry-all was carrying the General and his staff.

When the convoy neared the river, the carry-all and the rear truck stopped two hundred yards short of the crossing site while the lead truck drove directly up to the river. When the first truck reached the end of the roadbed, it stopped, and the soldiers piled out and secured the area. What appeared to be the officer in charge then loaded a squad of eight soldiers into a sampan, and they were ferried across the river. When they reached the other side, they did a thorough check of the far bank, then spread out and secured that area as well. Luckily, they came nowhere near the shooting site. When that had been accomplished, the officer waved the carry-all and the second truck forward.

When the carry-all and second truck arrived, all the soldiers in the second truck piled out and spread out around the carry-all. That accomplished, the two Russian trucks turned around, went back down the road fifty meters, pulled off into a shaded area, and parked.

The officer in charge then called for three sampans. The first sampan was loaded with a squad of troops, and it pushed off from the bank. But instead of heading for the far bank, it moved to a spot about twenty yards offshore and remained stationary. When it reached that position, the carry-all doors opened. Five uniformed officers climbed out and got into the second sampan. They were joined by two soldiers and the officer commanding the security detail. A moment later, another seven soldiers climbed into the third sampan.

"Your targets are in the second sampan, Dunaway," Taylor said quietly as he lowered his binoculars.

"I can see them."

"The General is the fourth man in the sampan from the front."

"Take him out now."

Dunaway ignored him as he gazed through his spotting scope.

"Didn't you hear me?" Taylor hissed a moment later.

"Quiet, Captain," Dunaway snapped in anger. "this is my detail."

Macklin didn't say a word. He just kept his eyes glued to the scope and waited for instructions from Dunaway, just as he'd been trained to do.

Breslan listened to the entire exchange and wondered what the hell was going on. The Marine corporal had just told his Captain to shut the fuck up and back off! Apparently, there was more to Dunawayal than he had initially noticed. He didn't take shit from anybody when he was in charge.

Chapter Eighteen
The hit and the getaway

Suddenly, the second and third sampan pushed off from the bank, and their paddlers began taking them across the river. The first sampan took up a station in front of the first two, maintaining a steady position in the small three boat convoy. Still, there was no word from Dunaway. Taylor was agitated now and about to repeat something when Dunaway finally spoke.

"Primary target is in the third, repeat third sampan, second man from the rear," Dunaway told Macklin.

"He's dressed as an ordinary soldier, not as an officer."

"They've pulled a switch on us."

"The other four targets are presumably in the second sampan." Acknowledge."

"I've got the primary," Macklin said a moment later.

"What about the other four secondaries?"

"There are six potential targets in that boat."

"After you hit the primary," Dunaway ordered. "take out everybody in the second sampan except the two paddlers; the security officer first."

"He's the second man in that sampan."

"Acknowledge."

"Got it," Buster said, settling in.

Taylor's mouth fell open; he was so surprised.

Suddenly Pao's face loomed up in the scope. Buster could see the wrinkles around the corners of the General's eyes as he squinted into the morning sun and the small wart just below his lip with a single black hair growing out of it. It was Pao, all right. Macklin has been studying his picture for the past three weeks. By now, he knew his face as well as he knew Dunaway's.

Since the sampan was moving, Buster centered the crosshairs in the scope an inch forward of the man's temple and waited. His hold on the weapon was rock steady, so the crosshairs moved slightly laterally, never leaving his aim point.

"Stand by," Dunaway said as the three sampans approached the center of the river. Buster clicked off the Sako's safety.

A moment later, Dunaway quietly said. "Send it."

There was an instantaneous Crack from the Sako, and the General's head exploded. Buster threw the bolt automatically, chambering another round. Almost immediately, there was a second Crack and then a third a second later. Then three more, all in rapid succession.

"Hit," Dunaway said. "Primary is down."

"Hit. One secondary is down."

"Hit. Another secondary is down."

"Hit. Another secondary is down."

"Remaining two targets are now in the water."

Buster didn't acknowledge; he just fired again and two seconds later again.

"Hit," Dunaway said. "Another secondary is down."

"Hit. The last target is down."

There was return fire now, coming from the Pathet Lao squad securing the far bank, but it was ineffective since they were out of range. However, Dunaway knew that wouldn't last long.

"Shift fire to the far bank at ten o'clock," Dunaway ordered.

Macklin moved slightly and then shoved a fresh load of .308 rounds into the weapon.

"New target," Dunaway ordered. "Troops in the open."

"Range five hundred fifty yards at ten o'clock."

"Fire at will."

Macklin began firing again.

"Hit," Dunaway said.

"Hit." He said again and again as Buster continued to kill with cool efficiency.

Buster went through another complete reload before he was finally finished, and there were no more visible targets. By that time, only an occasional round of return fire was heard, and there were bodies spread out all over the far bank. Everyone else on both banks was either hiding or running.

Taylor and Breslan watched the entire scene through the high-powered binoculars in amazement. Every time there was a loud Crack, a man's head exploded in the distance. Running or standing, it didn't matter. Their heads simply erupted in a splash of blood and brain matter as the boat tail hollow points plowed into them and mushroomed. Even before their dead bodies hit the ground, there was another Crack from the Sako, and another man died. Macklin was a killing machine, and he never missed. It was like watching a Technicolor Sam Peckinpaugh movie in slow motion.

"Cease fire," Dunaway finally ordered a few moments later as the remaining soldiers in the distance finally found cover and disappeared.

"All targets are down, Sir," Dunaway reported to Taylor.

"It's time to move."

"God all mighty," Breslan said in awe as he lowered his binoculars.

"If I hadn't seen it with my own eyes, I wouldn't have believed it."

"Macklin, you just killed seventeen men in less than thirty seconds."

"Not a single miss at five hundred yards."

"Jesus, I've never seen anything like that before in my entire life."

"Where in the hell did you learn to shoot like that?"

"Everybody back to the sampan," Taylor ordered softly before Buster could reply.

"Keep low when you move."

Everyone grabbed their equipment and moved back through the reeds crouching to avoid being seen. A half a minute later, all six men were in the sampan hidden in the foliage behind them. Lop was bent over and silently poling it through the reeds headed back down river, keeping it close to the bank to avoid being detected.

There was renewed firing once again, going on behind them now as the other two sampans reached the shore. Rounds were flying everywhere. But since it was not concentrated on the shooting position, and the sampan was out of range, it wasn't effective. Hearing it, Dunaway doubted if most of the firers even knew where the team had been hidden since most of the remaining security detail appeared to be firing in pure frustration.

When the team reached a bend in the river a few minutes later, Lop and Chuy steered the craft out into the current, and then both men began paddling like hell. Behind them, back at the crossing, which was now out of sight, sporadic firing was still going on, but it was still blind. The remaining Pathet Lao were shooting at shadows in anger now because their leader was dead.

"Keep an eye on our six, Breslan," Taylor ordered. "just in case."

The big NCO nodded.

"Macklin, you did a flawless job," Taylor said, turning to face him.

"As Breslan said, if I hadn't seen it, I wouldn't have believed it."

"And Corporal Dunaway," he continued. "I owe you an apology."

"I let my mouth run away with me back there, and it overloaded my ass."

"I identified the wrong damn target," Taylor said, obviously embarrassed.

"But despite that, you saved our asses anyway."

"How did you know?" Taylor asked curiously.

"The Marine Corps trains its spotters to positively identify their targets, Sir, " Dunaway explained. "before they give consent to fire,"

"When I checked the second sampan and could not identify our primary target, I checked the other two and located him in the third sampan dressed as a simple soldier."

"But he had a hat on pulled down low, so it took me a moment."

"When I had a positive ID, I gave Private Macklin his location."

"But how did you know the guy in the second sampan, the one I thought was the General, was the wrong target?" Taylor asked, still puzzled.

"After all, he sure fooled me."

"You were looking at his uniform, Sir," Dunaway explained. "That's what threw you."

"I was looking at his face," Dunaway explained.

"I memorized General Pao's back in Saigon."

"As soon as I saw the man dressed as a General, I knew they had put in a decoy."

Taylor just looked at Dunaway in awe and smiled.

"They sure trained you well, Corporal," he finally said.

"If it had been up to me, the General would still be alive, and this entire mission would have been fucked."

"Thankfully, you saved it." He admitted.

Dunaway blushed slightly but remained silent.

"Taylor san," Chuy said twenty minutes later. "Our extraction point is very near." He said, pointing at a spot on the right bank in the distance.

"There."

Taylor looked at the spot for a moment. It was a completely open area on the riverbank with little to no concealment and devoid of cover.

"It would be an ideal spot for an ambush." he thought absently.

He hadn't noticed anything about the site the night of their drop-off because it had been so dark. Now its disadvantages stood out like a red flag.

"Take us past it," he ordered unexpectedly.

"Pull into those reeds about hundred yards downstream on the left."

"The left?" Chuy asked, puzzled.

Taylor nodded.

A minute later, the sampan was beached on the left riverbank and hidden by the reeds. The Team was in the thick vegetation just off the bank in a small semi-circle shortly after that.

Chapter Nineteen
Sold out

"This'll do until it gets dark," Taylor said, as everyone automatically formed a small perimeter around him.

"Everybody, relax," he said. "we've got a long wait."

Dunaway was puzzled by Taylor's sudden action but remained silent. After all, Taylor was in charge, and if there was anything they should know, Dunaway felt sure he would tell them.

"Breslan," the Captain unexpectedly ordered a moment later. "recheck the radio."

"See if it's working now."

Breslan took off his rucksack, took the radio out of it, extended its telescoping antenna, and began fiddling with its knobs and dials.

"The fucker's still dead," he reported disgustedly a minute later.

"Goddamn piece of communist shit."

Taylor was silent as he thought for a moment.

"Open the back of it and check inside," he ordered.

"Maybe something's loose."

Breslan looked at him oddly, then took out a Swiss Army Knife, unscrewed several screws, then popped the metal cover off the back of the radio. Afterwards, he scrutinized the inside.

"Well, I'll be goddamned," he said a moment later as he looked up at Taylor strangely. "the crystal's missing."

Taylor looked puzzled.

"This radio has a fixed crystal that controls its band width," Breslan explained.

"It fits in this little slot," he said, pointing.

"Without it, you can't transmit."

"It's missing." He said unnecessarily.

"And it didn't fall out accidentally," the big NCO added angrily a moment later.

"It's not inside of the radio."

"I've already checked. "

"It's completely gone, and it damned sure didn't disappear all by itself."

"That means somebody took it out deliberately," Breslan said angrily.

"And the only time this radio has been out of my sight is when it was in the truck cab with the spook that drove us to Charlie's."

"That means he took it out, the sonofabitch."

"But why?" he asked, puzzled.

While everyone else was shocked, Taylor just nodded, seemingly unfazed by the dramatic announcement.

"I thought that might turn out to be the case," he finally said calmly.

That floored everybody.

"I don't get it, Sir," Breslan said.

"What the hell's going on?"

"Why would he deliberately sabotage our radio?"

Dunaway, Macklin, and the two Nungs were all listening intently too. They also wanted to hear the answer to that.

"It's simple," Taylor explained. "We've been used."

"We've been deliberately set up by the goddamn Agency."

Nobody else on the team said a word with that bombshell. They were too shocked. So, they all waited for Taylor to explain.

"I don't know all of it," Taylor began a moment later.

"And I'm just guessing about some of it." He admitted.

"But I do know enough to know we've been set up and deliberately used."

"I had my suspicions earlier," He explained. "and they started with the radio."

"I thought about the radio not working when we got to the target but working perfectly before we left the staging area," He continued.

"Later, I realized that no radio meant no helo to extract with."

"It also meant no calls for help to anybody either," he pointed out. "if we needed it."

"Finally, it guaranteed we'd have to use Charlie again as our extraction platform."

"All that got me to wondering why."

"But when Dunaway said that they had put in a decoy for the General, that's when I finally figured everything out and realized the truth."

"I still don't get it, Sir," Breslan said, puzzled.

"You're going to have to explain it to me by the numbers."

Dunaway was thinking the same thing.

"Look at our drop-off point carefully, Breslan," Taylor said, pointing across the river. "It's open as hell."

"There's no cover anywhere near it."

"Anyone waiting there for a pickup tonight would be a sitting duck."

"Maybe Charlie made a mistake when he put us out there," Taylor opined, reminding everyone of the wide-open extraction site. "but I don't think so."

"I think that's exactly where he wants us to be tonight when he picks us up."

"Because when he gets back here," Taylor predicted. "I think he's bringing some friends with him."

"When they get here, they're going to try and kill every one of us!"

"But why," Dunaway asked in astonishment. "I still don't understand, Sir?"

"Why would the Agency hire Charlie to take us in, then tell him to kill us after we accomplished our mission?"

"The Agency is big into drugs in Laos, Corporal," Taylor explained.

"Just about everybody in SF knows it."

"It's the worst kept secret of the war in the Special Forces community."

"The word is, they're even using some of the proceeds to finance their own little war here in Laos."

"But what's not commonly known," Taylor continued. "is that a lot of that same money is also being skimmed off by some of the Agency personnel, and they're getting rich off it."

Dunaway's and Macklin's eyes widened at that. This was the first they had ever heard of the Agency's connection with drugs in Southeast Asia.

"I should have picked up on that when Chambers briefed us that Pao was meeting a drug lord," Taylor said, almost to himself in hindsight. "but I didn't."

"Later, when we got tasked with a mission the Agency could have easily handled itself, that should have been another red flag," He told the group.

"But I missed that too," he said disgustedly.

"Hell, the CIA controls all the allied activity in this entire country," Taylor explained.

"Laos is an all-Agency show, so they run everything here, and they have everything and everybody to do it with."

"So, you have to ask yourself:

"*Why would they want a DOD team to conduct a mission their own people here in Laos could have easily accomplished themselves?*"

"The answer to that question is easy," He explained.

"They needed a convenient scapegoat to blame everything on."

"Why?" Breslan asked, still obviously in the dark.

"For two reasons," Taylor explained.

"First, if anything went wrong, the Agency could point the finger and say it was the fault of military assets DOD sent them."

"That's us," Taylor pointed out.

"Remember, we planned and mounted the entire operation, and then conducted it."

"The Agency only gave us the target and then supported us with some assets."

"At least that will be their side of the story."

"And since we'll all be dead, who can refute them?"

"Further, since we are all members of the military, if there was ever an investigation into Pao's death, they will provide ample evidence to prove all that."

"The fact that we were working for the Agency at the time we were tasked with the mission will be conveniently lost in the shuffle when the blame game starts," He explained.

"That would let the Agency off the hook, at least as far as Pao and the Pathet Lao are concerned."

"And anything to the contrary would be almost impossible to refute because neither Pao, us, nor anyone else would be in a position to make any counter-charges."

"Second," Taylor continued. "we're expendable."

"After this operation was over and we were dead, the entire affair could be buried very easily by the Agency."

"Especially since they are the only ones privy to any of the details of the mission, or even the mission itself."

"The Agency would just tell MACV or our units that we were all killed on the mission, and with no proof to the contrary, who's to challenge them?"

"Afterwards, they'd slap a Top-Secret security classification on everything, and that would be the end of it."

"That's the primary reason the Agency wanted this mission done covertly," He explained.

"That was just added insurance in case somebody started asking questions about it later on down the road."

"You've lost me again," Dunaway said.

"I still don't understand, Sir."

"I keep forgetting he and Macklin are Marines and not SF." Taylor reminded himself.

"So, they know very little about the Agency and its activities here in Southeast Asia."

"So, I'm going to have to explain this by the numbers, so they'll understand."

So, he began again.

"General Pao is a legitimate military target since he is the Pathet Lao's head man," Taylor explained.

"Therefore, he's fair game for the military because he is a surrogate of the North Vietnamese."

"If that's so," Taylor asked rhetorically. "ask yourself this."

"Why would the mission to kill him need to be classified as covert?"

"That doesn't even make good sense, even on the surface."

"That's something else I should have picked up on and didn't," he added disgustedly.

"But, if the Agency wanted him killed because they wanted to take over his drug empire, and not because he was just a legal military target, that makes this an entirely different ball game."

"Then a covert mission makes perfect sense."

"No one would ever know that his death was ordered because of his drug activities because the mission was classified as covert."

"In addition, anyone looking at the circumstances of his death would just think that as a legitimate military target, he got taken out when the opportunity arose."

"That would mean that only the Agency would be privy to any of the details concerning the real reason behind his termination."

"Everyone else would just assume the mission was conducted because Pao was an enemy combatant."

"Jesus," Dunaway thought to himself apprehensively. "This is starting to make more and more sense, and I don't like where it's going at all."

"If what I think is going on is true," Taylor continued mysteriously. "that's make everything very convenient."

"I'm lost," Breslan said.

"I think I may be too," Dunaway parroted. "Again."

'I'll try to explain it in simpler terms,' Taylor said.

"I probably should have done that to start with."

"I keep forgetting you two are Marines and aren't privy to all the gossip about the Agency us guys in SOG hear all the time."

"So here it is in basic terms."

"My guess is that the late General Pao was cutting into the Agency's drug profits here in Laos too deeply," Taylor explained.

"We already know he's into drugs in a big way to support his military efforts and to make himself rich simultaneously."

"Hell, Chambers told us that."

"What he didn't tell us is that in the process of doing all that, Pao has become a big competitor to the Agency's people who are also in the drug trade in Laos."

"That's what this whole thing was all about, to begin with."

"Some selected elements of the Agency decided that the simplest way to eliminate some of their competition, namely Pao, was to get rid of him," Taylor continued.

"And the simplest way to accomplish that was to set up a meeting with him on the pretext of setting prices and offering to buy all his product."

"But that was just a pretext to lure him out of his headquarters."

"What they really wanted to do was kill him."

"When they did, they could take overr everything he controlled for nothing."

"Killing him was our job," Taylor told them.

"So, if anything went wrong, the Agency could blame it on the military."

"But if everything went as planned, since the operation was covert, no one outside the Agency would know the real reason for Pao's elimination."

"Of course, after we killed him, good old Charlie, acting on Agency orders would eliminate us."

"That would seal up everything nice and tight, with only the Agency knowing the truth."

"But somehow Pao got suspicious of the meeting itself," Taylor continued. "or maybe he was never a trusting soul, to begin with when it came to dealing with the Agency."

"Regardless, that was the reason for the decoy."

"Even though he agreed to the meeting, he didn't trust the CIA."

"You've lost me again, Sir," Dunaway said, puzzled.

"Chambers told us Pao was scheduled to meet with a drug lord."

"Where does the Agency fit into that picture?"

"And if Pao was suspicious," Dunaway asked. "why would he still agree to meet with the drug lord anyway?

"That doesn't make any sense to me either."

"Maybe he wasn't meeting with a drug lord, Corporal," Taylor opined. "Maybe that was just a cover story Chambers fed us."

"After all, we only have his word for that."

"Maybe he was meeting with somebody else entirely," Taylor suggested.

"Somebody he didn't trust."

"Maybe somebody that just might try and kill him."

"Somebody like an employee of the Agency who was the lead man in their drug operation."

"Pao probably already knew him because they had done deals before."

"Despite that knowledge, Pao realized that if he could make a deal with the CIA to sell them all his opium yearly, that was a once in a lifetime opportunity he couldn't pass up, and he would be filthy rich because of it."

"Still, however, since he didn't trust the Agency fully, he decided to use a decoy as added insurance."

"You don't get to be a drug kingpin in Southeast Asia because you are a trusting soul."

"So Pao protected himself accordingly."

Suddenly the light bulb went on, and Dunaway understood.

"That makes perfect sense," Dunaway thought. "All the puzzle pieces that worried me before now fit."

"Personally, I don't think Pao ever intended to meet with a drug lord," Taylor explained.

"I think that was just a bullshit cover story Chambers fed us to account for Pao's meeting."

"Probably with another drug lord in the region."

"The Agency found out about that through their asset and decided to kill him when he did because it was convenient and supposedly, they weren't involved."

"And, of course, the meeting itself was a perfect way to get Pao to a place where he could be eliminated."

"Futhermore," Taylor told everybody. "I don't even think this was even a sanctioned Agency operation."

"I think a certain element in the CIA just took it upon themselves to conduct it to protect and expand their existing drug empire."

"I think Pao was going to meet with another asset in the drug trade they controlled," Taylor said. "to talk about control of the opium trade here in the region, and maybe set a price for all the opium being grown and processed."

"You know," he suggested. "who was going to get what and how much they were willing to pay for the product."

That was the real reason for the meet, but it also presented the Agency with a perfect opportunity to eliminate a major competitor."

"So they took it and used us to do their dirtywork."

"Bingo," Dunaway thought as the pieces all suddenly fell into place.

"Opium makes strange bedfellows," Taylor said with a thin smile. "Money and control of the opium trade are key here in the region."

"Whoever controls the most opium makes the most money."

"And the people who currently control most of that trade," Taylor informed everybody. "is an old KMT division based up in the Golden Triangle."

"Chaing Kai Chek deliberately left them there when he got run out of China back in the forties."

"They were big into the opium trade in the region even then, working, of course for old Chaing."

"Now, they control about seventy percent of it, and guess who they work for?"

"The Agency," Taylor told everyone, not waiting for an answer.

"They've been supporting and supplying them ever since Chaing and the KMT fled to Taiwan and established a government in exile."

"In return, they get intelligence about mainland China from Chaing's intelligence service, who still has assets on the mainland."

"So, in reality, the Agency already controls a significant portion of the drug business in the entire region thru them; about 50 to 60 percent is the figure I've heard."

"General Pao and the other two ethnic tribes in Burma and Laos control the remaining forty percent," Taylor said, finishing up.

"My guess is that they decided to get that forty percent by eliminating Pao."

"That would give them complete control of nearly all product grown in the region."

"And since the region supplies nearly all of the world's heroin, that means that with a monopoly, they could set the price on the world drug market."

"If they did that, everybody would get richer."

"General Pao included. "

"That's probably why he agreed to the meeting in the first place."

"It was simple greed."

"But then, the Agency, or someone in it, got greedy and decided to eliminate Pao and put their own man in to replace him," Taylor explained.

"That way, they could effectively control all the opium trade in the entire region and not have to give Pao anything."

"Pao's replacement was probably the Agency's mysterious "asset" that gave us all the information on Pao's itinerary and route," Taylor said, summing up.

"The Agency probably cut a deal with him and planned to put him in as the General's replacement after we killed him."

"That explains everything very neatly," Dunaway thought bitterly as he remembered all the other little things he had observed earlier that hadn't made any sense at the time.

"But where does that leave us?" he worried.

"In truth, the *"war"* here in Laos is just a sideshow for the Agency," Taylor said absently.

"The real key here is control of the opium trade in the region."

"It generates multi-millions of dollars a year after it is processed into heroin."

"Think of what the Agency could do with that kind of money."

"Or think how rich some of its corrupt case officers could get," He opined.

"They don't call it the "Golden Triangle" for nothing," He snorted.

"Everything you've said makes perfect sense, Sir," Dunaway said. "but there's no proof."

"It's all just assumption and supposition."

"You're right, Corporal," Taylor said. "Every single thing I've said has been unsupported supposition."

"The proof, if there is any," he explained. "will come tonight."

"If Charlie shows up with a bunch of people and they try to kill us, we'll know I'm right for sure."

"If that happens, Sir," Macklin asked, speaking for the first time. "What do we do then?"

"Interesting question, Buster," Taylor replied.

Chapter Twenty
Run for your life.

"One option is to try and kill Charlie and all his friends and then take his boat," Taylor suggested a moment later.

"If we don't get killed in the process, theoretically, we could all be back in Thailand by tomorrow morning."

"But after we get back," he asked everyone. "what would we do then?"

"If the Agency tried to have us killed in Laos and failed," Taylor reminded them. "and we show back up in Thailand, alive and pissed off; there's no doubt in my mind that when they find out we're still alive, they'll try again."

"And I don't think they'll fuck around and use another Charlie the second time."

"They'll use their own people, and they'll make sure they get the job done this time," he said flatly.

"The second half of that problem is," Taylor continued. "even if we can avoid the Agency in Thailand, how do we get back to Vietnam, and what do we do when we get there?"

"We're all black, remember," He reminded everyone.

"We don't have any IDs, uniforms, or even any money."

"Hell, we can't even prove we're Americans."

"So, where do we go to get any help?"

"The US Embassy is out because the Agency has a Station there," Taylor explained. "So, they'd turn us in or scoop us up as soon as we made contact."

"And returning to NKP and contacting the Air Force units stationed there is out too," Taylor explained.

"Because nobody there even saw us come in."

"We weren't even listed on the aircraft's manifest." Dunaway thought.

"So, they don't know even know we're here."

"In addition, nobody on the base knows us from Adam."

"And since we have no IDs," Taylor pointed out. "we can't even get back on the base, to begin with."

"Even if we were able to somehow manage that, with no proof of anything, who would believe us?"

"Lastly, we're still under the control of the Agency," Taylor reminded everyone. "Even though we all may be military, that doesn't mean shit."

"Until the Agency officially releases us, we belong to them."

"And believe me, nobody in the military is going to challenge the Agency when it comes to operational control of its assets."

"So, until they give us back to MACV, they own our asses."

"Lastly, to convince anyone else of what happened would require some pretty strong proof," Taylor said. "And we don't have one single scrap of evidence."

"Wonderful," Breslan growled. "just fucking wonderful."

"So, where does that leave us, Captain?"

"I'm not sure," Taylor said. "Up shit creek for sure, but other than that, I just don't know."

"I'm still thinking."

"If we could somehow manage to get back to South Vietnam, we might be able to contact our parent units, explain the situation, and maybe they could help us," He said almost to himself.

"But with no military IDs or uniforms, just getting back in country would be a miracle."

"So obviously, we'd need some help to accomplish that."

"Special Forces has 46th Company permanently stationed in Thailand at Lop Buri," Taylor said a moment later. "so, there might be an outside chance we could convince someone there to help us."

"Assuming, of course, we could get there."

"Unfortunately, I don't know anyone assigned to that unit."

"And again, with no IDs, we can't even prove we're in the military, much less in SF."

"So that's a big fucking maybe at best."

"Other than those two options," Taylor concluded. "I'm fresh out of ideas."

"I know somebody in 46th Company," Breslan said unexpectedly, a big grin spreading all over his face. "and he's a good friend of mine."

"If I can contact him, he'll help," He said.

"I can guarantee that."

"We go back a long way." He explained.

"Are you sure?" Taylor asked, looking up and now highly interested.

"Positive," Breslan said as he nodded.

"Are you sure he's still there?" Taylor asked hopefully. "He could have already rotated back to the States."

"He hasn't."

I'm sure of that too," Breslan said.

"I saw him when I went to Bangkok on R&R three months ago."

"He's got another year left on his tour, so he's still there."

"And you're sure he'll help us," Taylor asked.

"I guarantee it," Breslan replied.

"Then I guess we're going back to Thailand," Taylor said with a smile.

"Now we just have to figure out how we're going to get there."

For the first time since Taylor had begun his explanation, Dunaway felt a ray of hope. Maybe they could get out of this mess after all. At least now they had a chance.

"Can you hit anything with that Sako at night?" Taylor asked Macklin minutes later.

The team was now discussing whether they should try and hijack Charlie's boat.

"If I can see it, Sir," Macklin said confidently. "I can hit it, day or night."

"If you and Dunaway could take out a few of Charlie's friends," Taylor said. "assuming, of course, that I'm right about all this, then I have an idea."

"Let's hear it, Sir," Breslan said, barely able to control himself.

"Right now, I'm about as pissed off as I can get, and the Agency and everybody in it is right at the top of my shit list."

"I'm ready to kill every CIA asshole I can find, and that includes good old Charlie, the rotten little sonofabitch."

Ten minutes later, Taylor had laid it all out. It was risky, but there was no other option, and everyone realized that. Dunaway and Buster would play critical roles. Macklin would stay on the river's left side while everyone else went to the pickup point on the right.

Dunaway would conceal himself upstream of the drop-off point in the foliage, with Macklin doing the same on the other side of the river. They would both be upstream of Charlie's boat when they started firing downstream. In that manner, they could both fire simultaneously without fear of hitting each other. Taylor and Breslan would be waiting near the riverbank in the open as bait, with the two Nungs behind them providing cover.

Everyone would wait for Charlie and his boat to show up at the pickup point later that night, with Taylor and Breslan standing in the open and everyone else concealed. At the first sign of trouble, Macklin and Dunaway would take out anyone on the boat showing themselves with a weapon. When or if they fired, Taylor and Breslan would drop to the ground, and Chuy and Lop, the Nungs behind them, would cut loose, providing them covering fire. Afterwards, they all would unload on anybody on the boat, and everyone would keep firing until there was no more resistance.

"This has got to be done quickly," Taylor warned everyone.

"The firing is going to alert the entire countryside, and there are probably still some of General Pao's security force around, plus the local Pathet Lao unit in the village."

"Furthermore," Taylor informed the group. "I can practically guarantee that there are other Pathet Lao elements in the area too."

"After all, they control this entire section of Laos."

"So, unless we take care of business quickly, then get the hell out of here before they can find us, we're liable to wind up getting into another firefight with them after we finish with Charlie and his crew."

"And since we're still sixty miles from the border, that could complicate our continued survival immensely."

"I don't want to get into a prolonged firefight with the Pathet Lao forces that could last from here to the border because if that happens, we'll never make it, understand?"

Everyone nodded. A long-lasting, stand-up firefight with the Pathet Lao after taking out Charlie was a nonstarter. If one occurred, they'd all wind up dead. And even if they somehow survived that, since they were still sixty miles from the border, that was too far to run with the Pathet Lao chasing them the entire way and alerting even more Pathet Lao forces ahead of them to stop them. They'd never get out of Laos alive.

"Macklin," Taylor ordered. "When Charlie shows up in his boat, check it out carefully with your scope."

"If he's got armed people with him, you shoot first."

"Take out whoever is operating the engine first," He ordered. "That way, Charlie can't simply sail away once the shooting starts."

"Once Macklin shoots, everybody else opens up," He then explained to everyone else.

"But when you do," Taylor warned. "make sure you have a target."

"I don't want a boat that won't float because it has a bunch of bullet holes in it after the firefight is over," He explained.

"There's a three-quarter moon tonight, so we'll have some visibility," Taylor noted.

"That should be enough to let you find a target and hit something."

"And one more thing," he added. "once the shooting starts, keep firing until everybody on the boat is down. Understand?"

"We have to kill everybody on it to take it over."

"Everyone got that?"

Everybody nodded.

Afterwards, everyone ate their last freeze-dried ration and then cleaned and checked weapons. At sunset, everybody except Buster got in the sampan, paddled back across the river to the pickup point, and got into position. Meanwhile, Buster made his way back upstream until he found a suitable shooting position, where he settled down to wait too.

The river wasn't as wide at Buster's new position as it had been at the crossing site, but its banks were steeper. That gave Buster a slight elevation advantage when the boat arrived, and he planned to take full advantage of it.

Buster estimated that the far bank was less than two hundred yards away. His scope was still set for five hundred yards. But he didn't want to screw with the scope after dark, so he told himself he would just have to aim low. But only slightly because he was still above where the targets would be.

Once it got fully dark, he checked his visibility through the scope and found that he could see Taylor and Breslan clearly in the moonlight on the far bank. That was all he needed. He was ready now. And like Breslan, Macklin was extremely upset at being deliberately used, then being set up to be killed. Now he was more than prepared to deal out some payback.

Nothing happened for the next two and a half hours once it got dark except for everyone's constant fight with the mosquitoes. They came out in droves with the darkness, and the GI insect repellant Macklin put on was useless against them. That and the time involved in just silently waiting made the time pass slowly and made staying still just that much more difficult.

Finally, four hours after sunset, there was the faint sound of an engine in the far distance. Buster put his scope on the bend in the river, and minutes later, a boat appeared. At first, he could barely make out its outlines in the distance because it was close to the right bank and moving very slowly. As it got closer, Buster recognized it as Charlie's because of its length, high sidewalls, and the small, covered cabin in its center.

As the boat got even closer, Buster watched it intently through the scope looking for armed personnel. Initially, he didn't see any. But suddenly, on the left side of the cabin, hidden from view on the right bank of the river, he saw three armed men crouched down low, just their heads and the barrels of their weapons visible as they hid behind the cabin.

As he scanned the rest of the boat a moment later, he saw two more in the bow crouched below the gunnels and another in the rear hiding just below the man manning the engine. All of them were trying to prevent anyone at the pickup point from spotting them.

"That's six," Buster said to himself. "but surely there's more."

"There's six of us, so there has to be at least ten or twelve of them."

"Otherwise, they couldn't be sure of getting all of us."

"So, they're either on the other side of the boat or in the cabin, maybe both."

Moments later, Charlie must have spotted Taylor and Breslan because the engine stopped, and he edged the boat towards the bank. Just before he reached it, Buster took out the guy operating the engine. The shot rang out clear as a bell, and it was soon joined by Chuy's, Lop's, Breslan's, and Taylor's AK's. During all that, Dunaway's Remington also barked.

Although Macklin heard all that, he disregarded it and quickly shifted to the three men behind the cabin. He killed two in as many seconds, but the third man got up and tried to run around the cabin before Buster could get him in his sights. When he did, his body was suddenly flung backward as someone on the other bank shot him.

Buster was already lined up on the two in the bow a second later. They were firing from below the gunnels and hidden from view by anyone on the other side of the river, but not from Buster. He killed both a moment later. Then there were more shots from the far bank, but before Buster could locate another target, the firing suddenly slacked off. A moment later, he heard Dunaway yell, "Cease Fire," so he put the Sako back on safe. Five minutes later, Chuy appeared with the sampan and picked him up.

"How'd it go, Chuy?" Buster asked anxiously.

"We kill them all," Chuy replied excitedly, his eyes wide and shining in the dark. "but they shoot Taylor san."

"Shit," Macklin said, wondering if anyone else got hit too.

But before he could ask, Chuy was already paddling like a madman back across the river, so he decided to wait.

When Macklin and Chuy beached the sampan on the far bank minutes later, Buster saw a small crowd gathered around a figure on the ground. He and Chuy ran up to them.

"It's the Captain," Dunaway said as Buster arrived. "he's dead."

"Goddamn it," Buster responded, frustrated and scared, all at the same time.

Taylor had been their brains. He had figured out what was happening to them and that the Agency had set them up. He had even come up with a plan to start getting them out of the mess they were in. Now that he was dead, Buster wondered what they would do?

Breslan, kneeling by the body, looked up with tears running down his cheeks.

"What am I going to tell Jim's wife?" he asked. Then he started sobbing.

No one said a word.

A few moments later, professionalism took over. Dunaway snapped out of it and took charge since Breslan was obviously in no condition to assume command.

"Lop," he said. "you and Chuy get the bodies off the boat and throw them in the weeds but strip the clothes off them first and put them on the boat."

"Buster, you collect all the weapons and put them in the cabin."

"When you're finished, use your flashlight to check the boat for any leaks made by the firing."

"If you find any, cut some pieces of rope from the loop hanging on the side of the cabin and plug them," He ordered.

"Meanwhile, I'll see if the engine still works."

"And hurry everybody," He said urgently. "Every asshole in Laos heard that firefight, so it won't be long before they'll be all over us."

Five minutes later, it was done. Although the boat had several bullet holes in it, fortunately, none were below the waterline. Buster plugged the ones nearest the waterline anyway, just to be sure.

While he was doing that, Chuy and Lop threw twelve naked bodies into the reeds, including good old Charlie, the bastard who had set them up.

When Macklin finished plugging the bullet holes, he and Dunaway collected all the AKs and web belts and stacked them in the cabin. Moments later, Macklin picked up the bloody clothes Lop and Chuy had dropped and dipped them into the river several times to wash away some blood. Afterwards, he threw them onto the boat deck to dry.

"What the hell are we going to do with those?" he asked Dunaway, pointing to them.

"We'll wash them in the river again to get them clean after we get underway," Dunaway replied.

"After they dry, we'll put them on."

"These uniforms are too conspicuous." He explained.

"They make us stand out like whores in church, and that's the last thing we need right now, more attention."

"What about the Captain's body?" Buster asked. "What are we going to do with it?"

"I'll strip it, and then we'll leave it," Breslan ordered in a choked voice, walking up quietly behind them.

He had finally snapped out of his grief and was getting control of himself again.

"He won't mind," The big Sgt said sadly as he turned back towards Taylor's corpse. "Not now."

"He knew this was part of the job going in."

"All of us do."

Minutes later, Dunaway cranked the engine, and they were moving. Macklin looked back at the riverbank as they shoved off and saw the naked white corpse of Taylor in the moonlight as they departed. It looked lonely and somehow very helpless. He shook his head sadly because everything had seemingly turned to shit. The Team had been betrayed, Taylor was dead, they were seventy miles inside Laos, and Breslan was on the verge of losing it.

"What the fuck are we going to do now?" He wondered as the boat chugged steadily downriver.

"The Goddamed Agency tried to kill us, so who do we turn to for help?"

With Chuy handling the engine, minutes later, Breslan, Dunaway, and Macklin were in the cabin looking at the map that had belonged to Taylor with the aid of a flashlight.

"Here's where we are," Dunaway said, pointing at a marked spot on the map. "Captain Taylor marked the crossing site."

"I know; I was with him when he did it."

"We just need to follow this river downstream until it connects with the Mekong."

"How long do you figure that will take?" Macklin asked, impressed that Dunaway had taken charge so quickly, had a plan and knew what he was doing.

"The trip up here took over five hours," Dunaway said, remembering.

"I know because I timed it."

"But it was all upstream, and we were fighting the current."

"So, the trip back should be much shorter."

"Even going this slow," He predicted. "We should hit the Mekong by dawn at the latest."

"If we can make it that far without running into trouble, we should be okay as far as the Pathet Lao are concerned."

"At least that's what I'm assuming."

"Don't you think so, Sgt Breslan?" Dunaway asked, trying to get Breslan back into the conversation and back to normal.

"Yeah," Breslan finally replied. "I do."

"As long as we're on the river, we should be all right."

"Since the Mekong is the border between Laos and Thailand," he explained. "the Pathet Lao don't try and control any of the river traffic because they don't want the Thai Army all over their asses."

"They stay on their side, and the Thais stay on theirs."

"That makes the river itself neutral ground."

"So, when we hit the Mekong," Breslan continued. "we'll head south till we hit Vientiane."

"That's about three hundred kilometers south of here."

"When we get there, we'll let Lop and Chuy sell the AK's we just took off those assholes."

"They should bring about three hundred apiece on the black market, and that will give us traveling money."

"Then what?" Macklin asked, incredibly happy that Breslan was seemingly back to his old self.

"We'll continue south for another hundred miles or so," Breslan explained as he traced their route on Taylor's map.

"Lop Buri, the headquarters of 46th Special Forces Company," he continued as he pointed with his finger. "is in the center of the country, about here," He said, pointing at the map with his finger.

"But that's a long way from the river."

"I don't want to have to try and make that trip overland unless it's necessary because we don't have any papers."

"We're okay while we're on the river," He explained. "because it's neutral ground."

"But we start moving overland, we'll need IDs sooner or later, and we don't have any."

"So, before we try that approach," he explained. "I want to call my buddy at Lop Buri first."

"He knows the country a lot better than I do, so we'll need his advice."

"If I can get him on the phone, hopefully, he can meet us somewhere closer."

"That will save us both some time and be a hell of a lot easier and a lot more secure."

"When we meet, we'll figure something out."

Hearing that, Macklin felt relieved. At least they had a plan now, so there was a chance.

"If anything happens to me before I can contact my buddy," Breslan said, finally getting all his composure back. "his name is SFC Jerry Spencer."

"He's about my size with brown hair and blue eyes, and he has a small scar on his chin."

"I know," Breslan said. "because I gave it to him years ago during hand-to-hand training."

"His wife's name is Joan, and her nickname is "Shorty.""

"She lives in Metairie, Louisiana."

"My wife's name is Carol, and we have a dog named Rufus."

"All those facts will be your bona fides and confirm that you know me and he can trust you," Breslan told Dunaway and Macklin.

"With them, even if I'm not around, he'll still help you."

"Can you remember all that?" he asked Dunaway and Macklin.

They both nodded.

"And one more thing," Breslan retorted. "if something does happen to me, I want you to kill that sonofabitch Chambers."

"He's the one that set us up," Breslan said angrily.

"We owe him for that and Taylor, and I want to make sure the bastard pays."

"Count on it," Macklin promised before Dunaway could answer.

Later, Dunaway and Macklin were talking by themselves as the boat continued down the river.

"What are we going to do if we ever do get back to Vietnam?" Dunaway asked anxiously. "especially now that Taylor is dead."

"What does the Captain's death have to do with what we're going to do when we get back to Vietnam?" Macklin asked, puzzled.

Dunaway looked at him and shook his head.

"Taylor was the only one who had any control over Breslan, Buster," Dunaway explained.

"Now that he's gone, Breslan can and probably will do as he pleases."

"That means as soon as we get back, Breslan is going to kill Chambers the first chance he gets, in revenge for Taylor."

"That as certain as the sun coming up tomorrow."

"So?" Macklin said apathetically. "Chambers deserves it, the sonofabitch."

"We can't be a party to that, Buster," Dunaway said in frustration because Buster still didn't get it.

"If we do, we'll go to jail as accessories."

"In his current state of mind, they'll catch Breslan for sure, and then they'll try him for murder."

"Us too, if we're involved."

"No, they won't," Macklin said.

"How do you know that?" Dunaway asked.

"Because I'm the one that's going to kill Chambers," Macklin said. "not Breslan."

"He's too screwed up in the head about Taylor," Buster said. "If he tried, he'd fuck it up for sure."

"So, I'll kill him, and I'll get away with it."

Dunaway's mouth fell open and formed an "O" he was so surprised.

"That bastard ain't gonna get away with what he's done," Macklin told Dunaway quietly. "Taylor's dead because of him."

"And if the Captain hadn't figured out what was going on," Buster reminded Dunaway. "by now, we'd be dead too."

"Or have you forgotten about that, Marty?"

"We owe him, Corporal Dunaway," Buster said in a deadly serious tone. "And I am going to see that our debt is paid personally."

"If you wanna help me," Buster snarled. "fine."

"If you don't, then stay out of my way, and I'll do it myself."

"And I want you to know this is not just some juvenile quest for revenge," he added.

"Chambers dies because he deliberately used us."

"And unless somebody kills him, he'll go on using other Marines in the future and get them killed too."

"That's just not gonna happen," Macklin vowed hotly.

"I won't let it."

"And killing the bastard is the only sure way to prevent it."

"Well. I'll be goddamned," Dunaway thought to himself. "Buster has suddenly grown up on me."

"And he's right about everything."

"I was so busy trying to cover my ass; I lost sight of everything Taylor did for us and how Chambers used us."

"Shit," he thought disgustedly. "I'm ashamed of myself again."

"I apologize, Buster," Dunaway said a moment later. "You're right."

"Chambers deserves to be taken out, and you're the logical one to do it."

"But when that happens, we'll do this together."

"That way, I know we'll get away with it."

Macklin smiled. Marty had finally got his head out of his ass and was back on board again. That was good because for a minute there; he was beginning to sound like a stuffy old maid again.

Five hours later, they reached the Mekong River. By that time, everyone had changed into the clothes they had taken off the dead Pathet Lao, and the Nungs were handling the boat.

When Buster looked at everybody, he thought they all looked like half-assed pirates parading around in dead men's clothes in some low-budget B grade movie. His, Dunaway's, and Breslan's legs were so white they stuck out like sore thumbs.

"Who the fuck are we fooling?" he wondered.

So, he, Breslan, and Dunaway stayed out of sight in the cabin as they motored down the river because even in the native mufti, their legs, arms, and torso stood out because they were so white. That was a dead giveaway they were Caucasians. And they didn't need anybody spotting them and wondering what the hell a bunch of round eyes were doing on a boat in the middle of the Mekong River, masquerading as Laotians. They already had more than enough problems to deal with.

At noon, Chuy told Breslan that they were headed into shore, because they needed gas. When Breslan pointed out they had no money to buy it with, Chuy said he would trade some of Charlie's trade goods for it. After all, the boat was loaded with them. Breslan nodded.

However, Buster unexpectedly gave Chuy some money he had found in the clothes he had dipped in the river. That surprised everybody. Apparently, only Buster had been smart enough to check the pockets of the men they had killed. Unfortunately, the wad of notes was a collection of Laotian Kip, Thai Baht, and Chuy didn't think it would be enough anyway.

In the end, it wasn't. Chuy still had to barter some of the trade goods on the boat to get the gas. But when he brought it back to the boat, he also brought some food and beer along with it. He had used the money Buster had given him to buy it. An hour later, everyone was back on the river and eating.

They had to stop two more times for gas and food before they finally reached Vientiane two days later, just before noon. Both times Chuy bartered more trade goods to obtain them. Overall, the trip had taken them almost forty hours of nearly nonstop sailing. But in a way, it had been helpful. It had let everyone get their heads back on straight after what had happened back in Laos.

In addition to being Laos' capital city, Vientiane was a sprawling collection of thrown-together shacks and makeshift houses courtesy of the war and had a huge waterfront district. There were various types of boats of all sizes moored all along it, and people were everywhere. It was much larger than either Dunaway or Macklin had expected and by far the largest city they had yet encountered since their trip had begun. Fortunately, although the place was practically crawling with people, no one appeared to notice one more boat as Chuy pulled old Charlie's craft into a small harbor and tied it off.

Afterwards, he casually walked down the pier and disappeared into the crowd a few moments later. Twenty long minutes later, he returned, bringing some food with him. Breslan briefed everyone on what they would do next as they all ate.

Chapter Twenty One
Back to Thailand

While the rest of the team waited on the boat, Chuy and Lop went to find buyers for the AKs. That was one of the things Chuy had asked about when he had left the boat earlier, and he had quickly gotten the right kind of information with his questions. It didn't take long because weapons were a hot commodity in the Laotian capital city because of the war. So, there was always a market for them. After their meal, both Nungs again left the boat in search of an appropriate buyer.

The two Nungs were back at the boat an hour later with an old man they had found who had agreed to pay for the weapons in Laotian Kip after he had examined them. Breslan, who seemed completely normal now and back to his old self once again, said "No" to that transaction immediately, telling the buyer they wanted US dollars instead. The old man bitched and haggled some more, but he offered two hundred and fifty dollars each in greenbacks after seeing the weapons' condition. Breslan negotiated with him some more and finally got him up to three hundred apiece by agreeing to throw in the web gear, extra magazines, and ammo.

The old man returned an hour later with four armed bodyguards to complete the transaction. Their presence initially scared everyone, but the buyer had the money, so the deal was done. Breslan sold him a total of ten AKs for three thousand dollars, including the one belonging to Taylor. He kept the other two for security.

Immediately after the sale, Breslan had Chuy shove off. They headed down the river before the buyer had a chance to return and try to take his money back with his new weapons. A half-hour later, before they left the city entirely, they stopped for supplies and more gas, then continued.

The next day, after six long, hot hours on the river following sunup, Breslan had Chuy pull into a sizeable Thai river town they encountered. Taking Lop with him as an interpreter, he went to find a telephone. After four separate tries, an hour later, he finally found a grocery store with a phone and a Chinese owner who also spoke some English. Thirty minutes later, with the store owner's help, Breslan finally got through to 46th

Company Headquarters, only to find out that his buddy Spencer was gone for the day on an exercise and wouldn't be back until late that evening. Breslan left a message for him, saying he would call again at nine the following day.

Since it was already late, and everyone was tired, when Breslan and Lop returned to the boat, the team decided to stay in the village overnight and have a meal in a small Thai restaurant on the river. It was the first time everyone had completely relaxed since before the mission started. Even Macklin had a beer at the urging of Dunaway. Afterwards, they all went back to the boat and slept there overnight.

The following day at nine, Breslan finally got in touch with Spencer and had a long conversation with him, giving him an abbreviated version of what had happened on the mission. Spencer agreed to help. After some questions and answers to a suitable location, he finally decided that the easiest and best place for both him and the team to link up would be at the Florida Hotel in Bangkok the following week. It was a place known to both he and Breslan, and that was the earliest Spencer could get away. Spencer also told Breslan the team could take the train into Bangkok, without any IDs provided they dressed as SF personnel in Tiger fatigues. After the conversation, Breslan came back to the boat, briefed everyone, and the team departed downriver again.

Three days later, after stopping at various waterfront villages en route for information, they pulled into another large Thai river town that they had been told boasted a railway station. Since they still needed additional money for their future expenses, Breslan and Dunaway agreed they should sell the boat.

It took almost the entire day of canvassing the waterfront. Still, Lop finally found a buyer for the boat and everything on it. Because they had no title or proof of ownership papers for the vessel, they got raped on the price. Still, they managed another five thousand dollars, half in greenbacks and the other half in Thai Baht. Afterwards, Chuy told everyone that the only reason they had gotten that much was that the boat had so many valuable trade goods still on it.

After the sale, everyone went to a nearby open-air market/cum shopping area and bought new clothing, two used suitcases, and three long cardboard containers to put the two Sakos and the other three AKs in. All the optics and personal web gear went into the two large suitcases.

Everyone kept their rucksacks for everything else. Since rucksacks were an item already familiar to many native Thais, they were not out of place. Once outfitted in Tiger stripes and boots, the Team piled into two pedicabs that took them to the railway station to buy railway tickets to Bangkok.

The trip to Bangkok by rail took another two full days. They had to change trains twice and stay overnight in another village en route because their original station had been on an outlying line. In addition, the train had broken down once and took four hours to repair.

Making the trip seem even longer, the train stopped at every village along the entire line, en route to the main line that led to Bangkok. All that, taken together, amounted to a long, boring, and tedious trip that was hard on everybody's ass because the train seats were wooden with no cushions. Worse, the train had no food for sale on it, which meant that everyone existed on snacks and soft drinks they purchased at the various stops. That made the entire trip a real thrill. But late on the third day, they finally arrived in Bangkok, sore assed, exhausted, and hungry.

They quickly discovered the Florida Hotel rates were much too high for their budget, so the Nungs asked around and finally found a small Thai hotel nearby to stay in the next two nights. After they checked in, Breslan called and left a message and phone number for Spencer at the Florida Hotel desk. Afterwards, everyone slept like the dead for the next twelve hours, and when they awoke, they ate. Late into the morning of the seventh day, Breslan got a call from Spencer, and they arranged to meet at a small open-air restaurant not far from their Thai hotel.

An hour later, following introductions, Breslan told Spencer the entire story, including all of Taylor's suppositions, as they all sipped iced drinks under a large umbrella-covered table in the back of the restaurant's open-air courtyard.

"Unfortunately," Spencer remarked after hearing the story. "I think the Captain was exactly right."

"Bangkok has most of the processing labs for the opium coming out of the region, and the people that control that trade are common knowledge here."

"I've heard the name Pao before," he said unexpectedly.

"He was a r player in the drug business around here."

"Taylor was also right about the KMT Division." He continued. "They control a lot of the opium trade in the region; about sixty percent."

"And Pao controlled most of the remaining forty percent."

"He was definitely a major player," He explained.

"Now that he's gone, whoever takes over his share is going to make a shit pot full of money."

"I've heard a lot of talk about both those organizations from the BBP (Thai Border Police) who we advise up at Lop Buri."

"They keep track of them because they're both big players in the drug business around here, and that makes them big players in several other areas, not the least of which is Thai politics."

"Since we trade information and intelligence regularly with the rest of the agencies in the Thai government, we know a lot about the drug trade in the region."

"And it would be just like the Agency to knock off Pao and try and get control of everything rather than trying to bargain with him," Spencer opined. "That's just their style."

"They'd probably get an "attaboy" from the politicians for getting rid of him, and at the same time, they'd get almost total control of all the opium here in the region."

"That would be a major coup and be worth hundreds of millions of dollars once the opium was refined into heroin."

"With that kind of money at stake, you guys are in some deep shit," Spencer said the more he thought about it.

"Those assholes in the Agency find out you're still alive; they'll come after you with a small army because they'll want the truth buried deep and forever."

"Or they'll send some of the drug people after you."

"Either way, you'll be dead, especially with this much money at stake."

"And this time, they won't fuck around and miss."

"I've dealt with those bastards before," Spencer revealed. "and they don't play by any rules."

"And if Taylor was right about this whole thing being about drugs, and I think he was, they'll kill you without a second thought."

"Here or back in Vietnam."

"It won't matter."

"They got people everywhere, and there's too much money on the line to let you live and possibly expose their operation."

"But I can help," he said with a sly smile. "at least a little."

"Hopefully enough to get you back to Vietnam, where you can at least get back to your units."

"I got a buddy who works at Heavy Hook," Spencer explained.

"That's SOG's western launch site here in Thailand," He said, explaining to Dunaway and Macklin.

"They use it when everything gets weathered in back in South Vietnam, and an RT has to be inserted."

"After I got your call," Spencer explained. "I got my buddy there to send me six SOG ID cards."

"I couldn't get you regular military IDs because they are a controlled item, but the SOG cards are the next best thing."

"At least they'll identify all of you as military and get you on a military aircraft."

"I also brought some jungle fatigues with me; enough for everybody."

"But I can see you don't need them."

"I've got a little money too if you need it." He added.

"It isn't much, but it's all I could scrape together," Spencer said.

"I also typed up some bogus travel orders for all of you on 46 Company letterhead stationery," He said.

"Between them, the uniforms, and the SOG cards, you should be able to hop an Air Force flight back to Saigon with no questions."

"They have two or three flights out of here a day, so that shouldn't be a problem."

"Unfortunately, that's it."

"Sorry, Buddy," he told Breslan. "but that's the best I can do."

"You did fine, Jerry," Breslan said. "That's more than I expected."

"We can get back to Saigon on what you've given us, and that's all we need."

"Once we get there, we can get home easy."

"And you can keep the money," he told a surprised Spencer. "we don't need it."

"We sold some AKs and Charlie's boat, so we're good."

"But after we leave," he warned. "you never heard of us, Jerry."

"Understand."

"There's going to be some heavy duty shit coming down the pike once we get back, and believe me, you don't want to be involved."

"You're going to waste this guy Chambers, right?" Spencer said, guessing correctly.

Breslan nodded.

"Bet your ass we are," he said. "That's the first item on the agenda."

"Figured as much," Spencer said. "The fucker deserves it."

"Here," he said, handing Breslan a box. "this might come in handy."

When Breslan opened the box, it contained a silenced Belgian Browning 9 mm pistol and two full clips.

"Thanks, Jerry," he said. "But won't this get you into trouble?

"Nah," Spencer said with a smile. "I got it from my buddy at Heavy Hook."

"It's sterile and completely untraceable, so I'm covered."

"Shoot the sonofabitch in the kneecaps first," Spencer suggested angrily as he stood up. "that's what he deserves."

"After he hurts enough, then kill him."

"I've dealt with those assholes before too, and they're all alike."

"They'd sell their mother out if they had to."

Then he shook Breslan's hand and left after wishing the team good luck.

The next day, dressed in the tiger stripes and jungle boots Chuy had bought on the black market, the team left the hotel. Armed with their fake travel orders and SOG IDs, they went to the airfield, then caught a ride to the flight line. Three hours later, they were on C-130 hauling supplies to Tan san Nuht AFB outside Saigon, thanks to an obliging pilot. Breslan spun him a bullshit story about the team being an RT returning to SOG from Heavy Hook, and he was glad to help. He didn't even ask for IDs once Breslan showed him everyone's SOG card, and they didn't have to show him the bogus orders either.

An hour and a half after landing, they were back in downtown Saigon at a small seedy hotel just off Tu Do street. The entire episode was an almost surreal experience.

"Well, we're back," Dunaway said after they settled into the hotel rooms. "What now, Breslan?"

"I been thinking about that," Breslan replied.

"First, we put surveillance on Chambers' compound," He ordered. "Find out when he comes and goes and where."

"Once we have his routine down, then we'll figure out how to snatch him or to take him out."

"And afterward?" Dunaway asked.

Breslan blinked in confusion. He had gotten that far yet in his half-assed planning but no farther, and it showed on his face.

"I guess you go back to your Scout Sniper Platoon, and I'll go back to SOG," he finally replied.

"Just like that, huh?" Dunaway asked icily.

"Something wrong with that?" Breslan asked, looking uncomfortable and sort of confused by the question.

"Only about five things that I can think of, right off the top of my head," Dunaway replied.

"Like what, for instance?" Breslan asked.

"Well, for starters, what do you plan to tell your superiors at SOG regarding your sudden reappearance?" Dunaway asked. Especially with Taylor missing.

"You tell them what really happened; they'll go apeshit."

"Secondly, your Captain is dead and his body is still in Laos."

"They'll want to know all about that too, like how, why, where, everything."

"They'll also want to know where his body is and why you had to leave it."

"They'll also want to know who killed him and how it happened."

"Then you'll be forced to tell them about Charlie and the Agency, and, believe me, that'll open up a whole new can of worms."

"The more they find out, the more they'll want to know, so your situation will just get bigger and worse."

"Finally, it'll get so big it will be out of control, and remember, you have no proof of anything."

S it will be just your word, and I don't think that will cut it."

"It certainly won't be enough for SOG to take any legal action against the Agency, even if they edcide to."

"Remember, SOG is classified TOP SECRET, so that will certainly be a decisive factor in what they do."

"If they decide to anything, to begin with."

"Because the last thing the Army needs is a war with the CIA."

"And this incident has all the necessary ingredients to produce one."

"Third, after you kill Chambers, there's going to be a huge investigation," Dunaway continued.

"Remember, he's not just some simple grunt; he's a senior case officer in the CIA."

"So, when he's found dead, and you suddenly show up back at your unit a day or so later, the first person the Agency is going to want to talk to is you?"

"What do you plan to tell them, or have you evenr thought about that?"

"Fourth, we're still attached to the Agency," Dunaway reminded the big NCO.

"So how are you going to explain why you are suddenly back at SOG when you haven't even been released by the CIA yet?"

"Don't you think somebody is going to think that's very strange?"

"Especially when the Agency thinks you're still back in Laos dead?"

"And fifth, how are you going to explain how you got back to Vietnam on your own?" Dunaway concluded.

"And why you had to get back on your own to start with?"

"Theoretically, if you hadn't been killed, the Agency should have gotten you back."

"But instead, you came back without even telling them."

"That's another little item a lot of people are going to be extremely interested in."

"And once again, you don't have a single bit of proof concerning any of this; just your word."

"So, in summary, if you're not very, very careful, Breslan," Dunaway warned. "and you keep going down the road you're on, you're going to wind up in jail for the rest of your life!"

"That is if the Agency doesn't find you and just kill you first."

Breslan thought for a moment; then, his face looked crestfallen.

"Yeah," he finally admitted. "I guess I didn't think things through very well, did I?"

"I don't think you thought about anything at all," Dunaway said angrily.

"I think you just want to kill Chambers so bad you can almost taste it and said fuck everything else."

"And you expected the Agency to just forget all about it afterwards."

"That's about as far as your thinking went."

"Well, Sgt," Dunaway snapped. "that's just not going to happen."

"First, although we may be back in South Vietnam, we are a long way from being safe," Dunaway reminded Breslan.

"Second, this operation is far from being over."

"Third, the CIA is neither stupid nor forgiving."

"And lastly, in case you've forgotten," Dunaway reminded the green beret Sgt. "there are four other people involved in this mess besides you."

"And their future is dependent on what you do next, especially if you kill a senior CIA case officer."

"So, if you want to stay out of jail and stay alive," Dunaway said. "there's a lot of work that has to be done before you can even think about killing anybody, much less going back to SOG."

Breslan remained silent because he knew Dunaway was right.

"Go ahead and put surveillance on Chambers," Dunaway said a moment later. "that's got to be done anyway."

"But let the Nungs handle it."

"This is going to take some time, and they'll be less conspicuous."

"Meanwhile, you and I need to do some thinking and then some planning before we do *anything,*" Dunaway told him.

"We'll get Chambers because it's the moral thing to do," Dunaway promised. "But when we do, we'll do it the right way and at the right time."

"And, we'll have a suitable cover story already in place to cover our asses."

"I don't intend to go to jail or let Private Macklin go to jail over this," Dunaway said. "So, unless you can come up with a better course of action, we'll do things my way from now on."

Breslan looked at Dunaway with new respect. The Marine was smart, and he had just proved it.

"That's fine with me," Breslan finally said. "planning was never my strong suit anyway."

"Good," Dunaway said. "then let's get started."

"You can set up a surveillance schedule for the Nungs, and they can start watching the compound tomorrow morning."

"Meanwhile, I've got some thinking to do."

"Jesus," Buster thought after hearing the entire exchange. "Marty sounded just like Gunnery Sgt Casey."

"He took charge, and he's junior in rank to Breslan."

"That means he's our new leader."

"I'm proud of him."

Chapter Twenty Two
Back in the Nam...Now what?

For the next three days, Dunaway came up with, critically reviewed, and then rejected, several potential cover stories the team could use once they killed Chambers. He also considered a variety of methods regarding how they could do it when they got the chance. But in the end, he didn't like any of them. During that same time, the Nungs watched the compound.

At first, Dunaway tried to get Breslan to help him with the planning. But he quickly concluded that although the SFC was a good soldier, he was not the brightest bulb in the chandelier. His planning ability was sufficient for tactical military operations, but something like this was beyond him. So, Dunaway realized that he would have to create the plan for the cover story himself and then devise the plan to kill Chambers. Otherwise, everybody would wind up dead or in jail.   Ideally, in Dunaway's thought process, the team would still be out of the country when Chambers was killed. Still in Laos or Thailand trying to get back to Vietnam now that their mission was over. That was the perfect cover story and the best option. If they weren't in Vietnam, they couldn't have possibly killed their case officer. At least that was Dunaway's reasoning.

However, now, that was impossible. They were already back in-country. Getting back to Thailand incognito was not a risk Dunaway was not prepared to take.

So that left coming up with a believable story that would make the Agency *think* that they hadn't arrived back in country until *after* Chambers had mysteriously disappeared. Coming up with an idea like that proved to be exceedingly tricky. Finally, after another day of brainstorming, Dunaway had an idea. It was risky, but it was all he could come think of that had a resonable chance of success.

First, the Team would take out Chambers, but not publicly. They would do it very quietly and then hide his body. That done, they would catch a hop to Da Nang, using their SOG IDs, but they would travel separately.

Dunaway didn't want anyone remembering them, and going as a team would make them stand out. So Breslan would go on one flight, Macklin and Dunaway on another. The Nungs would hide in Cholon.

Hopefully, they would all be one of the hundreds of GIs hopping Air Force flights around the county daily, and no one would remember them, especially if they used false names. The Nungs would stay in Saigon and hole up in Cholon while they were gone because they were too conspicuous on an Air Force flight.

Upon arrival in Da Nang Breslan, Dunaway and Macklin would all link back up and then go underground in the bar district. Thanks to Buster's intimate knowledge of the area, Buster already knew a safe place to stay. After four days, they would call the American Embassy in Saigon, telling the Station assets, the Team was now located at Da Nang, having hitched a ride there from Thailand. They would also tell them they were en route to Saigon and had tried to get in touch with their case officer named Chambers.

Of course, Chambers would be unavailable since he would already be dead. But since Saigon Station didn't know that, they would probably pass the Team's message on to the compound. Regardless, it would appear to anyone investigating later that the team hadn't even gotten back in country until *after* Chambers had disappeared.

When Breslan, Dunaway, and Macklin got to Saigon, they would link back up with the Nungs at Tan San Nuht, then call the compound and ask for someone to pick them up. When their Agency transportation arrived, they would all go back to the compound. When asked about Chambers, or his whereabouts, as would undoubtedly happen, they would play dumb. They would also tell the Agency case officers that they had already contacted their units, telling them the mission was over and that they were back in country waiting to be released by the Agency. Hopefully, that would prevent the Agency from trying to eliminate them again.

It was a story that, with any detailed investigation and checking, could probably be easily unraveled. But Dunaway was betting that because of the nature of the mission, with the Agency having knowingly used the Team as expendable throwaways, that wouldn't happen. Especially after trying to have them killed to ensure complete deniability on the mission itself. Because of that, Chambers' superiors would be more than happy to accept Dunaway's story and sweep the entire incident under the rug.

Especially since they didn't know Chambers was dead.

Later, when they found out, Saigon Station certainly wouldn't want any widespread investigation of the case officer's death either. If that happened, there was the possibility of the real story coming out, and that would be a disaster of the first magnitude for them.

At any rate, as he reviewed his plan, Dunaway decided that it was the best he could devise given the circumstances. So, in the absence of anything better, they would have to go with it.

A few days later, Dunaway and Breslan debriefed the Nungs on their surveillance. By then, the Nungs had been watching Chambers for over a week and had a good idea of his daily habits and routines. According to them, Chambers left the compound every day at around noon, went to lunch at either the Rex Hotel or at some other upscale restaurant, then dropped by the American embassy for an hour, probably to check in with Saigon Station proper. Afterwards, he returned to the compound around two-thirty. The only change in that routine had been on a Friday when he had gone to Happy Hour at the

Rex in preparation for taking the weekend off, something he had done twice.

Hearing that, Dunaway had another brainstorm and suddenly changed all his plans. Instead of simply killing Chambers, the team would kidnap him instead, then interrogate him to find out just how far up the chain the conspiracy went. If they could get their hands on that kind of information, Dunaway was sure he could keep the Agency from killing them by threatening to release it. Even better, with it, maybe they wouldn't have to kill Chambers at all!

Accordingly, he planned to snatch Chambers when he left Happy Hour at the Rex that coming Friday. Chambers drove his own car and lived in a private room at a government-run hotel, so that would make things easier. If they timed it right and snatched him early Friday evening, he wouldn't even be missed until the following Monday. That would be more than enough time to implement their cover story.

Dunaway briefed everyone on his new plan, omitting his desire to just squeeze Chambers for all he knew rather than kill him. Llate Friday afternoon found the team concealed and in position at the Rex.

When Chambers arrived, they noted where he parked his car. After Chambers had parked and went inside the hotel for Happy Hour, Macklin unlocked the car door using a coat hanger, and Breslan got in the backseat on the floor. Afterwards, everyone else concealed themselves behind the car next to it and waited.

Two long hours later, after it had gotten dark, Chambers finally came out of the hotel, walked up to the car, unlocked it, and got it. A second later, before he could crank it, Breslan sapped him behind the ear, and he went out like a light, slumping over the steering wheel.

Breslan whistled softly, and the rest of the team came out from behind the other vehicle and up to Chambers' car. A few moments later, Chambers' unconscious and bound body was in the trunk, and the rest of the team were seated in his car and driving out of the parking lot.

An hour later, they were back at their cheap hotel with Chambers duct-taped to a chair in their room and his car parked in the alley behind the hotel.

When Chambers came to and saw Breslan, Dunaway, and the rest of the Team, he went wild-eyed. He struggled with his bonds, but that did no good. Instead, the cold sweat of fear popped out on his face immediately, and his eyes started darting frantically around the room. He had been caught by the men he had ordered killed, and he was terrified.

"What's the matter, Sunshine," Breslan snarled. "surprised to see us still alive?"

Chambers groaned, and he stunk of fear. He was scared right out of his wits.

"Well," Breslan continued. "Taylor didn't make it."

"On your orders, your friend Charlie and his buddies killed him."

"And you're going to pay for that, you bastard."

"But before I finally kill you," Breslan promised. "I'm going to let Lop and Chuy go to work on you with a K-Bar; a nice sharp one."

"They're going to cut about five pounds out of your sorry ass because they liked Taylor and want a piece of you too."

"A few minutes with them, and you'll be screaming like a little girl," Breslan promised, smiling nastily.

"They'll carve nice thin slices out of your sorry ass when they aren't chopping off your fingers and toes."

"And believe me, Sunshine, you'll beg me to kill you just to get them to stop."

Chambers' eyes turned white with fear, and he thrashed hopelessly against his bonds. The thought of being sliced and diced by the two Nungs was terrifying. Sweat gushed uncontrolled off his forehead, and he moaned desperately. But it did no good, especially when he looked at Chuy and Lop, who already had their K-Bars out and were sharpening them as they looked eager to get started.

"Hold up a minute, Breslan," Dunaway said, in the pre-rehearsed routine. "I want to talk to him first."

"Afterwards, you can let Chuy slice and dice his ass."

"Go outside, have a smoke, and cool off a little."

"Revenge is always better when you're cold and calculating anyway."

"Not pissed off like you are now."

"He's not going anywhere, and we have plenty of time."

Breslan appeared to think about the request for a moment and then nodded reluctantly, playing his part perfectly. A moment later, he, Chuy, and Lop left, leaving Dunaway and Macklin alone with Chambers.

"Chambers," Dunaway began. "because I don't want to chance going to jail for your murder, I'm going to give you one chance to live, and only one."

"So, you better not fuck it up."

"Answer my questions, and I'll keep Breslan off you," Dunaway promised. "Afterwards, I'll get you out of here, and the courts can take care of your sorry ass."

"Lie to me, even once, or refuse to answer my questions," Dunaway snarled. "and you're dog meat."

"Chuy wants to slice up your ass so bad he can practically taste it."

"He and Taylor were good friends, and he knows you ordered him killed, so he wants a piece of you badly."

Chambers's head nodded up and down rapidly, clearly indicating he was willing to do anything to keep the two Nungs off him. He was terrified of getting cut, and Dunaway had just offered him a way out. There was no way he wasn't going to take it. Macklin took the duct tape off his mouth.

"Taylor figured out most of it before he died," Dunaway told Chambers before he could speak.

"I just want you to fill in the blanks, Chambers."

"The whole thing was about drugs, right?"

"Yes," Chambers moaned, realizing there was no sense in lying now. "The Agency wanted Pao eliminated so we could take over his territory."

"And put your asset in his place, right?" Dunaway added quickly.

"How did you know that?" Chambers asked in surprise.

"We're not stupid, Chambers," Dunaway said. "and like I've already told you, Taylor figured out everything and told us before he died."

Chambers face fell.

"They don't know everything." he thought *a moment later as his emotions subsided. "But do I want to risk getting my ass carved up to protect the others?"*

"Maybe I can bullshit just a little and get away with it." He told himself.

"Who ordered us killed?" Dunaway asked.

"I don't know for sure," Chambers mumbled, trying his first lie. "the orders just came down to me as a part of the mission statement from Saigon Station."

"I don't even know who sent them."

"I warned you not to lie," Dunaway said disgustedly, getting up.

"Macklin, call Chuy and Lop back in and make sure they bring their K-Bars."

"Apparently, this asshole doesn't believe me."

"Wait," Chambers screamed as Macklin stood up, suddenly changing his mind.

"It was Patterson, Donald Patterson."

"He's the Chief of Operations in Saigon Station."

"What does he look like?" Dunaway asked.

"He's fat," Chambers replied. "really fat."

"And he's short, maybe five foot six or seven, with brown eyes and balding."

"He looks like a bowling ball with arms and legs," Chambers said.

"He runs things here in Saigon as far as the drug operation goes."

"He's the one Breslan and the Nungs want," Chambers wailed. "Not me."

"I just passed on his orders."

"It wasn't anything personal."

"He's the one who ordered you all killed," The case officer said as tears rolled down his cheeks.

"I just briefed you on the mission."

"Please," he pleaded.

"How far up the chain does all this go?" Dunaway asked.

"Pretty far," Chambers wailed. "all the way back to Langley, I think."

"And the Agency is still controlling the KMT Division in Burma that controls nearly all the drug trade up in the Golden Triangle?"

"Yes," Chambers confirmed. "we have been for years."

"What happens now that Pao is dead?" Dunaway asked.

"With Pao gone," Chambers explained. "we will control the vast majority of the opium trade in Southeast Asia."

"That was Patterson's plan."

"That's why he sent you to kill Pao," Chambers wailed.

"Tell us how the set-up works and who else is involved," Dunaway ordered.

"And don't try lying to me again, asshole."

"You do, and that's it."

I'll feed to Chuy and LOP and you'll die screaming."

Crying and moaning, Chambers started talking, really talking. Names, plans, places, everything, and once he did, the words came out in a gusher. He told Dunaway everything he knew. When he finally finished, the strain was too much for him, and he started sobbing uncontrollably.

Dunaway nodded, and Macklin put the tape back over Chambers' mouth.

"Did you get it all?" he asked Macklin.

"Every word," Buster said with a smile as he held up a miniature cassette recorder.

Chambers' eyes widened, and he moaned, low and guttural when he saw it. He knew then he was finished. His own words had probably killed him. With the tape, even his own people would kill him now, just to keep him quiet.

A few minutes later, Dunaway played the tape for Breslan and the rest of the Team. When he finished, he said.

"Now we know who ordered us killed."

"And we also know the names of the rest of the CIA assholes involved in this entire operation."

"This is our ticket out of this mess," He said, smiling.

"We don't have to kill anybody."

"We're home free."

"I don't give a shit about any of that," Breslan snarled unexpectedly. "I want this asshole Patterson dead, then afterward, Chambers too."

"He was the guy who ordered Taylor killed, so he pays with his life."

"Now, are you going to help me take him out?" Breslan asked. "Or will I have to do that myself?"

Dunaway thought for a moment.

"Why not," he said desperately, trying to buy some time. "in for a penny, in for a pound."

It was evident that Breslan was over the edge now. He was ready to do anything to kill Patterson. In his state of mind, he would screw up everything and everybody around him in the process. As a result, they'd all wind up going to prison. Still, with a last glimmer of curiosity and maybe a plea for help, he asked Dunaway.

"Okay, smart guy,"

"How?"

"We'll never get near the sonofabitch in the Embassy," He said. "That place is guarded like Fort Knox."

Dunaway thought for a moment, realizing that whatever he came up with had better be good and sound believable. Otherwise, Breslan would almost certainly go after Patterson the next day without even a plan, and that would be disastrous!

"Buster," Dunaway ordered. "Go back to the other room and ask Chambers where Patterson lives."

Buster nodded and left.

It turned out that Patterson lived in the same government leased hotel that Chambers did. It was located near the embassy in downtown Saigon. But because Patterson was a big shot in the Agency, he had a penthouse on the top floor, not just some normal room in the building. That gave Dunaway an idea, which he partially explained to Breslan. Fortunately, Breslan was still sane enough to listen to him. Dunaway's concept had a much better expectation of success than his plan did, so he reluctantly agreed to wait before he acted.

The following day, Buster left the hotel with Lop and Chuy with specific instructions from

Dunaway. Two hours later, they found the spot they were looking for. Meanwhile, Breslan had slipped a little further into the abyss of rage and insanity and was almost foaming at the mouth in his newfound urge to kill. So much so that Dunaway was having a hell of a time trying to maintain control of him and keep him from doing something idiotic.

Chapter Twenty Three
A Plan and Another Disaster

"You know when we kill this asshole, Patterson," Dunaway said to Breslan, trying desperately to reason with the big NCO. "the shit is going to hit the fan."

He was trying to talk Breslan out of trying to kill Patterson that very day, but it wasn't working. Breslan was nearly gone by that time, almost salivating at the prospect, and no amount of logical explanations by Dunaway, or anyone else, was going to change his mind. He wanted blood, and that was it. Nothing else would satisfy him, and that was obvious.

"Killing Chambers is one thing," Dunaway said, trying to explain the situation logically to Breslan one last time. "killing the Director of Operations for Saigon Station will be something totally different."

"Patterson is the number two man in the Agency in South Vietnam, for Christ Sake," Dunaway pleaded.

"So, killing him will generate a shitstorm of almost biblical proportions."

"One so big, we will probably not be able to survive it, no matter how careful we are, how tight our cover story is, or how well we plan the hit."

"Don't you see that?" he begged.

"I don't care," Breslan said, unfazed and barely rational anymore, the hate almost visibly leaping out of him.

"He deserves to die," he said, repeating what he had said earlier.

"He's the one that gave the orders that got Taylor killed, so he dies for that."

"I realize that, and I agree with you," Dunaway said, still hoping for some miracle.

"I was just letting you know upfront that killing him opens up an entirely different can of worms for everybody on the team, not just you."

"I told you I don't give a shit anymore, Dunaway," Breslan said irrationally. "He still dies."

"I'll kill him myself if I have to; Chambers too."

"Somebody is gonna pay for Jim's death," Breslan said, his eyes gleaming with hatred. "and I'm tired of waiting."

"And as far as I'm concerned, that means Patterson, Chambers, and anybody else in the Agency that was involved that I can get my hands on."

"I'll kill every fucking one of the bastards if I can find out who they are," Breslan threatened wildly.

"And if I can't, after I do Patterson and Chambers, I'll just go back to the compound and kill everybody there," Breslan promised insanely. "They were all in it anyway."

"Take it easy, Breslan," Dunaway said, eyeing the big NCO carefully. "Cool off a little."

"We'll get Patterson. I promise you that. Just let me think."

"Well, you better hurry it up," Breslan retorted. "As I said, I'm tired of waiting."

"We already know who to kill, so let's get on with it!" he demanded angrily.

"All right, all right," Dunaway finally said reluctantly. "we'll do Patterson tonight."

"But it will be better if Macklin and I do it," he told Breslan. "at least we have a chance of getting away with it."

"We let you try; we'll all wind up dead or in jail."

"At least we have a workable plan."

Breslan just glared at Dunaway sullenly. Dunaway didn't know whether he had convinced him or not.

"What is it?" Breslan finally asked.

When Dunaway told him, Breslan had just enough sanity left to realize that Dunaway's plan would work. So, he promised to wait until they made the hit. Then he planned to kill chambers. That would satisfy his desire for his pound of flesh. At least that's what he told himself.

That evening, Dunaway and Macklin went to the hotel Macklin, and Chuy had reconned earlier. They took the elevator to the top floor, then found a door that led to the roof. It was locked, but using a small piece of plastic, Macklin slipped the lock.

"Where did you learn how to break into shit?" Dunaway asked when they were on the roof. "First Chambers' car, now the door."

"You're a regular burglar."

Buster smiled.

"Product of a misspent youth," he grunted.

A few minutes later, using the spotting scope, Dunaway zoomed in on Patterson's penthouse apartment that was several hundred yards away, across several lower rooftops, but in a different building. Macklin and Chuy had deliberately selected the rooftop he and Dunaway were now on because it offered a clear and unobstructed view of Patterson's penthouse. That's where they had been earlier in the afternoon, checking possible shooting sites in the buildings surrounding Patterson's apartment. This one had been perfect.

Patterson's penthouse had a large sliding glass door that opened onto a terrace and balcony. Dunaway could see the entire living room since the drapes had been opened. Since the lights were on in the apartment, the view was perfect. Unfortunately, after a few minutes of careful observation, Dunaway confirmed to Macklin that Patterson was not home. With that, both men settled down to wait.

During the wait, Macklin suddenly realized that this was the first time another American would be his target. Every other man he had killed had been an NVA soldier, so their deaths had never bothered him. He was in a war, they were the enemy, and that was what he had been trained to do. But with Patterson, it was different. Even though he had been the person who had ordered the members of the Team killed, he was still a fellow American; because of that, Buster's conscience started to bother him. But he didn't let on to Dunaway.

Buster realized that trying to simply contain Breslan while attempting to find a way out of the mess they were in was already weighing heavily on his partner's mind, so he didn't need any additional stress.

"It's my problem," he told himself." and I'll deal with it.

"Still, I have some genuine concerns about what I'm about to do."

Earlier, Dunaway had convinced Breslan that he and Macklin would take Patterson with the Sako. At the same time, Breslan woul mind Chambers until they returned. Afterwards, Breslan could have Chambers to himself. That plan seemed to placate the big NCO, but just barely. He was on the very edge of rational thought now, and it was evident that more and more of his sanity was slipping away by the hour.

"You know, Buster," Dunaway said while they waited. "before this whole thing is over, we may wind up getting killed or going to jail."

"Breslan is a time bomb just waiting to go off."

"I don't even think he's quite right in the head anymore; he wants revenge so badly."

"So, there's no telling what he might do before this is over."

"I picked up on that last night too," Buster said. "and again, this morning."

"So did Lop and Chuy."

"They even asked me what was going to happen."

"I told them just to hang loose and keep an eye on Breslan," Buster explained. "To ensure he didn't do anything stupid while we were taking Patterson out."

"Why didn't you tell me about that?" Dunaway asked in alarm.

"You already had enough on your mind., Macklin replied. "So, I handled it myself."

"It was no big deal."

Dunaway looked at Buster quietly.

"He's grown up since we left the Platoon," Dunaway thought as he gazed at his partner.

"This mission has done it."

"He's changed."

"He isn't that wild teenager he was before; he's become a man."

"We got movement in the apartment," Macklin said a moment later, breaking into Dunaway's thoughts.

"A fat guy just came into the apartment with another guy," He reported as he gazed through his scope.

"From what Chambers said, I think the fat one is Patterson."

Dunaway put his eye to the spotting scope and focused on the apartment.

"Yeah," he confirmed after a moment. "the fat guy fits Chambers' description."

"You sure you want to do this, Buster?" Dunaway asked one last time.

"We can still change our minds," He said, pleading. "It's not too late."

"It will have to be two shots," Buster replied, ignoring Dunaway's question.

"The first one to break the glass, the second one to take out Patterson."

"That's the only sure way."

"Well," Dunaway thought. *"I guess that answers my question."*

"What about the second guy?" Buster asked a moment later. "Do I take him out too?"

Dunaway looked at the second man through his spotting scope and debated for a moment. If the second guy was Agency, then he didn't have any qualms about letting Buster kill him.

"Why not," he thought to himself irrationally. "they can only send us to the electric chair once."

"What's another life in this entire fucking mess anyway?"

"Hell, we're already guilty of kidnapping, and we're about to commit premeditated murder, so what does another life matter?"

"They can only hang us once."

"But what if he isn't Agency?" he thought a moment later.

"What if he is just a friend of Patterson that isn't even in the CIA?"

"There's no way to be sure," He finally decided.

"Let him be," he told Buster. "He may just be an innocent bystander."

"We don't know for sure, so we won't take the chance."

"Christ, we're not coldblooded murderers," he said, trying to rationalize what he and Buster were about to do. "Not really."

"Bullshit," Buster thought to himself. *"If what I'm about to do to Patterson isn't murder, then I don't know what is."*

"But if it helps Marty to get through this, then he can call it whatever he chooses to justify it to himself."

"He's right on the edge of losing it himself right now with all this stress."

"You're the Boss," Macklin said with a shrug a moment later, bringing up the Sako to a firing position and chambering the first round.

"Anytime you're ready," Dunaway said in a choked, almost hesitant voice. "you can fire."

"Here goes the rest of my life." He thought sickly. *"Right down the fucking tube!"*

"I'm going to wait till Patterson gets closer to the sliding glass door," Buster said.

"That way, I can get two off immediately."

Dunaway nodded absently, gazing at the apartment. He was sickened at what was about to happen, but at the same time, he knew he wouldn't stop it. One part of his brain screamed at him to stop this madness before it was too late. Still, the other part told him that Paterson had coldly ordered him and Buster killed, so he deserved what he was about to get.

Meanwhile, Buster was utterly relaxed. He got a good spot weld and acquired a good sight picture, the crosshairs centering up on Patterson's head as it loomed up in the scope. Then he shallowed out his breathing and started to take up the slack in the trigger. All thoughts of right and wrong, good and evil, and everything else were suddenly gone. Now he was focused entirely on the shot. In the next few seconds Patterson would be a dead man.

Suddenly, however, Patterson moved away from the window without any warning and headed back towards the apartment door. Buster frowned, losing his sight picture, then took his finger off the trigger and waited.

"What the fuck is going on?" he wondered. "Where's that fat little shit going?"

A moment later, with Buster still watching, Patterson walked across the room to the front door and opened it. What happened next was not only completely unexpected, it was astonishing

Dunaway gasped as Breslan came barging through the door with the silenced nine-millimeter in his hand. Rage was written all over his face, and he was highly agitated. He started screaming at Patterson. Although neither

Dunaway nor Macklin could hear the words, they both had a good idea of what Breslan was saying. The look on Patterson's face was one of sheer terror a moment later when Breslan shot him in the stomach. Patterson clutched his fat belly and fell to the floor writhing in pain and his legs kicking spastically.

Suddenly, the other man in the apartment, who Breslan had not seen, jerked a pistol out and fired at Breslan, hitting him at least twice. Breslan staggered, raised the nine-millimeter, fired back, shot the second man in the head, and killed him instantly. His brains splattered against the apartment wall, staining it red, with his blood slowly dripping down the wallpaper. A second later, his body fell to the floor lifeless, and his automatic skittered across the rug as it dropped from his dead hand.

Afterwards, Breslan turned and emptied the magazine into Patterson's head blowing it to pieces and splattering blood, bone, and brain matter everywhere. Suddenly, the big green beret staggered slightly, and then he too collapsed on the floor. In the process, his body went completely limp, the silenced nine-millimeter sliding from his hand and blood seeping out of the two holes in his chest, staining the carpet, and collecting in a dark red pool beside his fallen body.

"Jesus H Christ," Buster exclaimed in shock. "Did you see all that, Marty?"

"Yeah," Dunaway said, wholly numbed. "I did, and I don't fucking believe it!"

"That crazy sonofabitch Breslan finally lost it, I guess."

Buster remained glued to his scope, still staring at Breslan's lifeless body.

Minutes later, two other men came rushing into the apartment, drawn by the shots. One ran out a few seconds later while the other checked all three bodies on the floor. Less than five minutes later, there were the sounds of sirens wailing from the street. Shortly after that, the apartment was filled with MPs, followed moments later by medical personnel.

A few minutes later, Breslan, Patterson, and the third man's bodies were covered with sheets and taken down to the ambulances. It was apparent all three men were dead. The ambulances left silently a few minutes later.

It took well over an hour, but finally, the crowd in the apartment thinned out, and everyone eventually left. All that remained were three dark splotches on the wall-to-wall carpet, and the stain on the wallpaper, and even they disappeared when the lights were finally turned out by the last person to leave. Macklin and Dunaway witnessed the entire incident through their scopes without a word being spoken. They were still in shock by what had happened.

"Break the Sako down and let's get back to the hotel," Dunaway finally said.

Buster complied wordlessly, while Dunaway sacked up the spotting scope; the recent events numbing both men. An hour later, they were back at their hotel.

When they entered the hotel room, Dunaway knew right away something was wrong. Lop and Chuy were both extremely agitated and excited. Then he saw the corpse.

"Shit," Macklin said, looking at Chambers's body folded over and still taped to the chair. "I should have guessed."

"Breslen did Chambers before he left for Patterson's."

"He finally went completely fucking nuts."

The air in the apartment was foul, and blood stained the cheap linoleum floor under the chair.

"Breslan, go crazy and shoot CIA man," Chuy said excitedly, pointing at Chambers corpse still taped to the chair. "We no can stop him."

"He wild man and go crazy."

"Scream and curse, then shoot Chambers."

"Then he run away."

"He is crazy, man," Chuy continued. "We wait for him, but he no come back."

"We not know what to do after he leave, so we wait for you, Dunaway san."

"What we do now?"

Dunaway thought for a moment.

"Cut Chambers loose and wrap his body in the plastic shower curtain," Dunaway ordered, thinking quickly.

"Tape it up good so it won't leak blood."

"Afterwards, we'll take it out the hotel's back door and put it in the trunk of his car."

"Later, after we've cleaned this place up, we'll drop the car off somewhere downtown and leave the keys in it."

"Somebody will undoubtedly steal in less than ten minutes," He explained.

"Then they can deal with his body when they find it."

"Meanwhile, let's get this room cleaned up," He ordered. "And I mean, I want it spotless."

"Like we've never been here."

"Afterwards, we'll all get the hell out of here and drop the car and Chamber's body off."

"What about Breslan?" Lop asked. "We wait for him?"

"He won't be coming back," Dunaway said flatly. "He's dead."

Lop and Chuy just stared at him open-mouthed as Dunaway explained what had happened at Patterson's apartment. After hearing the story, neither Lop nor Chuy acted surprised.

"I tell you before; I think Breslan go crazy," Chuy told Macklin sadly.

"He very sad Dai Uy Taylor gets killed, and he wants to kill all CIA men for that."

"What we do now?" He asked a moment later.

"CIA be very angry now, so they will look for us in a big way."

"If they find us, they kill us all for sure."

"I very afraid now," He continued.

"I not know what to do."

"Everything big fuck up now for Lop and me."

"We'll all have to disappear," Dunaway told Lop and Chuy after a moment's thought. "Permanently."

"That means that neither you nor Lop can go back to SOG," Dunaway explained. "Ever."

"All that's finished for you two," He warned. "Understand?"

"You go back to SOG, the CIA will find you, and they will kill you," Dunaway explained.

"Breslan killed their Big Boss here in Saigon tonight, right after he left here."

"Macklin and I saw the whole thing."

"Now that Patterson is dead, and Breslan did it, they'll start looking for the rest of us."

"They find out you two are still alive; they'll kill you for sure."

"But only after they torture you to find out what you know," He explained.

"You understand?"

Chuy nodded, fear written all over his brown face.

"We understand," he said. "We finished in SOG for good."

"Finished working for all Americans for good, too."

"Breslan fuck up everything for us."

"So, we go back to Cholon and family and change names."

"We have many relatives there, and they help us and hide us."

"We be all right."

"Nobody ever finds us again."

Dunaway smiled.

"Here," he said, handing Chuy what was left of the money they had accumulated getting back in country, about three thousand dollars.

"Take this with you; you both earned it."

Chuy looked down at the money and then back at Dunaway as tears formed in his eyes.

"Thank you, Dunaway," Chuy said. "You and Macklin are good friends."

"You must go and hide too," he warned unnecessarily. "If CIA finds you, they kill you too."

"You can come with Lop and me if you want," He offered. "We will hide you and take care of you until you can leave this country."

Dunaway nodded.

"Thanks for the offer Chuy," he said. "But we'll go our own way."

"Don't worry about us; we'll be fine," He assured his friend.

Chuy nodded, smiling.

"Now, let's get this room cleaned up and wiped down," Dunaway ordered.

"I don't want there to be a trace of any of us ever having been here."

"No fingerprints, no blood stains, no garbage, nothing."

"The same goes for Chambers' car," He added.

An hour later, the room had been cleaned up, and all traces of their presence had been erased. Chambers' car had also been wiped clean of prints and left near the waterfront, with Chambers' body in the trunk, minus the shower curtain, and the keys still in the ignition. Chuy and Lop had dropped it off and then departed for Cholon.

Since Chuy had rented the room and the desk clerk or staff had never seen either Breslan, Macklin, or Dunaway, there was no worry on that score. And since Chuy was a Nung with over a million of them in Cholon, there was no worry there either.

When the car had been disposed of, Macklin and Dunaway shook hands with both Nungs and wished them good luck before they departed. Afterwards, they left the hotel by the back door without being seen and caught a pedicab to the airbase. Now they were at the Tan San Nuht terminal, once again dressed in Army fatigues and waiting for a hop to Da Nang. Everything else except the Sako's had been dumped. Macklin had refused to part with them.

"The Agency owes us," he told Dunaway. "So, I'm keeping these as payment."

"I'm taking mine home as a war trophy," He explained. "Yours too if you don't want it."

Dunaway didn't have the strength to argue with him.

"Think Lop and Chuy will be okay?" Macklin asked later as both men sat outside the terminal in the sultry night air.

"They'll be fine," Dunaway replied. "They aren't stupid, and they know what to do."

"Once they get to Cholon, they'll disappear."

"Chuy told me over a million Nungs are living there, so they'll just be another two Chinese in a sea of many."

"Once they change their names, the Agency will never find them."

"What about us?" Macklin asked.

"That's an entirely different matter," Dunaway said. "And before you ask, I don't have a goddamn clue as to what to do about it."

"What *are* we going to do when we get back?" Buster asked, ignoring Dunaway's previous statement.

"I don't know," Dunaway said. "All I know is that we can't stay here. Not now."

"When the CIA puts everything together," he explained. "And that won't take very long once they identify Breslan's body; they will start turning this entire city upside down looking for the rest of the team."

"When that happens, we have to be long gone."

"Other than that, I'm fresh out of ideas."

Buster nodded in agreement.

"This whole thing has turned into a first-class disaster," Dunaway moaned, shaking his head a moment later.

"Everything I planned for is now completely useless because of what Breslan did."

"We can't even use the cover story I took so much time dreaming up because it's completely useless now."

"With Breslan dead in Patterson's apartment, the CIA is going to know that at least some of the team survived," He said. "So, they are going to come looking for the rest of us, especially when they find Chambers missing too."

"It won't take them long to figure out we're probably responsible for that too."

"I just hope they don't start a full-blown search for us until tomorrow," Dunaway said. "Hopefully, we'll be out of here by then."

"But even when we get back to Da Nang, we'll have to be goddamned careful."

"They'll undoubtedly be looking for us there too."

"We're Marines, that's our home base, and they know that," Dunaway said. "So, they'll have people watching for us."

"Hell, they've probably already sent people to the Platoon looking for us."

"If all that's true, Buster," Dunaway said in exasperation. "then I don't know *what* we should do after we get back."

"All I know is that Da Nang is home to us over here, so that's where we're headed."

"At least we know the town."

"We don't Saigon for shit, especially now that Breslan and the Nungs are gone."

"What do *you* think we should do when we return to Da Nang, Buster?" Dunaway asked a moment later.

"So far, all my planning has done is get us into more trouble."

"So maybe you should figure out our next move."

"You mean that?" Macklin asked.

Dunaway nodded.

Buster thought for a moment.

"Well," he said thoughtfuly. "first off, we didn't kill anybody in the CIA; Breslan did."

"All we did was complete the mission they assigned to us, and for doing that, the CIA tried to have us killed."

"We may have helped Breslan kidnap Chambers," Buster continued. "but now that both of them are dead, nobody else but Chuy and Lop know that."

"And they sure as hell aren't going to tell anybody because they were involved too.

"So, the way I figure it," Buster explained. "Breslan is probably going to be blamed for everything."

"Nobody has any proof that anyone else was even involved."

"The CIA may have suspicions, but they still have no proof, and we've covered our tracks pretty well since we left Laos."

"That being the case, we don't have any reason to hide from anybody," He concluded.

"We keep our mouths shut; the CIA can't prove shit."

"You know," Dunaway thought to himself in amazement. "Buster's right."

"We haven't done anything the CIA can prove."

"And they probably will blame everything on Breslan."

"Especially since they'll want to cover up this entire mess before it becomes front-page news."

"They sure as hell won't want any details of the mission revealed, and that might very well happen if they start a full-blown investigation."

"Buster's pretty goddamned smart for a Tennessee hillbilly," He thought with a smile.

"But that doesn't mean we're off the hook," Buster continued. "The Agency may still try and kill us anyway, just to shut us up and ensure everything stays buried."

"So, in case they're thinking about doing that," Buster concluded. "I think we ought to tell Gunny Casey the entire story and see what he thinks we should do."

"If anybody can figure a way out of this mess, he can," Buster said confidently.

Dunaway thought about Buster's suggestion for a moment.

"You know, Buster," he finally said. "That's not a bad idea."

Chapter Twenty Four
The Gunny takes charge.

It took another nine hours for Dunaway and Macklin to finally catch a ride back to Da Nang. They had to change planes twice to do it. That was the scary part. Dunaway kept waiting for either the CIA or the MPs to come bursting into a terminal looking for them while they were waiting, but luckily, that didn't happen. They finally boarded a C-130 with about twenty other soldiers early the following day. They were back at the Da Nang airfield before noon.

"I've been thinking," Dunaway told Macklin as they walked towards the terminal.

"I think that instead of just going straight back to the Platoon, maybe we should call Gunny Casey first and meet him somewhere."

"Then we can tell him the whole story."

"For all we know," he explained." The CIA may already be at the Platoon waiting for us."

"And if they are, they damned sure aren't going to let us say shit to anybody before they police us up, especially the Gunny."

"They'll just going to haul our asses out of there as fast as they can, and nobody will ever see us again."

Buster agreed. So, using a phone at the airfield, Dunaway called the Platoon.

"Scout Sniper Platoon," the clerk answered. "Private Henry speaking, Sir."

"This is Major Spears at Division Headquarters," Dunaway said, muffling his voice. "Let me speak to Gunnery Sgt Casey."

"Just a moment, Sir," Henry said.

"Gunnery Sgt Casey, " the Gunny said a moment later as he came on the line. "What can I do for you, Sir?"

"Gunny," Dunaway said quietly. "it's me, Corporal Dunaway."

There was silence on the line for a moment.

"Who the fuck is this?" the Gunny roared. "I ain't in no mood for any sick fuckin' jokes."

"Especially about some of my people that are dead."

"It's me, Gunny," Dunaway said desperately. "Corporal Martin Dunaway. Honest."

"The half-assed NCO in charge of Private Roan Macklin, the teenaged Platoon fuck up; Mutt and Jeff."

There was a silence, and Dunaway could hear himself breathing into the phone. Finally, Gunny found his voice.

"Jesus H Christ," Casey said, expelling breath in complete surprise. "It really is you."

"The fucking CIA told us you and Macklin were both dead," Casey said a moment later. "Told us that a week ago, the lying bastards."

"Said the entire team got killed in Laos, and they were unable to recover the bodies."

"Christ," Gunny moaned. "we've even notified your parents."

"Where's Macklin?" he asked quickly. "Is he alive too?"

"He's with me, Gunny," Dunaway said. "He's fine."

"But we got big fucking problems."

"Can we meet you somewhere and talk?"

"Where are you, now?" Casey asked.

"At the Da Nang Airfield," Dunaway replied. "I'm calling you from the terminal."

"Stay right there," Casey ordered. "and keep out of sight."

"The fucking CIA has already been here earlier this morning nosing around and asking stupid questions, so they know you're alive too."

"If they do, they'll want to talk to you and Macklin in a big way, the lying pricks."

"But not before I find out what the hell is going on," Casey said heatedly.

"I'll be at the airfield in twenty minutes," He promised.

He then hung up without another word.

When Dunaway put the phone down, he wondered.

"Was the Gunny just acting, or was he shocked?" He asked himself.

"And even if he was really on the level, would he risk his entire career for two people who were known fuck ups in his eyes?"

"Especially if the CIA threatened him and his career if he did?"

"What did the Gunny say?" Macklin asked after Dunaway hung up.

"The CIA told him we were dead," Dunaway said.

"Until I called, he thought we were."

"He said he'd pick us up here in twenty minutes ,and we'd better be prepared to explain things."

"Relax, Marty," Dunaway said, sensing Dunaway's uneasiness. "Gunny Casey won't let us down."

"He takes care of his people, no matter what."

"That's what Gunnies do."

"He'll get this whole mess sorted out," Buster said confidently. "Wait and see."

"He'll take care of everything."

"I sure as hell hope you're right, Buster," Dunaway replied. "If you're wrong and he doesn't, we are well and truly fucked."

Twenty minutes later, Gunnery Sgt Casey pulled up in a jeep. Looking around, he finally spied Dunaway and Macklin by the corner of the building and waved them over to the jeep.

"Get in, you two," he ordered sternly.

When Macklin and Dunaway were in the Jeep, the Gunny drove off, but not in the direction of the Platoon, Dunaway noted nervously. A few minutes later, he pulled in behind some warehouses near the airfield where the Jeep was out of sight and stopped.

"First, the CIA tells the Skipper and me that you two are dead," He began. "killed in the mission you were on."

"Then yesterday some CIA clown shows up at the Platoon asking questions about you two."

"Now you call, and it turns out you're both still alive."

"What the fuck is going on?" he asked hotly.

"It's a long story, Gunny," Dunaway said.

"I'm listening," Casey said. "Start at the beginning and tell me everything."

"Don't leave out a single detail, and don't bullshit me."

"I can't wait to hear this," He said disgustedly. "It ought to be some fucking fairy tale."

It took almost an hour of explanations before Casey had the entire story. He listened patiently as both Dunaway and Macklin explained precisely what had happened since the day they had left the Platoon. Finally, both men finished talking.

"Jesus," Casey said as he shook his head in disgust. "When you two get into trouble, you don't fuck around, do you?"

"This story ranks right up there with the Kennedy assassination."

"It has more twists than a fucking pretzel."

"No wonder that guy from the CIA was at the Platoon yesterday," He said almost to himself.

"Shit, I'll bet those assholes have got a countrywide alert out for you two right now," He opined. "especially after this Breslan character knocked over their number two man in the country."

"What a fucking screwed up abortion," He said, his exasperation evident.

"And now that you two are in shit up to your fucking eyeballs," he concluded in disgust. "you come to me, wanting Daddy to fix everything, right?"

Dunaway's heart sank.

"I don't suppose you have a single ounce of proof about any of this?" Casey asked in disgust. "Just your word."

Macklin switched on the cassette recorder with Chambers' confession on it.

"Just this, Gunny," He said.

After the tape finished, Casey smiled.

"That will do nicely, Private Macklin," he said, taking the tape player.

"You seemed to have grown some since you left and gotten a little smarter in the process."

"So at least one good thing has come out of this goat fuck."

"With this," Casey said, holding up the tape player. "I think I can safely take over from here."

"This is not the first time I have had to deal with complete assholes, so I am fairly certain I can deal with the CIA."

"Glad to have you, two men, back," The Gunny then said unexpectedly. "After hearing your story, I want to say that you two did a fine job, and I'm proud of you."

"The Skipper will be too when I tell him what happened."

"You accomplished your mission, and you did it like Marines."

"We couldn't have asked for more."

"Under the circumstances, no one could have done any better," He exclaimed happily.

"Now, let's get you back to the Platoon, changed into the proper uniform, and fed."

Dunaway could hardly believe what he was hearing. Buster had been right. The Gunny was going to take care of things.

"I'll take charge of everything from here on," Casey told both men as they drove back to the Platoon HQ.

"You two just keep out of sight until I tell you differently."

"Keep your mouths shut and let me handle everything," He ordered.

Macklin smiled.

"I told you the Gunny would take care of us," he told Dunaway quietly.

"Thank God you were right," Dunaway thought.

The next day two civilians showed up at the Platoon asking for Macklin and Dunaway again. Although they didn't show any IDs, it was apparent they were CIA. Their cute little safari suits gave them away immediately, plus they had asshole written all over themselves. The clerk showed them into Gunnery Sgt Casey's office.

"I understand you want to see two of my Marines," Casey said with a tight smile that had all the warmth of an arctic summer.

"That's right, Sgt," the older man said. "In fact, we're here to take them back to Saigon with us."

"We're not finished with them yet."

"Oh yes, you are," Casey said flatly, in a no-nonsense voice.

"I beg your pardon, Sgt," the CIA officer said, taken aback.

"Macklin and Dunaway still work for us."

"We haven't released them yet."

"Oh yes, you have," Casey said menacingly.

The CIA agent started to say something, but the flash of anger in Casey's eyes warned him to shut up instead.

"Corporal Dunaway and Private Macklin have done everything the CIA asked them to do," Casey said angrily.

"They completed a difficult and dangerous mission superbly."

"And as thanks for all their efforts," Casey said in a low menacing voice. "the fucking CIA decided to eliminate them."

"Oh shit," the agent thought when he heard that. *"he knows everything."*

"But they failed," Casey continued.

"The number two man in Saigon, some clown named Patterson, ordered the murder of a serving officer in the United States Army as part of that mission and also planned to eliminate the rest of the team as well, including my two Marines," Casey continued.

"I'm sad to say that that officer was killed as a result."

"Afterwards," Casey continued. "when the CIA tried to have my two men killed in Laos, they came back here to their unit on their own."

"They had to," Casey thundered. "because the sorry fuck ups in your organization left them to die in Laos."

"That's preposterous." The CIA agent said in mock anger. "Who told you those lies."

"Macklin and Dunaway did," Casey said. "and they don't lie."

"Unlike you and the assholes you work for, they know what honor is, so they don't have to."

"And their story was corroborated by the confession of their case officer on the mission; another asshole named Chambers."

"I have it all on tape," Casey said, holding up the recorder Macklin had given him. "and it's very informative."

"Chambers confesses that your man Patterson ordered the murders, and they were to cover up the Agency's involvement in the drug business in Laos."

"He goes into great detail about how everything in your slimy little drug empire works, who is involved, and why the mission was ordered to begin with."

"He says your fucked-up organization used my men to take out your primary competitor in the drug business in Laos," Casey said, now really furious "The one cutting into your opium profits."

"Some fucking zipper head name Pao."

"Later, after my men had done your dirty work," Casey said sneering. "you tried to have them killed to hush the entire affair up and ensure no one found out about your involvement in the drug trade."

"But they survived instead and made their way back here."

"Now you want to finish the job to keep the entire affair stays quiet."

"But that's not going to happen, Sunshine," Casey said angrily.

The agent glared at Casey, who gave him a dirty look.

"I don't have the words to describe just how slimy you and your organization are," Casey told the case officer menacingly. "Or to what degree of contempt I hold both you and them."

"Everything you've said is complete hearsay." the agent said. "You don't have one ounce of proof."

"I've got your man Chambers' entire confession here on tape," the Gunny roared as he switched on the tape player. "Is that good enough?"

As the tape played, the faces of the CIA agents fell, and they had no retort. Chambers' confession was damning, and he named names up the chain, and all the way to Langley. If that tape were to become public, a national level disaster would follow, heads would roll in the entire CIA, and they both knew it! More importantly, their names would be first on the list.

"So," Casey said in a low dangerous voice after the tape ran out. "let me tell you what's going to happen now, you useless little prick."

"You two assholes are going to crawl back under whatever rock you crawled out from under, contact your superiors, and you're going to tell them that it all ends *right fucking now*," Casey roared.

"This entire sorry little affair is over."

"The CIA is guilty of murder, conspiracy to commit murder, and drug dealing."

"You and your buddy here, as part of that conspiracy, are accessories," Casey pointed out.

"That means that your asses are now on the line too."

"That means if I release this tape to the public, you, your bosses here in Vietnam, and some people at the head of the CIA in Langley, along with you two, are all going to prison."

"But I know how you assholes think and operate," Casey said. "I've dealt with you before."

"You think you can go to MACV, invoke the coverall cloak of national security, and that will keep my people and me quiet, and all your assholes that are involved will simply walk away."

"Then later, my men will suddenly disappear."

"But that's not going to happen either," Casey vowed.

"This time, you're going to do things my way."

"You don't, or you try going over my head," Casey warned. "I'll take this tape, along with Macklin and Dunaway, to the Division Commander and play it for him."

"Afterwards, I'll let Macklin and Dunaway tell him the entire story."

"He's a friend of mine," Casey said.

"We go back a long way, back to the Chosin Reservoir, so he knows I don't lie."

"And he's a man of honor, so he won't let this slide or two of his Marines be taken by your people."

"Afterwards, we'll all go to the Division Staff Judge Advocate and have your Station Chief and his subordinates in Saigon charged with murder for the death of Captain James Taylor, attempted murder of my two Marines, and conspiracy."

"We'll also include your Station Chief."

"Because he's a part of this, just like your man Patterson was."

"Afterwards, just to cover all my bets, I'll call a friend of mine who's a reporter for the New York Times, tell him the entire story, and give him a copy of the tape."

"Langley will love that when they hear it being played on the six o'clock news with Walter Cronkite telling the world what a bunch of slimy bastards you are."

"And Congress will have a field day French frying your sorry asses when the investigation that Cronkite demands starts being televised."

"Congress will burn Langley to the ground before it's over."

"They'll have to; the public will demand it."

"And you two, along with and everybody else in the Agency that is even remotely connected to this affair will all go to Federal prison before it's over."

"You understand what I'm telling you, asshole?" the Gunny thundered. "Are you receiving all this loud and clear?"

The senior CIA agent paled, and he nodded. There was no doubt in his mind that Casey would do precisely as he had threatened. He was the type. And there was also no doubt about what would happen once CBS News got a copy of the tape.

"And one more thing, Sunshine," Casey added. "If everything I've said fails, or anything happens to my two Marines, anything at all, I'll turn this entire Platoon loose on you and everybody that works for your sorry organization here in country."

"You know who we are and what we do for a living, and you also know how good we are," Casey said steely-eyed.

"What you don't know is that we take care of our own," Casey revealed.

"You try fucking with us; we'll kill every fucking one of you sorry sonabitches before it's over."

"We'll gut your entire organization, you two included."

"I'll make sure of that," Casey vowed.

"And since we'll do it from a thousand yards, nobody will be able to either stop it or prove anything afterwards."

"You'll all just be stone fucking dead."

"You think I'm blowing smoke or just bullshitting," Casey threatened in a low dangerous voice. "you try me."

"They'll start burying your people a few days later, and it'll be a big fucking funeral before it's all over."

"You fuck with my Marines or me; I'll light a fire under your worthless asses that nobody can put out."

"Now you haul your useless asses out of my Platoon area and don't ever come back."

"If you do, I'll kill you both myself!" Casey threatened ominously.

Three days later, the Skipper got a phone call from Division telling him that Macklin and Dunaway had been officially released from the CIA detail and returned for duty with the Platoon. He was also informed that both men had received letters of commendation for their superior performance on the mission. The Platoon was receiving a citation of its own for outstanding support for a classified and sensitive operation. The report itself would be forwarded through the 1st Marine Division Commander back to the Commandant's office.

Later that same afternoon, Casey called Macklin and Dunaway back into his office.

"You two men did an excellent job on your last mission," he said. "I'm proud of you, and so is the Skipper."

"The Agency has sent letters of commendation regarding your performance, and they'll be posted in your records jackets; the fucking useless pricks."

"They didn't have any choice."

"You both may get promotions as a result."

"And I think I can safely say that your problems with them have all been resolved, permanently."

Macklin and Dunaway smiled.

"All that means that you are both back for duty with the Platoon," He said.

"And you are both once again starting here with a clean slate," Casey continued with a smile. "You deserve at least that."

"It seems like you have both matured some since the last time I talked to you," Gunny said. "so you both will start clean again.

"Even with me."

"That means you are finally beginning to understand what an extremely serious business we're all in."

"So, I expect both of you to take advantage of this new opportunity and continue to conduct yourself as the exemplary Marines that you have proven yourselves to be."

"You are seasoned professionals now, so I expect the best out of you from now on."

"And I'm fairly certain that I'll get it."

"From now on, it's your job to set the example for all the newbies coming in."

"Now, take three days off, go on liberty, and then report back for duty."

"Congratulations, Marines.'

Later, when they were back in their hooch, Macklin told Dunaway.

"You know Marty, the Gunny was right."

"I did grow up on that mission."

"And I think I finally understand what he was trying to tell us about the business we're in too."

"It really is about as serious as it gets."

"Before, I thought it was just a big game."

"Now I know different."

"I think it finally hit me when we were about to take out Patterson," Macklin revealed.

"I didn't feel right about that, and what I was about to do didn't sit right in my mind."

"I think what the Gunny said about this being about as serious as it gets finally hit home then."

"I'm glad I didn't have to kill that sonofabitch," Buster admitted.

Dunaway looked at Macklin with a new sense of respect. Buster had grown up, and his last statement proved it.

"You think the Gunny took care of all our other problems too?" Macklin asked a moment later.

"I'm sure he did," Dunaway replied.

"Private Henry told me about the conversation Casey had with two CIA officers in his office yesterday."

"According to him," Dunaway explained. "it was a world-class ass-chewing and a come-to-Jesus meeting that was monumental in both loudness and profanity."

"He said he had never seen the Gunny that mad before."

"He told me Casey tore those CIA guys' new assholes, then afterward, ran them off."

"Told them if they came ever back, he'd kill them himself."

"No shit!" Buster said in surprise.

Dunaway nodded.

"That's what Henry said."

"All that sounds to me like us and the CIA are done," he happily reported a moment later. "for good!"

Buster grinned. The Gunny hadn't let him down. More importantly, like all good Gunnies throughout the Corps, he had taken care of his men just like he had promised.

"One day," Macklin told himself. "that's what I'll be."

"And I'll take care of my people just like Gunnery Sgt Casey takes care of his."

"Because that's what all this is all about."

"We're professionals, and we act like professionals."

"We're serious about our mission, about our responsibilities, and about how we conduct ourselves; all the time."

"I finally know what Gunny Casey has been trying to tell me all this time; I finally understand."

"I think maybe I've finally grown up, at least a little."

Dunaway looked at Buster and smiled. He was amazed at Buster's perception of himself. He had grown up, and he realized it. When Dunaway thought about everything that had happened, he realized that he had grown up himself. The mission, the drama, the intrigue, and him having to assume command had done it.

"I think all that calls for a celebration, Buster," Dunaway continued, pleased about the way things had finally turned out.

"So, I'm going to take you downtown and buy you a drink for a change, instead of you trying to buy me one like you've always done in the past."

"I think you're grown up enough now to handle one."

"And I think we both deserve one after everything we've been through."

"How does that sound?"

Macklin smiled.

"Maybe just one," he said, smiling. "I don't want to go overboard and fuck up everything again."

"Remember what happened after the last time I did something like that."

Dunaway started laughing.

The End

Epilogue

The real legends. The extraordinary Marine snipers in Vietnam this story was based on.

By doctrine, a Marine Scout Sniper is: *"an individual highly skilled in both fieldcraft and marksmanship who delivers long-range, precision rifle fire on selected targets, from concealed positions, in support of combat operations, without being detected."* In less formal terms, he is simply called a sniper, and history tells us that the Marine version of these individuals are some of the best shots in the world. But being a Marine sniper also means that these highly skilled professionals usually operate alone or paired with a spotter as part of a team. Yet even when operational, they are normally independent of other Marine units.

Nowadays, Marine snipers receive highly selective and specialized training and utilize precision-made rifles and sophisticated optics to conduct their specialized missions. They also often have specialized communications equipment to feed valuable combat information they collect back to their units.

Lastly, in addition to marksmanship, they are also trained in camouflage, fieldcraft, stalking, infiltration, reconnaissance techniques, and observation. Utilizing these skills, they are especially effective when deployed within the terrain associated with urban or jungle warfare. They are both feared for their ability and despised by the enemy because they are so effective wherever they operate.

Scout snipers receive their training at one of the four Marine Corps schoolhouse locations in the United States. This training is both harsh and demanding, with a high failure rate. Still, those Marines who successfully graduate from Scout Sniper School are deadly in their effectiveness and unequaled in their shooting skills. Their motto is One Shot-One Kill, and they practice that creed in combat with cold-eyed efficiency. They now have a permanent Military Occupational Specialty or MOS and a permanent home within the Marine Corps. However, that hasn't always been the case.

Until the Vietnam War, Scout Snipers didn't even exist in the Corps. Although snipers have always been a part of the Marine Corps since its inception, they were never formally trained before Vietnam. They had no occupational classification identifying them as specialists. They were simply ordinary Marines identified as exceptional shots. They were subsequently assigned to various Marine units and employed on an as-needed basis. During the Vietnam War, thanks to a mustang Captain named Edward Land and several respected world-class Marine marksmen, a concept for creating a Scout Sniper was born.

A provisional unit was then authorized and established. A Scout sniper concept developed, tested, and later combat-proven in the jungles of Southeast Asia. That was all thanks to the extraordinary abilities and service of several distinguished Marines who were the people who helped to create the modern Marine Scout Sniper. Of this group, there were three Marines in particular, who distinguished themselves while performing that task.

The most well-known of the three was Gunnery Sergeant Carlos Hathcock. Hathcock was born May 20, 1942, and died on February 23, 1999. He was a United States Marine Corps Gunnery Sergeant and a legendary sniper with a service record of 93 confirmed kills. His record and the extraordinary details of the missions he undertook while in Vietnam made him a legend in the Marine Corps.

His fame as a sniper and dedication to long-distance shooting led him to become a primary developer of the United States Marine Corps Scout Sniper program. He was even honored for his feats by having a sniper rifle named after him, dubbed the Springfield Armory M25 White Feather.

Before deploying to Vietnam, Hathcock had won numerous shooting championships, including competitive rifle matches at the NRA-sponsored National Rifle Matches held annually at Camp Perry, Ohio. He had also won the prestigious Wimbledon Cup, the ultimate trophy for long-range rifle marksmanship in the world. By the time he began his tour in Vietnam in 1966, he was already a recognized and accomplished shooter. His assignment to Vietnam would make him a legend.

Ironically, Hathcock's initial assignment in Vietnam was as an MP. Later, he was reassigned as a sniper after Captain Edward Land pushed the Marine Corps leadership into raising snipers in Marine Corps units and created a dedicated scout sniper platoon at the Division level. Once that concept had been approved, Land began recruiting Marines who had previously set their records in sharpshooting to help validate his theory. Naturally, one of his prime recruiting targets was Hathcock.

Working as a part of Land's new sniper unit, Hathcock had 93 confirmed kills of North Vietnamese Army and Viet Cong personnel, an extraordinary feat in itself. But it was even more remarkable, considering the bureaucracy that existed at the time.

In Vietnam, Marine sniper kills had to be confirmed by a third party, who had to be an officer. That was in addition to the kill being witnessed by the sniper's spotter if the sniper had a spotter on the mission. Since snipers normally operated without a third-party present, this requirement often made confirmation of a kill difficult, if not impossible, especially if the target was behind enemy lines, as was often the case. As a result, without that restriction, Hathcock's actual record of kills would have probably been at least double that number, maybe even higher.

Hathcock was such a compelling and deadly sniper; the North Vietnamese Army placed a bounty of $30,000.00 on his life for killing so many of their men. Although the NVA put bounties on all snipers because it was a simple and easy way to get rid of them, none was as significant as Hathcock's. Rewards put out for other U.S. snipers by the NVA typically ranged from $2,000.00 to $8,000.00. Hathcock, however, held the record for the highest bounty ever placed on a sniper's head because he was so effective; and he killed every North and South Vietnamese marksman who tried to collect it.

Hathcock was so deadly that he was well known to the Viet Cong and the NVA, who called him *Lông Trắng,* meaning "White Feather." He got the name because of the small white feather he habitually wore in the band of his bush hat. However, eventually, that small trademark became a detriment to his safety after a platoon of trained Vietnamese snipers was sent to hunt down. Marines in the area subsequently donned white feathers in their bush hats to deceive the enemy as to Hathcock's identity. Since Hathcock was already well on his way to becoming a legend in the Marine Corps, these Marines were aware of the impact Hathcock's death would have on the Marine Corps in general and their unit in particular, so they took it upon themselves to try and look like Hathcock, thereby deliberately making themselves targets to confuse the NVA counter-snipers. Such was the regard that regular Marines had for the Gunnery Sergeant.

One of Hathcock's most notable accomplishments was shooting an enemy sniper through his own rifle scope, hitting him in the eye, and killing him before he could shoot Hathcock. Hathcock and John Burke, his spotter, were stalking the enemy sniper in the jungle near Hill 55, which housed a firebase from which Hathcock was operating. The sniper, known only as "the Cobra," had already killed several Marines and was believed to have been sent specifically to kill Hathcock himself. Instead, Hathcock eventually found him and took him out first.

On the day of the incident, Hathcock and his spotter were stalking the enemy sniper in the jungle around the firebase. When Hathcock saw a flash of light reflecting off the enemy sniper's scope in the bushes, he fired at it almost instinctively. Incredibly, his round went through the NVA sniper's scope, hitting him in the eye and killing him instantly. Surveying the situation afterwards, Hathcock concluded that the only possible way he could have put the round straight down the enemy's scope and through his eye behind it would have been if both he and the

NVA sniper had been zeroing in on each other at the same time and Hathcock had fired first.

Given the flight time of the rounds, at the ranges involved, once Hathcock saw the flash of light reflected off the NVA's scope, he had only a split second to react. Both snipers could have easily killed one another had they fired at the same time. Fortunately, Hathcock's reflexes were faster, and he fired a split second before the enemy sniper did.

After the incident, Hathcock took possession of the dead sniper's rifle, hoping to bring it home as a "war trophy" because of the unusual circumstances of the event. Unfortunately, after he turned it in and tagged it, it was later stolen from the armory, so he never got the chance. Pity, because the incident was the only known circumstance ever recorded of such an unusual and extraordinary event.

On another occasion, a female sniper, known to be a Viet Cong platoon commander, was killed by Hathcock. She was also reputed to be a vicious interrogator, known as to the US troops by the nickname "Apache," because of her sadistic interrogation procedures and her penchant for making her victims suffer. She derived the name because of her inhuman methods of torturing captured US Marines and ARVN troops for information, then letting them bleed to death. Once Hathcock killed her, her death was a major moral victory because she had been terrorizing the troops around Hill 55 for quite some time.

Hathcock reputedly removed the white feather from his bush hat only once, and that was during a volunteer mission conducted just days before he redeployed. He was forced to crawl over 1,500 yards through a grassy, NVA patrolled field during the mission. To a shooting position where he could take out an NVA commanding general. That overall effort took four days and three nights, over ninety hours, and the total distance involved equates to almost a mile.

Hathcock had no sleep during all that time and was forced to crawl inch-by-inch, not move the grass and give away his position to the nearby NVA security elements. That feat alone was genuinely remarkable.

During his move, Hathcock was almost stepped on by an NVA soldier patrolling the area shortly after sunset during the second day of his stalk. Fortunately, the man never saw the camouflaged Hathcock. Unbelievably, later, during his three-day ordeal, he was nearly bitten by a bamboo viper. Fortunately, when the snake appeared, Hathcock saw it and had the presence of mind to cease all movement and freeze, rather than getting up and trying to get away from the reptile. That act would have not only given up his position but would have also aborted the mission and probably gotten him killed. Eventually, the snake crawled away because of his complete lack of movement, and Hathcock resumed his stalk.

Finally, after he had gotten to his shooting position, as the NVA general exited his tent, Hathcock fired a single shot that struck his target in the chest and killed him. Afterwards, Hathcock slowly crawled back to safety to avoid the NVA soldiers frantically searching for him.

Hathcock was not informed of the details of the mission until after he had accepted it. Had he known about them before that, he later said, he might not have volunteered. For when the mission was over, Hathcock stated that he regretted it because, in the aftermath of his killing of the NVA General, the NVA doubled their attacks in the area, apparently in retaliation Hathcock killing their senior commander. Unfortunately, those attacks resulted in a substantial increase in American casualties.

After that arduous mission had been completed, Hathcock returned to the United States in 1967and left the Corps. However, he missed the Marine Corps and later reenlisted, returning to Vietnam in 1969, where he commanded a platoon of snipers. At the end of his service commitment, Hathcock retired and later died of cancer. But before his death, he was a vigorous proponent of the Marine Corps Scout Sniper program and shooting sports in general. To this day, he remains a Marine Corps legend.

Charles Benjamin "Chuck" Mawhinney, the second legendary Marine sniper, was born in 1949 in Oregon and was the son of a World War II Marine Corps veteran. As an avid hunter in his youth, he had been around firearms most of his life and was already known as a fantastic shot when he entered the Corps. After his initial training, he was sent to Vietnam in early 1968. There, he spent the next sixteen months assigned to the Marine Division headquartered in I Corps and operating as a sniper, a capacity he proved to be exceptionally effective at. So much so that he ultimately became the Marine sniper holding the most significant number of recorded kills of any Marine in history. This record still stands to this date.

Mawhinney's record is an astounding 103 confirmed kills and 216 "probables" during his sixteen months in the Vietnam War. Given the climate, terrain, and conditions of Vietnam, that feat is nothing short of remarkable, as are some of his actions in recording that number.

On Valentine's Day 1969, Mawhinney encountered an enemy platoon and killed sixteen North Vietnamese Army soldiers, one after another, with headshots from his M14 rifle before the rest fled. At the time, he and his spotter were completely unsupported by any other friendly forces. Later, during an interview with a reporter from the Los Angeles Times about that feat, he was quoted as saying:

"It was the ultimate hunting trip: a man hunting another man, who was hunting me. Don't talk to me about hunting lions or elephants. They don't fight back with rifles and scopes."

"I just loved it, the whole experience. My rules of engagement were simple. If they had a weapon, they were going down. Except for an NVA paymaster I hit at 900 yards, everyone I else killed had a weapon.

"My one regret was the one that got away. I can't help thinking about how many

people he may have killed later, how many of my friends, or how many Marines. He messed up, and he deserved to die. That still bothers me."

After leaving the Marine Corps in 1970, Mawhinney returned home to Lakeview, Oregon, later marrying and then working for the U.S. Forest Service until his retirement in the late 1990s. However, during all that time, he never told anyone about his Marine Corps service as a sniper, not even his wife. As a result, his accomplishments as a sniper were almost entirely unknown for more than two decades. Even Mawhinney himself did not know how his record as a sniper compared to that of his peers.

In 1991, when his exploits were recounted by fellow Marine sniper and author Joseph Ward, in his book, *Dear Mom: A Sniper's Vietnam*, Mawhinney suddenly found himself involuntarily thrust in the public limelight, as his wartime service was highlighted. In the book, Ward credited Mawhinney with 101 confirmed kills. Still, that figure was controversial because it was generally believed that the 93 confirmed kills by the legendary Gunnery Sergeant Carlos Hathcock stood as the record for any American sniper during the conflict.

However, subsequent research into the subject, which included researching US Army sniper records, discovered that US Army sniper Adalbert Waldron actually held the record, with 109 confirmed kills by a United States serviceman. The research also showed that Mawhinney's original documented total was in error. In the end, Mawhinney was credited with a total of 103 confirmed kills, not with just the 101 he had previously been accredited with. He was also credited with an additional 216 "probables." Like Hathcock, Mawhinney's actual number of kills would probably have been much higher, but for the requirement for an officer having to certify a kill to confirm it.

In any event, Mawhinney was then recognized as the United States Marine Corps sniper with the most confirmed kills, and further identified as having the second-highest of any US service member. In appreciation of that feat, his M40-A1 rifle is now on display in the National Museum of the Marine Corps.

The third most renowned sniper in the Corps during the Vietnam War era was a Marine named Eric England. England was born in 1933 in Union County, Georgia, and joined the US Marine Corps in 1950. During his training, he quickly proved to be a fantastic shot, so much so that he became a National Rifle Match shooting champion by the age of 19 in 1952. Later, he became the All-time Long-range Rifle champion in 1968.

Interestingly, England received his first competitive shooting training during boot camp. From his cousin, Dr. James Harry Thurber. At the time, Thurber was a Marine Corps weapons instructor providing marksmanship training to Marine enlistees. Over the ensuing instructional period, England proved to be an avid student. It soon became evident that he was a gifted shooter. That realization led to a 24-year career on the United States Marine Corps Rifle Team. England won numerous national and international competitions, both as a participant and later as a coach.

When he was deployed to Vietnam, England put his skills to work. It served as a Marine sniper, racking up 98 confirmed kills, with dozens more listed as "probables." However, unlike Hathcock and Mawhinney, England's 98 confirmed kills all occurred within seven months. Following that, he was medically evacuated back to the United States. That means England acquired almost as many confirmed kills in seven months as the other record holders got while serving a normal twelve-month tour, or in Mawhinney's case, a sixteen-month tour. According to the Scout Sniper Association, England averaged an astounding fourteen confirmed kills a week; a figure that has never been replicated during his time as a sniper in the country.

It should also be noted that England, like both Hathcock and Mawhinney, had many solo sniping missions during his tour where witnesses were unavailable to confirm his kills. So, his number of kills, as with both Hathcock and Mawhinney, may have been much higher, as high as 200, as estimated by his superiors.

England himself has never mentioned his number of confirmed kills, either officially or unofficially. This estimate had to be obtained from former USMC officers who knew him and served with him in Vietnam. The same is true for Carlos Hathcock, William Dunam, Chuck Mawhinney, and other scout-snipers.

Although little known outside of sniper circles, England is highly respected and was the subject of the book *Phantom of Phu Bai*, written by Dr. J. B. Turner. Gunnery Sergeant Carlos Hathcock was once quoted as saying,

"Eric is a great man, a great shooter, and a great Marine."

That was the sniper legacy achieved during the Vietnam War by US Marines, shooters. Still, it has continued into the modern Iraq and Afghanistan Wars, where snipers have played a significant role. However, modern-day snipers have undergone improved training and have improved weapon systems. The accuracy of sniper weapons and the loads they fire have been modernized and upgraded. Consequently, all these changes and enhancements have resulted in modern snipers getting confirmed kills at extraordinary ranges.

Today, the longest recorded range for a modern sniper kill currently stands at an astounding 3,079 yards. That equates to almost one and three-quarters miles! It was achieved by an unnamed Australian sniper assigned to the Australian 2nd Commando Regiment and was accomplished in an engagement in 2012 in Afghanistan, using a Barrett M82A1 rifle chambered in .50 caliber BMG.

A computer, using QTU Lapua external ballistics software, with the appropriate data concerning that shot fed into it, predicted that such a shot traveling at a distance involved would have struck its target after nearly *six full seconds* of flight time. And once fired, the round would have lost 93% of its kinetic energy and would have *dropped almost 400 feet* from the original bore line during that time.

There was also a light cross-breeze of 6 mph reported at the time of the actual shot that would have diverted the round a total of *30 feet off its intended target line,* requiring the appropriate compensation by the shooter. That makes that shot not only genuinely remarkable but absolutely astounding, something that could probably never be replicated under combat conditions!

Mr. Tom Irwin, director of Accuracy International, the British manufacturer of the L115A3 rifle, which also fires a heavier round (8.59mm) for long-range accuracy, when commenting on the shot, was quoted as saying:

"The L115A3 is still fairly accurate beyond 1,500 m (1,640 yds), but at that distance and beyond, luck plays as much of a role as anything else in hitting a target."

That statement may well be true, but it is still just an opinion. Another, better one is that the shooter's ability still plays the most crucial part in an equation like that.

History has proven it, especially in Vietnam. And that fact has been consistently reinforced by the actions of modern snipers in both Iraq and Afghanistan.

The Marine snipers in the Vietnam War were a special breed of men. They were the forerunners of the current United States Marine Corps Scout Sniper Program. Their ability, courage, and sacrifice helped create that program. They have since become the stuff of legends, and that is exactly what all the men mentioned above are now considered.

This novel is fiction, with the main characters and their actions fabrications. However, they are loosely based on the three men described above and some of the actual events they accomplished and lived through.

However, the real men who fought in Vietnam as Marine snipers and their extraordinary accomplishments are even more unbelievable than the fictional events described in this novel. They were giants in their time, and they have become legends and icons in ours.

Glossary

A

AO military acronym for Area of operations

Across the fence Slang for across the border; being in or operating in denied territory.

Agency Short for the Central Intelligence Agency

Airborne Course A specialized military course that instructs soldiers to conduct parachute operations from aircraft; slang is jump school.

Airstrike A strike on a ground target by aircraft involving attacking ground targets with bombs, rockets, cannons, or machine guns mounted on an aircraft.

Area of Operations The unit's assigned area of responsibility; the area a unit is conducting operations in.

Army Marksmanship Unit The US Army's Competitive Shooting Team is located at Ft Benning, Georgia, AMU for short.

AK-47 Russian-made assault rifle chambered in 7.62 Parabellum, originally produced in 1947. Normally has a thirty-round magazine. It can be fired in single-shot, semi-automatic, or fully automatic mode; it and variants are still being used today throughout the world; so much so it has become iconic; normal weapon carried by both the VC and the NVA.

Ammo Short or slang for ammunition.

Ass Chewing Slang for a harsh verbal counseling session given to a subordinate by a superior (i.e., Private being counseled by his Sergeant); in the military, it normally involves the use of profane, vulgar, and debasing language; it is designed to let the soldier know immediately that he had erred in his behavior, conduct, or actions and had better take immediate action to correct it.

B

Base Camp Rear area in a combat zone where the unit has its fixed installations; the area where the unit's headquarters, personnel, logistics, maintenance, housing, messing, and training, and other combat support sites are normally located.

Base Station The radio station that normally controls all the other radio stations on the net; usually the base station is a fixed site with a large, fixed antenna array capable of sending and receiving long-distance radio transmissions.

BTHP Acronym for boat tail hollow point; the projectile on the end of a round that has its rear edges rounded off in the shape of a sailing boat; it is copper jacketed, and lead-filled with a small hole drilled into the center of the round which causes it to mushroom when it impacts its target, creating a large exit wound.

Boat tail See above.

Boot Marine Corps term for a newly enlisted trainee undergoing his initial basic training in the United States Marine Corps.

Boot Camp Slang for the initial training course each Marine recruit must undergo and successfully complete before he can be called a qualified Marine; conducted at either Parris Island, South Carolina, or Camp Pendleton, California.

Boxer Primed Brass ammunition using a Boxer primer, originally invented by Edward Boxer in England in 1866; most modern rifle cartridges are boxer primed because they can be easily reloaded. The primer is a small metal cup filled with pressure-sensitive explosive, affixed to the base of the brass cartridge. When the weapon's firing pin strikes it, it explodes, igniting the powder in the brass and the produced gases propel the round from the weapon.

Brass The metal casing of the round containing the powder; it has a primer on its base and a projectile on its other end.

Burp Gun Slang for a Chinese submachine gun; a weapon carried by Chinese troops during the Korean War; normally a Russian or Chinese made PPSh-41 chambered in 9mm and carrying a round, drum capable of holding fifty rounds.

C

Camo Short for Camouflage

Camp Perry A National Guard base located in Ohio on the shores of Lake Erie; this base has the largest outdoor rifle range in the world; it has been home to the NRA-sponsored National Rifle Matches since 1907 and is the hub of competitive rifle shooting worldwide.

Carry all Older slang term for an enclosed truck with seating for more than four and a cargo compartment; usually boasts a four-wheel drive; now commonly called an SUV.

Case Officer A nonmilitary intelligence officer employed in a variety of roles by the Central Intelligence Agency.

Case of the Clap Slang for an individual who has gonorrhea or some other STD.

CCN Short for Command-and-Control North; SOG's northernmost forward operating base in South Vietnam; located near the city of Da Nang.

Center of mass Refers to the center of a human torso in the heart region; this is a normal target for a sniper which typically results in the death of the target.

Central Intelligence Agency An independent, civilian intelligence agency of the US government. The primary intelligence collector of foreign intelligence for the United States. It also performs selected special operations when tasked; America's top spy agency.

Chaing Kai Chek The national leader of the Nationalist Chinese forces, called the Kuomintang during and after WWII until he and his regime were thrown out of China by Mao Tse Tung and the communists and forced to resettle on the island of Taiwan and set up a government in exile.

Chosin Reservoir The site of a brutal seventeen-day battle in freezing weather in North Korea between the United Nations X Corps, containing the 1st Marine Division and the Chinese 9th Peoples Volunteer Army. This elite unit had secretly infiltrated across the North Korean border with orders from Mao Tse Tung to destroy the UN Forces. It surrounded the first Marne Division with almost 70,000 Chinese troops and during the subsequent forced withdrawal, UN forces inflicted crippling losses on the Chinese units before being evacuated from the port of Hung Nam.

CIA Acronym for Central Intelligence Agency.

Clandestine An operation carried out by elements in such a way as to ensure secrecy or concealment; the operation usually goes unnoticed by the general public in the area, but its primary purpose is to conceal the operation itself from the enemy until it is conducted.

Confirmed Kill When a sniper's target is killed, and the death can be confirmed by another individual.

Come to Jesus Meeting A particularly harsh counseling session during which an individual or individuals are strongly advised to immediately change their conduct, actions, or normal way of doing things. These are favorites of senior sergeants when instructing subordinates in the error of their ways and usually involve a high degree of profane language.

Commo Short for communications; usually radio communications.

Company A military unit normally composed of a command element and three platoons. It usually numbers anywhere from 120 -160 personnel, based on the type of unit, and it is usually commanded by a captain.

Concept of Operations A basic idea of how a commander intends to conduct an operation; it is normally fleshed out to form a complete operations plan.

Corps large military unit normally consisting of several Divisions usually numbering three to five, and a Support Command. It is commanded by a three-star general and contains approximately 90,000 to 100,000 men or more.

Covert An operation conducted by elements during which the identity of the sponsor is concealed rather than just the operation itself; in a covert operation the sponsoring power is given plausible deniability concerning the operation, its purpose, its perpetrators, or any of the equipment used to conduct it. In other words, if you get caught or the operation gets blown, the government never heard of you.

Cover (1) the Marine term for a hat. (2) a believable but fictitious story or identity designed to either conceal or protect an individual or a project from becoming common knowledge. It is commonplace in both intelligence and special operations and usually involves paperwork, documentation, identification cards, or other material, either real or forged, designed to enhance the believability of the story.

Churls Knobs on a telescopic sight used to adjust for either elevation or deflection. They move the rifle's aim point so that the round will impact its selected target regardless of wind or height.

CH-53 A large multi-purpose, twin-turbine engine helicopter capable of carrying twenty personnel over long distances. Some are very sophisticated, are air refuellable, and boast numerous radars, airborne countermeasures, and other exotic avionics. They are in active service in almost all branches of the US military.

Creep Slang for the stealthy movement of a sniper to his shooting position where he will engage his target; movement to the target is usually accomplished by crawling.

Crotch Slang for US Marine Corps; I e. "the Crotch"

D

Deflection The lateral compensation a shooter must make to allow for wind or the movement of the target.

Delinquency Report A written violation issued by military police for unauthorized conduct by a soldier when he is off duty and in a social environment. It is usually proceeded by disciplinary action taken by the offender's commander.

Denied Territory Militarese for territory in which US military ground personnel are forbidden to operate. In the Vietnam War, Laos, Cambodia, and North Vietnam were considered denied territory for ground operations.

Dog Soldiers The slang term given by US troops to North Vietnamese soldiers operating in South Vietnam, because they lived in the jungle like animals.

Donut Dollies American female Red Cross workers who operated in South Vietnam throughout the country during the Vietnam War and provided donuts, snacks, and coffee to US servicemen, among other things.

Dicks Another slang term for NVA soldiers.

Dinks Another slang term for NVA or VC soldiers.

Dinky Dau Slang Vietnamese for crazy.

Division A large US military maneuver unit composed of a headquarters and staff and three or four combat Brigades and several support battalions. Its troop strength numbers anywhere from 16,000 to 27,000 personnel, depending on the type of Division.

DMZ Acronym for Demilitarized Zone. In the Vietnam War, the border area between North Vietnam and South Vietnam. Neither side was supposed to have combat elements in this small border area.

Drill Instructor The US Marine Corps Sergeant charged with supervising the initial training of Marine recruits after they enlist.

Drop Slang for a parachute drop; or in shooting terms, refers to the number of inches or feet the projectile falls below the bore line of the weapon once the round is fired; the longer the distance the more the drop.

Drop Off Point A preselected point on a map or on the ground where men or material are deliberately dropped off their insertion platform and left.

E

Elevation The up and down adjustment a shooter must make to compensate for the distance to the target.

E Silhouette A standard, half-man-sized, olive green, cardboard target used routinely by the US military in shooting exercises.

Exfil Short for exfiltration.

Exfiltration The recovery of personnel previously inserted into an area.

F

F-4 A MacDonald-Douglas manufactured US fighter bomber used by the US Air Force, Navy, and Marine Corps during the Vietnam War era.

FAC Acronym for forward air controller; these individuals flew small unarmed light aircraft and marked targets as well as controlled airstrikes by fighters and bombers.

Field Expedient Using available, on-hand equipment to jury rig something in the field and make it temporarily operational.

Fore Stock The front portion of a rifle stock situated under the barrel of the weapon.

G

Garand A WWII vintage, semi-automatic service rifle firing an eight-round en-bloc clip and chambered in 30-06 caliber; used by US Forces in both WWII and Korea; commonly called an M-1.

General Giap The military leader of all North Vietnamese forces during the Vietnam War.

Ghillie Suit A specialized suit/covering worn by a sniper to help conceal himself outdoors. It is made of various types and pieces of suitably colored cloth/fabric attached to a netted material that can have natural foliage woven into it and when worn by an individual covers his head and body.

Golden Triangle The confluence of the borders of Thailand, Laos, and Burma; this area is home to the largest opium-growing region in the world.

Green Beret Slang term for a member of US Army Special Forces; coined from the distinctive green beret they wear as part of their uniform.

Gunnery Sergeant A senior sergeant/rank in the US Marine Corps.

Gunny Slang for Gunnery Sergeant.

Groups Shot groupings on a paper target made by rifle projectiles penetrating it.

Guns Slang for helicopter gunships.

Gunships Armed helicopters that provide fire support to ground personnel using rockets, machine gun, or minigun fire.

H

Head shot A shot to a target's head by a sniper. It is almost always fatal.

High Value Target A specific target usually provided by intelligence that has been deliberately selected because of its importance.

Hit When a round impacts its target.

Ho Chi Minh Trail The name given to the North Vietnamese logistics artery that ran from North Vietnam, through the border regions of both Laos and Cambodia and culminated just short of the Gulf of Thailand. It was the primary supply route for all North Vietnamese and Viet Cong personnel operating in South Vietnam.

Hooker Slang for a prostitute.

Hollowpoint A projectile that has a small hole or tunnel drilled partially into it. When it impacts its target, it mushrooms and causes a large exit wound.

I

I Corps The northernmost Corps area in South Vietnam. It was the operational area for the 1st Marine Division.

II Corps The Corps area due south of I Corps. It contained the mountainous region of the country and the Central Highlands.

ID Acronym for Identification.

ID Card A laminated military identification card issued to everyone in the US military; it had his service number as well as his picture on it.

Infil Short for infiltration.

Infiltration The insertion of either men or material into an operational area; usually conducted in a clandestine mode.

Insertion Introduction of men or material into an operational area by ground, aerial, or maritime platform.

Insertion Platform How an insertion is accomplished, usually by a vehicle, an aircraft, or a watercraft.

In the weeds In the field or the jungle, usually on an operation.

J

Jungle Boots The distinctive footwear worn by ground personnel during the Vietnam War; They were designed for wear in a tropical climate and made of nylon and rubber with a cleated sole.

Jungle Fatigues The nylon uniform worn by military personnel during the Vietnam War. They were breathable, durable, fast-drying and came in olive drab or a mottled green camouflage pattern.

K

K-Bar A fixed bladed combat knife with a small hilt, leather grip, and a seven-inch blade issued by the Marine Corps. They could be honed to razor sharpness.

Kim il Sung The national leader of North Korea during the Korean War.

Kill Zone A preselected area in which you intend to kill the enemy, usually by ambush.

Klick One thousand meters on a military grid map.

KMT Short for Kuomintang; the nationalist Chinese Army and the political party formed by Chaing Kai Chek that ruled Postwar China until it was defeated by Mao Tse Tung's Communist forces and forced to withdraw to the island of Taiwan.

L

Lake City Match The specially selected, military-issued, match-grade, rifle ammunition used in National Match competitions and issued to snipers during the Vietnam War era.

Langley Langley, Virginia; Headquarters for the Central Intelligence Agency.

Laos A country in Southeast Asia that borders Vietnam, Thailand, and Burma. Its border regions were used by the NVA to establish a permanent large-scale logistics artery and basing area from North Vietnam to South Vietnam called the Ho Chi Minh Trail. Laos was supposedly neutral during the Vietnam War, yet it turned a blind eye to the NVA efforts and activities in its border regions during that period.

Liberty The Naval and Marine Corps term for a temporary pass allowing an individual to go into town in his off-duty time.

Link up Point A preselected point where individuals or vehicles link up/ come together/ rejoin.

Log Site Short for a logistics site.

LST Acronym for Landing Ship Transport. A naval vessel capable of landing or putting large elements of men or material over the shore/on the beach or recovering them for that same area.

M

M-1 A WWII/Korea vintage standard service rifle for the US Army and Marine Corps; see Garand.

Mao Tse Tung The national leader of Communist China during the Korean War.

Minute of angle A popular shooting term referring to the accuracy of rifles; a precision firearm's accuracy will be measured in MOA. This simply means that under ideal conditions (i.e., no wind, match-grade ammo, clean barrel, and a vise or a bench rest used to eliminate shooter error,) the rifle can produce a group of shots whose center points (center-to-center) fit into a one-inch circle when the weapon is fired at 100 yards. If a weapon is capable of a sub-MOA, then it is deemed extremely accurate.

Model 70 The Winchester Model 70 is a bolt action sporting rifle with similarities to Mauser designs and it is a development of the earlier Winchester Model 54. It was a weapon of choice used by the snipers in the 1st Marine Division's Scout Sniper Platoon during the Vietnam War and chambered in .308 caliber.

Mekong River The Mekong is the seventh-largest river in Southeast Asia and the 12th-longest in the world. Its estimated length is 4,350 kilometers. It runs from the Tibetan Plateau through China's Yunnan Province, into Laos, Thailand, Burma, Cambodia, and Vietnam until it empties into the Gulf of Thailand.

Moonshine Illegally made whiskey.

MOS Acronym for Military Occupational Specialty; the military job a soldier is trained to do.

MP Acronym for Military Police.

Muzzle Energy The kinetic energy of a bullet as it is expelled from the muzzle of a firearm. It is often used as a rough indication of the destructive potential of a given firearm or load. The heavier the bullet and the faster it moves, the higher its muzzle energy and the more damage it will do.

Muzzle Velocity The speed a projectile has at the moment it leaves the muzzle of the firearm; the higher the muzzle velocity, the less drop the projectile will have on its way to the target. It will also affect the amount of damage a round does to the target when it impacts.

N

National Matches The NRA sponsored National Rifle Matches held annually at Camp Perry, Ohio.

NCO Non-Commissioned Officer.

Noncom Slang for an NCO.

Non-Commissioned Officer A corporal or sergeant rank in the US military.

Neck Turned Precision seating of the projectile into the brass cartridge; used to promote extreme accuracy in rifle ammunition.

Number Ten Slang Viet/American term meaning bad.

Non-disclosure forms US government forms which when signed, require an individual to never divulge selected information under penalty of law.

Nungs A sect of Tay Chinese who remained in Vietnam when the country gained its independence from China. Disenfranchised by the South Vietnamese government, many worked as paid mercenaries for both US Special Forces and the CIA during the Vietnam War

NVA North Vietnamese Army.

O

Officer in Charge The commissioned officer who has the responsibility for ensuring that the task has been completed.

On the Pad Refers to aircraft, especially helicopters. Aircraft sitting on a landing pad, ready to be launched at a moment's notice.

Overt Open, unconcealed.

P

Parris Island The Marine Corps Recruit Training Depot at Parris Island, South Carolina.

Pathet Lao The NVA backed communist insurgents in Laos trying to overthrow the Royal Laotian Government during the Vietnam War era.

Pearled A term used in firearms vernacular referring to the smoothing and polishing of various internal moving parts of a weapon. Pearled actions are extremely smooth and synonymous with extreme accuracy.

Platoon A military unit containing three squads and commanded by a lieutenant.

Phantoms Vietnam era fighter bombers; see F-4

Pillar bedded A method of mounting and securing a rifle barrel and action onto a stock; Small metal posts are mounted and secured to the inside of the rifle's stock and reinforced with fiberglass for added stability. Then the rifle's barrel and action are secured to these pillars with metal screws; pillar bedding is used when constructing a rifle capable of extreme accuracy.

Point of Aim The point on the target where the reticule in the telescopic sight is fixed.

Point of Impact The point on the target where the round hits.

Product A term in the drug business referring to the type of drug being harvested or produced.

Projectile The part of the cartridge expelled from the weapon's barrel when it is fired; commonly called the bullet.

R

Receive The capability of a radio that allows the operator to hear the message being sent.

Recover In militarise, to return to a certain point.

Remington Model 700 BDL A US sporting rifle produced by Remington Arms that had a detachable magazine or a hinged floor plate over the magazine well. These rifles were sometimes used by Marine Snipers and were usually chambered in 30-06 caliber.

Reticule The crosshairs in the telescopic sight. There are many variants.

Round Military term for a cartridge or bullet

S

Safety The feature on a weapon that prevents the operator from pulling the trigger and firing the weapon.

Sako A Finnish-made, bolt action, rifle legendary for its extreme accuracy.

Saleeems What the Vietnamese called Salem menthol-flavored cigarettes. They were a favorite with them.

Sampan A small, shallow draft, wooden boat common in Asia.

Satellite Imagery High-resolution photographs taken by an orbiting overhead system.

Scope Slang for a telescopic sight.

SCU Special Commando Unit. The unit all paid mercenaries working for Special Forces in the Vietnam War were assigned to; a euphemism for an indigenous asset, working for US Special Forces.

Secure Safe, secure from attack; an area under total friendly control.

SF Special Forces.

Shitter A field latrine; a three to six holer.

Shooting Position The concealed and covered position a sniper fires from.

Shot Groups See Groups.

Silenced When a sound suppressor has been affixed to the end of a weapon's barrel to make the sound of the round being fired almost unnoticeable, it is a silenced weapon.

Silencer The implement that allows the report of the weapon to be silenced.

Skipper Marine Corps slang for the commander of the unit.

Slick Slang name for a UH-1H unarmed helicopter manufactured by Textron Corp. The standard, now iconic, helicopter used in Vietnam, to haul troops and supplies.

Snake Eye A fin retarded bomb commonly used in airstrikes by fighter-bombers during the Vietnam War.

SOG Acronym for Special Operations Group. SOG conducted unconventional warfare operations against the North Vietnamese in the Southeast Asian Theater during the Vietnam War.

SOG Card A laminated card issued to all personnel assigned to SOG which allowed them to carry weapons anywhere and have priority access to transportation assets.

Sorry Lazy, no good, worthless.

Special Forces A specialized element of the US Army that conducts unconventional warfare; also called Green Berets.

Special Operations Operations conducted by specialized, highly trained elements usually in a clandestine or covert mode. They are often strategic.

Spotting Scope A monocular scope used by a spotter to assist the shooter in target identification and getting rounds on target.

Spotter Individual on a sniper team that conducts target ID, assesses deflection, estimates range, and gives consent to fire.

Spot weld Shooter's term meaning placing your cheek against the stock of the weapon permitting you to get a stable and steady sight picture and holding it in that same position round after round.

Stage Prepare, provision, and/or rehearse for a mission.

Staging area The area in which a unit stages for the mission. Usually different from its launch site.

Stalk Stealthily move to your shooting position/hunt your target.

Sterile Nonattributable equipment used on a covert mission that could never be traced back to the sponsoring power.

STOL Acronym for Short Take-Off and Landing; refers to specialized aircraft that have this capability.

Strip Alert Aircraft sitting on a runway with their pilots already in them ready to launch at a moment's notice.

T

Take out Another name for kill.

Terminate Euphemism for kill.

Throw a bolt A shooting term; to eject a spent shell casing and then load another round into the weapon in one smooth continuous motion using a bolt action rifle.

Tour of Duty A twelve-month assignment in Vietnam.

Trail Sign Inconspicuous and secret signs or markings left on trails by the VC or NVA that indicated mined areas, water, rest areas, the direction of movement, etc.

U

Unloaded on Came down hard on verbally.

Utilities Marine Corps issue fatigues

V

VC Viet Cong.

Vientiane The capital city of Laos.

Viet Cong The non-uniformed guerrillas operating in South Vietnam that aided the NVA in the Vietnam War and were dedicated to overthrowing the Saigon government.

W

Waste Another word for kill or terminate.

Z

Zero Adjusting the sights of a weapon to its operator to allow him to bring accurate fire on a target at a fixed distance. Military service rifles are usually zeroed to 250 yards. When a weapon is zeroed, its operator's point of aim and the round's point of impact are the same at 250 yards.

Advance Preview

Tempting the Devil

Available on Amazon.com, and LegionBooks.net

Chapter One

"Everybody wants to go to heaven,
But nobody wants to die."

Unknown

The jungle was as silent as it was deadly, which was not a good sign. No birds chirping or monkeys yammering meant something had disturbed its natural rhythm and turned it mute.

"Christ, it's the NVA," Jarvis thought grimly. "They're here!"

"That's why everything suddenly got so quiet."

"Are they tracking us or just on a routine patrol?"

"No way to tell, but I need to know for sure," he worried.

He hand signaled Pretty Boy, the little Montagnard mercenary on point, to turn right, praying a radical change in direction might help. Later he would button hook back on his original trail to give him an answer. At least that was the plan.

Pretty Boy nodded his understanding and waved. He, too, had already sensed trouble but didn't know how close it was. Jarvis's radical direction change meant he and his slack man Luc would probably soon find out. They both departed silently but stopped suddenly minutes later, with Pretty Boy's hand shooting up in a fist, the danger signal. He quickly turned into a statue as the rest of the RT dropped to one knee, weapons at the ready. He and Luc slowly melted into the jungle foilage a second later.

"Oh Shit," Jarvis thought wildly. *"Pretty Boy has spotted the NVA."*

"Christ, I didn't think they were this close."

"Jesus, we're in deep shit now."

He began sweating bullets while waiting for the imminent firefight to crank up. His eyes told him there was no cover anywhere, which was more bad news. Without it, considering where they were, the RT would get chopped to pieces.

"We're about to get our asses handed to us, and there's nothing I can do to stop it," he groaned silently as he realized the danger.

"Where are the little bastards?" he silently begged, franticly searching his surroundings for a clue. *"Why don't they open up?"*

No such luck, so he waited, anxious and terrified, yet nothing happened. No rounds tearing through the greenery, no screaming when people got hit, and no chaos. Just continued tense silence.

"What the hell? He wondered wildly as he waited anxiously for another signal from Pretty Boy.

"Maybe he didn't spot any NVA after all," Jarvis wondered in confusion.

"But if there are no NVA, why did Pretty Boy and Luc flatten so suddenly?"

Jarvis continued sweating and remained apprehensive as the seconds ticked by. He glanced at the team behind him and saw they were as jacked up as he was and wondering mightily what the hell was happening. In this case, no news was bad news, maybe the terminal kind.

Moments later, Pretty Boy reappeared from the jungle floor and waved him forward, cautioning him to be slow and quiet with hand signals. He crawled towards him a moment later, expecting bad news. Pretty boy didn't disappoint him.

"Trail," the little Yard whispered, wide-eyed and pointing.

"Big one. Fresh tracks are all over it."

"We have a big problem, Boss."

"NVA are very close."

That was a massive understatement, and Jarvis realized it. He stared at the trail grimly, thinking, his heartbeat rising.

"No NVA yet," he thought, relieved, *"but it's time for a change in plans."*

"We'll have to head in a different direction to avoid them, and we'll have to do it immediately and quietly, so they won't know we're here."

He thought for a moment, then pointed out a new direction of movement. This one was completely different than the old one and headed another way. Pretty Boy nodded his understanding.

"A radical change in direction might work," he thought in approval.

"It certainly won't hurt."

"But we'll have to be extremely careful."

"If the NVA don't hear us, we may just skate through this."

The rest of the team also saw Jarvis's hand signal and understood. They all realized they were in serious trouble now with NVA behind them and probably more NVA on the way to cut them off if they were being tracked. That created a major problem that was getting worse by the moment, and if they weren't extremely careful, it just might jump up and kill them. To prevent that, Jarvis was obviously attempting something drastic. They just prayed it would work.

"The NVA's proximity accounts for the silence and the acidic stench of fear everywhere," Jarvis thought.

"The NVA brought death along with them when they arrived."

"Or maybe it's already here," he worried.

"It's hard to tell at this point because it's too close to call."

"But we'll soon find out."

"But the NVA aren't our only problem."

"This goddamn jungle isn't going to help our situation."

"It's going to hinder it instead."

"It's an equal opportunity eliminator," he remembered. *"always hungry, never satisfied, and requiring new meat every day."*

"Especially here in Laos."

"So we're in an extremely dangerous environment facing a toxic situation, and every man on the RT realizes that."

"You can see the fear etched on their strained faces, even though they're trying hard to conceal it."

"They're scared, its shows, and they have no desire for an oncoming face-to-face meeting with God ."

"They realize that if our situation doesn't improve quickly, that' s a distinct possibility."

"Since remaining undiscovered is our only real protection, we'll have to try and sneak out of here without the NVA hearing us."

"That will be extremely difficult, but not impossible."

"If that doesn't work, we're in grave danger of getting our return ticket punched."

The RT's fear was more than justified. Their mission was covert; they were illegally in Laos, outnumbered at least ten to one, and outgunned. Worse, the operation they were attempting was near suicide and in an area where the NVA controlled everything except the weather.

All that meant they were skating on very thin ice and in danger of falling through at any moment. It made them nothing more than expendable throwaways in the heart of Indian country and just asking for it. Although that was all part of their job, that didn't make things any easier, and they didn't want to die while attempting it. So they were doing everything they could to prevent it.

Seconds later, found the RT moving again, desperately trying to put some distance between them and the NVA tracking them without getting discovered in the process. That was no easy task since their minds focused more on staying alive than on silent movement. Still, they tried to concentrate on stealth.

Slivers of sunlight peeked through the jungle's thick canopy shedding barely enough light to move silently as they snaked forward. That limited their visibility, ten feet at most in the dense foliage, sometimes less. That demanded their movement be abnormally slow and painstakingly careful. Speed was a nonstarter in the equation since it produced noise, which was a killer, especially where they were.

"Hopefully, the jungle's dimness will also decrease our chances of being spotted," Jarvis reminded himself. *" but that's a double-edged sword,"*

"At the same time, it restricts our vision, and if we're blind, we're screwed."

"Limited vision, especially at this range, also guarantees certain death when the shooting

starts because we're so close to the NVA, they can't miss."

"No matter." his brain commanded. "you can't do anything about that, so keep moving,"

"Concentrate on the positives while you check out your surroundings."

"You aren't dead yet."

"So, look for anything out of place and move like a ghost while you try to stay that way."

The thin rays of the sun managing to penetrate the gloom were also a disadvantage, and Jarvis realized that. They cast the foliage around the RT in a soft, unnatural, yellowish hue. That dilution muted the normally emerald-green vegetation making it appear orange-like and dull while creating a mirage that made normal shapes blurry and indistinct. All that aided the small seven-man recon team's camouflage as did being uniformed in Tiger suits, their distinct pattern making them especially difficult to detect, even to a trained eye. However, it didn't make them invisible or immune to discovery which was their goal. It had to be. Discovery meant a firefight, and a firefight was the epitome of bad luck. That's when people started dying.

With that worrisome thought foremost in their mind, the RT stole their way through the dense green morass with barely a whisper. Concentration was paramount, and silence was golden because there could be no mistakes. That made their movement wary and fearful. So quiet they were as silent as smoke filtering through a screen door. No sound, no spoken words, total noise discipline, and complete attention to detail demanded all their attention. Their slow, cautious motion hinted at their presence, but just barely. That made the silence of the ambient environment almost deafening, which was another dangerous sign.

"A quiet jungle is a dangerous jungle," Jarvis thought nervously as he moved again.

"It means the NVA are nearby, and like me, every man on the team senses that."

"Christ, I can almost feel the bastards breathing down our necks right now."

Jarvis's hunch was spot on. The NVA were very near the RT and closing rapidly. Every indicator pointed to it, so not admitting it would be a bad mistake. All the signs were there and glaring. Gut instinct, no jungle sounds, that eerie feeling you got when you were about to get hit, and an icicle running down your spine.

The ambient environment made the anticipation even worse. The sun had baked the entire area all morning, turning the trapped, fetid air underneath hot and still. The continually rising temperature and high humidity made it even worse. It created a sluggish, lazy atmosphere that made it difficult even to breathe, much less concentrate.

Consequently, the resulting situation was almost as intolerable as it was dangerous. Something akin to a damp shroud descending over an about-to-be corpse with no way of stopping it. Jarvis's optimism about skating through this situation without a firefight was rapidly dissolving.

"Don't think about failure," Jarvis admonished himself. *"Concentrate on succeeding."*

"Keep alert. Stay focused. Keep moving."

"We're not dead yet."

"No, but without a miracle, that may not be the case much longer," his bain taunted.

"You're juggling nitro with greasy hands, Sunshine."

"Don't screw up and drop something."

Good advice that Jarvis was trying desperately to heed but barely succeeding.

"We've been on the ground three days with no contact," he remembered.

"That means we're either goddamned lucky, or our efforts to remain undetected have paid off."

"Or have they?" he worried as he thought about it some more.

"Maybe I'm just fooling myself," he reflected as his worry continued to mount.

"It's virtually impossible to move through the jungle without leaving some small tell-tale of your passing," he reminded himself realistically. *"Especially with seven men."*

"The NVA are very good, which means they've probably found our sign by now."

"If they have, they're undoubtedly tracking us."

"The question is, how close are they?"

Interesting question, especially since the NVA controlled this entire section of the border, blanketing it with an excessive number of troops. They considered it their own private backyard and were extraordinarily serious about its security because they had to be. It contained their primary logistics artery, which was vital to their war effort in neighboring South Vietnam. Without it, there would be no war. Therefore, threats to it weren't tolerated and eliminated immediately.

"The NVA are so conscientious about protecting this area," Jarvis remembered grimly. " they sometimes employ entire five hundred man battalions around their more sensitive sites to secure them."

"They even use special tracker teams and dogs to detect and ferret out RTs searching for them."

"Christ," he thought fearfully as the possibility suddenly hit him. "if they have dogs looking for us, we are definitely in deep shit."

"You can't outrun the four-legged bastards, and you can't hide from them."

"It's just a matter of time before they run you down."

"Please, Lord," he prayed fervently. "Don't let them have dogs."

More problems to worry about, more tension he'd have to control, and more fear he'd have to suppress. It never ended and only got worse. But it also meant the RT's survival clock was winding down fast. They were rapidly running out of luck, almost as quickly as they were running out of time. It was no longer a question of "if" they would be found but "when."

Their luck would run out completely when that happened, and the situation would turn terminal. When he realized that, Jarvis's fear ratcheted up accordingly, and his heart started beating faster. His rising anxiety became apparent and didn't go unnoticed by the rest of the team.

Consequently, tension began skyrocketing, and anxiety started pegging out. As mouths started to turn dry, body sensors began red-lining, and hearts began chattering like runaway sewing machines. Everyone was so jacked up they felt like they were practically swimming in their own sweat, another bad sign and another dangerous indicator.

Fear made their body odor apparent and was another reason for worry. Caucasians emitted a completely different body odor than Orientals, so if the NVA had tracker dogs, they would smell it immediately. More bad news, the kind people didn't usually recover from.

"Please don't let them have dogs," Jarvis *prayed nervously again as he inched his way forward.*

"Anything but that, Lord," he begged.

"Christ, I can smell myself, so I know a dog can pick up my scent,"

"Just give us just one more day."

"Twenty-four more stinking hours, and we'll be out of here."

"But we don't stand a chance with dogs tracking us."

"They'll run us down before we get a chance to extract."

By this time, Jarvis was extremely worried about the RT's future. Their situation was escalating so rapidly that he was in danger of losing control, and he realized that was dangerous. So did Pretty Boy, the little Montagnard mercenary walking point. He had already arrived at the same conclusion minutes ago and was scared, too, his body language telegraphing it when he moved. His jerky body movements revealed his tenseness as he obviously sensed danger, and his twitchiness became apparent.

That was probably partly from nerves and partly from experience. He had been doing this same job for two years, so he was an expert by this time. That meant when he felt the icicle forming in his gut; he knew what it meant and why it was there.

Consequently, his hesitancy and uneasiness spoke volumes to the six men behind him. Watching his actions, they sensed his rising fear and reacted accordingly. If something had scared Pretty Boy, they were scared too.

By this time, the entire RT was so tense they were ready to jump out of their socks at the first hint of trouble. With eyelids skinned back and ears tuned to catch the slightest whisper, they were primed for anything yet hoping for nothing.

"The NVA are very close, now," Pretty Boy *thought fearfully as his darting eyes examined every detail of the foliage in front of him.*

"So close I can almost smell them."

"I know they're tracking us."

"We've been on the ground too long for them not to know we're here."

"But are they ahead of us too?" he wondered fearfully.

"That's the big question."

"If they are, they've got us in a box, and there's no way we can avoid a firefight."

"Still, there's no way to tell for certain," he said, gnawing at his lower lip."

"But there's damned sure something out there, and it's getting closer."

"I can feel it in my gut."

"But exactly where, and how close is it? "he asked himself in desperation as his tension mounted.

A backward glance assured him the RT was still behind him, so he sighed in relief. They were still there, all eyeballs, ears, and strained faces. They had his back, and he could depend on them to cover him if things went south. Sweat covered their uniforms and revealed their anxiety. The fear in their eyes was rising faster than the temperature. Trouble was only an eyelash away with no way to avoid it, and they sensed it, just like Pretty Boy.

Still, the wiry Yard doggedly continued to edge forward, not hesitating. By this time, he was an expert and had learned to trust his instincts. Disciplined, repetitive training is a hard habit to break, and he had received untold hours of it. That's why his gut was screaming at him to watch his ass.

"Get ready, sport," it wailed.

"We're gonna get hit," it told him grimly. "any second."

"I can feel it coming."

"But the team will cover me," he reassured himself.

"They know we're in trouble too, and they're ready for it."

"I saw it in their faces."

"Please, Buddha, don't let me get shot first."

With heads on swivels and eyeballs almost clicking, they moved so rapidly, the RT searched for the slightest hint of danger. Furtive glances bored into every yard around them, looking for anything unnatural or out of place. Nothing. Ears strained to pick up the faintest, out-of-place sound. Silence. Still, the feeling of danger was overwhelming.

"If Pretty Boy is expecting trouble, it's on its way," the RT worried. *"or already here."*

"His instincts are never wrong."

"So, it's no longer a question of "if" we're gonna get nailed, but when."

"Please, God, don't let me die when the shooting starts," each man prayed.

"If I get killed, I don't want my body to rot here in Laos."

"Please let Pretty Boy find a way out of this mess."

The RT's trust in the little Yard was implicit because experience had rarely proved him wrong. Now, as twitchy as he was, they all realized contact was imminent, probably any second. That meant WIAs and KIAs were on the way, probably more than one. That was bad news considering their size and location.

*"We're twenty-five miles inside Laos," Jarvis
remembered. " a country we are legally forbidden
even to enter, and there's only seven of us."*

*"That's bad enough, but we're also here
covertly.*

*"No dog tags, or IDs, sterile weapons, and
unmarked clothing and equipment means we're
men without a country."*

"That makes us expendable throwaways."

*"If we're caught, we're dead because the US
will disavow us."*

*"That's because we're part of SOG, and
officially, SOG doesn't exist."*

"That means we don't exist."

All that made the RT's nervousness
apparent and their tenseness palpable. No one
wants to die. Even throw-away pawns on a near-
suicide mission.

*"If we get into a firefight, seven against a
hundred NVA won't even be a contest,"* Jarvis
thought as he continued to eye Pretty Boy.
"They'll go through us like crap through a goose."

*"Those are lousy odds that will only get
worse with time."*

*"Especially if the NVA have put a blocking
force in front of us to cut us off."*

"If they have, we'll have nowhere to run if things go south, so barring a miracle, that will mean a massacre."

"Yet we have no choice but to keep moving."

"Stopping or trying to hide is out of the question."

"If we're being tracked, the NVA will crawl up our ass within minutes if we even slow down, much less stop."

"Yet the farther we move, the higher the chances of us running into a blocking force."

"Shit, we're screwed either way!"

With that knowledge, sweat dripped, adrenaline surged, and sphincters tightened. Dry lips were unconsciously licked, and mouths turned chalky as selector switches on CAR-15s were switched to rock and roll. Safeties were thumbed off as sweaty hands gripped weapons tightly, and extra magazines were readied. At this point, anticipation was paramount as fear gripped the team tightly.

Every man was coiled tighter than an old, over-wound watch, primed to snap at the slightest sound. Still, there was only silence as they continued to quietly snake their way through the thick vegetation. However, the ominous silence relayed an ever-increasing sense of foreboding, making every step a potential death knell. It was so apparent that every man on the RT felt it, yet there was nothing he could do except concentrate on their job and pray.

"Quit worrying about getting killed," young Sgt Johnnie Johnson told himself grimly. "Just concentrate on checking your sector of responsibility and worry about silent movement."

"The rest of the team will cover your flanks and ass because that's their job."

"So don't worry about them; just concentrate on doing your own job."

"Move slow and watch where you put your foot down, you big ox."

"Step like you're walking on eggshells, and don't hurry."

"Speed is a killer because it generates noise, and you can't afford that."

"Just do your job and let Jarvis do his."

"He knows what he's doing."

"Don't fuck up, and he'll get you through this."

Endless hours of repetitive training had drilled him into focusing all his efforts on stealthy movement while searching his sector of responsibility. Letting their teammates worry about his flanks and rear. It was a proven formula for success. They even burned it into your brain housing group in training when you were at Recon School at Long Thanh in big red letters.

But repetition, determination, and training can only deflect anxiety; they can't eliminate it. These men could control their fear, but they weren't immune to it, and they had ample reason. It was wartime, their mission was covert, and by this time, they were in deep shit, and they knew it.

"We're almost certainly being tracked by this time because the NVA must know we're here," Jarvis finally admitted to himself as the last of his optimism faded and turned into reality.

"They control this entire area, meaning they've undoubtedly discovered our presence by now."

"That means they're definitely behind us and probably in front of us too by now," he reasoned. *"And with every step we take, the noose gets tighter."*

"Worse, they know the terrain and are using trails to move, which makes their movement quick and easy."

"In contrast, we're experiencing it for the first time and must bust brush to move since trails are deathtraps for us."

"That means we'll leave a trail, no matter how careful we are, and that's a guaranteed recipe for disaster."

That was the unvarnished truth, and Jarvis knew it. Everyone wasn't going home this trip, and that was a fact. He could feel it in his gut. He wondered who would get hit first. He wondered if it would be him. After almost eight months of running recon, he was overdue.

"You wanted excitement, Hotshot," his brain taunted disgustedly. *"That's why you volunteered for SOG."*

"Well, you've got it," it screamed sarcastically. *"Now that it's here try not to let it jump up and get everybody killed."*

"Cause you're driving this train, and you're about to run out of track."

"Shit!" he thought angrily.

"That's just what I needed right now."

"A fucked-up pep talk from my brain telling me how stupid I am."

Moving stealthily in the enemy-dominated territory is arduous, time-consuming, and challenging, a task that isn't always successful. When you fail, a lopsided firefight ensues, usually in the form of an ambush. If that happens, which isn't all that uncommon, the members of the RT who aren't killed outright have to run since they are too small to stand and fight against superior numbers.

Chapter Two

"Running for your life is an experience you don't need.
Because if you fail, you die.
"If you make it and live, you're scared shitless it will happen again."

Unknown

Being chased and running is the epitome of a worst-case scenario for an RT. Namely, because when you're in Laos, there are no friendly bases to run to. So you either run until you drop, until you get extracted or until you get killed,

Regardless, running through the dense jungle is no mean feat by itself. Worse, it always leaves an obvious trail. That means your only hope is to make it to an LZ and be extracted back across the border by helo before the NVA follows you, runs you down, and kills you.

"Despite all that, our recon plan seems to be working," Jarvis murmured to himself, trying desperately to regain some optimism.

"We landed on a clean LZ two days ago."

"Once down, we conducted our mandatory security pause to ensure we were alone."

"When no NVA showed up to investigate the sounds of the insertion, we moved off through the dense jungle apparently undetected," he reassured himself.

"That's a rarity nowadays because the NVA use watchers on almost all open areas that can be utilized as LZs around their hidden sanctuaries."

"Their job is to alert the other NVA security forces in the area to just such an intrusion."

"But they can't watch everywhere, and apparently, we got lucky and snuck into just such an area unnoticed."

"But luck alone isn't going to keep us safe."

"We need to stay salty and remain focused 24/7 to get out of here alive."

"And right now, we're right on the edge of the bubble."

"One more day, Lord, just one more lousy day," he prayed silently.

Unfortunately for Jarvis, his prayer went unanswered. Probably because it was based on a flawed assumption, a terminal one as far as he and the RT were concerned. The NVA had heard their insertion after all, then moved troops to the

LZ. Although the RT was gone when they arrived, they started tracking them once they found the RTs trail. That could only end one way, badly, and the wheels for that result were already in motion.

The trackers had radioed ahead once they found their trail. Although the welcoming foliage of the jungle surrounding the RT provided excellent concealment for them when they moved, it also hid the L-shaped ambush the NVA had prepared and was waiting for them. The reinforcements they contacted had used another trail to get far enough ahead of the RT to establish a death trap which meant the RT's luck was about to run out.

"The NVA are here," Luc, one of the Yard mercenaries, suddenly realized, wide-eyed.

"They're so close enough I can smell them."

"They're going to light us up any second."

Luc was right. His luck ran out a second later as shots suddenly fractured the tomb-like silence sounding like fine crystal shattering in an empty ballroom. An AK round blew the tiny Montagnard backwards violently, a crimson stain blossoming on his chest. He grunted in pain as he was blown down, the air rushing out of him as he lay still. Everyone else on the RT flattened immediately and returned fire instinctively. The jungle around them instantly erupted into a tsunami of weapons fire from both sides. The firefight they had been expecting was here. The RT's luck had just run out.

A nanosecond later, the jungle lit up like a tropical neon sign as green and red tracers appeared, illuminating the landscape as they searched for targets. 7.62 parabellum AK rounds zipped overhead from everywhere, shredding foliage into green confetti. 5.56 CAR 15 rounds answered them in retaliation, creating more confusion and detritus. Body sensors redlined as death found the unprepared, just as poor Luc had predicted.

Jungle foliage exploded into green bits of vegetation thanks to the chattering machine-gun fire. Their copper jacketed rounds zipped through the fetid air like angry wasps on steroids. Rocket-propelled grenades exploded when they hit low-lying limbs or tree trunks. Wood splinters and shrapnel rained down everywhere as chaos and fear skyrocketed. Death had finally arrived.

As lead flew everywhere, fear ratcheted up into terror, and sphincters snapped shut with an audible click. Dying suddenly got very easy. One tiny mistake was all it took.

Yet, training replaced fear a second later. Almost by rote, the RT fled behind a wall of return fire using a well-practiced *"immediate action drill."* They had no choice but to run. Death lurked like a giant cat, ready to pounce on anyone dumb enough to stick around and remain a target.

"Run," Jarvis screamed as the world blew up around him.

Scooping up Luq's limp body on the fly, he took off.

"Follow me," He yelled over his shoulder.

"Head for the extraction, LZ."

"Don't think," Johnson's brain screamed as *he obeyed. "Just run, fire, and reload as fast as you can."*

He relayed Jarvis's instructions to the men behind him as the remainder of the RT fled from the ambush like scalded-assed apes. Hearing them, the team took off so fast that their asses barely had time to catch up with them. Boots pounded the jungle floor as the one-sided firefight cranked up in earnest behind them. Rounds blew by indiscriminately, barely missing as they searched for targets.

"Run faster," their brains screamed! *"Don't slow down if you want to live."*

"The NVA are right behind us."

Consequently, they fled like madmen through the hail of gunfire. They evaporated into the mass of jungle greenery like puffs of smoke in a strong wind with a hurricane of 7.69 Chicom parabellum rounds waving them goodbye. Miraculously, no one else was hit.

"That will soon change," Jarvis thought angrily as he charged through the foliage. "There's too much fire pouring in, and our escape just started."

"And, Goddammit, it's all my fault," he cursed violently.

"I walked us into an ambush, and the tab for that mistake will be a big one."

"The goddamn NVA will ensure that."

The NVA were already certainly trying their best to collect. Yet, they had been shocked by the RT's violent reaction and sudden flight and were momentarily stunned. They had thought they had the RT cold, like meat on the table, ready to be carved, but they were wrong. They had overestimated their capability and underestimated the RT's violent return fire. Their momentary lapse was decisive and gave the tiny RT the few extra seconds they needed to break contact and disappear.

However, the reprieve didn't last long. The NVA were up and chasing them seconds later, cursing themselves for their overconfidence and incensed at their lack of success. They had lost face, an unforgivable sin in the Orient, so they wanted revenge as repayment and atonement. They were determined to get it. That made it a race now, pure and simple. If you lost, you died.

"With hundred-pound rucks strapped to our backs," Johnson thought wildly. "We'll never outrun them."

"We're all already winded and struggling to maintain the breakneck pace while they're gaining on us."

"They'll be all over us any second if this keeps up."

Even as big and as strong as young Buck Sgt Johnnie Johnson was, he could feel his weighty load slamming into his back and slowing him down with each pounding step. Moments later, his aching lungs felt like they were on fire as his legs began to feel rubbery from the strain. Even with his exceptional size and strength and the adrenaline pumping, Johnson knew he couldn't keep up the grueling pace much longer. Not with all that weight. He realized he had to do something, so he snatched a prepared claymore mine from his ruck just as Jarvis yelled.

"Drop your rucks," Jarvis screamed over his shoulder a moment later, reading Johnson's mind and realizing the team was on the verge of exhaustion. He then spied John with the Claymore, realized what he was going to do, and nodded.

"Follow me and don't slow down or stop for anything," he ordered."

"If it gets in your way, run over it or kill it."

"We have to get to the emergency LZ before the Dicks do."

"If we don't, we're dead."

"Christ, I hope Kelly called for an emergency extraction when we took off, " he prayed earnestly.

"If he didn't, we have no chance."

Johnson heard Jarvis and obeyed instantly, yanking the quick-release straps and feeling his heavy rucksack mercifully fall away. The relief was instantaneous, and a second later, he and the men behind him were reenergized and accelerating through the sea of green like sprinters coming out of the blocks. Everyone realized it was a flat-out race for survival now, a desperate run to see who could get to the LZ first, the RT or the NVA. Only first-place counted. Coming in second meant death.

The team continued to bulldoze through the dense foliage like it was tissue paper at a breakneck pace, ignoring the crisp, deadly zip of rounds clipping foliage around them. They hardly felt the leaves slapping their faces or the vines bruising their shins as they tried to trip them. They had no time to feel pain or turn around and return fire because the pursuing NVA were too close, almost on them.

"Something has to be done to slow them down, or we're finished," Johnson realized.

"Grenade," he yelled as he pulled the pin on the run.

He then lobbed an M-26 fragmentation grenade over his shoulder to the rear. The team had four seconds to get clear before it exploded.

The pursing NVA ran right into it seconds later, its shrapnel killing three and wounding two more. The survivors screeched to a halt and wailed in anger, vowing revenge. Johnson could hear them screaming in frustration and grinned evilly.

"Payback for Luc," he thought bitterly.

"That will slow the little bastards down some."

Johnson's grenade infuriated the NVA, and their anger turned to rage when they saw its effects. They began firing wildly as they resumed the chase, hoping for a lucky hit in revenge. No such luck. The few precious seconds the grenade bought them allowed the RT to vanish again and gain a few more precious yards.

Regardless, the NVA pursued the team relentlessly, following their trail, firing randomly as they ran while searching for targets, and hoping for a lucky hit. Johnson heard their rounds slicing through the foliage behind him, getting closer, then a sudden thump, followed by a loud grunt.

"Oh Shit," he thought wildly. *"Somebody's been hit."*

"I'll have to stop and carry him."

But when he turned to pick up his wounded teammate, both Kelly, Pak, and the other Yard, were still up and running, wild-eyed and terrified. Confused, Johnson continued to bull his way forward, crashing through wait-a-minute vines and jungle undergrowth like a runaway freight train, desperately tearing a jagged hole through the dense vegetation for the people behind him. Trying like hell to keep up with the two Yards and Jarvis, who were just ahead of him.

It was a flat-out race now. No more creeping, no more silent running, and no more stealth. Screw the noise; just run like hell.

"Our only hope is to get to the LZ ahead of the NVA," Johnson realized.

"Coming in second is not an option."

"Run, you big sonofabitch," Johnson told himself angrily. *"Faster!"*

"Jarvis isn't slowing down, and he's carrying Luq."

"So, find another gear and move your sorry ass."

Lungs seared, hearts pounded, and emotions exploded as the RT barreled forward. Grunting like gored bulls, they tore through the matted foliage like a steam roller through a lattice flower support. Leaves slapped faces, vines grabbed feet, and limbs slashed legs. But they barely noticed. Escape was the only thing that mattered now. Still, the NVA pursued them relentlessly.

John now realized the RT's only hope was to break contact permanently before they reached the LZ, and it had to be done now. He slowed and waved Kelly and Pak past him a second later. Stopping for a quick second, he knelt and jammed the Claymore into the ground, facing backward. It had a six-second fuse and contained hundreds of steel ball bearings that blew out in a lethal cone when it exploded. They killed everything, plants, animals, humans, and even insects.

When it detonated, the Claymore turned plants into coleslaw and humans into hamburger meat. Nothing escaped it. It was a definite attention-getter and a man-killer of the first order. Johnson's was even more lethal and effective because it had a plastic bag of powdered tear gas taped to its front.

The lead elements of the NVA chasing the RT ran right into it five seconds later when it exploded. The few remaining survivors immediately became much less avid about catching the team. They were desperately trying to stop the bleeding and patch themselves up while blind and throwing up, thanks to the gas.

Their dead were everywhere, mangled by the mine. Those still alive were disoriented and sickened by the gas. The RT continued to flee while the ravaged NVA tried to recover, and this time, they were successful. The Claymore had done its job spectacularly.

Terrifying minutes later, the jungle suddenly thinned, then unexpectedly disappeared. Waist-high, lime green elephant grass covering an open field replaced it. It blanketed the LZ that had magically materialized to the exhausted RT's front. Sweaty smiles and a collective prayer of thanks rippled through the team as they continued to run towards it like a welcoming refuge.

But all that excitement and thankfulness were suddenly stillborn. Relief faded instantly as the team's nightmare abruptly got worse!

The NVA had outsmarted them! The wily little North Vietnamese bastards had sent a unit ahead of them on a trail as a blocking force, just as Jarvis had feared. Now they had the LZ covered too. An NVA squad was already securing the jungle's edge near it, just waiting for them. They knew that if any of the team escaped their ambush, that's where they would head, so they were all set and licking their chops in anticipation.

Jarvis spied the NVA squad off to his left as they suddenly popped up like apparitions spread out in a line. That left him no choice, and he knew what he had to do instinctively, something totally unexpected. So instead of trying to run around the NVA formation, as they expected, he led the running team straight at them, blowing a gap in the human wall with his CAR 15 hammering on rock and roll. His slugs knocked down some of the surprised NVA like bowling pins as the rest scattered for cover. They hadn't been as ready as they thought, so Jarvis's unexpected tactic had momentarily shocked them because it was the last thing they expected him to do. But their amazement didn't last long.

Immediately afterward, rounds began zipping in from all sides again, behind the team and to its front and sides, as the NVA recovered and returned fire.

"Christ, the little shits are everywhere," Johnson told himself franticly as he ran.

"Don't stop; keep firing."

"Kill anything you see."

Jarvis had the same thoughts as the RT ripped through the surprised NVA formation like it wasn't even there, killing as they ran. They tore through the gap, accompanied by the crack of AK-47s seemingly coming from all directions. Johnson continued to run, holding his Car 15 out in front of him like a spear and spewing death.

Seconds later, he exploded a Dog Soldier's head like a ripe melon as he shot him at point-blank range. He kept firing as he ran, snap shooting two more when he spied them, then reloading. Afterward, he shot another two in the chest as he ran by them. Their faces reflected utter astonishment as they died wordlessly.

"There's too many of them," he thought *wildly.*

"I can't kill them fast enough,"

Suddenly, there was the terrifying blast of an RPG detonating, and everyone cringed instinctively. Johnson, running behind Thu, saw the Nung's head and upper torso suddenly disappear in a wild explosion of blood and gore as the RPG hit him chest high. He literally exploded, pieces of him flying everywhere.

The blast knocked Johnson down, his ears ringing as blood and fragments of the Thu smacked into his shirt and face. Appalled by Thu's violent death and still shaky and groggy, he got up and continued to run. He had no choice. Stopping meant dying.

"Too late to help Thu now," he thought *angrily as he took off again. "He's gone."*

"What's left of him is lying on the jungle floor like a torn ragdoll."

"His woman will wail when she gets the news."

John screamed in anguish, frustrated by the gruesome sight. What was left of his friend had already collapsed as he ran by the headless corpse, and he squeezed off an entire magazine on rock and roll in anger and frustration. He could do nothing else because there was no stopping now, not for anything, especially the dead.

Blowing through the shocked NVA formation a moment later, John waxed one with another headshot blowing his brains out in a technicolor splash of red blood, white bone, gray brain matter, and black hair. He blew another one down who had stepped out to help him a second later. Then another. Yet more kept sprouting up like new growth.

"Christ, they're everywhere," he thought wildly as he continued firing.

"We'll never make it," he thought desperately as he shot two more. "There's too many of them."

Yet amazingly, seconds later, he was suddenly through the NVA formation, and there were no more targets. The remaining NVA were either hiding or ducking for cover. The six remaining men on the RT flashed past their remnants seconds later. Afterward, they suddenly found themselves in the waist-high elephant grass before the NVA could recover.

Moments later, they disappeared completely, the high lime-green stalks turning them invisible as they continued to run in a crouch.

Within seconds, the NVA Dog soldiers sent hundreds of rounds flying everywhere to try and find them again. However, it was a vain effort to cut off their escape, and too late. They were shooting blind and hoping but had no targets. Hence, the enemy rounds flew harmlessly over their heads, snipping off bits of the lime green stalks in frustration. What was left of the RT had already dived headlong into an old bomb crater in the LZ's center.

By that time, Johnson's heart was beating like a jackhammer, and he was sweating so hard he could barely see. The salty beads stung his eyes as the exhausted youngster struggled to get his breath. He felt like he was trying to suck air through a hose in a steam bath and couldn't quite manage. The heavy humidity prevented his heaving lungs from cooperating. They couldn't inhale oxygen fast enough to satisfy his starving need, so he was drowning in the humid, lifeless air.

Seconds later, another RPG exploded outside the depression to his front, reminding him the NVA hadn't given up. The small RT had killed too many of them, and they wanted revenge. Their fury demanded it.

The concussion rocked Johnson backward, and he instinctively curled into a fetal ball, expecting to feel the red-hot sting of shrapnel, but there was none. Instead, chunks of black earth rain down on his back as he cringed. Johnson heard the rest of the team firing wildly and was suddenly ashamed he wasn't helping. Slamming a fresh magazine into his weapon, he peered over the lip of the hole and rejoined the action.

He ignored the rounds zinging by him and knocked down two NVA who had been foolish enough to break cover and follow the team into the field. They fell with a dull Thud as he changed magazines once again. He shot a third who came to their aid. Then a fourth. They were still coming, so he kept firing.

"Oh Jesus, the little bastards are getting ready to assault," he realized.

"I can't kill them fast enough to break it up."

The remaining NVA bastards were close now and already massing. If they weren't stopped immediately, they would overrun the team's small position any second. Knowing that, John lobbed a grenade, then began firing wildly at every hint of movement in the elephant grass in front of him. But weapons fire wasn't enough to blunt the assault, and John realized it. He heard screams when the grenade exploded, and later, more screams as more NVA Dog soldiers fell from the 5.56rounds from his CAR-15.

He threw two more grenades in as many seconds to break up the charge and heard more screams when they exploded. Then two more. As more targets appeared, he calmly got a good sight picture and downed them too, becoming a killing machine that never missed. He got so caught up in the killing he was completely unprepared for the sudden stillness that followed when the firing abruptly stopped minutes later. When it did, the sudden silence shocked him.

"What the hell," he screamed in wonder. "Why did the little bastards suddenly stop firing?"

"What are they doing, and where did they go?"

The instant silence and lack of targets astounded him so badly he couldn't fathom it. The NVA had inexplicably pulled back into the jungle, and he wondered why.

"For better cover?" he wondered. "Or have we somehow beaten them back?"

"If we have, it cost us," he noted as he glanced around the bomb crater in shock.

Jarvis, the team leader, was no longer firing because he was hit in the stomach. He was lying on his back, holding his intestines in with bloody hands and biting his lower lip to keep from screaming. The Yard, Luq, was lying beside him, face down and not moving. Apparently, he hadn't made it after all, despite Jarvis's efforts to save him.

Pretty Boy was unexpectedly missing. Kelly, the RTO, was also down, sporting an awkward-looking right arm and a splayed left leg, both bright with splotches of spreading crimson. Pak, the little Yard beside Kelly, was also face down at an unnatural angle and not moving either.

"Jesus," John thought wildly as he took in all the carnage. "the entire team has been shot to shit!"

"I'm the only one not hit."

As another round zipped by, he ducked and readied himself again, afraid the NVA were getting ready to assault once more. But when he peered anxiously over the grass, he saw nothing, and relief flooded his system.

"If the little bastards come at us now, we're finished," Johnson realized as he changed

magazines again and readied another grenade, his last.

"I sure as hell can't stop them by myself."

But inexplicably, the NVA also ceased firing a moment later.

"What the hell?" John thought anxiously as he laid out another magazine and risked another quick peek over the elephant grass.

He expected to see the NVA massing again for a final assault. Surprisingly, however, when he looked, nothing was moving, either in the field or on the edge of the jungle. Evidently, the NVA had decided to hold off on their attack for some reason.

"Why?" the young Buck Sgt asked himself uneasily. "What are the little shits up to now?"

"They certainly didn't stop firing because they decided to surrender, and I know damned well they ain't out of ammo."

Then it hit him.

"It's that Asian patience thing," John suddenly remembered.

"They've got us surrounded and pinned, and with the sun going down, that's all they're waiting for."

"When it gets dark, they can take us any time they please, with fewer casualties."

"We won't be able to see them coming in the dark."

"Shit," Johnson said to himself disgustedly as reality set in.

"We're all as good as dead right now."

With that, he settled back to wait. He cursed his luck as the hot Asian sun beat him unmercifully with its last few dying rays. He had only minutes left to live, he realized it, and he was pissed.

Chapter Three

"Courage is knowing you're about to get your ass handed to you but saddling up anyway."

Old Cowboy saying

As the afternoon rapidly waned and John waited to die, his anger got even more intense. The sun's fierce heat didn't help. With no mercy, it became an unrelenting fireball searing everything beneath it one last time as a final kiss goodbye. It was almost sundown, and although it had passed its zenith long ago, the sun's remaining heat was primarily focused on the small jungle LZ where the shot-up RT now waited.

The tiny clearing was unusual, one of the few open patches in the mass of endless tropical vegetation within a five-mile radius. It was an ideal extraction LZ but had now become a death trap for the team who was surrounded and stuck. They had nowhere else to run, even if they were able.

The terrain consisted of steep ridges and valleys covered with thick multi-layered flora that blanketed its entire topography. Double canopy jungle, endless climbing, clinging vines, and dense overgrown broadleaf vegetation covered the remainder of the surrounding landscape, as it did most of this region of northeastern Laos. Any opening in this sea of endless green was rare.

Any open space was usually overgrown with elephant grass or other hardy vegetation. Plants that were resilient enough to survive the withering Asian heat and the fierceness of the sun's direct rays. Even so, the sun's blistering heat was sufficient at this time of day to wilt some of the young shoots of even those hardy plants. It was the dry season in the region. The hottest time of year. Hell on earth if there was no shade.

Now, in the last part of the day, the cloudless azure sky ensured the blazing tropical orb was relentless. It had continuous access to the poor shot-up bastards in the bomb crater below. As a result, the heat, combined with the intense humidity, sucked the remaining moisture out of everyone, leaving a hot sticky clamminess that covered their skin like a wet shroud in its wake. With no shade and not a hint of a breeze, the mind-numbing heat continued to bake them in the small clearing's confines, like hand-made biscuits in a natural Dutch oven.

"Jesus," John thought. "I'm burning up."

"There ain't no shade here, and I'm sweating like a pig."

"And it's even worse for Jarvis and Kelly since they've been hit."

As if to confirm his thoughts, the air around the LZ shimmered with heat waves as they rose from the moist earth. They blurred the outlines of everything with a thin, whispery veil of steam, making the stifling air even hotter and its odor more pungent. It reeked of an odious mixture of cordite, new-mown vegetation, and centuries-old rot, all mixed with the newly added aroma of death.

But as the five desperate men lying in the old bomb crater patiently waited for the end, they barely noticed. Death was already on them, so heat hardly mattered. John drank the last few swallows out of a canteen, but it wasn't enough to satisfy his thirst, and he wanted more. He reached for his second one, then stopped. Water had suddenly become a precious commodity. Someone might need it more later on.

Ironically, the crater's bottom was partially filled with gallons of the brilliant aqua-colored liquid. It was as beautiful as it was inviting but a cheap illusion. It was the result of rain acting on the chemical residue of the explosive in the bomb that had created it.

So, the parched RT, exhausted by their earlier run to the hole and the ensuing firefight, lay charbroiled by the sun, waiting patiently for the NVA's next move and staring wistfully at the water around them that was unfit to drink. As delicious looking as the aqua blue water appeared, it was toxic and offered no relief at all. Sheer torment.

The adrenaline rush they had all experienced minutes earlier when the firefight had first begun was wearing off. Their minds were rapidly becoming sluggish and lethargic as they slid down the natural high the adrenaline had generated. They were unconsciously slipping into the black depression that was its result, and that was dangerous. Anything less than maximum vigilance would be terminal.

The Company of heavily armed North Vietnamese Dog soldiers had finally run them down like hounds treeing a fox. They now had them surrounded and pinned like flies on a specimen board. That left an aura of helplessness hanging over the RT like a darkening cloud. Worse, more NVA were already on the way to help, proving that bad news travels fast.

The entire area was eerily quiet now. A prospective cemetery just waiting for new occupants. The vicious firefight raging only moments before had abruptly subsided. Its only remnants were an occasional round or two zipping overhead every few seconds to let the trapped men know they were still pinned and the torn-up real estate around the bomb crater indicating they weren't going anywhere.

With good cover and concealment, the NVA now had time on their side and the advantage of numbers and firepower. They could take the small team any time they wanted. They wouldn't be such defined targets when it got dark as they emerged from the jungle and overran the surrounded round eyes. But, like all Asians, they were patient. They could afford to wait.

The clearing was a killing ground for them in broad daylight, and they knew it. Its high elephant grass was deceptive. Its thin green stalks offered excellent concealment but provided no cover. So, while it looked peaceful and serene, the field was a death trap.

Once darkness fell, and visibility dimmed, the NVA's movement would be much more difficult to detect by the Americans hiding in the bomb crater. Consequently, their chances of overrunning the small American recon team with minimum casualties would be significantly enhanced. So, they satisfied themselves by keeping the men in the depression heads down and rendering them immobile. They could wait. As Asians, it was a part of their nature.

But waiting was difficult for Johnson, Johnnie, NMI (No middle Initial), and Sgt E-5. The youngster's head was like a Jack in the box, popping up regularly over the rim of the depression and scanning the wood line for any signs of movement. The young Green Beret was sweating furiously, the salty beads running off his brow like torrents and staining his shirt with salt. After the team's frantic scramble for the hole and the subsequent savage firefight, he was still jacked up. Yet, he was desperately trying to slow down his runaway emotions because he expected the worst at any moment.

John knew he had to calm himself down to stay alive. So, decelerating his red-lined body sensors, slowing down his heart rate, and regaining control of his breathing were essential.

"Calm down, asshole," his brain urged the rest of his straining body.

"Throttle back a little and take a deep breath."

"You got good cover here, you ain't hit, and the NVA ain't dumb enough to try another frontal assault through the elephant grass again."

"They'd get the shit shot outta them again, and they know it."

"That's why they're still in the tree line, waiting for dark."

"So, settle down, boy," his brain urged. "before your excitement gets your ass waxed."

"Don't be in such an all-fired hurry to die."

"Give yourself a few more minutes of life."

But the sight of destroyed green foliage all around Johnson, combined with his realization of what was coming, was not reassuring. The NVA had the RT surrounded, and the nearby shredded elephant grass and clumps of torn-up jungle floor proved it. The entire area around the depression had been ravaged by exploding rocket-propelled grenades, and murderous machine-gun fire. The carnage that remained was mute testimony to the ferociousness of the just-ended firefight and the number of NVA that had created it. It was also a harbinger of even worse things to come.

"Shit," Johnson spat disgustedly as he eyed the damage. "we ain't going anywhere."

"They got us boxed up tighter than a tin of sardines."

"They can take us anytime they want."

"It's only a matter of time now."

The jungle birds, normally yammering away at any human presence, were deathly quiet now. The AK rounds eviscerating the jungle moments before had rendered them mute again. Even the ever-present insects were quiet, making the overall silence overwhelming. Death was everywhere, its presence almost tangible. Everybody could feel it coming, the members of the RT and the NVA.

But Death didn't seem to be in any hurry on this late summer afternoon. He was probably content in the knowledge that the intended victims were already his. Pinned in their hole, they certainly weren't going anywhere. Most were dead or shot to pieces. Those that weren't soon would be.

There would be no last-minute cavalry charge over the ridge to rescue them. The nearest friendly force was fifty miles away and in an entirely different country! That made reinforcement an impossible dream, which meant they were already dead. They just hadn't quit breathing yet!

"John," a pain-wracked voice behind him suddenly hissed. "I can barely move, so see who's left and what kind of condition they're in."

"We got to get set before the Dicks hit us again," he moaned painfully.

"Lay still, Tom," Johnson whispered, shocked by Jarvis's anguished voice.

"I got us covered, so don't fret yourself."

But training took over when the young Sgt suddenly realized that with Jarvis and Kelly down, he was now in charge.

"Sound off," he hissed a moment later, his eyes never leaving the tree line to his front. "status and ammo."

Initially, there was silence, then finally, a weak response.

"Kelly here, John." a weak whisper off to his left rear replied. "I'm still around."

"Most of me anyway."

"Took one in the back, and I think it broke my left arm when it came out."

"Every time I try and move the fucker, it feels like it's on fire."

John winced. He had seen that type of wound before, so he knew it burned like the devil. Kelly was hurting. So was Jarvis.

"Took a couple in my right leg, too," Kelly added. "but it's still mostly numb."

"Bleeding like hell, though."

"I'm pretty fucked up, partner," Kelly explained through gritted teeth.

"Getting lightheaded too from blood loss because I can't bandage my leg with just one hand."

"Pak's over here with me," Kelly continued raggedly a moment later. "but I think he's dead."

"He ain't moving like he was a minute ago."

"Ain't even moaning no more."

"I think he's done cashed out and bought the farm."

"He took a bad one through his chest right after we got here, and I think it killed him," he explained.

"The goddamn bastards."

"What about the radio, Jim?" John asked hopefully.

"It's finished," Kelly moaned as he gazed at the shot-up PRC 77 beside him. "I already checked."

"Got a hole through it as big as a baseball."

"Ain't nothing but sixteen pounds of OD-colored scrap metal and busted transistors now."

"Useless as yesterday's garbage."

"I'm low on ammo too," he added. "I only got one magazine left."

"Pak's got a couple on him," he groaned. "But I can't move good enough to get over to get 'em."

"Okay, Jim," Johnson responded gently. "Just lay still."

"I'll be over to tend you in a second."

"Pretty Boy," Johnson called a moment later when no one else responded. "you still here?"

There was silence as John waited.

"Luq?" he called hopefully a moment later.

"Luq's had it too, John," Jarvis replied painfully, off to his right. "he's over here next to me."

"He died a few minutes ago."

"Took a round through the chest back at the ambush and another right after we got here."

"It blew most of his head off."

"I got pieces of him all over me," Jarvis said disgustingly.

"Pretty Boy never even made it out of the wood line." He reported.

"RPG got him while we were still running."

"I saw him go down when it exploded."

"What's left of them is laying on the edge of the jungle back there, blown to hell."

"Me, you, and Kelly are the only ones left," Jarvis grunted, squinting at the sun.

"And we're ain't going to be around much longer," he predicted disgustedly.

"Sunset is all them little bastards are waiting on."

"When the sun goes down, they'll be coming."

"When that happens, we're all done here," He predicted ominously.

John could feel the hair on the back of his neck stand up when Jarvis said that. The youngster had never had anybody tell him he was about to die before. That unnerved him so much that he felt a sliver of ice slice through his gut, deep inside him, even as hot sweat poured off the rest of his body. The faces of a few friends and a pretty girl he had known long ago suddenly flashed through his mind unbidden, and he swallowed hard as he remembered life before the war. Then he returned to reality as he faced the upcoming probability of his own death.

Like most young people his age, John had never thought much about dying. Until moments ago, he had thought he would live forever. The exuberance of youth and his unquestioned immortality, known only to the young, had always shielded him from such thoughts. Now, he suddenly realized just how fragile and tenuous life was and how wrong he had been.

Right now, his own was hanging by a slender thread that was about to snap. Chances were, he would be dead within the hour. That knowledge made him grimace as he tasted the bitterness of bile as it rose in his throat. Suddenly another round zipped by his head, and he ducked involuntarily.

"Keep daydreaming, asshole," he told himself angrily, ashamed of his lapse.

"You'll be dead sooner than you think."

After a final peek at the wood line, John slid down the depression's side and crawled over to Jarvis. He had waited to tend to the wounded until now because he was the only one that could still shoot. Now that the NVA had apparently decided to wait for sunset to finish the team off, it was time to patch up the wounded so they would be ready when the NVA decided to come and end their misery permanently finally.

"Jesus, I hurt," Jarvis grunted as another spasm of pain shot through him like a red hot, steel rod.

"Feels like my whole goddamn gut is on fire."

"Gimme some water, John," he pleaded. "I got a terrible thirst."

"I'm dry as a bone."

John gazed at the bleeding hole in Jarvis's stomach he was trying to close with his bloody hands.

"You can't have no water, Tom," Johnson replied gently. "you're gut shot."

"I give you water, you'll get peritonitis, sure as shit, and that'll kill you."

"Shit, son," the short, squat, forty-two-year-old Master Sgt snorted painfully. "that ain't gonna make no difference now."

"I'm probably going to die in the next few minutes anyway."

"And long before peritonitis can set in and kill me."

"The Dicks will make sure of that."

"They're sitting out there right now just licking their chops."

"Come sundown; the little shits will come boiling out of that wood line like ants and kill every one of us."

"So, what's the difference?" He reasoned logically, with a weak smile.

"Now, gimme some water."

"Just a sip to wet my throat, John," He begged. "Please!"

"I want to be ready when it's time."

"Take a few more with me before I cash out."

"But I need a little water first."

Johnson debated for a second, finally realizing Jarvis was right. Perontinitous was a moot point now. Afterward, he awkwardly rolled on his side and reached back to the rear of his web belt for his one remaining canteen. Unscrewing the cap, he held the plastic water bottle to his team leader's lips as Jarvis sipped the warm water greedily and then coughed.

"Thanks, John," Jarvis said with a weak grin on his haggard face.

"Now gimme a smoke, boy."

"Might as well go out feeling good," He croaked as he clutched his stomach when another spasm of pain hit. "especially since they already know where we are."

As Johnson fumbled through Jarvis's fatigue pockets for his crumpled pack, the veteran Master Sgt looked up at him.

"Listen to me, boy," the grizzled old soldier said urgently as John finally found a Lucky Strike and lit it for him. "I'm done, and so's Kelly."

"Ain't neither of us getting out of this hole alive."

"Not as fucked up as we are."

"That leaves you."

"You're the only one left that's got any chance at all."

"I had Kelly call in a *Prairie Fire* emergency when we were running back here to the LZ," Jarvis told John through clenched teeth.

"I think he got through before the NVA got the radio, but I ain't sure."

"Either way," he said bitterly. "it doesn't matter to us cause we're both finished."

"But you ain't hit, John," Jarvis continued.

"You can still move."

"So, I want you to get the hell outta here."

"Ain't no sense in you dyin' here too."

"There's an alternate LZ only three klicks west of here, and it's marked on my map." He said as he fumbled awkwardly with one hand, trying to get it out of his pocket.

"It ain't much, but it'll handle one helo."

John gazed at him as he ripped a battle dressing's paper cover off with his teeth.

"If Kelly's message got through to the FOB, then the exfil birds are already on their way," Jarvis continued.

"After they overfly this place and don't find anybody alive, that's where they'll head."

"That's SOP."

"Since it'll be sunset in about ten minutes," Jarvis grunted, gazing up at the darkening sky. "that'll give you an edge."

"If you prop us up so we can shoot, me and Jim still got enough gas left in our tanks to make some noise."

"So, we can cover your move back to the wood line."

"If you keep low, the Dicks will never see you because of the elephant grass."

"Especially with us firing and holding their attention."

John listened impassively as he wrapped the battle dressing around Jarvis's stomach.

"All you gotta do is prop us up on the rim of this hole where we can see and still fire before you leave," Jarvis explained.

"Once we get the NVA's attention, if you're quiet and stay down in the grass, you can make it to the far tree line without them seeing you."

"When you get there," He finished raggedly. "you can put the sneak on the little bastards, then get the hell outta here."

When John tightened the bandage, Jarvis grunted with pain.

"But you gotta go now, boy, before the sun sets," The old soldier said a moment later, grimacing.

"You wait any longer; it'll be too late."

Made in United States
North Haven, CT
05 April 2023

35070957R00323